AN

EMERALD CITY

Sex Comedy

A novel

SUSANNAH WHITE

Benny Bee

B O O K S

FOR MIKAL AND TASHA
WITH ALL MY LOVE

"Fate and soul are two names for the same principle."
Novalis

"NY TOST NY TARD" ("Neither soon nor late.")
De Chiel (Dashiell) Family Crest Device

"Riding is said to be worst for horses."
Norwegian Rune Poem

BACK AT THE OKAY CORRAL

Matthew Barker was in love with the ghost of his sultry ex-wife, an up-and-coming cabaret singer. Haunted by day, hunted by night, by delightful and horrible visions of her. Promising him things. Making him grovel. And grieve for the lustful past that they'd shared together.

Beautiful red-haired Rosie O'Hara wasn't actually dead even though she floated around in his head like a billowy specter, obscuring his plans for the future. Mucking up his life as a footloose bachelor.

His whole life had gone to hell since she left him for a sloe-eyed lesbian thirteen months ago. But he was damn well going to correct that. Learn to live again. Learn to cope. Have some actual fun.

And tonight was the night.

He clipped his pen onto the margin of the yellow legal tablet he was scribbling investment figures on and threw it under the bed. He was rich, in spite of his better instincts.

"Come in, shit-kickers." He twiddled the FM dial of his newest rehabilitated transistor radio, switching from business news to a rockabilly song on KEXP. He wouldn't mind kicking some shit tonight, although his usual MO was to get the shit kicked out of him after picking an unwinnable fight with a bully.

No, the sexy shade of his undead wife and pointless worries about his economic future were gonna be kicked to the curb, as soon as he could change his clothes and get out of the house, he vowed, feeling a delicious flicker of excitement.

He had a date with destiny tonight, thanks to his new friend, the celebrated enfant terrible and illustrious writer, Jackson Brand.

His best friend, Terry, called right as Matthew was pulling on his socks. "How's it hangin', Ol' Bean?" Terry said, just like he always did.

"Hangin' fine, 109," Matthew answered automatically. Crap, he should have let the call go to voicemail.

"Friday night, dude! Friday fuckin' night!" Terry chanted, like a drunk guy at football match.

"Which means exactly what?" Matthew asked, knowing exactly that it meant since he'd been spending every Friday night with Terry since his divorce.

"It means we're gonna party!" Terry yipped. "We're gonna score!"

Matthew shuddered. "Score" seemed sad coming from a celibate loser, and they hadn't "partied" in years.

"You and me are gonna get us some ladies!"

Terry didn't mean ladies at all, he meant pussy, even though he didn't really want to get laid, he just wanted to sound like he did. He said the same thing every damn week.

Been there, done that, all the way back to Wyoming.

Matthew took a deep cleansing breath, his new version of prayer, different than the way he begged the *Great Whatever* to bring Rosie back. Attending to his breathing made him feel more centered, less anxious, but he wasn't going to explain his way of breathing to Terry right now. He was in a hurry.

"You go for it, dude, I've got to finish this crazy security project I'm working on," he lied.

Terry was a Taurus of determined disposition, impossible to put off. "Nah, man, yer fuckin' up the plan. It's Friday night!"

"Sorry dude. Gotta go!" Matthew hung up quickly and switched off his phone. Hunting around for a pair of jeans and shirt acceptable for an evening in the company of a famously flamboyant writer, he suppressed a shudder of guilt. He was a weasel for lying to Terry, but tough shit.

Another shudder as he viewed his ridiculous quiff of red hair and rimless glasses in the oversized bedroom mirror where once he'd watched Rosie's face change from sexy to sublime while he fucked her from behind, his own face aflame with pleasure and love—now he just looked dorky and worn out.

Maybe some speed would help? But he didn't have any. And it wouldn't bring back the love in his eyes, anyway. Some excitement then, tonight. Maybe a chance to feel popular!

He collected his wallet and keys, and went out to the corner to wait for his town car. He wondered if Rosie and Alexa were having sex, although it wasn't yet eight o'clock. He was diverted from his masochistically prurient thoughts by a shiny black Lincoln pulling smoothly up to the curb. The beefy driver got out of the hearse-like vehicle and opened the back door for him.

Matthew settled back in his traditional mode of civilized paranoia, hands loose in his pockets like a wary gunslinger, alert for any signs of ramped up synesthesia—the weird sensations, smells, and visual images of sounds and words that regularly troubled him—but his brain was obedient tonight. Nothing but familiar sensory anomalies and pangs of social anxiety. And the ever present sense of longing that felt like a stone on his chest oppressing him.

"The Underground," he said, giving the address of a nightclub in Georgetown he'd never been to. It was a trendy dive with a reputation for blatant drug use, a popular place with the arty in-crowd. He thought maybe he'd enjoy using some drugs himself, whatever it was everybody was using these days to quell their terror of the future. He guessed he'd leave that up to Jackson.

Matthew rode along watching the traffic lights dim and brighten in a complicated urban pattern which made him feel awed and disoriented, like a Podunk tourist new to Seattle. How odd not to be driving his trusty old Honda through familiar potholed streets.

"I'm on a hero's quest!" he confessed to the back of the driver's shaved head. The guy didn't respond but that was okay as long he wasn't drunk or stomping an angry foot on the gas pedal.

After fifteen minutes and a short stint on the freeway the car pulled up in front of the nightclub. There was a long line of vaguely ominous people in fancy clothes stretching around the corner towards an alley where god-knows-what was going on.

For a mad second Matthew considered saying he'd changed his mind, he wanted to go back home, but he handed the silent driver a hundred dollar bill and his business card and warily got out of the car.

"Come back at two unless I call for you earlier!" he yelled as the town car sped off.

The Underground seemed to be where it was happening, at least to the assembled crowd of duded-up coked-up

Seattleites. The Latinx contingent was amply represented, ditto the gay population, and rich city slickers unsheathed from leather car interiors for an evening of inebriated fun.

Matthew didn't fit into any social category he could identify as he joined the untidy queue on the sidewalk. Identifying anyone by their clothes, apparent economic status or other external characteristics was dangerous anyway. You could get killed making wrong assumptions.

"Fucking Studio 54," the woman in front of him muttered, gesturing to some big-haired girls arguing with the doorman who wouldn't let them into the club. Eighties throwbacks with neon eye makeup, they made a pretty contrast to the skeletal doorkeeper and the stringy tough GRRL's in roller derby duds and scuffed stilettos slouching at the back of the line.

Matthew considered coming to their rescue but his chivalrous impulse was quelled by the arrival of the girls' boyfriends who turned out to be pals of the doorman. The old buddies thumped each other in the brutal way Matthew was never any good at. The sight of the backslapping bozos made him feel queasy. These dudes weren't handshakers, they were Viking potheads, ready to kill any dumb-ass club crawler stupid enough to hit on their girlfriends.

For a few seconds he was back in Casper, trying to figure out which drunk mean bastard, smoking a doobie outside The Wonder Bar, was likely to attack him before the end of the night.

Shit, he almost wished Terry was here.

The doorman let the berserker couple inside the club and resumed arguing with some other hapless people who weren't his long-lost friends. Matthew skirted the line and handed Skeletor a C-note and his business card. Jesus, he was a real little businessman tonight.

"I'm with Jackson Brand," he announced to the accompaniment of boos and catcalls from the queue for cutting ahead. A Grace Jones lookalike standing up front gave him the finger.

"Big fuckin' deal." The doorman pocketed the money then ripped up the card without looking at it and handed the tiny pieces back to Matthew's outstretched hand.

"Enjoy yourself and don't get killed," he chortled, opening the nightclub door and waving Matthew in.

A dark tunnel the color of dried bull's blood greeted Matthew as he stepped into the venue's foyer. Up ahead bright lights beckoned like something out of a near death experience. The tunnel opened out into a several adjoining rooms painted in disturbing psychedelic colors. He took an intuitive turn towards the right where he thought the bar might be located.

Primal music, heavy on bass and reverb, mimicking the sound of wet bodies spanking and/or fucking each other, assaulted him as he wove through throngs of noisy people drinking and snapping photos of each other on their cell phones. There were naked go-go girls in cages hanging from the ceiling; most of the patrons were watching videos of their gyrations projected on the walls instead of dancing.

"ACK! ACK! ACK!" The machine gun fire of a panic attack threatened to overtake him.

Matthew reminded himself to breathe his calming breath—about as effective as telling a Tourette's sufferer to just shut the fuck up. He felt like a sweaty shuddery mess. Still, catching sight of Jackson sitting across the room, perfectly placed under a purple spotlight, almost did the trick of unfreaking him, since his target destination was in sight.

Pushing his apprehension away he stumbled towards Brand's tiny table for two which was surrounded by a tightknit crowd of hangers-on looming over the handsome writer. Jackson lounged in his cheap wooden chair as if he were sitting on a plush banquette in the Paris Ritz, the other chair was empty. He waved an elegant wrist at Matthew, gold cufflinks flashing in the spotlight.

"Ah dear boy, there you are… You made it after all. How sweet to see your anxious face… Sit down before your disability undoes you," he drawled in the voice of an amused God, if God was Peter O'Toole, born and raised in Confederate Virginia.

With his dazzling blue eyes and blonde hair slicked back from sculptured cheekbones, he did resemble Lawrence of Arabia or some other leonine adventurer the dashing actor must have played, but his face wasn't the face of a movie star. Jackson Brand looked like the fucking King of the World. King of the Underworld, too.

One of the hovering minions pulled out the empty chair and Matthew sat down. It felt weird that everyone was standing but him and Jackson, like nightclubbing movie stars being swarmed for their autographs—if fans still queued for something as prosaic as written autographs in the glorious age of selfies.

The Viking boys from outside were standing at Jackson's elbow swigging a bottle of Jägermeister and mugging for him like clowns in a burlesque show, even though the languid writer wasn't looking at them. It was reassuring to see the cocky berserkers acting like kowtowing sycophants. Matthew took his chance and smiled at their pretty girlfriends but their raccoon eyes were fixed firmly on Jackson.

"This wretched man's named Matthew." Jackson nodded at him, then waved the fingers of one slim hand at the phalanx of tableside groupies.

"Sorry I can't remember who in the world you are ..." He pinched the tattooed arm of the closest Viking. "Umm . . . Frank Lloyd Wright, was it? Or was that Mr. Wrong?" The groupies dutifully tittered.

Jackson pushed a bottle of Stolichnaya towards Matthew after pouring a hefty shot into one of the smudged shot glasses that littered the table. Matthew surreptitiously wiped the rim of the cleanest-looking one on the hem of his T-shirt and took a shot, then slugged back another one for good measure.

"Drink judiciously, dear boy. . . So disappointing to find one's memories of an incandescent night permanently erased. . . Don't you agree?"

Brand turned towards his fawning audience which was starting to look pretty drunk. Matthew was reminded of Hieronymus Bosch paintings where the peasants wear tormented bestial faces, although these tableside donkeys and pigs were smiling contentedly, smug in the amplitude of their public hero worship.

"Some privacy for me and dear boy, if you please," Jackson gently requested, his intonation sweet as a mint julep. But his intention was clear, even before his dismissive follow-up remark of "Get along with you now." He fanned his beautiful fingers at them. He wanted them all to clear out.

The little crowd of fans melted away after a brief bout of ritualistic hand clasps and cheek kissing. The ass kissing was over for a while, too, it seemed, although Jackson patted the eighties-girls' taut fannies as they sashayed past in the clutches of their banished boyfriends. Matthew gawped lustfully and again they ignored him.

Now it was just him and Brand beneath the regal spotlight. Apparently the people Jackson had invited him to meet hadn't been part of the tipsy group which had just been sent away.

But where were they? Matthew hoped they never came. Being alone with the author made him nervous, but the thought of meeting another flock of strangers felt even worse. He dug a Xanax out of his jeans' pocket and swallowed it with another shot of Stoli. In his mind he heard Terry saying "Courage, Ol' Bean," but he told the interfering presence of his fuddy-duddy old friend to shut up.

Jackson refilled their dirty glasses. "You're wondering where the fascinating people you're supposed to meet are . . . But be patient, dear boy. Relax, enjoy yourself! The night is young . . . "

The next thing Matthew knew he was scrunched up against the wall of an unfamiliar bathroom, a ladies restroom by the look of it. Better decor than the men's room in The Underground, which he vaguely recalled visiting, to pop another Xanax, but that was to be expected. Urinals made even the cleanest gent's rooms seem disreputable. Ladies' loos were almost always of a higher aesthetic caliber, or so said fastidious Rosie who knew these things.

He couldn't remember how he got here, with his hands down the pants of a woman who was kissing a woman who was sitting on the closed lid of a cherry-pink toilet. There was cocaine involved somewhere in the strange scenario and too much alcohol and a cab driver who was wearing a kilt—so this wasn't still The Underground—and a cat sitting in his lap but maybe that was just pussy.

Before the pussy he was presently fingering, that is, but he couldn't remember anything else about leaving the club with or without Jackson, aside from a fleeting recollection of someone yowling who wasn't an actual cat.

"We need to pee! Let us in!" The tiny room, too small to hold him and the two strange women even though they were bunched up together like three peas in a pod, reverberated with the noise of unhappy female patrons pounding on the door.

Matthew's mouth was pressed against the blonde girl's breast, and the girl who'd been on the toilet was now standing up, rubbing his crotch with a Fu Manchu claw, and the next thing Matthew knew he was watching their faces in the mirror as he traded off fucking them from behind while they bent over the rust-stained sink.

He felt as if his penis were on fire, as if his lips pressing against the women's necks and shoulder blades were inflamed with some kind of horrible irritant like Spanish fly. He wasn't numb any more but he was still drunk, although sober enough to realize that he was acting well out of character.

BANG! BANG! BANG! He felt himself flying to bits like a cheap firecracker. His orgasm was shattering. Then suddenly it was all over and he was hanging over the bathroom vanity like a wet washrag and the two girls were trotting off like happy puppies, promising to call each other rather than him.

For a brief moment, less than an eye blink, he considered calling Terry. His cellphone was still lodged in his back-pocket even though his pants were down. No. Better to keep this whole crazy debauched night to himself until he could make sense of it.

But where was the fuck was Jackson?

WISTFUL DAY IN THE NEIGHBORHOOD

Terry's next door neighbor reminded him of Eleanor Rigby, the sad old lady in the Beatles' song. She had silver hair and an unreadable face—the kind that might be kept in a jar if such an odd thing were possible—and solemn eyes that never caught his when he waved at her. There was something sphinxlike about her which appealed to him.

She sat a few feet from her front window almost every day, ensconced in a high-backed armchair. She was there by seven in the morning when he left for his UW hospital janitor job, still there when he came home at night. Presumably she moved from her perch in the interim, to eat and use the toilet, but somehow he doubted it. She looked like she lived on air.

Terry had wondered if she was disabled, survivor of a stroke perhaps, but intuited that she was not. Even though her gaze was diffuse he was sure that she was aware of everything that transpired on their quiet tree-lined street, including his workday comings and goings and weekend mechanical bouts, his cries of distress over minor dents on his motorcycle.

He hadn't seen anyone come to her house, aside from their mail carrier, since he moved next door a little over six months ago. But this morning a pretty hippie chick in a flounced cotton skirt had come knocking on her door while he was out in the driveway dicking with his Harley.

He watched her climb the steep stairs up to the porch, admiring her boyish ass and short feathery haircut. Her goofy-looking dog lolled in the open window of her old Volvo like a drunk sea captain blearily searching for land on the dull horizon.

The girl turned around and waved at her pooch when she got to the top of the stairs. Terry was entranced. He hoped she was the old lady's prodigal daughter come home for a tender reunion. Not so fantastic perhaps—her smile was definitely sphinxlike.

He put down his ratchet and waited for the old lady to answer her door, glad that she had some company. He caught a glimpse of her slipping past her window in what looked like a ghostly caftan but she didn't come to the door. After several minutes of unanswered hammering, the now scowling girl went away, muttering about "stubborn Scorpios."

Even the disappointed girl's dog looked glum when they drove away and Terry felt sad for the unhappy pair of them, and for poor unresponsive Miss Rigby. He wondered if he should go and check on her. Maybe she was one of those sad-eyed ladies of the First-Alert nation who keep falling down.

Or maybe she was just a reclusive old bitch who wouldn't like him prying and spying on her. He decided that he didn't want to find out and went back to diddling his Harley.

But he was careful to include her parking strip when he mowed his lawn later that afternoon. He wanted to do something nice for her. Take care of a few of her practical needs, the way he wasn't doing with his father. Not that Mr. Thompson would have noticed if he had.

It was enjoyable to think of himself as a selfless hero which he hadn't done since he'd tried—vaingloriously—to stop

Matthew from marrying Rosie three years ago. And look where that got him. Stupid Matt was still stuck on his cheating ex-wife. Like a medical leech. Or a love-struck vampire.

Or no, it was the other way around. The Ol' Bean was the victim here not femme fatal Rosie. He was the one who'd been used and sucked dry, like the crazed old professor in Marlene Dietrich's *Blue Angel,* captive to a heartless singer.

Whatever, Matt was never going to give up on Rosie.

Just like Terry was never going to get away from menial jobs supervised by people who were dumber than him. Several of his janitorial co-workers were obvious tweekers, who swirled through the hospital like scrubbing tornados, and their uptight boss treated *him* like the weirdo of the whole fuckin' bunch because he talked about UFOs and read Sci-Fi.

Terry's life was going nowhere fast but he reckoned poor Matthew's life was going nowhere even faster, even though it probably looked like a perfectly notched arrow speeding towards the succulent apple of success to his bigwig clients and brokeback twin brothers stuck in the doldrums of Wyoming.

But Terry knew the truth. From second grade on, he'd watched the Ol' Bean attempt to jettison his neuroses through various grand romantic gestures and fuck-tons of work, down to his obsessive tinkering with broken analog and digital stuff, and fixation with sultry women, all of whom ended up running out on him when they found out he was busted inside.

Lying bastard had been out with Jackson Brand last night. Terry had gotten a text from him around 3 a.m. — in hindsight meant for the writer guy—which read, "Where are you? And where am I?"

Terry had responded with, "What's up, brother?" feeling worried, and flustered, having fallen asleep on the couch in front of the TV, still clutching his weed pipe.

When he didn't hear back, he'd called Matthew five or six times before the dumb-ass answered, mumbling something about cats and silly mistakes, before a background clatter like breaking dishes, and a shriek of feminine laughter, was interrupted by a ghoulish voice proclaiming, "I'm here, dear boy!"

Matt slurred the name Jackson, then clicked off the call, leaving Terry feeling jealous and angry.

He was pretty sure the Ol' Bean didn't actually want to fuck his fancy new writer-friend—like all the bowled-over celebrity-worshipping literary critics apparently did these metrosexual days—but guessed there was something subliminal going on. A budding bromance—very vanilla, but still, it was pretty insulting when he thought about it.

Because he—Terry—was Matt's true-blue best friend, his classic sidekick, the one guy who knew him inside and out and didn't get sick at what he saw, didn't run from the poor bloke's sloshing mishmash of pain and self-hatred.

No one knew the Ol' Bean better than him, felt sorrier for all the bad shit he'd gone through, or more sincerely championed his happiness. But it was hard, mighty damn hard sometimes, not to tell him to just *take a fuckin' hike.*

What with being haunted by Rosie and hating his programming job and not knowing what to do about the frantic outbursts of his weird electrical circuitry—other than try to take the edge off by monkeying around with busted radios and cuckoo clocks—the poor dude was suffering. Which made him terrible to be around. Worse than the tweekers Terry worked with at the hospital.

No wonder he gravitated towards a suave poseur who pretended to *really like* him, when he didn't much like himself. His whole fucking life was a pretense. Except for loving Rosie, that is. And him, Terry hoped. They were the two exceptions. But lately he didn't feel very exceptional when Matt was around. Just felt like a worn-out dildo.

Terry remembered how excited Matthew had been after meeting Jackson at some kind of lavish do at a tech investor's house, described in excruciating detail over a round of overpriced drinks at a chic new oyster bar in Ballard, Matt practically slavering over the charms of his new literary bud, while Terry fiddled with their pile of bivalve shells.

Afterwards, they'd walked several blocks to the Chittenden Locks to check out the fish ladder. A decade-old tradition that made them feel like native Pacific Northwesterners instead of expats—escapees—from the landlocked prairies of Wyoming.

But instead of watching out for chinooks and sockeyes, Matthew had continued extolling the virtues of the fancy-pants writer, acting out the salient parts of their fortuitous meeting, complete with verbatim dialogue, until Terry wanted to hit him.

Terry had frogmarched him over to the algae-smeared window in the fish-viewing room but the besotted dude still wouldn't fucking shut up. It was infuriating! And he hadn't even looked at the beautiful salmon migrating upstream to their spawning beds.

"Fuck him and the horse he rode in on," Terry muttered for the umpteenth time as he stood on his back porch after dinner, savoring his anger and waiting for the moon to rise, even though he knew it wouldn't show through the thick gauze of clouds gathering on the darkening horizon. Rain was coming. He could smell the evening air freshening as he gazed morosely upwards.

He was still hungry after eating four slices of leftover pizza but he didn't want to go back inside to hunt up a beer and a donut until he gave the night sky a chance to enliven him. He was hoping for the Aurora Borealis or a spectacular meteor shower, or even just a brilliant full moon, but it was the wrong time of the month and the wrong time of year for astronomical comforts. Just like it was for everything.

With a sad frisson, he realized he was thinking about his mother, remarried now, after shipping his demented old dad out of Casper to a rinky-dink Alzheimer's home in Cheyenne a month prior to divorcing him. He hated her for that, but he still missed her. She seemed like the only reliable female influence he'd ever had, not counting Matt's mom, who was long ago dead, burned up in a car crash along with Matt's dad.

He wondered if his silver-haired neighbor was back in her chair, but he didn't walk down the driveway to find out. He wished he had a cigarette even though he didn't smoke and a rum and coke, with a paper umbrella in it, even though he didn't like mixed drinks. It would be good to have something meaningful or fun to celebrate but he couldn't think of anything that moved him, besides his growing disappointment with Matt.

So *shee-it*.

Maybe it was time to let loose of his mixed-up friend, even if it meant watching him hook up with a modern Marquis de Sade or a castrating bitch like Rosie. Probably be happier without his balls anyway, the way Matt railed about the sexual benefits of lesbianism, although based on what Terry had heard about Brand's sex soirees, he'd probably spent last night teabagging a bevy of literary socialites.

Memories of his own sexual escapades buzzed like cicadas in Terry's now drowsy head. Women's voices asking him to do exciting things to them. But the wild night sounds, silenced by years of willing and not-so-willing celibacy, were as dim as tactile memories of his ex-girlfriends' sweet-smelling flesh.

He was sick of masturbating in a lonely bed, chilled to the bone by old regrets. He wanted to lie in a field of wildflowers, pressing his sun-warmed body against some pretty girl's naked chest. Like how it used to be up on Casper Mountain when he felt like Pan, aroused by the eroticism of nature. When every teenaged weekend was a bacchanalian romp and the touch of female breasts a cause for Yeatsean rapture.

Of course there'd been women after he came to Seattle. A baker who pandered to his prodigious sweet tooth, a coy pediatric nurse, an ASL teacher who signed obscene words when he went down on her. He'd been friendly with a lot of clitorises and his sensual moves had been good, but somewhere along the line his juicy libido had dried up.

His problem hadn't been hormonal, nor was he strictly depressed. It was something indefinable, worse than ennui, a secret unnamable embarrassment that bugged him, even though he could still "get it up." But he hardly ever wanted to. There was no going back to those innocently voluptuous days, sure as shit no going back to Casper, no reason to get all het up, so what was the fucking point?

Terry wanted something he'd never had before. Something exhilarating that was real at the same time as it was science-fiction, something momentous and alien and otherworldly, filling up the holes in his life. Not sex with robots, God forbid, but a kind of transcendentalism in the love act. The ASL lady had scoffed at the idea, without signing anything.

But he'd forgotten how to fall in love. Not that there were any women around to fall in love with. No one at work, no one in the neighborhood, no one in his social circle—the Union of Underpaid Janitors—no one to succor and suck him. Not that he'd put things that crudely.

He looked up again. Nothing happened in the sky over the next several minutes, except that it got as dark as an urban sky with cloud cover ever gets, which isn't very dark. Antithesis of the inky skies of Wyoming, dotted with a billion stars like sprinkles on a giant blue-velvet cupcake. So gorgeous you could eat it. The image made his stomach growl.

He took a hit off his pot pipe, pondering his options for tomorrow. Other than taking his Sunday motorcycle ride which wasn't that much fun anymore, anyway.

"*Shee-it.*" He grumbled, suddenly aware that he'd been muttering aloud.

What with the out-of-control traffic and the Mcfuckin' crazy-assed aggressive bicyclists, who made the Hell Angels look like kids at a Victorian fete riding along in a donkey cart with old Granny, it was a nightmare on the streets of Seattle.

Not to mention that every other block had a giant hole in the ground where a row of old Craftsman houses had been pulled down to make way for another stinkin' condo. Or drugstore. Or Starbucks. Rents were sky-high and utilities were climbing, so his view of the affordable nature of living in Seattle kinda stank. Lake Union was turning into a giant puddle surrounded by tin cans. It was getting so he couldn't remember why he came here.

Ah, but he was sick of complaining. He was getting to sound just like Matt. Even though he was just talking to himself on his porch, in the wondrous privacy of being a nonentity in a city full of dope-smoking entrepreneurial movers and shakers, it was embarrassing sounding like such a dumb-ass.

He had to try something else. Maybe AA? He wondered if there was an organization for forsaken friends other than Facebook. Would there be pizza at the Meet Up?

Terry lifted his head, no longer drowsy, smelling something green and sweet that smelled like home. Like pine trees in the Wind River Canyon. Which for some inexplicable reason, biologists probably knew but he didn't, didn't smell like the pine trees around Puget Sound. The memory of ancient crevasses and rocks struck him like a summer lightning storm, only gentler. His Rocky Mountain heritage must be seen as a gift, he supposed, yet here he was in Seattle. What did that mean?

He looked higher up at the clouds.

Oh! Lovely! Lovely! There was a bit of the moon. Saved by the cosmic bell! There really was light in the Universe, something beautiful he could count on.

Swiveling around to face Ms. Scorpio's house, he shot a volley of good thoughts and neighborly good wishes her way. Then he went inside to call Matthew.

21

LIVING THE VIDA LOCA

J ackson Brand was a good kind of guy to be friends with when you wanted to see yourself in a flattering light, Matthew reckoned, totting up the number of times he'd gone out with the celebrated fellow in the past few weeks—ten or twelve meetings, at least.

Even when he took you to a seedy den of iniquity in some unnumbered circle of Dante's Inferno, and you were snorting coke off the sweaty backside of a transgender hooker, you imagined that being with Jackson made your motives and behaviors less venal, more poetic than they actually were.

Everybody from the valets at the chichi restaurants he frequented to the production assistants fussing about him in green rooms wanted a piece of brilliant charismatic Jackson. To suck, fuck or be fucked by Jackson, preferably in real time, online, with a paying audience. To be seen in his company was to have finally "arrived" in society even if social acceptance was something you formerly hated.

Matthew hated just about everything and everyone but he was enthralled with his masterful new friend. Sometimes he imagined going down on Jackson in the tarted-up bathroom of some culinary hotshot's *fuck-me-with-food* restaurant, while the patrons in the dining room licked duck fat off each other's faces, but couldn't quite finish the fantasy.

Too bad he was basically heterosexual and, recent experience to the contrary, didn't enjoy having sex in public bathrooms. He hoped his innate prudery, if discovered, wouldn't offend his priapic new pal. It was not a good thing to be mocked by Jackson Brand.

Jackson's extemporaneous expositions on the joys of "giving it to the bitches"—tight young unmodified-by-plastic-surgery bitches, since natural beauty suited his self-identification as an aesthete—were no help in straightening out Matthew's sexual confusion. He was getting fucked all the time now, mostly by decadent girlfriends of Jackson's, but there was no joy in the sex acts and only a modicum of physical relief.

Matthew's couldn't quite remember what the *it* Jackson bragged about was, or how you gave it to anyone, although he was sure he had possessed *it* at one time, back when Rosie's adroit understanding of his sexual psychology made him feel as if his penis could open the floodgates of eternal love, and vice versa.

It was strange remembering how assertive his manhood had felt back when he was getting lawfully-wedded sex on demand, but not quite as strange as knowing that he and Terry were no longer best friends. His guilt over his deliberate ruination of their friendship made Matthew feel unbearably anxious, but he racked up his self-loathing to cocaine-induced panic attacks, skirting his misery with more decadent sexual encounters.

Rosie disappearing into the deep pink labyrinth of lesbianism with Alexa hadn't been half as bad, in many ways, as losing the only man he could trust. Terry had never wanted anything from Matthew except friendship—no abject apologies, no alimony, no public sex acts—and even that requirement had generous parameters.

"Just don't fuck me over, man," was Terry's only demand, from the age of twelve onwards, and that's exactly what turncoat Matthew had done two weeks ago. Told him off at their favorite restaurant when Terry was drunk and he wasn't. It didn't make any difference that Terry had started the fight; he was the one who'd ended their friendship

Everything has been going fine until Terry said, "What kinda tricky secret life are you livin' now, anyway, man? I saw your freakin' photo in *The Stranger*, at some rich douche bag's party, sniffin' Lit-Prick's armpit like its Chanel Number Five. You told me you were workin' that night… So what the fuck's goin' on?"

"Nothing's going on. I was at a party for godsake not mutilating your mother." Jesus, why had he said that? Terry was very fond of his mother. Matthew tried to laugh it off but Terry puffed out his cheeks and bugged out his eyes like a blow-fish.

"That's what you're like, bro. The fuckin' Michelin man. Nothin' but hot air. And you don't even wanna know what comes out of your mouth these days. Mcfuckin' pathetic."

Not this old palaver, Matthew had thought, the same damned sin he's been sticking me with since the seventh grade when I dumped him on the school grounds to go hang with some popular kids. How I'm cheating on him if I have other friends.

"Talk about puffed up idiots. You should see yourself, Terry. You might as well have a badge pinned on your chest that says you own me. You don't own me just because we're friends…used to be friends."

"Whaddya mean *used to be*?" Terry had been slumping, fidgeting with his napkin, but now he picked himself up, sat up straight, and looked directly at Matthew.

He was drunk as a lord, he must have been, he'd drunk several double whiskeys before placing his order, but suddenly Terry seemed solemn as a judge. And the next thing he said was a proclamation.

"Well fuck you and the blindfolded horse you rode in on even if that dumb ol' horse was me. Fuck you and fuck your whole family, including the dead and the crazy ones you were always a shit to. But hey, now that you're bein' a cock-breath to me you can go fuck yourself sideways until you figure out that Brand is screwin' ya, too, and not in a good way… Stupid-ass motherfuckers."

It was Terry saying "motherfuckers" that hurt Matthew the most. As if they were on opposite sides of some civil war battle, and he was in Brand's battalion. That was when, for better or worse, he decided that their friendship was over.

Being without Terry at his side, even though he'd pushed him into the outer darkness himself, made Matthew feel as if he were alone on the planet, like the Little Prince in Saint-Exupery's book. There was a line in it that Rosie had used when she was still in love with him: "One sees clearly only with the heart. Anything essential is invisible to the eyes."

Matthew wondered, not for the first time, if that was why he could no longer see the real Terry or value him the way he truly deserved to be valued. He'd been Matthew's stay-at-home man and boy-o-solace for so long that he'd become invisible, like a predictably solicitous wife—easy to take for granted, stale, unfuckable.

Every act of kindness, every naked confidence Terry shared from their kid clubhouse days to the terrible Joe Cocker catharsis at the restaurant, paled in comparison to the glittering pronouncements of Jackson, the shining King of Letters who enthralled the world with his suck-my-adjectives attitude.

The nihilism of loving this preposterous poseur was intoxicating in its pointlessness. Jackson didn't deserve to be loved although his vivid well-arranged words certainly deserved to be admired. Bumbling Terry with his histrionic temperament and hangdog devotion deserved every iota of affection which could be scraped from Matthew's half-charred heart but he couldn't summon the energy necessary to attempt the life-saving curettage.

"Don't hate me I just need some time," he'd texted as soon as he thought Terry had made his way home from the Salmon House. There were tears in the poor guy's eyes when he roared away from the parking lot on his Harley. Thank god he was an experienced drunk driver.

Matthew hadn't attempted any further communication with Terry, as pointless, in its way, as trying to get Jackson to pick up his phone. Terry presented the opposite challenge—he was always ready and willing to talk, but his flimsy old cellphone couldn't hold a charge. Their conversations, punctuated by the beeping signaling the imminent demise of his phone's battery, were exercises in coitus-interruptus, his texts, forever responding to outdated messages, goofy non sequiturs.

Matthew's whole life was coming askew, tilting like the deck on the Titanic, flying apart—sinking or exploding? He couldn't tell which. Whatever state of mind he ascribed to himself, he had no adequate words to express what he was experiencing, no diagnosis of his actual condition. He knew he probably ought to see a therapist but didn't.

Random phrases accompanied by disturbing mental images—decapitated rats, starving children—popped into his head throughout the day, especially right after his pointless phone calls to Jackson. The obsessive flow of words and thoughts made Matthew feel possessed. He ordered his brain, "Stop making me think these horrible things!" but his brain said, "Go fuck yourself," instead of "Yes, master."

And his nightmare went on, even when he was partying, getting his picture taken with a crowd of fantabulous hipsters stoned to the top of their cockily-angled fedoras on the heady smell of media-worthy insider gossip, of which Matthew was now an integral if self-conscious part.

As if he was undergoing a sadistic sort of mnemonic acupuncture, aural memories also stuck in his head along with the random phrases, until he felt like a pincushion wired for sound. Rosie's husky voice saying she was leaving him. His mother's tremulous invitation to a family reunion he'd refused to attend, a few weeks before she died in the car crash with his dad, on their way to Seattle. Terry's angry shout when he dumped him.

The cacophony of voices, the terrible unforgiving relentless voices of the dead and lost and betrayed kept at him until he could barely sleep, barely eat, barely remember anything other than the volcanic rumblings of his unhappy past. He snorted more cocaine and worked on his broken toys and clocks and tried not to care that he was burning up from the inside out.

Lying in his top-of-the-line Sleep Comfort bed, adjusted to maximum firmness so that he felt like a yogi reclining on a board of foam nails, Matthew texted Jackson some kind of folderol about a women they'd met at a bar on their last hump-day in Fremont.

True, Jackson would probably never pick it up, or if he did, never respond, at least not in a timely way. But sending out a trivial little message about some poor girl's fuckability with a snide remark about the hair on her upper lip—which Matthew secretly admired—was a manageable way to get through a few minutes of the endless evening which stretched ahead of him.

Amazingly, Jackson texted back almost instantly. "Took an amazing dump... try it sometime & get that load off yr guts... Id give mustache grl a twirl if evr saw her again... luckily, won't... & neither will u..."

Jackson's misspelled texts were riddled with ellipses and frequently scatological. Matthew wondered if he'd been subject to strict toilet training as a child or just liked talking about feces. His last novel, purportedly autobiographical like everything he wrote, featured the hero enjoying a high colonic while jacking off, come to think of it.

The esteemed auteur's apparent copromania made him seem more approachable, though, less a literary lion than a figure of fun. Terry would have stepped right up to the plate when it came to lobbing insulting nicknames at him—Mr. Loo, Poo Fighter, etc.—but if Matthew had anything to say about it, the two men would never meet. Not likely the way things stood between him and Terry at the moment, nevertheless an idea which couldn't be countenanced.

Matthew's back was starting to hurt. The Hindu Guru Comfort bed was more like a torture chamber than the cosmic flotation device he fantasized washing him into the ethers. If only there was some reliable way to fly off into the clouds that didn't involve skeezy sleeping pills like the succubus moth Lunetra, which landed on people's faces in TV commercials, or darker more seductive drugs like heroin.

He might as well just lie back and watch the drapes on the open bedroom window stir sluggishly in the evening breeze, partially obscuring his magnificent view of Lake Washington and the opportunity it afforded him for drowning himself.

Not that he would, of course. Not that he would.

LONDON CALLING

J ackson was going to London and wanted Mathew to come along. Dinner with Mick and Keith, a stroll by the Thames with Zady, a guest spot on the Graham Norton Show. His calendar groaned with important appointments he was already blogging about.

"Don't be a ghoul stuck in dim Seattle-land. I need your company!" he said as they careened along Portland's Terwilliger Curves in Jackson's rental car.

Ghouls were party poopers, politicians and academics, and, worst of all, unfuckable women. Doggy-ghouls, Jackson called them, mimicking some poor bitch howling at a spinster's moon. His falsetto, while coyly Beatlesque, was alarming. Matthew was mortified by his cruelty yet strangely impressed by his ceaseless narcissism.

How did such an insensitive shit get to be so fucking popular?

Sales of Jackson's dystopian novels were soaring thanks to a gushing article in *People* magazine he never referred to, preferring to quote *The New York Times* which called him "the acerbic conscience of literate millennials," even though he was a greying gen-exer.

The writer was famous as hell but Matthew wasn't so sure about Jackson anymore, wasn't even sure he liked him. Impossible not to come to the conclusion that he was jealous of the guy's success, but it was something more insidious than envy that was starting to give him the creeps. A dawning recognition that Jackson's dark vices were getting darker and darker, and he was increasingly complicit in them. Still he'd willingly accompanied him to Portland to visit a private sex club, so obviously he was either a slow learner or a hypocrite. Rosie always maintained he was both.

It took only a few minutes to find the place once they turned off the twisty boulevard. They screeched to a stop in front of a low-slung house on the side of a woodsy hill which looked no different than the expensive suburban homes on both sides of it, and got out of the car.

"No need to be nervous, dear boy," Brand proclaimed as they walked up the flagstone pathway to the big front door. He handed Matthew a pink guest pass with his name calligraphed in dramatic lettering.

"The ladies who will be honoring us with their presence are part of my perks as a founding member. It's my privilege to break in the interns. Remember, *do what thou wilt is the whole of the law*. So have fun . . . Etcetera."

Jackson drew a large pink key from his pocket and stuck it in the door lock as casually as a man returning home from the grocery store. There was no one to greet them when they stepped inside but there was a pink princess phone sitting on a little table in the foyer next to a pink announcement which said "use me to sign in."

Jackson picked up the pink receiver, said a few words, presumably securing their right to be there, while Matthew tried to case the place. There wasn't much to see except a large gilt mirror on the wall above the foyer table and an empty hallway leading off somewhere to the right.

After a few moments a beautiful woman came into the room from a doorway Matthew hadn't noticed at the end of the hall. Her long blonde hair was gathered up on top of her narrow head in a ponytail as long as a horse's mane. She was wearing a tight latex apron, thigh-high latex stockings and black leather boots that skimmed the top of her kneecaps. Matthew could see her ass in the mirror when she turned to face them. She wasn't wearing any underpants.

"*Guten Tag,*" the concierge said in a husky voice as she executed a satirical curtsy. "Welcome back, *Herr* Brand. Everything has been arranged for your servicing."

Jackson bent low at the waist like an effete Victorian and kissed her pale white hand. "Charmed, once again, Miss Wagner." *VAHG-nur.* The fin d'siecle atmosphere was getting thicker and thicker and Matthew wasn't sure that he liked it.

"As am I," she returned, inclining her head so low her ponytail swished on the floor. She did a little pirouette on sharp high heels and gestured for the men to follow her down the long pink corridor lit with pink-colored lights.

"Like going back to the womb, dear boy," Jackson commented as they trotted along behind her.

When they came to the end of the hallway she opened a door to a dimly lit room and beckoned them inside before blowing a kiss and striding away on her spindly heels. Two nude woman were sitting on a low couch drinking diet Pepsis, a dishwater blonde and an olive-skinned brunette, both with silicone breasts and denuded pubic hair. For a confused second Matthew thought they were sex dolls.

Shelves of whips and rubber dildos, anal plugs and vibrators lined one pink wall, the opposite end of the room held a four-foot wooden post with metal rings at the top and a wide massage table adorned with canvas straps. An array of enema bags, blindfolds, and nylon cords was draped over a portable coatrack.

"Come here, masters," the blonde one said, opening her skinny legs and showing her pink vagina.

The brunette let her last swig of Pepsi dribble onto her enormous breasts. "Wanna lick it off?"

Yes! Yes! Matthew's cock swelled as he approached them. But Jackson seemed to be hanging back so he paused, taking his hands off his belt buckle. What was the etiquette regarding who fucked first in a sex club?

"Do what thou wilt, dear boy." Jackson drawled from somewhere behind him, coaxing him forward.

The brunette unzipped Matthew's pants with fingertips painted the color of menstrual blood. There was something unsettling about her ashen lips and heavy eye-makeup, a hint of vampirism that made him sweat, even as his cock throbbed inside his underpants.

He fumbled with his jeans and flannel shirt and took them off. As he knelt down to suck the Pepsi-girl's nipples he felt a sudden stinging lash on his back.

"What the fuck!" Matthew staggered to his feet and swung around to see Jackson in a gladiator stance holding a short leather whip which he brought down again on Matthew's chest before he could dart away.

"Like that, don't you, darling boy?" Jackson crowed, prancing around Matthew like a demented Nijinsky, naked except for his trademark argyle socks and a cord tied around the base of his enormous penis.

"Whip *me*, master!" The blonde girl sprang to her feet and lunged towards Jackson, inflated tits bobbing like mooring buoys, but he evaded her and stepped back en garde, tossing Matthew the leather whip.

"Beat them black and blue, dear boy . . . Twisted bitches seem to like that kind of brutal thing . . . Surely I'm not mistaken?" Jackson's Virginia drawl was thick as molasses poured over something nasty.

Matthew recoiled as he caught the whip, shocked into instant revulsion. He lunged towards Jackson and struck him in the face with the rubber whip handle as ancient images of his angry father hitting him with a belt exploded in his head.

No sadistic prick was ever going to beat him again!

The pink-girls, quivering with unappeased lustfulness or indignation, crouched on the couch, relegated to hieroglyphic status, while Jackson and Matthew grappled.

"Fucking pervert! Get me out of this hellhole!" Pushing Jackson away with both hands, Matthew snatched his clothes and fled to the corner of the room behind the massage table.

"Unlock the door, goddamn it! I am fucking freaking out, you crazy son of a bitch!" he shouted as he shoved his arms and feet into his clothes, a massive panic attack hurtling along the frayed tracks of his nervous system, but Jackson just stood there, his obscene erection swinging like a drunk cop's truncheon, a skein of spittle hanging from his bloody lips where the whip handle had hit him.

Finally the blonde, grumbling to her vampire friend about Matthew's gauche behavior, rose from the couch, unlocked the door and let him out.

"Pussy," she smirked as she shut the door in his face.

Slumped in the pink corridor outside the stultifying sex box, throbbing head pressed against the wall as he waited for Jackson to come out, Matthew wondered if he was finally having the breakdown he'd always feared, the one that would summarily kill him. His asthma, chest pains and heart palpitations were going to zap him dead, unless he could catch his breath.

Then again, his morbid anxiety, so long his nemesis, might be his salvation, if he could only succumb to it, throw himself into the vortex, the empty howling space of a friendless universe, where every trace of lustfulness and sexual curiosity he possessed might turn to ashes from which no phoenix flicker of life could ever erupt.

Speaking of friendlessness, here was Jackson now, emerging from the tawdry sex room, re-dressed, thin lips stretched in an impersonal smile from which the smear of fresh blood had been carefully erased.

"How unfortunate," he said blandly, pinching Matthew's tear-stained cheek. "You made me look like a fool in there… I hope that wasn't your intention, dear boy."

Jackson pressed himself against Matthew's back, hands wrapped around his waist like a lover's. For a brief moment Matthew felt consoled by the hot breathe against his neck, Jackson's indefatigable erection pressed hard against his ass, the ridiculous sense that he was going to be rescued by the sadist he'd just insulted.

But of course Jackson had a different idea, one befitting his favorite themes of moral and mental corruption. In a masterfully synchronized movement he bit down hard on the tender flesh between Matthew's shoulder and neck while simultaneously twisting his balls with one brutal hand and clawing his thigh with the other. Screaming in pain, Matthew slumped to the floor, waiting to be kicked, but the vicious hands which had just assaulted him were gentle as they helped him to sit up.

"Poor boy." Jackson knelt next to Matthew, a look of seemingly genuine concern flitting across his aquiline face, yet there was a terrible malice in his eyes which warned that he was cold-bloodedly dangerous.

"Don't mess with me again… Terrible idea to bite the hand that feeds you… Particularly when it's mine…"

A stranger might imagine that the well-dressed man attending to the crumpled man in the corridor was an empathetic doctor on hiatus at the sex club tending to a medical emergency. Jackson's melodious voice sounded like a ministering angel's as he tut-tutted over Matthew, even though it was the Voice of Doom hinting at his punishment to come. Something much worse than having his neck bitten and his testicles squashed like squeeze toys.

Matthew levered himself to his feet unaided and limped away from Jackson who had risen from his knees and was punching the keypad of his smartphone with the nonchalance of a man ordering takeout food.

"Message to the management to take you off my guest list," he intoned as he pushed Matthew out the fire exit which led into the parking lot behind the sex house, as if Matthew would ever want to penetrate the entrails of *Big Pink* again.

Jackson beeped his keychain at the rental car and unlocked the doors.

"Get in the back and keep your mouth shut," he said, and Matthew did, feeling like a criminal or a runaway kid being returned to a harsh military boarding school as he buckled his seatbelt.

All the way home from Portland to Seattle, Matthew sweated over what he was going to do about the monstrous Mephistopheles who'd sprung up in his life and was now in the driver's seat of their rental car, buzzing in and out of traffic like an angry wasp.

The Theremin waves emanating from Jackson's knotted brow emitted a horrible vibration that made Matthew feel sick. He wanted to roll down the window in case he had to throw up but was afraid the crazy bastard might run the car off the freeway, shoot him with a gun hidden in the glovebox, or re-grab his throbbing balls, if he felt in the least insulted. They drove in silence while he stewed and fretted and Jackson smiled a series of disturbing smiles, each one creepier than the satyr's grin he'd smiled inside the sex club when he was wielding his leather whip.

Stumbling through the doorway of his town house at ten o'clock, Matthew practically wept at the sight of his familiar furniture and picture window, his unobstructed view of Lake Washington where he was now sure he would never want to drown himself.

He was done with thinking about death after driving for three and a half hours with a potentially homicidal maniac who had it in for him.

"I'm sorry. I'm sorry." Matthew had said as he exited Jackson's rental car.

"No worries," Jackson had answered before he drove away. A phrase Matthew had always found menacing. Everything was menacing now except for one sweet moment of bliss when he laid his jangled head on his cool cotton pillowcase and picked up the phone to call Terry.

HOUSE CALL

Terry looked across the side yard into his mysterious neighbor's kitchen window. Her slim silhouette stood out like a black-and-white illustration in an old *Life* magazine, as she stood in the light of her open refrigerator in an otherwise darkened room. In her short summer nightgown she looked as svelte as Tinkerbelle as she pulled a carton from the shelf.

Funny how young she looked, much younger than he'd originally guessed, although his view through her voile curtains was indeterminate. She looked innocent and experienced, both old and young, a bit like a magical creature in the weird electrical light.

"Let me in," Terry whispered, a few minutes later, as he walked across the uneven grass between the two houses a few minutes later, holding a bag of *Mighty-O* donuts.

Climbing her broad back staircase, Terry felt less like a neighborly knight and more like a criminal about to commit an offense. Jail would not be his punishment, but rather a forcible exclusion from the female society he craved, if he blew this unlikely assignment.

What if the silver-haired stranger was like all the other women he'd pursued, aside from his mother who still picked up her phone when he called? All those wary women who backed away when his ardor got out of hand or his eccentricities became overwhelming. What if she just didn't like him?

Terry laid his trembling index finger on the old lady's doorbell and pressed the button. The kitchen was dim except for the moonlight which bathed the neighborhood, no gauzy clouds obscuring it as it had two weeks ago.

He watched through the back door window as his neighbor came towards him after flipping on an overhead light. She opened the door wider than he expected and stood squarely in the threshold like a major-domo ready for a fight. The sad story Terry had invented about her took on a thrilling new dimension in which she was less a victim and more of a fighter, although the expression on her face was wary rather than hostile.

She was middle-aged, not elderly, and she was beautiful to him.

Before he could introduce himself, she reached forward and plucked the donuts from his grasp.

"You might as well come in," she said. She pointed towards the kitchen table. "Have a seat. I'll make some tea. Then you can tell me why you've been watching me."

"Didn't mean to make you uncomfortable, ma'am," Terry said as he sat down, wishing he was still standing up with his old cowboy hat in his hand—the one he didn't have any more—that made him look like a cowboy TV sheriff. Better to look like a lawman hero than a scoundrel in her vivid green eyes which flashed with guarded good humor when she smiled at him.

"*Ma'am* . . . I usually hate the term, but from you it sounds like a compliment. Bet you weren't raised around here." She filled an electric teakettle with water and plugged it in, then plated the donuts and set them on the table along with two pottery mugs and the milk she'd taken out of the refrigerator earlier.

"Nah . . . I mean, no, I wadn't. Wasn't." *Shee-it*, he couldn't even talk to her.

"Okay, you can tell me your name and where you're from, after you tell me why you mowed my lawn."

"Just bein' neighborly," Terry said, wishing she'd stop looking at him, and maybe go put on a bathrobe so he couldn't see her nipples winking at him through her nightgown. Her breasts were small but supple, as was the rest of her, which made him think of dancers and old-timey farm women toiling in fields of sunny-colored grain. Not the body of a woman who sat on a chair all day.

She unplugged the kettle and poured hot water into a red teapot, then reached into the cupboard for two glasses. "Gin or whiskey? There's beer in the fridge."

He wanted the beer but said, "Tea's fine," wincing as she poured herself a shot from an expensive looking bottle of Scotch with a soaring eagle on the label. *Dumb-ass.* He really needed that beer. But he'd ask for one later. If he stayed that long.

Waiting for the tea to steep gave him a chance to marshal his thoughts and to keep looking at her while she looked at him, although they weren't quite having a stare down. After she poured them both a cup and sat down, he held out his hand and said, "Terry Thompson. Pleased to meet you, *ma'am.*"

She clasped his hand. "Likewise. Isabel Dashiell. My husband Charlie is dead." She laughed and took a quick swig of whiskey. "I don't know why I said that."

"'Cause it's true?" They both laughed, she more uproariously, showing her very nice teeth.

"I'm sorry. That must be awful for you."

"Yeah, you could say it sucks, although Charlie wouldn't appreciate the vernacular."

"How 'bout *fuckin' sucks*?" he said and she laughed again. Now he was getting the hang of it. The feel of her.

He broke a donut in halves and gave one to her. "My favorite."

"Mine, too," she said, devouring it in two hungry bites. "How did you know?"

"Somethin' like ESP. Or maybe just an educated guess."

Isabel's frown was satirical. "So I look like a cinnamon girl?"

"You bet. Pretty damn tasty . . . er, spicy." He blushed and she laughed, this time politely. He hoped she wasn't going to throw him out.

"Mind if I have that beer?" He struggled to his feet, feeling clumsy.

"Help yourself. Then tell me why you've been watching me."

"'Cause you look like a woman in distress," Terry said, hoping she'd laugh, even though he was serious. And that laugh of hers was a ruse, anyway. Deep inside, she was crying.

He opened his beer, took a long swallow, leaning against the counter instead of sitting back down. He felt antsy as hell, and uncomfortably aroused by her stoic performance, afraid that she thought him a fool. To cover his embarrassment he asked about Charlie and what had happened to him.

"Died of a heart attack in a parking lot on the UW campus. He left for work that morning and I never saw him again. Alive, that is. I saw his body when he was dead, but it wasn't him anymore."

"I work there, too," Terry said, inanely, since it seemed pretty obvious that Charlie Dashiell was an academic instead of a lowly hospital janitor. They'd worked on the same campus but in entirely different worlds.

To his relief Isabel didn't ask what kind of work he did, just stared into her half-empty mug as if she was reading her tea leaves. She poured another slug of whiskey into her glass. "Sure you won't have some?"

"Beer's fine with me. And tea. The tea's good, too." Shit, he sounded like a dimwit again, but he didn't know what to say. He wished he wasn't glad that her husband was dead but he was.

"We're supposed to be in France right now, visiting Gothic cathedrals. His field was Renaissance history, but he loved medieval church architecture more than anything. Aside from Emily and me."

So they had a daughter and what seemed like a tight relationship, although how you could tell what a strange widow's life had been like before her husband died, factoring in survivor's guilt—which Terry was already experiencing, even though no one he loved had died—no, that was impossible.

He finished his beer and sat down.

"What's your daughter like?"

Isabel smiled, and the sad look left her face. "Emily's wonderful! Smart, accomplished, funny, nice. The light of her father's life and mine. Recently married to an Indian scientist and a research scientist herself. She and Deepak work at the University of Minnesota, but I wish they lived here."

Emily was thirty, tall and dark like her dad who had French ancestry, "not a blonde-haired Norwegian like me," Isabel said, although her hair was more silver than gold. *Ash* blonde, Terry stopped himself from saying, in case Charlie had been cremated. Gol-dang, but he was getting as weird as Matt about words, and he didn't even have synesthesia.

For a long while they didn't say anything while they finished off the pot of tea, Isabel alternately sipping from her mug and her topped up glass of whiskey. Terry rejected her offer of another beer, saying he'd wait awhile since the night was still young. He sounded more like a loser from Hicksville than a guy on the make, which is how he wanted Isabel to see him, until he could get a grip on his feelings for her.

"That wasn't your daughter I saw coming up on your porch last weekend, then." He didn't mention that Isabel hadn't answered her door.

"No, that was my cousin, Madam Zodie. She's a professional astrologer. Quite a bit younger than me."

"Good lookin' lady," he said, hoping she didn't think he'd wanted to fuck her cousin, even though for a minute he had, imaging the girl's hippie skirt pulled up to waist while she sat on him, her doleful dog watching them as they rocked in unison.

"So tell me about yourself," Isabel said, disappointing him with the predictable command which so often meant the end of any real conversation. But she seemed genuinely interested in him, although he didn't know why, unless she was trying to access the likelihood of him being a psychopath.

So he told her about moving from Wyoming to Seattle with his old friend Matt, who was a bona fide computer genius, and a dork who didn't know his ass from a hole in the ground when it came to red-haired women and love, both of which he was addicted to.

"Sounds like he needs his chart done."

Terry suspected she was talking about astrology but it was hard to tell since she was beginning to slur her words.

"Ya mean his horror scope?" he said, meaning to make her laugh again, but she didn't. Fuck it, maybe it was time to go home.

Isabel's face was flushed and her hands were trembling as she abruptly pushed herself to her feet. "Thinks I has ta lie down," she muttered, sounding like Gollum only drunker. She'd gone from sober to seriously sloshed in the space of five minutes it seemed. Now what was he going to do with her? Well, lead her to bed, of course. *To the bed*, he clarified to himself. Not *lead her in bed*. There was a big damn difference.

Putting his arms around her he kind of joggled her into place, matching his long-legged steps to her mincing ones, as they walked through the hall to the staircase. A bit like leading a recalcitrant dog. A very tipsy one. Not that he'd put it like that if she brought up the subject later. But why would she? Even chronic drunks hated to be reminded of their drunkenness.

Getting her upstairs was a bit of a feat, but she was cooperative. A nice change from Matt who was usually combative by this stage. They stumbled into her bedroom like graceless participants in a three-legged sack race, out of breath and almost hysterical with laughter. By the time they fumbled their way to the bed she was crying full force, as if a spigot had been turned on, mucous and tears running into her mouth. Please God, he prayed, don't let her vomit.

She was barefoot and dressed for bed, so there was nothing for him to take off as he pulled back the covers and tucked her in, holding her carefully so she didn't fall over before her head touched the pillow. A quick picture of his dad reading him a bedtime story flashed through his mind when he sat down beside her. Maybe she'd read the same book to Emily.

Isabel closed her eyes as her tears subsided. "Hands are gentle," she said, as he wiped her face with the corner of the sheet. In a few minutes she was asleep.

Terry got up and turned off the light then went around to the other side of the bed and got under the covers with his clothes on. He wanted another beer and two or three donuts but he was afraid to leave Isabel. Almost anything could happen when he was gone.

Imagining himself rummaging around her kitchen while she fell out of bed or called the police—or did God knows what—made him sweat, but secretly he felt considerable relief about the state of her. He'd been so worried that she was helpless and weak, but she seemed strong and resilient in spite of her tears and drunkenness.

After a while he figured he could safely take off his jeans and go to sleep in his T-shirt and shorts, if he sandwiched himself between the blanket and top sheet, so he got up to use the bathroom and get himself sorted out.

Walking back to the bedroom he passed Charlie's office where a desk lamp was still on, illuminating the bookish contents of the room. Gol-dang but the place looked like Faust's personal library with its etchings by Durer and

Renaissance prints of angels and other divine intermediaries on the walls. He couldn't resist going all the way in instead of standing awestruck in the doorway.

So here was where *Il Professore* labored over his biography of Machiavelli—a copy of it was center stage on his crowded desk, surrounded by shelves of other people's books. Historians and philosophers who paved the way for advances in intellectual thought, in civility and culture.

Charlie's black-and-white photo on the back of the book made him look like a 19th century explorer, more intrepid backwoodsman than Victorian scholar with his swarthy complexion and smooth dark hair, one of those French Canadian trappers—a *voyageur*, if Terry remembered the word right—living an exciting life.

Terry's life was not exciting, exempting his spur-of-the-moment introduction to Isabel. Scrubbing sinks and mopping bathrooms got pretty damned old when you did it forty hours a week. Even the recent ups and downs with the Ol' Bean hadn't given his heart a good lift or a kick. It was just same old same old, all the way back to Casper.

He turned off Charlie's lamp and went back to Isabel's bedroom feeling anxious and out of sorts. He really was *a loner with a boner*, like Matt always said, and a loser, too, not a mensch like the apparently beloved professor. What the fuck was he doing in a grieving widow's bed, he wondered, as he stripped off his jeans and got in—under the top sheet, in spite of his previously chivalrous intentions.

Nestling closer to Isabel, he could smell the scotch on her breath, feel her exhalations gently tickling his face, and the heat of her upper body radiating towards his chest. Moving a fraction of an inch closer, he took her limp hand in his, and caressed her palm with his thumb.

"Sleep well," he whispered, knowing that he probably would not.

47

BREAKFAST AT ISABEL'S

Terry was dreaming about cathedrals. Great looming soaring spaces with domes made of silver and gold, under which couples dressed in medieval garb circulated, arm and arm, around a heart- shaped fire. The flames flicked at his eyelids and then at his mouth, even though he was watching from above, as if perched on the roof and looking down through a stained glass skylight.

He saw Isabel and her dead husband at the head of the promenade, dancing a stately waltz, then Charlie stepped into the fire and Isabel stood alone, like a priestess with her hands raised to the sky, in a shower of embers and sparks, which wafted upwards, searing his lips.

Waking with a start in Isabel's bed, he realized that she was kissing him.

He opened his eyes and closed them again, savoring the warm sensation of her mouth pressed softly against his, the feel of her hand on his thigh, perilously close to the bulge in his shorts. The hardest hard-on he'd ever experienced—in more than physical terms, since he wasn't sure he should be having it.

He started to say something, to ask Isabel if she was alright, but the words never got out, even after she pulled away and laid her head on his chest.

"Thank you for staying with me last night," she said, stirring in his arms which he realized had gently enfolded her.

"You're welcome," he said, wishing he had something brilliant to say that would tell her who he was and why he was there, although he wasn't sure himself.

Her hair smelled of musk and lavender, or maybe it was just her naturally delicious scent pinging his pheromone receptors. Her touch, her smell, filled him with desire, but he held himself back for fear of taking advantage of her.

The sudden tenderness which filled his heart frightened him. This was not sex, nor was it love, or even empathy and compassion. It was just the way she affected him.

"You sleep okay?" he finally said, breaking the pregnant silence. His erection, thank God, was subsiding.

She raised herself on one elbow and looked at him. "Like the dead," she said, laughing the nervous laugh he was getting used to. Like a woman sitting on the head of a pin about to fall off, he thought, wondering where the weird image had come from. It seemed like something Matt would say. Or maybe it was just seeing Charlie's wall of spooky glittery-eyed Fra Angelico angels before going to sleep last night.

He was fully awake now and the idea of things—people— falling downwards from a great height bothered him, tying him to his dream, which had felt beautiful and heartbreaking and threatening. To allay the throbbing sensation in his head—odd, since he didn't have a hangover—he got out of bed, after asking Isabel if he could get her anything. Tea? Or a cup of coffee?

"I could use a glass of water but I'll get it myself, while you use the bathroom." She smiled encouragingly. Of course she needed some time and privacy to change out of her nightclothes, so he skedaddled after pulling on his jeans.

Walking down the hall past Charlie's office he forced himself not to shut the door or look in. The scholarly room was a menacing place, reminding him of his personal deficiencies—high school education, menial job, mispronunciation of common words in spite of reading voraciously.

"Duddn't matter what I do, I'm never gonna be good enough for you," he muttered under his breath, while he stood at the toilet and peed, wishing Isabel would hear him somehow and tell him that he was wrong.

But it was true. He was a low-level guy whose heroes had always been snaggle-toothed cowboys, not handsome virtuous knights. He didn't have any exalted ambitions, no hunger for academic awards, or success in the corporate boardroom. He didn't even want to be like Matt, making six figures a year doing a job he was good at. He just wanted some peace. And a little bit of love from a woman who wasn't his mom.

The smell of brewing coffee percolated up from the kitchen while he brushed his teeth with a washcloth, and splashed his face with cold water. His sideburns were a frazzle of scraggly hairs creeping down towards his chin, and yesterday's clean-shaven face was pockmarked with stubby whiskers. Christ, could he look any more like a shit-kicker?

With no other shirt to put on, he went downstairs in his grease-stained black T-shirt, padding barefoot into Isabel's kitchen which she'd already tidied up. A jaunty looking daisy in a bud vase, a brimming sugar bowl and two steaming cups of black coffee graced the scrubbed pine table, replacing the smudged whiskey glass and tea things from last night.

Dressed in cargo pants and an old white T-shirt, Isabel bustled around, pulling warmed donuts from the oven, pouring milk into a pitcher, getting silverware and plates from drawers and cupboards. Seeing that she was barefoot, too, made Terry feel a little less self-conscious and edgy. His plan to sneak away before breakfast melted away as he took his first sip of invigorating coffee.

Isabel brandished a large cast iron frying pan, before putting it down on the stove. "In the mood for eggs?"

Terry started to say "no", but he was famished, so he said "yes, ma'am," elongating the "ma'am" to make her laugh, which she did.

"Fried or scrambled? Baked or boiled? Soft or hard? Omelet or frittata? Hot sauce or salsa?" she singsonged, extending the joke.

"All of the above!" Terry answered, wishing that Isabel was on the menu.

Watching her deft movements as she diced green onions and red pepper for what turned out to be scrambled eggs reminded him of watching his mother cook for him and his dad back when they were a happy little family. He wondered if Charlie had watched Isabel cook with the same sense of nostalgia and intensity.

Watching Isabel eat was almost as much fun as watching her cook with a threadbare tea towel tied around her waist. She was on the scrawny side—it was good to see enjoying her own food and two of the leftover donuts.

Terry scooped a forkful of eggs into his mouth. "You always cook like this?"

"Like what?"

"Like a fuckin' goddess . . . *Ma'am* . . ."

Isabel pantomimed a stuffy schoolmarm face, overarching her eyebrows. "Well, yes, *sir*. I very much think I do."

"That husband of yours was one lucky guy." Terry said, instantly regretting his joking tone, since the well-fed guy's sudden heart attack might have involved clogged arteries.

Why the fuck was it people died, anyway, he wondered—in an offhand way—too busy enjoying his breakfast to really give a shit about anything that wasn't sensual. Dumb damn scheme anyway, death. Pointlessly contaminated with existentialism. Shamelessly promiscuous and prodigal. Always too late or too early, too fast or too slow, heroic or pitiful. A total rip-off.

And it would happen to him, just like it happened to Charlie.

No offense to Isabel, but he didn't want to think about dead people or talk about Mr. Chartres Cathedral anymore, even though he'd brought him up. So Terry talked about himself for a while, to assuage his crazy hunger for her which the delicious food couldn't touch.

In pretty short order he'd covered his crappy janitorial job, passion for Harleys, love of cats and suspicion of dogs, and touched on his troubles with Matt, which hadn't been fixed yet. No mention of his long dry spell without sex, his sad sack dad in the Alzheimer's Home, or his abiding interest in the supernatural, for fear of warning her off.

She seemed to be a good listener even though she was preoccupied with some inner reality he couldn't quite fathom yet. He'd never met a widow as young as she was, relatively speaking. He guessed she was fifty. His mother's widowed friends, with their permanent waves and leathery skins, had never reminded him of Tinkerbelle. He had to keep reminding himself that underneath Isabel's fey attractiveness was an ugly loss he hadn't experienced yet. The sudden death of her mate.

A little worm of guilt burrowed into his chest when he realized how dismissive he'd been about death just a few minutes ago. It was more than a rip-off, but what, he just didn't know.

Looking at Isabel's somber face made him want to hold her tight and take care of her. Ridiculous, given their tenuous relationship and differences in age and status. She came from a working class family—she'd mentioned that while she cooked, reminiscing about her millworker parents starting their day off with big mugs of coffee and hardtack with homemade jam.

But she'd gone to college and married a professor, her daughter was a talented young scientist. And what was he, but an uneducated refugee from a Wild West ethos that he'd never understood or believed in. Sidekick to an equally exiled maniac with neurological problems who was hung up on his ex-wife's ghost.

But, shit, he didn't want to think about Matt when he was sitting at Isabel's sweet little table with its matching chairs and colorful pottery, with her big old tabby cat Delilah head-butting his legs, and the morning sun streaming in, painting the white kitchen yellow.

From Natrona County High School onwards, the story of Matt's fucked up family life—angry dad and passive mother, being tormented by his creepy twin brothers—coupled with thrice told tales of erotic treachery from all the tainted teenaged Jezebels he'd ever dated, had dominated every heart-to-heart they'd ever attempted.

They'd be sitting up on Casper Mountain passing a joint and drinking some long necks, shooting the breeze about some nice peaceful Wyoming thing or other—the fall leaves on the shivering aspens on Togwotee Pass, the same color as the beer they were slugging—and all of a sudden, Matthew's mouth would start flapping like sheets on a windy clothesline shaking out a litany of complaints.

Pretty soon the fragrant healthy air they'd sucked into their lungs along with reefer would be thoroughly polluted with Matt's neurotic effluvium, floating over their heads like a buzzkill smoke cloud. The joy was gone, the day was dead, and it was time to go back to the Wonder Bar and get drunker than they already were.

Hell no, Terry thought, we're not ever goin' *there* again. Fuck the fuckin' Wonder Bar, the past and Matthew's slutty old girlfriends.

Once upon a time he'd entertained thoughts of becoming a chef, or the owner of a bed-and-breakfast out in the sticks near Hat Six Road, but nothing had come of his culinary dreams aside from a stint as a hamburger cook at a funky A&W.

Still, he loved cooking shows, and old sitcoms with housewives in aprons, and cookbooks like his mother used to have, with recipes for tuna fish casserole and upside-down cake. A big yard with a barbeque, a wading pool for the kids, a fridge full of beer in a tool-filled garage—these were the things he used to dream about before he moved to Seattle. But somehow those dreams flew away.

"More coffee?" Isabel asked, interrupting the nostalgic images that momentarily occupied his mind.

"Sure. But lemme help you clean up." Terry got to his feet and began ferrying plates and silverware to the counter to be rinsed and stuck in the dishwasher.

"I wash them by hand," Isabel said, filling the sink with hot water and soap suds. "Less noisy and more contemplative." She gestured to the quiescent machine, then turned her back on him as she scraped off plates before lowering them into the plastic dishpan.

Ah, so maybe that was his sign that he ought to go home? Should he hug her or just say goodbye, with so many things left unsaid.

"Well, I guess I better be moseying along. Thanks for the breakfast and . . ."

Isabel interrupted him before he could say whatever innocuous words popped into his mind. "No, thank you for staying with me last night."

When she turned to face him, he saw that she was teary-eyed.

"About that kiss . . ." she began, then halted, a faint blush staining her cheeks.

Terry took a few steps towards her and stopped, afraid to put out his hand. "Hey, we don't have to talk about that, even though it *was* a mighty nice kiss. *Ma'am.*"

She laughed, as he hoped she would, but her discomfort seemed to increase as she looked at him—*examined* him, he might say, when he replayed the scene to Matt, describing the pupils of her eyes dilating in something akin to fear as she groped for appropriate words.

The thought that he was scaring her felt intolerable. He should go and leave her alone. But then, maybe not. Maybe being alone all the time was what was scaring her.

"You don't need to explain anything," he said. The truth and a lie, like so many things.

Isabel frowned, looking down at the old cat lying on the sun-lit linoleum, then back up at him, gaze still wary but devoid of that dismal terror, which he knew now was abject grief.

She pulled off the thin tea towel tied on her waist, twisting it in her wet hands until it looked a rain-soaked garden snake.

"There was never anyone for me but Charlie. He was . . . is . . . the love of my life. I'm so sick of being without him. Yet here I am . . ."

Terry didn't need to ask where *here* meant. He was there, too, on the dark side of the fence where abandoned lovers go no matter how much they crave the light, corralled by circumstance and happenstance and fate, which he firmly believed in but could no longer tolerate, overdosed as he was on loneliness and failure, and the existential angst Matt seemed to thrive on which he steadfastly deplored.

It could have been a romance movie moment, except that Terry's favorite flicks were sci-fi, but when he took Isabel in his sinewy arms, she allowed him to comfort her, hold her close while she cried. No outer-space monsters lurking inside her, just a dead husband named Charlie, who would always win out, when it came to a suitor's contest.

How he'd scoffed at the Ol' Bean being haunted by Rosie, but now he thought he understood. The awesome power of love over time. The commanding architecture of commitment.

"Pretend you're walkin' the labyrinth at Chartres Cathedral," he said, stroking Isabel's tousled blonde head. "Or lookin' though those awesome stained glass windows."

She lifted her tear-streaked face to his, revealing wet blotches on his grungy T-shirt. "Like the one named after you?"

A wry smile transfigured her face at his look of confusion. "The Good Samaritan Window," she said. "It was always Charlie's favorite."

MATTHEW MAKES A MOVE

Stalking Rosie was easy. *Miss Communication's* performance schedule was on Matthew's iPhone. One brush of the pad and Rosie was under his thumb like a bug. Or at least the right times to find her, singing her heart out under the spotlights at Teatro Zamboni. Thank God he was just a love-stuck guy trying to see his ex-wife and not some maniacal stalker.

Over the past few feverish weeks since his kinky run in with Jackson, Matthew had been fast at work devising a solution to the dilemmas which were wrecking his life. A perfect program for perfect happiness was perfectly impossible; eventually some part of the most elegant system was going to break down. But a simple workable plan shouldn't be that hard to follow.

The system he was cracking was one he was intimately familiar with since it revolved around him. His input, his psychological code, his weird DNA which preprogrammed him to trust the wrong people and screw over the people who loved him.

He didn't have to search for the right attitude or spiritual mantra, see a therapist or pay a repeat visit to the astrologer Terry had sent him to, although he was dimly aware that Madam Zodie beguiled him. He didn't even have to change his life. All he had to do was follow three simple steps and he would be free of the troubles which haunted him.

LET GO. REJECT. FORGIVE.

Like all directives, easier said than done. But there was real power in the words and what they stood for. Or rather who they stood for, the triumvirate of troublesome people at the heart of his tortuous problems: Rosie, Jackson and Terry.

The first part of his plan started tonight with a surprise visit to the theatre. Rosie would probably flip her lid when she spotted him in the audience; the prospect gave him a hard-on. He jerked off in the shower, which made him feel depleted and anxious, then put on his favorite black cowboy shirt and an old pair of jeans.

A double shot of gin, tossed down his gullet like a mega dose of Rescue Remedy, quelled his sudden inclination to add boots and a knee length duster to his outfit. "Drugstore cowboy, I ain't," he muttered as he laced up his usual high-tops.

He stuck the pint of Tanqueray in the pocket of his battered old bomber jacket and went outside to wait for the baldheaded guy who'd taken him to The Underworld, his driver of choice now that he no longer rode shotgun with Jackson.

When the car arrived, he climbed into the backseat with a terrible sense of déjà vu. Not residual images of the debauched lost-time nightclub night, but memories of midnight cab rides with Rosie, their mouths fastened on each other's like drunken singers crooning into overheated microphones.

He drank a mouthful of gin and asked the driver to turn on the radio to drown out the dipshit Hall and Oates song that was playing in his head. Rosie's kisses were still on his fucking list, no matter what feisty admonitions he'd written to himself in his cheap new notebook. They'd held him like a tight lasso, until one day she cut the rope and left him hanging onto nothing but grey Seattle sky.

"Ever been to Teatro Zamboni?" Matthew asked, picturing the driver cozied up to the bar with Rosie clinging to his burly arm. Shit. He took another swig of gin.

The bald guy shook his head. Thank god for small favors, not that the guy was Rosie's type. But then again he'd never thought a dykey lesbian plumber like Alexa was her type either.

The car pulled up to the curb under Teatro Zamboni's glittering marquee, where Rosie's décolletage was replicated in gold and pink lights in a side-ways figure-eight. *Miss Communication* was spelled out on one enormous breast, *Starring Rosie O'Hara* on the other, with the O right smack-dab on her nipple.

There was a long line at the ticket window—agitated procrastinators and returning fans avid for another dose of zingy titillation. The last days of the show were drawing in the wife-swappers and the hoi polloi. Matthew got out of the car, stepped around the crowd and gave his ticket to a top-hatted usher.

I've seen that guy somewhere before. Oh, God, it's the doorman from the Underworld! Is this some kind of sign?

It probably *was* a sign—but signs were good, weren't they? Wasn't that what Terry always said he should be on the lookout for—some kind of sign to lead him in the right direction? Away from Rosie and his old way of defining himself by his love for her. Feeling alive because she lit up the dark center of his private world. Wasn't he supposed to get away from that?

The doorman looked at Matthew out of one cocked eye, the other fixed on his ticket, and simpered, "Welcome sir to our 'umble abode, sir!" genuflecting him into the rococo theater with a theatrical bow.

Welcome indeed to the mixed up world of Teatro Zamboni, a hodgepodge of the Wicked Olde West and Gay Paree from some time period that never existed. Cancan girls, over-rouged demoiselles, goateed artistes in billowing smocks and villains in undertaker coats, all wove through the crowd, impossible to distinguish from the waitstaff.

A mahogany bar as long as steam locomotive, maroon velvet banquettes, glittering chandeliers, silk lampshades the color of spilled champagne, the smell of roasting meat; the sensual ambiance was overwhelming. Where in the fuck was he?

Matthew wished he *had* worn his high-heeled cowboy boots. The carpet was so plush, he felt as if he were walking on Velcro. Or maybe it was inhibition setting in, nervousness, fear, palpitations, mayhem, suicide, murder that made his feet feel stuck to the floor. Maybe it was worse than murder, maybe it was zombification and castration and horrible reawakened frustration. Maybe it was curtains or payback time or the end of the road where an arrow shoots out of the forest and your stupid skull's the target. And maybe it was just fear of still loving Rosie, of being one of the legions of unlucky men and women who wanted to possess her.

"No way out..." he muttered, making his way to his expensive table for one, a little left of center stage where Rosie would soon be singing the insouciant ditty she'd once sung for Matthew in their bathtub while she soaped her armpits, showing off the song her gay composer friend had written in her honor.

Ode to fucking transient joy should have been its title. Ode to here comes Alexa's super-sized tits and super-sized dildo as soon as his back was turned. Ode to I'll make your life a living hell even after I leave our marriage. Ode to Miss Understood. Miss Directed. Miss Begotten. Miss I want someone else instead.

But no, *Miss Communication* it was and nothing else—the song, the operetta, the selfish vibrant girl the whole shebang was created for. There was no fucking mystery aside from Rosie's intractable hold on him. The seductive songs, the smash hit show, the leggy beauties kicking up their heels until their vajaysjays squealed, was just ordinary entertaining sex.

When she finally took the stage he felt sick with apprehension, as wobbly as if he had some kind of energy-sucking virus. It was impossible for her not to see him sitting upfront, the red roses on his cowboy shirt shining like pinpricks of blood underneath the bright spotlights, but Rosie sang her opening number without looking at him, as if Matthew were invisible.

The same way she hadn't looked at him the day she was packing to leave, shoving the framed photograph of them tidepooling at Carkeek Park and the menagerie of stuffed animals he'd bought her at Woodland Park into cardboard moving boxes.

Matthew ordered a drink, clapped at all the right intervals—when Rosie sang, when Rosie wept, when Rosie and her pretty cohorts danced. It was surprisingly easy just to sit back and pretend that every cell in his body wasn't raging to kill or fuck her. Probably a lot of other guys were hiding erections and evil intentions behind placid faces, downloading a bunch of solicitous crap to clueless wives as they fantasized doing unspeakable things to Rosie.

Back in the day—as people said these weirdly imprecise days, meaning ten years ago or a million—before he was thoroughly disenchanted with being alone, he might have consoled himself for Rosie's defection by thinking he was better off without her. But he knew better now. Being alone sucked. It made fighting with Rosie, contending with her moods and fickle temperament, seem like a life lived in paradise where, however bad things got, there was always change on the dim horizon.

Matthew watched Rosie's frilly knickers twirl by five feet above eye level, her dimpled white fanny shaking enticingly, in numb admiration of her effervescence. She was enchanting, sublime, the perfect *Miss Communication*. How had he ever managed to marry a redheaded dream girl like that? Surely their life together had been a fantasy?

Her voice was angelic as she sang the song he remembered from the bathtub. Only now she was wearing a sexy scarlet-red costume instead of a handful of shampoo bubbles.

Red-haired girl meets red-haired boy.
Boy meets karmic match.
Girl and boy fall for each other
 But love will never last.
Girl wants one thing, boy another.
One a father, one a mother.
Opposite things pull them asunder
Amidst a lot of noise and blunder.
Misspoken words and coy charades,

Happenstance and trouble made.
Although they try to meet somewhere
There's no "there" there when they arrive.

Rosie teared up as she sang the last line: *How sad their little lives.*

But Terry said the same thing even better back in the day before they got married, although not as prettily.

"She's confused, man! She's rilly rilly confused! Mark my words, Miss Rosie's gonna to reel you in with her pretty pink tits and her sultry voice until she sees you sweatin' in the dark, stuck in the nihilistic nightmare of a panic attack, and realizes that you don't know the answers to life's persistent problems any better 'n a warsh-rag."

Terry had been right but that was no consolation for disappointing her. For making her want to leave.

Rosie's face was turned up to the spotlight as if she were singing to a higher power in accordance with her preacher-daddy's wishes. But surely her august Episcopalian father, The Right Reverend O'Hara, had never sat drinking French 75's in the peach-and-bum-colored interior of a circus night club, counting the jiggles on his daughter's backside as she flounced around miming variations of fellatio.

By the end of the show Matthew's head was ringing and he was psychically exhausted, although like most of the men in the audience, he had a hard-on that didn't subside until the curtain went down following a raucous standing ovation. He was barely aware of the tipsy crowd dispersing, the scrape of chair legs against the polished floor as diners and drinkers pushed away from littered tables, heading for the restrooms and glittering lobby.

Stumbling off to Rosie's dressing room with his pathetic alibi as her long-lost brother clutched in the forefront of his mind, he felt like a trespasser in the corridors of a busy brothel. Performers, stagehands and waitstaff, indistinguishable from each other in extravagant garments reeking of perfume and sweat, scurried by in and out of cryptic doorways, but no one gave him a second look.

A laughing girl in a feathered boa and periwinkle-blue corset, arm in arm with a leering judge in long black robes and curly wig, passed him in the narrow hallway. Then suddenly he was stumbling inside Rosie's dressing room like a befuddled cop in a Marx Brothers movie or Alice falling down the rabbit hole. Except that this was neither celluloid nor sardonic fantasy but a heightened moment of distillate terror capable of catapulting him into a full-blown panic attack.

The calm of Rosie's dressing room, the humming buzz of the quiet space around her messy makeup table where she sat like some kind of royal effigy in her slim white dressing gown unpinning her voluptuous hairdo, unreadable eyes as big as a barn owl's in the tarnished mirror, did nothing to reduce his anxiety.

The silence after the hullaballoo of the theatre—and years of listening to Rosie rant and holler—felt unnatural, like some kind of trap. Mustering his fortitude, he waited for her to say something with his head bowed.

"Time for the Last Gasp Conversation?" Rosie inquired politely, without turning to look at her hyperventilating ex-husband, slumped against the door jamb.

Everything that she needed to know about the reason for his visit—not as unexpected as he thought, she'd been expecting him for weeks—was written on Matthew's frightened expression in her looking glass.

He knew she'd seen his stricken face a thousand times, when they were fighting, when they were having unsatisfactory sex, whenever she looked into his eyes and saw the grinning ragdoll of self-loathing staring back from dilated pupils, and the realization shamed him.

Matthew tried to paste a convincing smile on the crazy clown face he could see in the mirror as he approached Rosie's magnificent satin-covered back. He looked like a deranged murderer about to rape and strangle her but still she said nothing.

He bent to kiss the nape of her neck, brushing aside her undone curls. "I want to fuck you!" he blurted, when what he really meant was "I love you."

In their halcyon days Rosie would have answered "I know," turned up her pert nose and turned on her dimples, run her hands down her body while she purred like a well-fed cat. They would have had sex and that would be that.

But now she said, "No, you don't," without even turning around.

Matthew dropped to his knees beside Rosie, glad he wasn't wearing his cowboy boots. He'd look like even more of a hick with a pair of four-inch heels jabbing him in the ass while he begged her for sex, although having a panic attack in high-tops was just as pathetic.

He scooched around until his chin rested on Rosie's lap, grateful that she didn't swing around and knee him in the balls or push him away with a cry for the Teatro security guards.

"Yes, I do! But I didn't come here to say that," he lied. "I just wanted to see you doing what you always dreamed about. I'm sorry we weren't still together when you finally got your chance."

"I could have had whatever—stardom, success—when I was with you, if I'd been ready for it. It's not your fault that I wasn't."

Rosie smoothed the hair on Matthew's temples, almost the same flaming color as hers, which had always amused them. An old gesture so intimate he felt himself swooning with longing, but he forced his mind and penis into penitent submission.

It was horrible—the ghastly desire to repossess her that made his limbs tremble with futile anticipation, the need to hold his desperation in check so that she wouldn't chuck him out on his ear, the ear now pressed to her warm thigh, damp from his tears. So different from how he had imagined their reunion but he pressed on.

"Please come back," Matthew gurgled into her crotch.

"You know I can't." She kept stroking his head but her voice was exasperated.

Of course he fucking well knew *that*. But he had to beg—it was in his shitty karmic contract, just like Terry said: "Ah, man, don't be fucked up just because you're pussy-whipped! Accept your lot, Ol' Bean. If you gotta beg *La Belle Dame Sans Merci* for whatever it is, then do it with a smile. It's your thing—do what you gotta do!"

"Do what you gotta do" was crap advice when what you had to do was kill your romantic dreams without remorse and move on like the dispassionate adult you were supposed to be but actually weren't. Moving on didn't work when you were a tortoise, a snail, a lump, a fragment of a once-beating heart, when there was no place you wanted to go except underneath the skirt of the woman who'd scorned you.

Matthew raised his head. Rosie was looking at him with such a peculiar expression his heart soared then dropped with a thud, as he realized her faraway expression was aimed not at the sparkling amorous ambiance he'd imagined floating Klimt-like around the tableau of their sentimental tête-à-tête, but at the open door of her dressing room.

In the narrow threshold, framed like a man from a diabolical Cubist painting, stood Jackson Brand in his black-and-white checkerboard jacket, looming over them like a ringmaster. He might have had a whip or a gun in his hand, something to subdue the animals, a prod or a brand to mark them as his property. But he was only holding a champagne bottle.

"Pardon me, dear boy! I seem to be the unwilling instigator of yet another incidence of coitus interruptus in your mirthless sex life… A state you're quite familiar with, it seems… Wouldn't you agree, Rosie-my-own?" drawled Jackson, extending his enormous hand towards the huddled couple.

Odd how panic attacks can come to your rescue, Matthew thought as he leapt to his feet and punched Jackson on the jaw.

BANG! WHACK! A resounding OOMPH!

Words lit up inside his head like cartoon balloons when his fist connected with Jackson's flesh, so Matthew hit Jackson again, this time in his hard flat stomach. Ah, the glorious synesthesia of physical violence chemically intermixed with his obsessive visualization of symbols!

"Matthew! Stop!" Rosie screamed, lurching out of her makeup chair as Jackson reeled backwards, clutching his gut, and the champagne bottle crashed and burst on the floor.

A white wave of bloodlust swept through him, washing away the quirky mental dialogue boxes like words written in sand, and Matthew punched Jackson again, another direct hit to the solar plexus. He didn't give a shit if murdering Jackson McFucking Brand was ethical right at the minute, when blood was beginning to be drawn and Jackson, staggering against Rosie, was beginning to fight back.

Rosie was gripping Jackson by the arms as if she was trying to force him into a straitjacket, Jackson was flailing, and Matthew was flying apart at the seams as if a Viking berserker was lose inside him, ripping his ego-identity to shreds.

Nothing was going to stop him now, he thought, just as Jackson's hand shot out and grabbed him by the neck.

"Got you now, you naughty boy," Jackson panted, squeezing his hand ever so slightly, his rock climber's grip fitting perfectly into the crease beneath Matthew's chin. The pain, like everything else about Jackson, was excruciating.

"I've been fucking your ex-wife for quite some time… Long enough to get her acclimated to my personal tastes, if you see what I mean… "

And unfortunately Matthew did.

MEETING MADAM ZODIE

My friend made me call you. I'm not into this," Matthew said to Terry's girlfriend's psychic cousin when he phoned to book an appointment. He tried to keep the anxiety out of his voice, but his resentful tone was hard to disguise.

"Why does your friend want you to see me?" Madam Zodie asked in a measured voice that didn't sound like a crazy astrologer's.

"Because I screwed him over and he wants to get back at me."

"And seeing me is your punishment? How flattering!"

"Well, yeah, you could kinda say that," Matthew sneered.

"I don't usually take clients who feel forced to consult with me. Maybe you ought to try someone else?"

"No, sorry. I really do want to see you, even though it's Terry's idea."

"And why is that?"

"Usual problems with life, I suppose." His dissembling sounded almost as cringe worthy as his open hostility.

After a long pause on Madam Zodie's side, he blurted out, "Please! It would be really good if you could see me," surprising himself by pleading with her. Now he really did sound like a two-bit loser. His planets were probably all malevolent or retrograde—whatever that meant.

"Okay, then, we'll give it a try. I have a free space tomorrow at ten."

Shit. So soon? He wasn't prepared. But he gave her his data anyway, muttering something about not being completely sure of his birth time even though he was holding his birth certificate in his hand that said he was born at 1:10 a.m. Central Mountain Time.

He paced around his office after he got off the phone, wondering if he should call back and cancel, or call Terry and ream him a new one for forcing this occult indignity, which, as absurd as it seemed, scared the pants off him. Eventually he settled down to work on his newest programming contract, losing himself in the soothing repetitions of code. His annoying synesthesia was a boon when it came to numbers and symbols. He could taste the rightness of his thinking when he was immersed in tricky security issues.

Several hours later he took his iPhone off airplane mode. No calls or voice messages from Terry, which pissed him off, even though he'd told the dummkopf to leave him alone. His brain was so frazzled from low blood sugar that he didn't realize he was hungry until he caught himself rummaging under his seat cushion for stray M & M's.

Giving up chocolate had been almost as hard as giving up Rosie. And just as Terry had predicted, it was a terrible idea, so he put in an order for an Uber driver to bring him three chocolate milkshakes from Dick's, which he guzzled while watching a YouTube video about cocoa production.

Belly full and belching with gusto, Matthew hobbled off to bed clutching his special collection of marital trophies. He took each treasure carefully out of the shoe-box-sized plastic container labeled *Rosie and Me,* setting it down on the duvet in front of him, like a little boy lining up toy soldiers, leaving his divorce papers inside.

A rubber-banded stack of photos and postcards from various road trips. The tiny ceramic giraffe Rosie bought him at Woodland Park Zoo. A sheaf of Post-it notes she made into a flip book for his 34th birthday, showing a ginger-haired man and a flame-haired flapper doing the Charleston when he fanned the tattered pages. Her lipstick-stained napkin from the dive bar where they met sporting her old phone number in lurid green ink.

Matthew pressed the napkin to his lips, remembering the heady smell of the potent cocktail she'd been drinking when he sidled up to her barstool and asked Rosie to dance. He, who never danced, in a dark room where no one else was dancing, willing to make a fool of himself for a haughty-looking redheaded stranger. How empowered he'd felt! Yet how small in the neon glow of her majestic aura, reduced to a small dot of pure longing, humbled to be so consumed.

He woke up in the morning with his head resting on the box, like a man on the guillotine, still dressed in his work clothes, which were stained with chocolate and semen, thanks to his late night whack fest. With just fifteen minutes to shower, shave and get dressed before it was time to drive to the astrologer's, he managed to make himself presentable in a clean pair of jeans and severe white shirt that on Terry would have made him look like a gangster.

Terry's girlfriend's cousin lived on the wrong side of Ballard, the part that was getting mowed down and turned into Condoville, in a little house that looked like a Dickensian chimney pot stuck between two concrete monoliths. She looked peeved when she answered the door, perhaps because Matthew was inadvertently scowling or maybe because her neighborhood was being destroyed.

She didn't look anything like he'd imagined she would. Small, pixie-faced, a slim wood nymph instead of a frumpy old witch, her smile seemed genuine enough although he sensed she might be holding a grudge over his insults last night.

He stuck out his hand and said "Howdy," then feeling like a rube, said, "Glad to meet you," even though he certainly wasn't. Madam Zodie's handshake was firm, which he always admired, but there was something a little bit off-center about her that made him uncomfortable. Maybe she really *could* read his mind!

He sat down politely when she offered him a seat at her dining room table, where a cozy-covered teapot sat next to a small plate of cookies and an open ephemeris, but he kept checking his watch, an old Casio digital, while she explained a few basics about his astrological chart after pouring their tea.

His Virgo Sun was square his Gemini Moon, with Neptune in Sagittarius challenging both of those planets. Apparently he was seething with intellectual energy, but desperately needed more grounding. She pushed the plate of chocolate chip cookies closer to him, and flashed a mischievous smile. "Maybe some food would help?"

He was hungry and the cookies smelled wonderful, but he shook his head no. He desperately wanted to go home. All he could think about was their allotted minutes counting down, the ticking of his watch, the way that time had slowed down until he felt like Madam Zodie's voice was playing at half speed on one of those broken reel-to-reels he bought at Goodwill.

"We're not talking about my sex life," he said, as soon as she moved on to his Venus and Mars.

"Relationships, then," Madam Zodie temporized. "You came to see me because of your friend Terry."

"I don't want to talk about him either."

Work was the one thing he would talk about. He hated most of the projects he worked on except the few he accepted from NGOs and charitable organizations. Even then, the sloppy work and limited vision of the people in charge of the people who might benefit from the efficient elegance of his computer programming, made him seethe with disgust.

"You'd be surprised how many CEO's, even technical ones, don't know their asses from a hole in the ground. Even though some of them used to be—maybe still are—bright little wizards, they don't understand how to synthesize information, how to make beautiful code without screwing up something else in the system."

The astrologer took a quick sip of her tea. "This inability to synthesize, to put things together gracefully—why do you think it bothers you so much, aside from the being-bad-for-business factor?"

"Oh, I don't really care about business." Matthew looked at Madam Zodie disdainfully.

"What do you care about then?"

"Making information work, not just as data, but philosophically. Making sense of different levels of language, I guess… although that sounds dramatic. Really I'm just anxious to get on with things."

"Does getting on with things extend to people? Is being here with me, because your friend asked you to, part of you getting on with things?"

"No, it's more like getting away from things. This isn't real life in your hokey, albeit cozy, little astrologer's den, you know… or maybe you don't?" His tone was derisive.

"My home *is* the real world. You seem quite real and you're sitting in it," Madam Zodie retorted, looking even more peeved than when she opened the door.

The reading was going nowhere.

In exasperation, she put down her pen and stood up from the table. Her hands were trembling but her voice was steady. "Well, that does it then. We've got time left but I think you've made adequate penance. I'm not sure how being here has helped you relate to your friend, but if you think that he'll be okay with you now then I guess I've done my job."

"Keep your shirt on." Matthew half stood, reaching forward to pull Madam Zodie gently back into her chair. "Please, sit down.

"I'm sorry I'm being rude," Matthew professed, although the sardonic look was still on his face.

"No, not at all," she said, which he could tell was a lie.

"Don't be so nice! I don't get why you're being so nice to me. Nicer than I have any right for you to be, no matter how much Terry paid you. He did pay you, didn't he?"

"Your consultation with me was his gift. What you do with it is your business."

"But you're pissed at me, right?"

"Not at all," Madam Zodie lied again.

"No, you *are* angry with me," he insisted.

"Well, what if I am!" she snapped. "You deserve it! For all your vast intelligence, you're still acting like a fucking narcissist!"

"Jackson Brand's the narcissist. I'm the masochistic guy with the hots for his ex-wife who keeps screwing over his best friend."

Matthew's confession went on, picking up speed. "I'm the jerk. Terry's the hero. He's the one who sticks up for me and keeps me from going insane. Told me I was buying trouble when I married Rosie, but I didn't listen to him. He tells the truth. But I don't know how."

Madam Zodie put her hand on his arm, but he shook it off.

"I gotta go. Time's up and I'm sure you're sick of me. I really am sorry I was rude but I have to tell you that I don't believe in psychic powers or astrology.

"No offense," he added, the way people do when they mean something offensive but don't want to get clobbered for it.

"None taken," she lied for the very last time.

Walking through the colorful caravan clutter of the tiny house, Matthew suddenly turned around and thrust a crisp hundred dollar bill into her hand.

"See ya around," he said, tipping an imaginary hat as turned towards the door.

"Wait a minute, I have something for you," the astrologer said, handing him a thin bundle of stapled papers. "A copy of your horoscope and my chart notes. And something else I wrote, which I know you'll hate."

"Then why are you giving it to me?"

"Because my dog told me to." Oh so that was who was making the far-off whimpering noises he kept thinking was the sound of children playing games in the neighborhood school yard.

Matthew stifled a laugh when he saw how serious she was, and bowed ironically. "I look forward to reading it." Which he definitely did not.

NOT SUNDANCE AND CASSIDY

Matthew grabbed his coat and headed out the door, making one last phone call to Terry. No answer, damn it, so he left yet another message, "I'm going to kill Brand. And I need you to come and help me."

But Terry wasn't anywhere that would help his friend's tactical dilemma. He was snuggled naked in his bed, with his telephone turned off, dreaming of an ebony sky pockmarked with stars under which he and Isabel, wearing medieval robes and antelope horns, cavorted and danced.

Driving through the dark towards Jackson's ritzy neighborhood, Matthew checked his rearview mirror nervously, half expecting something anomalous on the rain-slicked streets of the Arboretum. A hovering UFO, Men in Black following in a black limousine, pointing assault rifles menacingly. But his Honda was the only thing on the road.

"Get a grip, motherfucker," he scolded himself.

He cut his lights before he pulled into Jackson's driveway, peering through the darkness for Terry's Harley, knowing it wouldn't be there. The windows of the tony pied-à-terre were shuttered from within but Matthew had the feeling that Jackson was lying in wait for him, licking his chops over the heady scent of his blood.

The polished door shone like an onyx beacon under the porch light, pulling Matthew forward in spite of his churning anxiety. Climbing the graceful staircase, he stopped on the landing halfway up and speed dialed Terry.

"Dude! Are you on your way to Jackson's house or *what*? If I don't hear back from you in sixty seconds I'm going in without you!"

As luck would have it, Terry had woken up at the exact moment that Matthew parked his car outside Jackson's door, thanks to the mysterious physics of quantum entanglement. He reached for his phone to check the time. It was 2:30 a.m. and there were six messages from Matthew, none of which made any sense.

Terry tried calling back while he put his jeans on, peering out the bedroom window to see if Isabel's lights were on, but Matthew wasn't answering.

The tale of Brand's brutality at the sex club, and the news that The Bastard was now fucking Rosie, which Matthew had poignantly confessed earlier that same evening, reverberated in his mind. Shoving sockless feet into his battered biker boots and pulling on a dirty T-shirt, he prepared for a worst-case scenario, wondering if he should rustle up a crowbar or a baseball bat.

Damn-it-all-to-hell. He'd told the Ol' Bean that he had his back, but he hadn't meant that he wanted to play second at a dueling cockfight! So much for their fine reunion and rejiggered friendship. Now they were both in the soup.

He called Matthew again and left a quick message. "Wait in your car! An' call me back with McBastard's address!"

Maybe he should have warned Matt to get the hell away from there, because even though he didn't know the wily writer's house numbers, he had Brand's numerology down pat. Grade-A Number-One Asshole who was probably gonna stomp him and his best friend to death.

He powered up his old PC and Googled "Jackson Brand." A reference to the kinky creep's favorite Madison Park breakfast hangout, stating that it was only two blocks away from his luxurious home, was enough information to get Terry within sniffing distance.

"En garde, mofo!" he growled as he zipped up his leather jacket.

He backed his motorcycle out of the driveway without turning on the engine, in deference to Isabel's chronic insomnia, hoping she'd drunk the chamomile and valerian tea he'd given her, and was dreaming of him like he'd been dreaming of her.

Nothing, including Terry's special herbal formula, had put Matt to sleep after Rosie left. He stayed up all night, dismantling his crazy cuckoo-cuckoo clocks and scabrous appliances, until the dot of seven when he recommenced creating his intricate security programs. How he'd survived long-term sleep deprivation with his brain intact was anybody's guess.

But then again, maybe he hadn't.

The stupid dude was out in the dark, cruisin' for a bruisin' from Jackson Brand, right this goddamn moment.

Racing through the Arboretum, the smell of wet leaves wafting in under the face shield of his helmet, reminding him of Halloween even though it was only the tail end of August, Terry assessed his chances of getting home without incurring serious damage. Based on what he'd heard about Brand, they didn't seem very good. Not to mention what he knew about Matthew.

Once he'd spotted the neon sign of the upscale restaurant, Terry began searching for Matthew's Honda. In spite of the low roar of his motorcycle and the gleam of streetlights on his leather jacket he felt invisible, invincible, like a stealthy warrior sneaking through the woods on a moonless night.

He'd been hauled out of the Wonder Bar, more than once, for just sitting on a barstool minding his own business. Even the cowgirls who liked his jackalope grin expected a much darker tone to his makeup. He was genuinely sorry to disappoint them, but it wasn't his fault he'd been born with a devilish face. Inside he was tame as a pussycat. Except when it came to Matt, whom he'd sworn to protect and defend.

But Matthew's devilish side wasn't so modest. It had grown at least a foot in every direction in the time it took for him to drive from Laurelhurst to Jackson's neighborhood. Extending further outwards as he climbed the first flight of Jackson's long staircase, until it was a hulk of a shadow, the color of marijuana pipe gunk and dirty motor oil.

It felt glorious to feel his shadow-self expanding, his masculine flesh puffing up amidst the radiant coils of vengeful thoughts which lit him up like a stovetop. If this was power he wanted more of it, step by furtive step up to the door of the dragon's den, where his nemesis lay inside feasting on Rosie's succulent flesh.

Any qualms he had about confronting Jackson were erased by his vision of Rosie pinned beneath The Bastard's ropey thighs, being fucked insensible so she'd never go back to Alexa or her moony ex-husband.

He could smell their intermingled juices on their rumpled cotton bedsheets, the garlic chicken they'd eaten for dinner, Rosie's anise toothpaste. His enemy's coital sweat seeped through the door like steam through a bamboo cooking basket. The maddening scent of sexual treachery, as sweet as treacle, pulled him forward towards the second landing. An irresistible urge to bang the heavy brass doorknocker, demanding to be let in, shook him from inside out, and his raised his fist and did it, loving the drum-like sound of his fury.

What a fool he'd been! Telling Brand about Rosie. Spilling his guts about their incendiary sexual life, the magic of her touch, the sweetness of her laughter—even when she was laughing at him.

He'd rhapsodized while Jackson took notes—notes!—in his moleskin notebook, feeling pleased that the famous writer was listening to him. Thinking The Bastard was going to use his soulful confessions as fodder for the book he was writing on modern marital relationships. Believing the creep was his friend.

He banged on the door again, wishing it was Jackson's face.

But not Rosie's, no matter how angry he was. Her artful lies, alluring promises, the way she used him—cashing out their bank account, swiping his collection of vintage Matchbox cars—how he swallowed it all like a good little boy—were nothing compared to Jackson's treachery.

And The Bastard was going to pay.

Matthew's shadow didn't give a fuck that his call for justice was lost a long time ago, that there's no going back to a halcyon heyday. He wanted to eat Jackson alive, tear him limb from limb, and then go down on Rosie with his enemy's blood fresh on his snarling lips.

He was just about to ram his bony shoulder into the implacable door when along came Terry, thank God!

Springing up the staircase with feline grace to save his best bud from moral and likely physical destruction.

Too late, though! Lights were going on inside Jackson's house and a steady hum, as if a swarm of bees was massed on the inside of the doorway, was swirling out into the night, hypnotizing both of them.

"Shee-it! What the fuck you doin', man?" Terry grabbed Matthew's arm, attempting to drag him down the staircase, but he wrenched away and lunged towards the door.

"Getting some frontier justice, dude! We're gonna kick Jackson's cock-breathin' face in just like you said you wanted to!" Matthew's eyes were big and glassy—he looked like an enraged Yosemite Sam whose head was about to pop.

"That was hours ago. I didn't mean anything…I was just talkin'!"

EEEEEKKKK!

The big black door creaked horror-movie style as an unseen hand pulled it slowly open. A silhouetted figure loomed in the doorway, backlit by lurid spotlights so its face was dark, and glossy fabric dripped from its arms like wings rising up to strike them.

A swooshing adrenaline rush made Terry's heart thump, putting to shame the testosterone high he'd achieved earlier rushing to Matthew's defense on his trusted Harley.

"Oh my God…What the fuck?" somebody breathed in wonder, and for a happy change it was neither Matthew nor Terry but the faceless angel or devil, halo of bright red hair blazing like a stained-glass window, who was verbally overcome.

"What's going on you guys? Are you all right? Why are you pounding on our door at three o'clock in the morning?"

"What do you mean *our* door?" Matthew shouted, stumbling over the threshold to get a hold of Rosie.

For of course it was brave and impulsive Rosie, not Jackson, who answered the door in the dangerous dead-of-after-midnight. Matthew's heart went out to her as she fought off his feverish embrace. What kind of lily-livered jerk would let his woman take his rightful place on the front lines of home defense? The despicable coward Brand was nowhere in sight.

"You can't be living with that perverted creep—you can't possibly be that dumb!"

"Of course she's that dumb!" Terry roared, wishing he were back at Isabel's talking about the highlights of Renaissance philosophy. He pushed past the grappling couple into the blinding foyer, knocking into a small mahogany mail table as he groped for a light switch. He had to get those prison yard search lights out of his smarting eyes!

"I'm nothing of the sort." Rosie huffed. She spoke in old fashioned phrases when she was upset.

She'd managed to push Matthew aside or maybe it was the sight of her—resplendent in a lacy lavender nightgown, tousled hair falling across enormous milk-white breasts—that stopped the poor fellow in his tracks. Terry marveled at her instant effect on his blundering friend. After all this time, she still made Matthew cower like a schoolboy being reprimanded by their second-grade teacher, their mutual childhood crush.

Terry found the dimmer switch in the hall and turned the lights in the wall sconces down, making Rosie appear only slightly less supernatural than she'd seemed in their blinding glare. She might have been a ghost for the breathless way

Matthew was staring at her, as if she'd risen from an ancient grave and was holding skeletal hands out, beckoning him into her moldering crypt.

She *was* holding her hands out—they were planted firmly on her ex-husband's shoulders, pushing him backwards.

"I live with Jackson now, Matthew. I don't know what you thought you'd accomplish by coming here. Unless you plan to kill me, which seems unlikely, but go ahead and try it. There's nothing you can do to make me come back to you and you know it."

"Where's your fucking hero, then?" Matthew yelped. "Screwing some *other* bimbo in your bedroom while you rush out in your negligee to defend him?"

Oops, watch out, Ol' Bean! Don't go insulting her new boyfriend.

Terry had already spotted the emerald-encrusted platinum band on Rosie's left hand. He guessed the usually perspicacious Matthew had missed it.

"She's a bitch not a bimbo, man. Be careful what you're sayin'!" Terry averred with a friendly nod towards his old nemesis, the prettiest redhead he'd ever laid eyes on and probably the most dangerous.

It was up to him to keep some kind of order, otherwise it would be murder city at Brand's, with one of them lying in the foyer with a knife in his back. Envisioning poor deluded dying Matthew clutching the trailing hem of Rosie's seductive night dress—or himself, crawling along the baseboards leaving a slug trail of mucus and catsup-thick blood—both of them exsanguinating in a flurry of pedantic insults delivered by the bastard writer—was easy.

It didn't take a psychic like Isabel's cousin Madam Zodie to see that they were going to be massacred if they didn't get a move on.

Terry started to say "Come on, Kimosabe," tugging hard on the back of Matthew's nylon jacket, but Rosie interrupted him.

"Jackson's in New York on a book tour. I'm here by myself if that makes you feel any less inclined to do something dangerous. You've already hurt me enough, Matthew. You need to go."

Rosie's face was wreathed in an ironic smile. "Oh, and one other thing… Jackson already told you we're together but he didn't tell you we're getting married. I was going to do that myself and now I have."

She waved a royal hand at the open door. "Good night and good luck, fellas, you're both going to need it."

Guts churning, nausea vying for supremacy over a heart-racing panic attack, Matthew turned to Terry. "Let's get out of here, before I kill her."

It's the other way around, buddy.

But Terry didn't say anything. He just pushed Matthew out onto the porch and watched in grudging admiration as Rosie shut the door.

RESURRECTION OF MATTHEW

Matthew's panic attacks were gone. Poof! Just like that! As if a fairy godmother had tapped his skull with the sparkly pentagram on the end of her magic wand, declaring *"Be gone, evil affliction!"* And it was.

He was able to drive through tunnels and take elevators without fearing he was going to pass out, work on hated software contracts without a terrorist monkey digging its claws into his back. Two weeks without an anxiety attack meant that he could *cope* even if he was blindsided by events, the way he'd been when he found out that Rosie was fucking Jackson.

Goddamn but he was proud of himself! He was practically *being here now* like Terry's hero, good ol' Ram Dass.

Rosie's ghost was gone for good and in her place was a joyous sense of emptiness. No one and nothing could fill up the bottomless pit inside him, so he could finally give up. Stop obsessing and keening and crying over, fantasizing about and fetishizing and—according to her—dehumanizing Rosie, in the hopes of re-winning her love.

And he *had* dehumanized her. He'd made her superhuman, super surreal, super scrumptious, a paragon of desirability in every possible sense—a veritable Venusian love goddess, not a woman. No wonder she couldn't stand him rooting around like a baby on big mama's tit. She accused him of sucking her dry and he probably had.

Thank God he'd caught himself before he went too wrong with Terry. That he'd actually *listened* when his angry pal called him out for fucking up their friendship. That they were back in the saddle again, riding the rough terrain of booming cold-hearted Seattle together.

Good old Terry, always hedging his bets and coming out on top somehow, like a fucking jack-in-the-box. Look at him taking the widow down from her lonely perch, acting strictly on heroic impulse. The way he'd been at Jackson's house, rushing to Matthew's defense. The guy was a living fairytale.

Matthew and Terry were back at the Salmon House tonight, officially celebrating their recently repaired friendship and talking about the new woman in Terry's life. The sad widow Isabel.

"So the fact that she's old enough to be a grandmother doesn't bother you?" Matthew asked Terry, deliberately bating him, as usual.

Terry punched Matthew on the arm. "Ow! Motherfucker! I have to make a living with that thing!"

"You gotta meet Isabel and come to some decent conclusions. You're delusional if you think I'm gonna give up on this woman. What does a dead husband and a measly fourteen years age difference have to do with whether or not we can get along?"

"You think you're never going to feel like murdering her?"

"That's a down right shitty suggestion. What's with the pervasive perception that every relationship has to end in a hot fuckin' mess with two people hatin' each other? That gets really old after a while."

Nodding at an elderly couple across the aisle sharing a piece of cheesecake, Terry went on in his earnest baritone, "You break up when you don't feel safe anymore. But see, I'm always gonna have faith in Isabel because she's a trustworthy person. Like those rocks we used to hunt in the Powder River Valley. Duddn't matter if you polish 'em or not, they're still somethin' precious to keep in your pocket."

Matthew narrowed his eyes, his owlish spectacles flickering in the table's candlelight. Terry gave him an exaggeratedly quizzical look before tossing his head back to chug the last of his beer. It was so comforting to be back at it again! Two Musketeers communicating with the twitch of their eyebrows.

Terry twisted the bottom of his sideburns into two untidy points. "But hey! I know you're just pullin' my dick. What's left of it, anyway, after all good sex I been enjoyin' with my beautiful *old lady* while you've been off chasin' Rosie with your head up your ass."

Another, harder not-so-friendly punch on the arm accompanied Terry's friendly diatribe.

Matthew rubbed his forearm ruefully. "Okay, okay. I admit it. Aside from a few sordid episodes compliments of Jackson, I haven't been with a woman who took my mind off Rosie in what seems like a lifetime."

"Doesn't feel too damn bad about herself these days, does she, Ol' Bean? What with stardom and money and Jackson's famous come slitherin' around in her belly and an engagement ring on her finger the size of a dinner plate. Rosie's got it made in the shade, man."

Oops, Matthew was looking a bit green around the gills. Terry steered the conversation towards less incendiary topics than the debacle at Jackson's house. The merits of Matthew's grilled salmon versus Terry's pan-roasted halibut, the Eagles songs they remembered from the cranky old jukebox at the Wonder Bar.

They'd left Casper for good almost twenty years ago. Hadn't been back to visit since 2009, when one of the Matthew's twin brothers had been found wandering around the Cemetery over in Evansville without any clothes on.

They'd bailed Frank—or was it Fred?—out of the pokey, taken him home to the Barker's where he swore he hadn't been drunk, just tracking the ghosts of befuddled dead soldiers, and headed for Thermopolis as fast as Terry's funky old Ford could take them.

"You ever think of goin' back there?" Terry asked, already knowing the answer. *Yes, no, never* and *maybe*, the same things they both always said when asked if they planned to revisit Wyoming.

"First fuckin' state to give women the right to vote!" They chortled in unison, hoisting their drinks in commemoration of their feminist frontier heritage.

Thinking about *going home* was a good way to bring on a panic attack, but Matthew's breathing was even and steady as he contemplated Terry's big hands spread out on the table. Two broken fingers on his right hand, one on his left— evidence of a bad bicycle wreck as a kid which hadn't stopped him from moving up to the big boys when he was old enough. Harley Davidson, Honda, Kawasaki, Yamaha—he'd ridden them all.

The sight of Terry perched on a motorcycle still gave Matthew a thrill. He didn't bike, he couldn't swim, hadn't even been able to keep up with Terry when they were kids skittering through the underbrush searching for conkers to throw at each other.

Bad-ass Terry could've beaten Matthew up any old time he felt like it—then and now. Could have roared up to *his* door instead of Jackson's, with a chip on his burly shoulder and an old bone to pick, and taken him apart like balsa wood. But he never did.

Aside from Terry's terrible attitude towards Rosie, he'd behaved like a gentleman from the start, waving Matthew to the seat next to him in second grade as if he was sharing a prince's throne.

They ate in silence for a while, watching the wakes of passing boats undulate across the dark lake. Stories of sea serpents in nearby Lake Washington seemed entirely credible for a moment, which Matthew commented on, wishing that he and Terry could float away right out the big picture window. But Terry was in love and wanted to stay put.

They were almost drunk but not quite, teetering on the brink of sober. They continued staring out the window for several moments. The subtle note of diesel fumes seeped in through the restaurant door when customers came and went, mixing with the alder smoke and nutty smell of cornbread. The olfactory experience was as exhilarating as a drug trip.

"Where *are* we, man?" Terry suddenly said, just like he said the first time they took acid up on Casper Mountain.

That mountain was haunted, for damn sure, alive with ghosts, well beyond Crimson Dawn where the spirit of western paganism lived on in the ranch's meandering grounds and log house, now a museum, decorated with longtime homesteader Neal Forlings's spooky paintings of witches.

Up there on those half-familiar slopes amidst the creaking lodgepole pines and shivery silver aspens it seemed like anything could happen. You could soar off the ridge like a hawk without ever taking your feet off the rust-colored footpath, feel the high prairie clouds being pulled over your head, commune with the bugs in the wildflowers.

Where they sat now looking out into the lapping dark, drinking too much as a prelude to getting stoned once they managed to crawl off to Terry's place, this over-decorated fish house on the shore of an urban lake, was nothing like the mysterious space they'd inhabited on Casper Mountain. Yet it had its own undeniable charm and a certain low-level magic, a hint of the transcendent if you looked around just right.

Laughing families, couples courting beneath the hanging war canoes, waitresses who'd served Ivar's famous *Keep Clam* chowder for over twenty years, with the rainy Seattle skyline twinkling theatrically in the background. As good a place as any to rekindle a friendship, to start an evening of getting ridiculously loaded.

Intending to get high hadn't even come into it back then, when they were up on Casper Mountain. Drugs and alcohol, shared with pretty Natrona High School girls, were adjuncts to the mountain's magic not the cause of it. Now they had to work at being magically transported.

Going back to Casper the last time had been an eye-opener.

Aside from his delusional brother bringing shame on the family, there was a lot wrong with Wyoming that Matthew realized he'd forgotten. Windswept skies, hot springs bubbling with multicolored minerals, even the sight of elk, knee deep in lily pads, drinking from the blue waters of the Wind River, couldn't erase the sorrowful feeling that being back there gave him.

Moving to Seattle where there were no scorching summers or blizzardy winters only teardrops of chilly rain, where no one said "duddn't it", or called their glove compartment a "jockey box", or invited you to dinner when they really meant lunch—or joked about fucking sheep—had been as momentous a change as being released from a gulag.

Matthew forgot all about his fucked up family sizzling on the skimpy backyard patio of the dinky little house on Walnut Street when he and Rosie sat together on a cool summer evening under an awning of maple trees on the goose-poop-studded lawn at Green Lake.

Forgot about murdered mule deer, antelopes and cougars tied to the front ends of monster pickup trucks, dead eyes devoid of forgiveness, when they strolled along the paths at Woodland Park eating ice cream from the gourmet food pavilion.

Forgot about drive-up liquor windows and basement meth labs and sexy-cowgirl mud flaps and the Dick Cheney Alumni Stadium at their hated old high school, when he and Terry queued up at a Mexican food truck and no one drove by drinking beer in a truck with a gun rack or hawking spit onto the asphalt.

His Rocky Mountain past was dead when he walked out with Rosie, except for the good part with Terry, who'd followed him to the Pacific Northwest anyhow, and sat beside him now in a modified stupor, waiting for the check to come.

"We should've gone up to Casper Mountain," Matthew said, knowing his half-drunk old friend would know what he meant. "What the fuck was wrong with us?"

"Had to get outta there fast, man, your brothers were drivin' your parents berserk and Rosie was callin' you every fuckin' minute sayin' *come back, come back* like you'd gone off to Tahiti like Gaugin."

"We both could have done with one last visit to Crimson Dawn. *Crimson Dawn, man! Crimson Dawn!* We shouldn't have saved it for the end of the trip."

"'Member that time we made it up there in a fuckin' blizzard in that crappy old Jeep you got off Weasel Wilkerson and it died on the way back down? Shee-it! Pushing that gol-danged bugger off the mountain was how bein' in Casper felt. We were so exhausted from trippin' over the cracks in your family that drivin' to Seattle in the middle of the night was the only solution… But we'll get up on the mountain again, I promise."

But they wouldn't. They weren't ever going back up on Casper Mountain—except in their memories and imaginations—because it would require going to Wyoming to get there. After Matthew's parents died and Terry's dad got dementia and Terry's mom divorced him to marry a house painter, they promised themselves that they'd never go back to the town of their births unless Jesus himself gave them their marching orders.

Matthew thought that Terry was as close to Jesus as he was ever going to get. Built like a carpenter with a throw-out-the-money-changers swagger, an honorable guy with a loving heart who wouldn't be too hard to worship —but up until now he'd agreed that visiting Casper was *verboten.*

"You sayin' we ought to go back?" Matthew asked, almost desirous of hearing the wrong answer. He was on his fourth gin and tonic and dropping his G's like Terry.

"Well, you want to anyways, doncha? You been waitin' for me to say the word since two thousand and fuckin' ought nine—ever since we drove outta Casper. I'll bet you were missin' the place even if you weren't missin' your fam'ly by the time we got to Idy-ho."

Terry twiddled his scarred blood-brother thumb at Matthew, stroking his sideburns with the other one like a villain in a silent movie. "Am I right?'

Of course he was right. Terry was always right about the big stuff like who you could trust and who'd cut your balls off. But damned if he'd say so.

Frontier towns always had the smell of the graveyard to Matthew, and Casper was no exception. The sound of the perpetual wind whipping the branches of the straggly cottonwoods seemed like a dirge for dead losers.

Look who's the loser now the loser inside his head said to Matthew, meaning himself, not Terry, although he was looking right at him, watching him fork the last piece of halibut into his mouth.

Terry was never a loser. No matter what dumb-ass people said about him being better than his janitorial job, a bigger person than the parochial life he'd chosen for himself. He *was* a big person—he'd give Matthew his head on a platter, with a cherry in his mouth, if his friend ever asked for it. But he didn't need some kind of fancy job or smug reputation to prove it.

Matthew wished he were as impressive a specimen as Terry, physically at least if not in moral stature. There was nothing good about being a skinny redheaded geek back in the day in Casper. Only his scrappy nature had kept him from getting strung up on a fence post like poor Matthew Shepherd. The tweaked-up taxidermist in the Wonder Bar who threatened to skin him alive and tack his hide to the wall hadn't been the only Wyoming whack job he'd been faced with.

In Seattle he only had to be smart and technically facile to gain the admiration of colleagues and impress his uber-respectable pretend-to-be friends. No need to be physically tough to make his way in the skitchy caffeinated landscape, to protect himself from personal threats. But being a brainiac hadn't kept him from losing Rosie who liked her men harder than their hard-ons. Even when the men were women.

Erections aside—of which he'd had plenty—he just couldn't live up to her unconscious nevertheless imperative definition of what it means to be a *man*. He'd joked that she should've hooked up with a cop or a gangster or maybe a *real* tough cowboy, somebody who could break the back of anybody who blocked him.

And then, of course, she had.

Curdled memories of Jackson's acid aphorisms and visions of Rosie warm from The Bastard's bed almost made Matthew want to flee back to Casper, where his old ghosts weren't so sexualized. But there was no going back to Wyoming in his immediate future and he said so to Terry.

"So what're you gonna do about Rosie then. Stay home an' mope?"

No, he'd driven himself crazy trying to catch hold of her, like chasing a scarf in a tornado. "I think I'm done with her,"

Matthew said, surprising himself. Oh my God, it was almost true, if not quite.

"It's a goddamn miracle!" Terry crowed, clutching two pieces of cheesecake in a Styrofoam box, as they exited Ivar's, continuing their post-dinner conversation about Matthew's expired love as they stumbled towards the parking lot.

Matthew was driving even though Terry was a better driver, a habit from the early days when he pledged allegiance to motorcycles, although he'd inherited an ancient Ford sedan from his doting grandfather.

"Taking your life in your hands," Matthew warned as they got into the car, but then again so was he.

Just six months ago he would have relished the thought that they were in imminent danger, not that he wished any harm to Terry. Several quixotic left turns and run-through red lights in the weeks after Rosie's departure had given him enough jittery adrenaline punches that he figured he'd reached the threshold for casual self-destructiveness.

Still, the urge to drive into a freeway wall or the crumbling precipice of an old bridge sometimes crept up on him. Tonight though, in spite of the alcohol and his blurry vision and the emotional catharsis of reuniting with Terry, he felt centered and secure in his determination to be a triple-A driver, following the rules of the road.

"I'm with ya, man," Terry drawled, leaning back against the car seat with his eyes closed.

Looking carefully left to right, but forgetting to look left again, Matthew pulled the car out of the parking lot—there was no oncoming traffic so his inattention to detail didn't matter.

"Gog's my co-pilot," Matthew declared, as he stepped on the gas pedal.

An old joke, harking back to an "end of days" sermon at the evangelical church they'd snuck into as middle-school kids. They'd been galvanized by the fiery rhetoric, terrified by the implications of a war at the end of the world as they knew it. A battle between good and evil which would wipe them and their pets and parents clean off the planet. The beginning of Terry *wrastlin' with God* as he called it, his budding belief in the ineluctable power of the supernatural.

Well, they'd need a fuck-ton of supernatural assistance to get the ten blocks to Terry's, creeping slowly along Northlake Way to keep from skittering across the asphalt like a water-boarded beetle.

"A metric fuck-ton," Terry growled, reading Matthew's mind or maybe just tapping into the well of coincidence he argued hid the truth of the *sublime*.

"Quantum physics, pure and simple…downwards causation…the hand of the eternal ever gropin' . . ." Terry's words were slurred, their meaning obscure, but Matthew got their drift.

Being drunk did something weird to the rational mind — no wonder so many saints and philosophers were alcoholics. And being with Terry, riding along more than half lit with the spell of the night and the meter of his awkward thoughts voiced aloud inside the quiet shell of the car, only his boon companion to hear and judge him, was—as ever—intoxicating.

If I could only go back to living like this, he thought, I'd be able to fake it the rest of the time without feeling so sorry for myself.

"Not so sorry," Matthew said. And right before they swerved into a parked truck next to the Burke Gilman trail, Terry got what he meant.

"Right, Ol' Bean!" Terry shouted, just as his head hit the dashboard.

TERRY TAKES A BREAK AND MEETS UP WITH ALEX

Luckily for Terry his skull was as hard as a Wyoming rock but he was still nursing a hangover-type headache nearly a week after getting skull-fucked by Matthew.

Just one big turn of the asshole's skinny little wrist on his steering wheel and *tick-a-lock*, Terry's face got bashed by the back of a pickup truck.

Oops, I didn't mean it Occifer, I was drunk.

Not fucking drunk enough, Mattie boy, not by a long shot.

Thank a whole bunch of bobble-headed demi-gods Matt brought the turn up short, veered away from a head-on crash and just body-skimmed the truck. The gnarled hippies smoking doobies in the steamed up cab didn't even seem to care that they'd been hit once they realized that Terry's head took the brunt of the collision and Matt gave 'em a fistful of buy-off cash.

Terry shook his head vigorously, raindrops falling off his grease-stained watch cap onto his dripping nose. *Shee-it.* He could have been lying in a bargain-rate cemetery plot on the outer edges of some windswept prairie instead of sprawled on a wet plastic tarp fiddling with the starter on his motorcycle, if the crazy dude had succeeded in offing him.

Of course if he were dead, he wouldn't be a fuckin' wreck, worrying about where Isabel was, what she was doing, if she was tired of him yet. Might be some solace in having your brains bashed out—presumably your crappy self-trashing inner dialogue ceased and you got some well won peace. The kind you never got from romance.

He hadn't seen Isabel all weekend although her house lights went on in the morning and off at night signaling some sort of human activity.

"I'm going to be busy for a while," she'd said, the last time he went over to her place for coffee, and Terry hadn't ask with what.

He'd been watching her house all day with the fervor of Harriet the Spy. There'd been nothing to observe but the comings and goings of cats and birds in her yard and the sun moving from the one side of her house to another.

He rubbed the stiches over his left eyebrow while he put his tools back in his battered old tool box after determining that his starter was working okay. Fuck! If he only knew where Isabel was!

And Matt. What was he gonna do about Matt?

Well, he sure as shit wasn't goin' over to psycho-geek's house to hear one more goddamn pathetic apology from him. Gol-dang waste of gas even though his Harley needed a good long run.

Nah, he'd cruise over to South Park where there were actually people that didn't look like folks in a Nordstrom ad and all the old buildings hadn't been torn down or prettified yet. Neighborhoods were places for people to *live,* not for block after block of rabbit warrens, he grumbled, self-righteous in his Lesser Seattleism, although there was nobody around to appreciate his rant.

Making good time on the freeway and over the South Park Bridge made him so happy he almost forgot how worried he was about Isabel, how pissed off he was at Matt. Nothing like flying over the asphalt on a gigantic motorized bike, with insects and road shit flying into your visor to make you feel beholden to no one, not even your own fantasies.

He found a parking space no problem, squeezing between a cool-looking old Dodge and a crummy pickup truck similar to the one Matt had crashed into. It had finally stopped raining and a pitiful little sun had come out, reminding him that it was the autumn equinox today or tomorrow. Time for a gol-dang celebration then.

Resisting the impulse to pat a Hispanic-looking kid on the head as he passed a strolling family on the sidewalk, Terry hurried towards his favorite market. The bodega smelled delightful as always, the bells over the doorway tinkling gaily as Terry entered the tiny shop.

"Howdy," Terry said to the comely young woman behind the counter, who looked a bit like Flora, his old flame from Casper.

"Buenos días," she replied with a twinkle in her lively brown eyes. "Is there anything special you're looking for?

"Nah, just lookin' for some spices and things. Dried chilies, maybe some cornmeal and pumpkin seeds. Pretty much know where everything is, ma'am, but thanks."

As he strolled around the well-stocked shelves, he let his mind wander, imagining drinking coffee in the backroom of the shop with Flora's doppelgänger, pouring out his worries about Isabel. She'd pat his hand consolingly and tell him not to worry.

"Buy your querida a bag of dulces, to sweeten her heart," he could almost hear her saying.

Jesus, he really *could* smell coffee brewing. And something sweet and comforting baking in a hidden oven. Olfactory hallucinations, sensations of longing, he reckoned, until he heard a mellow female voice call out, "Agave or azucar in your cafe, sweetheart?"

A flicker of surprise rippled through Terry as a small slim boy stepped out from behind the backroom curtain. Two ropes of black hair fell below the young man's shoulders like Rapunzel's plaits, an odd contrast to his 1940's zoot suit, yet perfect for his long thick eyelashes and the natural redness of his mouth. The boy looked as much like a woman as he did a man, although his general air, the expansive way he gestured with his hands, seemed confidently masculine.

Not being sure of the gender of the handsome stranger made Terry nervous, although he had nothing against men who sound like women or women who dress like men. It was just that relationships were weighing on his mind, and he wanted everything regarding sex to be straightforward as a sort of personal talisman. He was well aware that he was, until just recently, a love virgin.

Gathering up his purchases, fewer than he'd planned, he strode to the counter, anxious to finish his transactions and be on his way back to Isabel. Reawakened worries about her whereabouts were swooping through his head like precursors to the kinds of migraines Matt got. Dreaded signs of the lovesickness which was stealthily trailing him and making the recent bad days with his fucked-up friend seem breezy in comparison.

"I know you," the feminine man said, peering closely at Terry.

Terry thought *no, not me,* not wanting the lithe little creature to have any power over him other than the visual. He already felt like he was gawking—just observing the agile form leaning languidly against the counter was like seeing a hermaphrodite in a Dali painting, or Prince channeling a Minoan snake goddess.

Androgyny had never seemed so viscerally attractive or so frightening. Even the walls of the shop seemed to be pulsing orgasmically, pulling him in.

Then suddenly he got it! He would have slapped his own forehead if it wasn't already bashed in.

The guy behind the counter was Rosie's lesbian lover, Alexa! Matt had a hated picture of her helping Rosie move out of their condo on his cell phone. Terry had been there that awful day, restraining the Ol' Bean from punching her.

Pre-frontal cortex over-stimulation alert!!

Shee-it! Had he said that out loud? Would have if he were Matt. Considering their most recent disturbing experience, thank God that he wasn't. He was still feeling pretty damn rocky. With his bruised and battered head he probably looked like a dope. No need to increase his crazy-assed quotient.

"See Rosie anymore?" he asked before he could stop himself.

"Just her show." Alexa's heavy eyebrows lowered ominously but her eyes got a tad bit teary. "If you ever see Rosie, tell her I'm *fait accompli*…I'm Alexander—Alex—now . . . She'll get the picture."

"Uh, sure."

Terry wondered what his former nemesis would do with the picture when she finally got it—not from him—hoping the shredded remnants of it would cascade down on Jackson in a fuckin' shit storm instead of on Matt, who'd begged Rosie not to get hooked up with a budding trans person.

He halfway hoped that Alexa/Alexander would ask about Matthew, acknowledge that her/his unquenchable ardor for Rosie had ruined the poor bloke's marriage, but was relieved when she/he—no, *he,* he reminded himself—or maybe *they*-- did not. The stitches in his forehead were hurting and he was getting confused about pronouns. He wanted to go home.

"Gotta get back to the little lady," Terry practically yodeled as he slapped down his debit card. He pictured Isabel standing in the window where she liked to sit, waving for him to come in.

"Lucky lady!" Rosie's conundrum of an ex-partner exclaimed, breaking Terry's reverie as the pretty clerk who looked like Flora handed him the purchases she'd rung up and bagged.

"Have a good day." Terry waved his fingers at the stunning duo behind the counter, and stepped out on the sidewalk with a sigh of relief.

They weren't there when he looked back through the storefront display window, which was decorated with tiny Mexican flags and a dusty piñata. Presumably they'd gone into the backroom to drink the coffee that Alexa/Alexander had prepared for them. Or maybe, a crazy voice in his head, said—probably Matt's—they'd never been there at all.

The chattering families pushing strollers on the sidewalk, haggling over what to buy for dinner, looked ordinary, bland, like passersby he'd see on the streets of white-bread Wallingford. The magic was gone. And he'd forgotten to buy pumpkin seeds.

Checking his phone as he straddled his bike, he found several groveling messages from Matt, all saying the same damn thing.

"Fuck you and your broke-down war horse," Terry texted back. "Get thee to a shrink."

When he parked his Harley in the driveway some thirty minutes later, he couldn't remember driving back from the mercado, or where he put his purchases until he found them in his saddlebag under some overdue library books. Might as well be concussed, he thought, even though—amazingly—he wasn't. All he could think about was Isabel and, even then, it was a rat's-nest jumble of inchoate subjects that occupied his thoughts.

Isabel still wasn't home so he went inside and made himself a burrito using canned beans he already had in his cupboard. The masa he bought at the bodega seemed like a rebuke to his socialization skills. No one was coming to dinner except him. He'd have to supply his own hors d'oeuvres and dessert and the flowers as well, which would pretty much have to be dandelions from his dried up backyard.

He saw Isabel's Subaru pull into the driveway around six o'clock, but didn't get out of his so-called easy chair—the used floor model from Macy's—to see if she was alone or what. It was the *what* that made him feel stupefied. Eventually he called her on his cell phone, on the pretext that he was worried about her. Which he actually was. But mostly he just wanted to be with her.

"Hey, lady," he started, sounding like a dipshit from a Doobie Brothers' song, but Isabel didn't seem to mind.

"Hey, Terry," she said, fairly warmly, although she seemed somewhat preoccupied, since that was all she said.

"Out with Madam Zodie today?" he inquired, somehow knowing that her answer would be negative, but hoping it was just some girl thing that kept her away all day while he was getting a psychedelic mind job from a pair of gorgeous characters.

"Actually, I went to work."

Work! What the holy fuck! Somehow he'd never thought that Isabel actually *worked*.

"Yeah," she continued, even though he'd merely grunted, like he knew what the hell she was talking about. "Figured it was about time I got back to it. My brother's a patient guy and he's been nice about me working at home, but the fish processing plant needs a reliable eye, someone on the scene to go over the financials other than him, since he can't read a spreadsheet to save his own life."

Fish plant! Financials! WTF! He had the sense to pretend that he'd always known she was an accountant, even though it was news to him.

"But this is the weekend," he complained, as if nobody worked on a Saturday.

"I worked all week," she said, as if he hadn't noticed that she'd been gone. As if he hadn't been mooing around like a motherless calf, calling for her to comfort him.

"So okay," Terry said, not knowing where to take the disappointing conversation, clueless about wooing her, stuck in his head—and he hadn't even been smoking weed.

He could hear her rooting around in her fridge, pouring herself a glass of wine, judging from the clink of glass bottles as she opened and then shut the door. He wished he was a wine connoisseur like Charlie instead of a cheap-beer drinker and pothead.

"Maybe you could come over for dinner tomorrow?" Isabel said, right before he was going to say he had to hang up for some stupid reason, although he did have to pee.

He wanted to tell her about the magical mercado, and meeting up with Alexander and his brown-eyed young girlfriend, but that wasn't a conversation for the phone. The story of Matt and Rosie, and her lesbian lover who turned herself into a man, probably wasn't a dinner conversation either, so he reminded himself not to say anything later. He hadn't even told her about Rosie screwing The Bastard yet.

Once he hung up the phone and went to the bathroom he felt a little bit better than he had for the past several days. At least he knew what Isabel was up to and could stop imagining her fucking some cool old college professor who'd known her dead husband. But he still felt out of sorts.

Calling the Ol' Bean was not the answer for relieving his stress. He opted for a YouTube lecture on time travel even though it made him feel antsy and out of sync with himself. He went to bed before midnight and dreamed about Charlie turning into Isabel, and Isabel turning into Matt, waking up at two a.m. with one of Rosie's show tunes stuck in his head.

Of course he'd always wanted to fuck her, but so what? The psychology of sex held no reliable answers for his ongoing distress.

Things seemed a bit brighter in the morning after he made pancakes with the masa he'd bought, although he couldn't get a grip on whether maple syrup or salsa should accompany them. His mother never made pancakes which was a mystery to him. He made a mental note to call her which didn't say when. Time, as he'd learned, was relative.

When dinnertime rolled around, he moseyed on over to Isabel's house nonchalantly, as if his heart wasn't leaping clean out of his chest, carrying the jar of mole he'd bought for her yesterday tucked inside his work-shirt pocket like an amulet.

Hoping for sex, praying for sex, yet clear in his unconditional acceptance of Isabel—however chaste she was—Terry consciously extended his aura, concentrating on spreading his inner light even though it probably looked kind of murky. The car wreck, the mercado, his long spate of existentialism, had taken their toll on him. Not to mention the physical effects of the accident, leaving his forehead as scarred as a pirate's.

But Isabel was wonderful. As soon as she welcomed Terry into her aromatic kitchen, she clung to him warmly, holding his body close to hers after her gave her the mole sauce.

"I made enchiladas with tomatillos and pumpkin seeds," she said.

Terry chuckled happily. But, of course!

MATTHEW WAS IN A FUNK

Terry wouldn't take his calls and Madam Zodie hadn't returned his voicemail. All he could do was work on his software projects and busted windup toys that were starting to remind him of malevolent creatures from a Stephen King novel. He'd exhausted his stock of old watches and clocks, putting the ones he couldn't fix back in the box from Goodwill. But he didn't go out hunting for more broken things to fix since he was supposed to be fixing himself.

At his low point—not the lowest, that would come soon—he dialed up Fred and Frank, who shared the same phone, just to have someone more fucked up than he was to talk to. The last time he'd called, almost two years ago, they'd been alternately surly and jovial, regaling him with mean-spirited tales from his childhood until he hung up on them. Luckily this time they didn't answer and he didn't leave a message.

The contretemps at Jackson's had all but cured him of his passion for Rosie but there was nothing to take its place. Even the Amazon digital editor who'd gone down on him at one of Brand's fuck parties seemed abashed when he asked her out for a drink. He was shit out of luck and on his own, and desperately worried about Terry.

What if the dummkopf was irrevocably brain-damaged? Or not damaged enough, so that he wouldn't stay stupid enough to take Matthew back as his best friend, common sense finally ruling the day.

Going to the Salmon House was out of the question, since it was too close to a lake where he might drown himself. Not that he actually would, of course. Living in a city built around water had pretty much cured him of wanting to pursue that suicide fantasy, although it was difficult not to think of himself sinking to the bottom of Lake Union with a gnawing rat on his face helping to push him under.

So rats it was and more fucking rats because the word kept playing in his head.

RATS in big shining letters like the sign on Rosie's marquee. Trying to substitute weasels or badgers didn't work for some stupid reason, nor did other short animal words like CATS or DOGS, so he ended up going to a pet store and looking at rats until the word dropped out of his head.

On Saturday, in despair mixed with boredom, he got out his horoscope and the chart notes from the pissed-off pretty astrologer. Maybe there was some cosmic wisdom in there that might take the razor-sharp edge off his looming self-hatred. He thumbed through the pages and there it was, the note that Madam Zodie said was okayed by her dog—

3 boys in a mad house
2 dead in a car
1 all alone with his brain on fire

What the fuck! But there was more.

A trip to the past
Then back but not to the future
Safe at home with a very good friend

Then the last freaky tercet.

Laid ghosts and healed sorrows
Although stalked by an enemy
New joy with a water sign

And then just one stark final line, by itself pretty creepy.

The monster finally embraces his daemon

A surge of angry electricity shot through Matthew's hand. He balled up the piece of paper and threw it in his office wastebasket before stalking into the kitchen where he downed a hefty slug of vodka, followed by several more.

Sparks shooting off in his head, fingertips burning like lit sparklers, he raced through the condo, on fire from the alcohol, angry at the world. And Madam Zodie. Shouting for Terry, "Where are you, motherfucker!? I'm dying!"

But he wasn't dying. He was never going to die because he was cursed. And even if he did somehow manage to die, he'd still be alive in the bardo, doing the same things again and again, because he was nothing but a robot, programmed to live on REPEAT.

To further extend the metaphor he decided to watch *Groundhog Day* and put his old DVD in the player. He'd just settled down to jerk off to Andie McDowell's freeze-framed face when he heard a gentle tap at his door. Figuring it was the pizza he'd ordered for six-thirty, even though it was only five after six, he zipped up his pants and stumbled to the door, throwing it open with gusto as he fished for his wallet.

Then POW!! A gloved hand pushed him backwards, while another hand wearing a tight black leather glove slammed the door behind him, then grabbed Matthew by the throat.

It was only when he was kneeling on the floor, with a strong arm around his neck from behind, that Matthew realized that the savage home invader was Jackson. Come to kill him, of course. He had no doubt that this was likely and possible.

Had it been an old noir movie like Terry liked, the villain would have scoffed, "time to say your prayers, sucker," increasing the pressure on his throat while Matthew struggled for breath. But his attacker was The Bastard Jackson Brand who operated by his own special rules which favored extreme humiliation over violence.

Luckily for Matthew he was drunk, which meant that his body was profoundly detached from the martial arts action, even though his mind was crazily spinning. If only Brand would untighten his chokehold, he could fall on the carpet and dream. Perchance of being rescued by Terry.

"Oh you fucking bad boy," Jackson drawled, shoving Matthew's head to the ground. "You baaad fucking boy who's been messing with Rosie . . . With Rosebud, my little girl."

Jackson's breath was hot on Matthew's neck, but not as hot as his tongue which burned like a firebrand when applied to Matthew's crotch, even though his pants were still on.

"Ooh, look at you, dear boy," Jackson snarled, or hissed, Matthew couldn't tell which, but every move he made was animalistic, in the most bestial way.

"Ought to cut off your nuts . . . feed your kidneys to Rosie . . . shove my cock up your ass . . ." Brand's menacing voice kept getting softer rather than louder as he leaned his full weight on Matthew, scooching up from his crotch to his chest like a succubus caterpillar.

The Bastard's expert caresses were excruciating but the worst part was when he aimed the thick ball of spit from his purplish lips into Matthew's gasping mouth with the easy finesse of a basketball player.

"Suck it, little brother," the crazy fiend twittered, quoting a line from one of his kinky manuscripts, or so Matthew imagined.

Matthew kicked out at Brand with all his force, which wasn't very formidable, considering his lack of physical traction. His legs felt like tranquilized jellyfish.

But he had to get away! He just had to get away! Because he knew what was coming. Down to the depths of his soul he knew that in the next sixty seconds Brand's cock would be wagging its snake's head of venom right in his face.

Gagging with disgust, Matthew lurched upright with considerable force, goaded into action by visualizing what Terry would do, knocking Brand off his chest and onto the floor.

There was no time to think, much less time for revenge, so Matthew couldn't maneuver himself into a superior position over Jackson. Nevertheless, something fundamental in the fight had shifted, so that his thinking became less panicked, his movements more sure.

Jackknifing his legs, he pushed himself away from the cad on the floor, staggering to his feet with the dazed expression that meant he was on the verge of an absent seizure, and lurched to the door, just as the pizza guy knocked.

"You gonna get out when I open this door!?" Matthew shouted, hoping the Pagliacci guy might twig to the situation and call the police, if Jackson didn't leave. But The Bastard just laughed and took off his OJ gloves, after getting to his feet languidly, like a man who's drowsy from sunbathing.

"Go on and pay him," Brand said when Matthew finally opened the door to the incurious delivery man, who snagged his fee and generous tip and went away happy, impervious to the unfolding drama behind him.

What the fuck, Matthew thought. Or rather some distant part of his brain did. The other part was eyeing his unwelcome houseguest with something like stupefaction. Stunned that he could have ever hung out with a guy who looked so much like a cardboard villain. That he'd ever been impressed with Jackson's dickishness.

And suddenly he just didn't care what happened between him and The Bastard Brand. For now, he just didn't give a shit. "What will be, will be," like his placid mom always said. No use trying to kill someone who didn't even deserve to be killed, in a transformative sense.

He shut the door behind the receding back of the pizza guy and stepped back into the room rather gingerly, but his movements were strong. He felt like a Christian in a lion's den, or a lion who's very hungry. All he knew or cared about for this very drunk second was that he was *hangry*.

While Matthew was ferrying the box of pizza to the coffee table, Jackson sat down on the couch, and checked his sculpted mane of shining blonde hair in his pocket mirror.

Matthew glared ominously at Brand. "Told you to get the fuck out."

"Yeah. Yeah. Yeah . . . Dear Boy." Jackson drawled, grinning at himself in his mirror. "What kind of pizza?"

Matthew gulped, feeling his gorge rise. "What kind of pizza!?" he shouted. "What kind of question is that, after you just attacked me?!"

Jackson sighed theatrically and smoothed his perfect eyebrows with both thumbs. "Tit for tat . . . Or tat for tit, if we mean the well-designed Rosie."

"Don't talk about Rosie that way!"

Jackson leaned forward and opened the pizza box, sniffing orgasmically. "You mean, she isn't actually *fuckable*?"

"Of course she's . . ." Matthew paused before finishing his sentence. Brand's question was a trap, as usual.

Looking towards his bedroom, Mathew wondered if he should lock himself in and call Terry, but inexplicably he said, "Want some vodka?" —ever the good host, in spite of his unwanted guest's despicable spate of recent indignities.

Brand arranged his long rubbery body into a more comfortable potion on Matthew's couch, something like a Roman senator at a banquet that he's just crashed, assured of his eventual welcome by a crowd of toga-clad sandal-lickers although nobody else was around.

"She's quite the little lady . . . Rosie is . . ." The Bastard said, making Matthew's teeth hurt from clenching them.

"She's not—" Matthew started, but Jackson interrupted, "But yes she is. A lady through and through. From the tips of her shiny pink toenails to her tight little pink cunt . . . which we're both exceedingly familiar with, 'ey what?"

If there was ever a time to strangle Brand, this was it. But Matthew just sat there. He was stuck. Roiling around in his stupefied head, the multiple possibilities of recourse chased each other's tails like medieval snakes. Most of his choices ended in prison or at least some sort of abject social ostricization, which he couldn't afford, dependent as he was on contract jobs.

"Shut up about Rosie," he managed to blurt. "This is about you and me."

Of course that set The Bastard off laughing uproariously, and eventually Matthew started laughing as well, even though he should be kicking the shit out of his enemy or crouching in the corner crying. What else was there to do?

Brand picked up Matthew's glass of vodka and downed it all, then picked a green pepper strip off the pizza and ate it with his eyes closed, like a discriminating chef on a cooking show. "Should have been red peppers, dear boy . . . and maybe some capers . . ."

Matthew slammed the lid shut on the pizza box to disappointing effect. The cardboard was already greasy and damp. "My dinner," he said, sounding like a selfish kid, then, "tell me why you're here, asshole," like an equally unsociable adult.

Jackson sniffed ostentatiously. "I'd have thought that was obvious . . ."

Well, yes and no, Matthew decided, seeing as how he was still alive, and Brand didn't seem to have a gun in his pocket, merely an iPhone, which he took out now and flashed a picture of Rosie in a skintight outfit towards Matthew's face.

"Bit like a bloody Kardashian, but you have to love her . . . However, she doesn't have to love you . . . Am I right, dear boy?"

He was, but Matthew wasn't going to say so.

Brand nodded his head towards the frozen Andie McDowell. "Who's that pretty bitch?" Matthew blushed and shut off the TV as Jackson chortled gleefully, "Oh, I get it . . . A thousand humbles apologies for interrupting your hot date night . . ."

"Just get to the fucking point!"

Jackson raised his voice an octave, mimicking a Southern Belle. "Why, that's no way to speak to your gentleman caller! You ought to be ashamed of yourself, dear boy."

"Stop with the goddamn *dear boys* and tell me why you're here or get out."

Brand opened the pizza box again and picked up a piece of pepperoni which he flicked at Matthew. "Like you can fucking make me?"

"Yeah, I probably can," Matthew boldly answered, feeling like he had nothing to lose.

Apparently The Bastard took him seriously because he stood up and said—for once, quickly spitting out his words, "In deference to Rosie's inexplicable feelings for you, I'm not going to take you apart, even though I could with alacrity." He pulled on his creepy gloves.

"There's a no contact order waiting to be signed at my lawyer's office. Should you contact Rosie again, or come to our home, you'll find a very unpleasant future waiting for you once you get out of the hospital."

Brand smiled nastily as he opened the front door, "If you ever get out, that is . . ."

Leaning against the doorframe, seeing Jackson out, Matthew wondered what the fuck he was doing, just giving in to the brute, acting like a pussy. Yet an extended fistfight hadn't seemed like the way to go, either. The thought that it was a lose/lose situation refreshed his confidence a bit. What else could he have done?

Besides, the fuck-wit writer could keep Rosie anyway. Matthew was done with her. And then it dawned on him. He really *was* done with her! It was the end of the Rosie and Matt story. Not just the end of their marriage, but the end of every twisted haggard minute of its post-divorce aftermath where he'd stayed chained to her like a slave.

And then another thought struck him. It was the end of everything and everyone!

Rosie was gone. Terry was gone. His parents and brothers were gone. Madam Zodie and her pugnacious dog were gone. Even evil Jackson was gone. He was all alone.

No one was here to watch him crawl back onto the couch, clutching the box of cold pizza, and the TV remote which gave him power over Andie McDowell.

He suddenly realized he was lucky. He had exactly the life that he'd always secretly wanted. Time alone to be nothing.

TERRY MEETS MADAM ZODIE

Terry finished trimming the scraggly bits off his unruly sideburns with a rusty old nail clipper, then grinned at himself in the bathroom mirror, checking his freshly brushed teeth, before heading over to Isabel's house to meet her cousin Madam Zodie who was coming for tea at two-thirty.

He felt nervous but not entirely so, knowing there would be something homemade to eat to take his mind off social intercourse with the psychic astrologer. One of Isabel's apple cakes or poppyseed muffins, and pot after pot of hot tea, made with a master's touch. So much better than the expensive swill and flavorless snacks at the neighborhood Starbucks.

Isabel scoffed when he said she ought to open up a bakery, but it was exciting imagining her pulling loaves from the oven while he stood up front taking money from salivating patrons. Or better yet, working beside her in the kitchen, turning out masterpieces of comforting culinary art.

Of course he put himself smack dab in the picture whenever he thought about Isabel, which was often, but not obsessively so, now that he knew she was going to work on weekends sometimes, and was not avoiding him. The rest of the time he thought about Matt, when he wasn't fantasizing about quitting his job or worrying about his dad sinking ever deeper into a mindless quagmire.

He smoothed the wrinkles on the front of his long-sleeved black Henley after taking one last look in the mirror. He looked respectable enough, he guessed, with his curly hair freshly washed and his new shirt hiding the screwdriver hole in the back pocket of his 501's. Only a little bit like a hick—and sort of an attractive one, maybe, based on a recent remark of Isabel's complementing him on his "ruggedness."

He supposed his apparent toughness was what attracted her to him—if she was actually *attracted* to him in the way that he meant. But he wasn't tough, just tenacious, as demonstrated by his long-term allegiance to Matt, although, of late, that had grown pretty thin.

Still, he couldn't help wondering what the Ol' Bean was up to these days. There'd been no groveling phone calls or text messages from him for over two weeks, which was both worrisome and a relief. Maybe Madam Zodie would have some psychic clue about how to deal with his crazy old friend, if he could find a way to talk about Matt without shitting on him.

Isabel advised time as the great benefactor in their healing process—ironic, as she was still grieving for her dead husband—yet encouraging, since her kindly advice showed that she cared about him.

Grabbing a bottle of wine from the fridge, Terry took one last look around his dingy kitchen before heading over to Isabel's sparkling one, the contrast briefly depressing him. His bachelor pad seemed outdated, if not wholly pathetic. Although it was clean, it felt static, washed-out, devoid of the nurturing energy hers seemed to possess.

He should paint, get a cat, buy some new furniture. Get a goddamn new life. With Isabel more firmly in it.

Once next door, after the brief flurry of introductions and handshaking with Madam Zodie, and nervously patting her weird- looking dog before it was put out on the deck, he realized he was holding his breath, but stifled an audible sigh so as not to seem crass and unmannerly.

Sensing his distress, Isabel set him to work collecting glasses and opening the wine, while she got out plates for her almond cake which Madam Zodie cut into generous pieces and set on the kitchen table.

Pouring out steaming cups of Darjeeling, once they sat down, Isabel said, "I'm so glad you're here," which soothed him a little, but he was jonesing for a quick swig of whiskey to take the edge off his unaccustomed anxiety. He wasn't much of a wine drinker, but he gulped down a half glass of the Sauvignon Blanc, before starting in on his tea.

Madam Zodie smiled encouragingly at him. The cake crumbs on her chin made her seem very young and less intimidating than the vaguely disturbing image he'd formed of her as the nixie shaman who was supposed to heal Matt.

"How's your friend?" she asked, the twinkle in her eyes belying any hostility she might have towards a man who'd probably acted like an asshole from the moment they met.

"Same old, same old," Terry said. "Duddn't know how to make peace with his past. Or his present, for that matter."

"So he's just like most of us then." Madam Zodie laughed kindly and took a ladylike sip of her wine.

Isabel eyed her cousin thoughtfully, and smiled her usual smile with its tincture of ongoing sadness. "You talkin' 'bout me?" she growled in a gangsterish tone, to which Madam Zodie replied, "But of course!" in a silly French voice, which made them all laugh, breaking the subliminal tension.

After that things were easy, the conversation flowing from topic to topic, mostly benign, between somber asides about various troubling world situations, and the limits of human intelligence. Isabel made another pot of tea when the first one was empty, bringing a box of Fran's chocolates to the table with a bowl of a mixed nuts, while Madam Zodie poured out the last of the wine.

Both of the pixie-like cousins reminded Terry of subversive girl-child warriors and humorous heroines like Pippy Longstocking, but Isabel seemed far more physically substantial than Madam Zodie, who was about her same size, widowhood and motherhood having conferred a weightier earthiness to her, he supposed.

In her voluminous skirt and swathes of silk scarves the slender astrologer looked like a gypsy fortune teller, but so far she hadn't sounded like one. No prognostications or prescient remarks had passed her lips in the last hour, merely burbles of companionable laughter and snorts of indignation about politics.

Terry wondered if she really could see into people the way Isabel said she could, if she'd seen the twisted mess inside Matt and been disgusted. The thought wrung his heart. He reached for the bottle of wine.

Madam Zodie's eyes were the same startling green as her cousin's but the amber flecks in them flashed like fire—or so he imagined—when she turned to him and said, "Your friend will be fine. After he sacrifices his treasures, perhaps."

Terry gawped. "Uh, what?" *Shee-it*. He sounded like a moron.

"Nothing for you to worry about." Madam Zodie frowned. "No, that's a dumb thing to say. There's everything to worry about when it comes to *that* kind of guy."

"Well, hell, should I worry about him or not?" A truculent note had crept into his voice. He guessed he might be a little bit drunk.

Madam Zodie smiled gently. Her irises had stopped flashing. "Your choice entirely. But, as I said—eventually—your friend will be fine."

Terry rubbed his sideburns distractedly and tugged at an unruly curl, pushing it behind his ear. He wished he had a slug of Jamieson's, a big fat doobie cigar, and some sweet little Reggae tunes playing in the background, to take the edge off his creepy feeling that the alleged psychic was right about Matt. Not that he wished she wasn't.

He was about to say something maudlin and stupid when Isabel stepped in with the suggestion that they go sit on the deck with the dog. It was pleasantly crisp outside, she reminded them. So out they went, teacups in hand, with a bottle of wine Isabel pulled from her cupboard, Merlot this time, the color of the autumn leaves that were beginning to fall from the neighborhood trees.

While the cousins reminisced about Halloween, and the doleful looking dog nosed his mistress for treats, Terry sat back in his aluminum yard chair and checked out his cottage next door. Tiny, chunky, too cheaply built to be a Craftsman. Modest, and in definite need of duding up, but, thanks to his hard daily labors at the hospital—sweeping litter, wiping up vomit and blood—it was all his, as long as he could make his monthly rent payment.

It could be Isabel's, too, he imagined. Not that she'd want it. Everything she needed was here except her dead husband.

He closed his eyes, contemplating their romantic future for a few moments without putting that name on it. Tuning back in to the women's conversation, he heard Isabel jokingly chide her cousin. "Remember that time you took Emily trick-or-treating and stayed out past eleven? I thought Charlie was going to murder you. She was only seven!"

"Yeah and I was a sophomore in college, with a black belt in Aikido, so I don't know what the fuck he was worrying about!"

"You saying *fuck*, no doubt." Isabel retorted dryly, making both of them laugh.

The joyful tinkle of feminine laughter warmed him, augmenting the tepid touch of the late afternoon sun. Oh, the cousins' comradery was so nice! So much more comfortable than his relationship with Matt had ever been, even before their recent murderous night.

There'd been a fly in the ointment long before that, months—years—before the alienating appearance of The Bastard. Long before Rosie hit the scene with her dangling red curls and the piss-pants days of the Wonder Bar. Long before their spine-chilling afternoons hiding from Matt's raging dad. All the way back to second grade when their lifelong friendship began.

A sudden image of seven-year-old Matt sprawled on the playground with blood on his face sprang to mind, a gut-crunching memory, reminding Terry just what the hitch was. Matt's oft-broken heart. So much worse than his scrambled brain. Bullies flocked to his invisible injuries like bears to honey-roasted termites. But he kept on trying to be loved.

It was probably all karmic, Terry reckoned. The whole goddamn relationship kick with him and Matt. Him and his demented old dad. Him and his slow-going relationship with Isabel which was giving him the bends.

But she was so easy to love. So tender and vulnerable. Like one of those medieval tapestry ladies with a unicorn resting its head on her lap. But he couldn't get a grip on her. She drifted around in his consciousness, disturbing and intriguing him, making him yearn for things he hadn't wanted for a very long time. Things he was afraid of.

Good ol' Terry Thompson. That's what he was. *A good ol' boy.* Dumb as a damn fuckin' ox. Plodding along with a load on his back of other people's problems. Their sick treasures, not his. He shook his head vigorously and opened his eyes to shake off his troublesome thoughts.

The cousin's melodic voices, a bit like bird twitters, continued, only now he was watching them. Taking stock, noticing their differences, comparing them to the couple in the bodega who'd so confused and enthralled him.

He didn't know why he kept thinking about Rosie's ex-lesbian girlfriend who was now a beautiful young man, why he was sorry he couldn't tell Matt about meeting up with him. How fated that chance encounter had felt. He hadn't even shared the experience with Isabel, his sense that he'd stepped into the *surreal* in that Mexican shop, even though she might enjoy his odd little story, and its strange relevance to him.

"We need cake!" Isabel announced before going back into the kitchen to cut some more slices, leaving Terry and Madam Zodie sitting silently enjoying the quiet as they assessed one another, their frank open faces falling into shadow as the lowering sun moved westwards.

"Purty sure your folks didn't name you Madam Zodie," Terry finally said, "Although it's a mighty fine name."

"Well, yeah they did, but not when I was born. The nickname came later—when I was a teenager—after I had a vision about finding a lost dog. Tehuti's grandmother."

Terry chuckled, "Tehuti! Funny name for a dog."

"It's a variant of Thoth, the Egyptian god of magic and writing. Although he isn't very scholarly." She gave the sleeping dog a gentle nudge with her foot. "He's bat-shit crazy for me. But he doesn't like your friend."

"Who the fuck does?" Terry said, even though he still did.

Mindful of professional boundaries, he probed the astrologer about Matt in a roundabout way. "He's a complicated guy, doncha think?'

"Sure. Just like everybody else," came her disappointing reply, any further opportunity for evaluation interrupted by Isabel's return with more cake. He ate two pieces, washing them down with the rest of his wine, his desire for whiskey and pot fading into the background while he considered his options for the night, hoping he could spend it with Isabel.

At five-thirty Madam Zodie retrieved her bag and coat from the kitchen, woke up her grumbling dog, and began to say her extended farewells, needling Terry about his sweet tooth, commenting on the upcoming holiday season, and Isabel's first Thanksgiving without Charlie.

"I know how much you miss him," she said, hugging her cousin tightly, before turning to Terry with a fond goodbye and one last remark about Matthew.

"Your friend's coming back into your life. I'm sorry that someone else may be leaving it."

She smiled obliquely at Terry's look of distress, but patted his arm reassuringly. "Don't worry, it isn't Isabel."

Returning to the kitchen after Madam Zodie had gone, and glad to be back in its fragrant warmth, he put their glasses and plates in the sink, while Isabel covered the remnants of her delectable cake with plastic wrap. The shared domesticity, while comforting, made him yearn for something more substantial than affectionate neighborliness.

He stretched out his hand as she passed him carrying the empty bottles of wine, catching her by the strings of the paisley chef's apron she'd been wearing all afternoon. Taking the bottles out of her arms, he enfolded her in his own, pulling her gently towards him until her head rested on his chest.

"What's gonna happen now?" he mumbled into the warmth of her hair, his hands light on her back, afraid of scaring her away.

"I don't know." She shifted away from him momentarily then moved back a little closer, her hands around his waist. "Maybe I should make us some dinner?"

Terry kissed the top of her head. "I'm not hungry," he said, even though he still was. But for her, not dinner food.

Isabel raised her head and looked up at him, their noses nearly touching. Her breath smelled fresh and flowery in spite of the wine they'd drunk which had left an acid taste in his throat.

Maybe now was the time to ask for that whiskey? Before he awkwardly and brazenly kissed her.

But when Isabel surprised him by pressing her lips to his, and clutching the back of his shirt with something akin to passion when he returned her kiss, he didn't feel awkward. He felt blessed.

Everything was going to be alright, somehow, in spite of her dead husband. And everything else hovering invisibly above and around them swishing angel wings of thwarted desire.

PARTY PARTY

How many goddamn times can a man whack off without losing his sense of proportion regarding the purpose of his dick?

How many times can a man lock himself in the bathroom with a bottle of gin and a pack of razor blades, lying in the tub till the water turns icy, without doing anything more decisive than gazing at the freckles on his skin?

How many times can a man face himself in the mirror, looking for clues to his inherent neurological state in the squint of his eyes, while besieged by a vicious migraine?

How many times can a man forgive himself for his sins when it's obvious that nobody else can or will?

Chalk at least three of these questions up to his own stupidity, and perhaps at least one to ill fortune. However Matthew looked at the problems that were not only facing him but sneaking up from behind, he couldn't come up with any worthwhile suggestions for relieving his rank state of mind.

He'd stopped trying to reach Terry by conventional means but occasionally succumbed to voodoo routines by burning spell candles with names like "absorb negativity", "needed changes" and "forgiveness", in a vain attempt to recapture his old friend's trust and affection. So far nothing significant in his inner or outer life had visibly changed, except his Visa bills, showing purchases from internet magick shoppes and a plethora of charges for delivery pizzas, one of which was still moldering in his refrigerator.

Last night he'd eaten a bag of corn chips washed down with a liter of Coke, followed by ten miniature Snickers bars from his copious cache of Halloween candy which trick-or-treaters were never going to get. The outside world loomed like a dystopian megalopolis, full of monsters and inquisitors, whenever he peeped out of his Levolor blinds. He slept on the couch all day in a funkified gloom of dyspepsia and moral despair.

Moribund by day, feverishly active at night, pounding out angry letters to Rosie and Jackson, and pleading ones to Terry, on his laptop, when he wasn't bent over his desktop pounding out code for cyber clients unaware of his ridiculous descent into madness. The tortured and torturous letters never got sent, but his software projects went out before time, scrupulously perfect—or as perfect as security ware ever gets.

"If you want a plan, I'm your man," he singsonged, when he had trouble concentrating on his work, butchering Leonard Cohen lyrics since he sucked at murdering himself. Aside from his fruitless letter writing, and repetitious self-blaming thoughts, he tried not to concentrate on his relationships which had either ended or were going nowhere quite quickly.

In the back of his mind, plans for revenge fomented and roiled, their object directed towards fate and his own stupid actions, rather than Jackson—or Rosie, who'd betrayed him. Talking to a shrink was out of the question since he hated people who purported to understand his brain chemistry, including the stalwart neurologists who couldn't figure out how to treat his cranial complaints without resorting to meds with worse side-effects than his various ailments.

Remembering Terry saying, "Yer fuckin' head's mess, but I love ya anyway," provided as much guilt as it did solace, so Matthew pretended that it was his best friend who had problems with him, not himself having problems with himself. Self-hatred, which he'd always been good at, had ceased to be fun.

Buoyed by the thought that he might escape himself for one night, he went downtown and looked for bars filled with deadbeats and ugly people, sitting in a dump on 6th avenue that didn't even qualify as a dive for so long that his ass felt glued to the barstool. The chichi places he used to go with Rosie beckoned from afar, but he stayed faithful to his nihilism by eating a stale mustard pretzel dunked in fake orange cheese while he drank his fourth or fifth round of beer. Puking it all up later proved ineffective as spiritual catharsis.

If only he could turn himself inside out and start all over again.

Succumbing to what seemed like a healthy whim, he decided to go to a long-term client's party on Capitol Hill on Halloween night, dressed in an old pair of pajamas and his favorite cowboy boots.

"Ghost of the Old West," he said, when curious partygoers, dressed as bloodsucking zombies and vampires, questioned him about his temporary archetypal identity. Quipping about Wild Bill Hickok—or Sam Peckinpah, if they were cinephiles—they floated away in a cloud of pot, after asking him where his gun was and why he wasn't wearing a mustache.

It was ludicrously easy to get drunk on the cauldron of Red Bull, vodka, and cannabis-infused pop, which bubbled on the dining room table in a vat of dry ice. After a few paper cups, Matthew was bobbing and weaving so much he was motivated to dance, even though his legs felt as wobbly as the gummy worms floating in the punch.

"Shoulda come as Gumby," he muttered to a tall black man dressed as a latex super-hero, who was nuzzling the neck of a tranced-out belly dancer on the makeshift dance floor, which was decorated with droopy poly-cotton spider webs. Neither the guy nor his dance partner paid any attention to Matthew, which—for a change—wasn't what he wanted.

Looking around for a suitable partner—someone who wouldn't ignore or mock him—he spotted a flash of long red curls bouncing in time to the music. Stumbling forwards to see if the backwards facing person was Rosie, he realized the tumbling hair belonged to a guy dressed like a foppish dandy from the court of the Sun King—his techno-chief host, who shouted "Whoa Matthew!" as he gyrated past in a disheveled conga line, crimson wig askew.

Now he was thinking about Rosie. Missing and wanting her. When he'd thought he was done. Shoving down his disappointment, he headed back towards the punch to drown out his sorrows, moving through the treacly crowd in slow motion.

But wait—just like in a comedy of errors—there she actually was! Fish-tailing at the end of the conga line, in a sexy green mermaid costume and silvery wig, Rosie swept by him in a swathe of familiar perfume, flashing an inebriated smile that seemed to light up the room.

FUCK. FUCK. AND TRIPLE FUCKITY FUCK.

He didn't think she'd seen him, or care if she did. His invisibility struck him as criminal, although he had no one but himself to blame for lately pursuing that state with the fervor of a maniacal stage magician. Intent on slinking out, he stumbled instead of slunk towards the living room to retrieve his cellphone and coat. No time to call an Uber driver or cab—he just wanted to get the fuck out of there.

But of course, along with Rosie had come Jackson, standing now in a tight circle of costumed admirers, directly in front of the door that was Matthew's exit point.

Shee-it, he swore, imitating Terry, whom he suddenly wished were beside him, muttering comforting admonitions. "Duddn't matter who's here. Go back and drink. It's *your* fuckin' party."

Well, it *was* his fuckin' party, if by party the imaginary Terry meant personal horror show—and not just because it was Halloween. Matthew turned around, scouting for another way out, shrinking himself down as he started to scuttle out, like an insect who's spotted a spider. He was just about to drop to his hands and knees to crawl around the snaking conga line, when he felt a heavy hand on his back propelling him towards the drinks table.

The hissing voice at his ear, the fatuous "Well, well, *dear boy*," made him faint with terror. His OCD ramping up, a migraine starting, numbers shooting off in his head, he clutched at the hem of his pajama top in a pointless attempt to ward off his inevitable panic attack, reciting "psycho killer, psycho killer, psycho killer" under his breathe, until the strong arm stopped pushing him.

Almost falling as he spun around, Matthew confronted The Bastard Brand for what he hoped was the very last time. "Mother-fucking-prick-son-of-a-bitch-cock-breathin'-ass-fuck," he snarled, grabbing Jackson by the pointed lapels of his steampunk circus-ringmaster costume. "I'll kill you once and for all!"

"Take it easy, *dear boy*," his sardonic nemesis drawled, attempting to brush him off like a fly, which further enraged him.

Matthew spat out, "Fuck you and the fuckin' horse you rode in on!" and shoved Jackson towards the exact spot where Rosie was undulating like an underwater sea creature, the sequins of her mermaid suit catching the light of the disco ball, turning her shapely form into a crème de menthe collage of sensuous scales and flickering fins.

Jackson slammed into Rosie, and Rosie fell backwards into the arms of the stupefied host, who'd been drinking absinthe all night. Rosie fell gracefully, her training as an acrobat coming in handy when push came to shove, which it had. Beaming at her drunken catcher, she pirouetted to a standstill in his outstretched arms and then kissed him, agile as Jane Avril.

Against all expectation, neither Jackson nor Rosie retaliated against Matthew. Rosie just kept flirting with the drunk French courtier, and—once steady on his feet—Jackson headed to the closest coffee table to snort cocaine out of his monogrammed snuffbox. Fuck! Those people were crazy! Crazier than him and the stoned conga dancers and poison-punch drinkers rolled into one.

Matthew headed for the bathroom to pour some water over his head. A buzzy hangover was coming on and he wanted some coke, but damned if he'd ask The Bastard for some. Looking at his wet face in the mirror, he had to laugh at the strange situation—him running into Brand and Rosie at a techie-type Halloween party—their inexplicable indifference to his fumbling attempt at assault.

It was stupid to waste his limited energy on them, no matter how much their insouciance might nag at him. Rosie and Jackson didn't give two shits about his ongoing grudge or the fevered obsessions that started it. Yet he couldn't stop thinking about Rosie's beautiful face and punching in bloody Jackson's.

When he came out of the bathroom—as if in a dream—there was the astrologer Terry had forced him to go to, waiting in line for the toilet with a couple of friends, all three of them dressed as animals. A voluptuous black cat, a heavily mascaraed raccoon, and Madam Zodie wearing a rough-looking dog costume made of papier mache and tangled skeins of fake fur.

"You obviously weren't going for sexy," Matthew said, giving Madam Zodie the blurry onceover as he sidled past her in the hall, hating himself for sounding like Jackson, except for the obnoxious drawl. Hating her, because even in her ridiculous getup, she looked fetching.

Madam Zodie smiled her annoyingly beatific smile. "Guess I could say the same about you." She nudged the black cat while rolling her eyes and made gagging sounds.

"Yeah, if you were a mannerless ass-hat like *that dude,*" the raccoon snarled, gesturing rudely at Matthew, before pulling the dog and cat into the bathroom with her, and slamming the door on their screeches of laughter.

"Those *mamminals* can go fuck themselves," Matthew muttered to himself as he headed back to the drinks table. Everybody seemed to be necking, taking drugs, or dancing instead of drinking from the ceremonial cauldron, so he honed in on the steaming punchbowl without interference and poured himself another cup of oblivion.

Backing up to the nearest wall, and careful not to spill his drink, he leaned back and closed his eyes, letting the sounds of the party wash over him. The throbbing music made him feel like he was on a fright-house rollercoaster, then like he was spinning around on a Ferris wheel made out of human skulls. Bones were clacking or maybe it was the sound of the heavy metal drums.

Once he felt a little steadier on his feet, he opened his eyes, scanning the crowd for Rosie and Jackson. It took a while for his eyes to adjust to the swirling gloom, but eventually he spotted them in the adjoining black-lit room, in a brazen tableau that took his breathe away.

Under the spinning disco ball, a trio of repeating figures on the dance floor flashed before his bleary eyes. Rosie, her slippery green arms wrapped around the swaying waist of the bewigged courtier, caught his attention first, then Jackson swam into view in his black top hat and funereal clothes, a shark looking for fresh meat.

With cruel finesse The Bastard latched onto the clutching couple, throwing his powerful arms around them in a crude hug sandwich. With him in the lead, the dubious ménage à trois waltzed slowly towards the staircase to the upper floor where the bedrooms presumably were, disappearing in a cloud of sequins and ruffled lace before Matthew had time to think.

He pushed himself away from the wall shouting, "Stop that satanic asshole!" before sliding off his feet and down to the floor, where he lay like an exhausted pup, waiting for somebody to kick him.

"Arrrg . . ." Matthew shook his head wearily as he raised himself on one elbow to inspect his pajama bottoms, wet from the drink he'd hurled towards the retreating lovers, his empty paper cup lying forlornly beside him like a discarded condom.

God, he wished Terry were here to protect him from himself, instead of holed up in some old lady's house, safe in her motherly arms. Ghastly images of his own mother's arms, burned to a crisp like over-fried chicken, threatened to surface. He took another big gulp of the cranked-up punch, hoping he wouldn't vomit.

"Time to get out of here, Kemosabe," Terry's voice said in his ear, but when Matthew turned to look it was the canine astrologer barking orders at him and pawing him on the arm, telling him he'd better get up.

"Grab your coat and hat, if you have one," Madam Zodie instructed as she marched him out of the room. "And don't say goodbye."

He did have a coat and old cowboy hat which she—not he—found on the floor of the CEO's media den, under a pile of feathery clothing discarded by the couple who were fucking in there. They'd been dressed as birds, presumably— angry ones from the look of them. Madam Zodie whispered an embarrassed apology but Matthew just chirped at them sarcastically.

Matthew jammed his hat on his head and struggled into his coat while Madam Zodie pushed him through the twisty-turny many-roomed house like a border collie herding sheep.

Every room they passed through, populated with outer-space creatures, vampires, and gyrating gypsies nuzzling and rubbing each other, exuded the hot scents of ambergris and wet animal fur. The allure of it all—the drugs, the sex—was intoxicating. Matthew wanted to stay at the party but he kept on walking, as if there was a gun at his back instead of a kittenish psychic in a ratty dog costume nipping at his boot heels.

"Wha'? Where we goin'?" he breathlessly inquired, when they finally made their way through the pulsating maze and outside, onto narrow porch of the fancy Victorian.

"What do you care?" the raggedy sheepherder said, as they descended the stairs under a dim first-quarter moon.

Clouds scudding by, chilly sweet air smelling of cider and licorice, and no rain for a change. A sort of happy Halloween, Matthew suddenly thought. He hadn't killed or been killed by The Bastard. Or fallen on his knees before Rosie. And here was this infuriating and intriguing girl beside him that he couldn't make sense of.

"Duddn't really matter to me," he drawled. Drunk, and sounding as chilled out as Terry—maybe that was good. He'd felt torpid for so long, but he hadn't been relaxed. Now he felt supple as a warm sheet of wax as he stretched his limbs on the sidewalk.

He inhaled a big breath, watched it color the air white as he let it back out, a cloud of released despair which made him feel lighter. He smiled into the possibly auspicious night. He was glad the weird Madam was here.

But she didn't seem glad. She seemed pissed off, although maybe that was just her wiry tail made out of a bent coat hanger wagging furiously behind her as they walked to her car.

He touched her hand which was clenched in a fist. "Sorry what I said about your costume."

She shrugged off his hand, and punched him hard on the arm, just like Terry.

"Know what?" she spat, "You should just go fuck yourself. Maybe then you'll get a grip on your nasty bad habits."

Chastened, he moved away from her, hoping a little distance would give her—and him—some relief from her simmering anger. Although it was her goddamn decision to abduct him, not his.

"I had a gig back there, by the way. Tarot reading at midnight, for cash—which I'm not going to get now. Not that you'd care."

"Here . . . wait." He fumbled for his wallet, but she punched him again with her glove-covered paw.

Once they got in her car, Madam Zodie seemed to calm down a little. In spite of resembling a lumbering dog, she thrummed like a hummingbird with energy that was instantly contagious. She drove the same way, with her foot pressed steadily down on the gas pedal, zipping along as if weightless, seemingly immune to red lights.

In just a matter of minutes they'd driven off Capitol Hill down Denny Way and were tootling down Eliott Avenue, towards 15th and the bridge to Ballard. So she obviously wasn't taking him home unless she was going a 'roundabout way for some random reason.

He wondered if she was taking him to her house but was afraid to ask. Hunched over the wheel in her ramshackle dog outfit she looked like one of the crazed doofuses from *Dumb and Dumber*, but he didn't mention that either. His arm still stung where she'd hit him.

In short order the car pulled up to a neat little house up the hill from the Locks. One of those dated places that makes people think of old Seattle with its dotted groves of ancient forest, long gone now. Wind chimes tinkled over the Smith Brother Milk box on the weathered porch reminding him of his parents' house in Casper. The sound was melancholy like the tone of the night, which had switched from frantic to wistful, if not downright contemplative.

Sitting in the dark after the engine was off, Madam Zodie gazed through the windshield with the concentrated air she'd had while she was driving, but the side of her mouth that Matthew could see looked softer, less angry than before. Almost as if she might smile.

He wished he knew what she was thinking. Then maybe he could tell her what he'd been thinking as he rode in her car as her captive—no, rescue animal, for surely her interest in him was maternal, nothing more. She was a nurturer, like Terry's widowed earth mama. He was just one of her strays. Asking her out on a date seemed absurd, after his many faux pas of the night, and his contentious attitude at their doomed astrological appointment.

Sensing that she was hip to his innate propensity for shooting himself in the foot didn't help. That just meant she could see through him, and didn't like what she saw. The same problem he had, which, so far, seemed unresolvable.

He took out his cellphone intending to call for an Uber driver, but then Madam Zodie turned her face and began talking to him, the penciled-on dog whiskers on her upper lip quivering with each firmly enunciated word.

"I shouldn't be taking you home with me. But, like an idiot, I have. So you'd better behave yourself or Tehuti will snap you up in one giant bite and chew you into bloody little pieces and spit you out on my rug. Understand?"

Matthew put his phone back in his pocket and nodded his head obsequiously. "Yes. Yes. I understand."

Madam Zodie took the keys out of the ignition and put them into her hobo bag, gave her subdued passenger a coolly appraising look, and got out of the car—rather gracefully, considering her costume.

Matthew followed Madam Zodie up to her front door which was decorated with small medallions and mandalas. Decals of Shakti and Shiva shined in the tiny stained-glass window, golden auras on midnight indigo, inviting guests inside.

She unlocked the door and stepped inside, pulling off her fleece driving gloves and furry dog ears as she went through the house, turning on lights, putting the kettle on after gesturing vaguely towards her couch, telling Matthew to sit himself down.

Sinking down on the green velvet couch—more of a psychoanalyst's divan really—he felt as if he were in a church filled with pagan tchotchkes and hippie stuff. The outré ambiance he'd sneered at, when he was here for his forced astrological appointment, felt comforting, even though Madam Zodie hadn't smiled once since she'd hounded him out of the party.

He closed his eyes, listening to her bustling about, savoring an unfamiliar sensation of bodily security and a soothing sense of release. His spine felt like a tube filled with warm water; he relaxed into the languid heat and felt himself sink even deeper into the couch cushions.

No need to drive. No need to speak. No place he'd rather be. In a few moments he was nearly asleep.

The clacking of the old-fashioned tea trolley that Madam Zodie wheeled in from the kitchen, rattling cups and saucers, roused him. He watched her sleepily as she sat down in a circular chair across from him and poured out the steaming tea.

Her transformation from scraggly dog—not to femme fatale but to femme magique—was so complete that, for the second time tonight, Matthew felt as if he were dreaming.

The ridiculous whiskers and rattails of paper and fur were all gone. She'd changed into a William Morris-patterned floral caftan, and put on a thin coat of pale lipstick and some dangly silver earrings that made her look like the Tarot's High Priestess, a little other-worldly, wise yet vulnerable. At that hypnogogic moment, she was beautiful to him.

He was enthralled by her, but his mind was jumbled, his mouth was dry, and a hangover loomed in Damoclean fashion. Anything he said in his disheveled state would sound woefully stupid, so he didn't say anything, just sat up straighter, sipping the floral tea that he wished was strong black coffee.

Whimpering sounds emanated from the bedroom where Madam Zodie's dog was shut in, a fitting soundtrack to the pitiful night, Matthew thought, wishing she would look at him, or read his mind.

Or no, maybe not. Underneath his new admiration for her lurked murky incriminating thoughts.

Madam Zodie fixed her kohl-rimmed eyes intently on his, the way he'd secretly wanted, and smiled impishly at him, more Nordic elf than mystical hierophant. "So why'd you want to beat up Jackson Brand anyway? And what's your deal with his wife?"

Matthew bristled. "*My* wife! Or, well, she was . . ."

"So you don't know they got hitched? I heard their wedding was earlier today, on Halloween morning. Brand's birthday, apparently—which strikes me as fitting."

"What the fuck!" Matthew started to rise from the couch, then lowered himself gingerly back down, as if his back was hurt. But it was his guts that felt punched, all the way down to his soul.

Rosie fucking—even living with—Jackson was aggravating, but the thought of her tying herself to the egotistical prick for some indefinite perpetuity made him feel sick to the core, knowing how insecure she was beneath her barbed cloak of ambition, how much she craved being loved.

Frightful images of Jackson jouncing around the Big Pink sex room, cock swinging like a nob's baton, made it easy to imagine The Bastard sucking every morsel of innocence out of Rosie like an octopus cleaning out a crab claw. Matthew shuddered as he sipped his hot tea. Hating Rosie's guts because she cheated on him didn't mean she should suffer. After all, he had loved the vulnerable side of her, as well as her indomitable will.

He was warring with his desire to pump Madam Zodie for more details about the unfortunate nuptials, when she leaned forward to top off their tea, exposing the upper curve of her breasts through the loose neckline of her caftan. When that happened, Matthew forgot all about Rosie's pact with the devil and how jealous and worried he was.

The angry lust he'd felt earlier that night, when he saw Rosie locked in a hot embrace with two horny stoned men, seemed inconsequential compared to the wave of desire which swept through him now. An expansiveness in the tight middle part of his chest. A flighty sensation. A surge of pure joy. Heart not hard-on desire.

He realized he was staring at Madam Zodie like he'd never seen her before.

"You can get an Uber, or stay here and sleep on the couch," she said abruptly, the vivid green irises of her narrowed eyes frankly assessing him as he squirmed under her scrutiny.

"Uh, yeah, I'll stay, if it's really okay . . . I mean, thank you . . ." He spluttered, knocked askew by her sudden change of demeanor.

"I'm just doing it for your friend," she went on, "who— from what my cousin says—inexplicably—still likes you. Even though you've been acting like an asshole."

"Terry said that? That I'm as ass?"

"No, I said that. Because you pretty much are."

Shit-fuck, she thinks I'm a dick, his inner voice ominously declared —although, thankfully, his outer voice didn't.

He didn't know what to think. Her smile was indulgent and she shrugged in a Gallic way, as if they were sipping champagne on a Cannes balcony. But her eyes were as piercing as daggers.

Maybe he should make that Uber call?

WIDOWHOOD AND LITERATURE

The sweet taste of Isabel's mouth was like nothing Terry had ever tasted before.

"Like lingonberries and Swedish pancakes," Isabel said, rolling her eyes and smacking her lips, mocking him.

But it was true, she tasted like summer and breakfast and kisses on the shore of a trout-filled lake ringed by white birch trees. Waking up next to Isabel made Terry feel like Adam waking up next to Eve on the morning after the first day of creation, so enchanted did he feel with her.

She was an enigma—like all women, he supposed—yet deeply familiar in an elemental way, as if they'd been created together, out of the same flesh, the same soul. Absurd, of course—far too romantic.

But he couldn't change how he felt about her. Like that old Average White Band song on the jukebox at the Wonder Bar, that atavistically proclaimed, *"I've got you in my blood,"* his very veins seemed like a conduit for Isabel's essence, her plasmic DNA.

Knowing that their situation was tricky only partially tempered his joy. Ecstatic but circumspect, he kept his own counsel about the surges of hopeful confidence that assailed him throughout each day. Isabel, for her part, seemed like a sleepwalker enjoying a transcendent out-of-body experience. There but *not quite there*, even when they slept together.

And sleeping was mostly all they did, aside from lots of tentative petting and passionate kissing, although last night they'd clung together in a heated ball, with his fingers stroking her clit and her hand stroking his cock until they came together in a whirl of electrical sensations that left them both breathless.

Almost there, he'd thought, glad he could make Isabel orgasm—or maybe help was the word. But how much better it would be if she'd take him inside her. *Let him all the way in.* He was a patient guy, he was willing to wait—but how long? That was the goddamn question.

Now she was lying in Terry's arms talking about what she wanted to cook for dinner that night. Listening to her made thinking about tough questions hard, so he didn't.

"How about Swedish meatballs, or maybe lefsa and lutefisk," she suggested, continuing the joke. "Or fried reindeer heart sprinkled with pine needles and hundred-year-old lichen?"

Terry laughed, ruffling Isabel's hair. "Nah, that's okay. That fancy Scandi shit is a too gol-dang weird for me, although I like pickled herring well enough with a good IPA."

She patted his flat belly. "I'll put it on my Christmas list for you then, dear."

Terry squirmed uncomfortably, pretending his foot was caught in the wadded up sheet.

Shee-it. Now what?

To say or not to say that he knew about Isabel's plans to visit her daughter for an entire month, from Thanksgiving through Christmas. To confess or keep quiet about hearing the tail end of their private conversation, wafting out of Charlie's office on her speaker phone, while he'd stood in her kitchen, holding the full recycling bin he was supposed to be dumping in the outside cart tight against his chest, as if to stop his heart sinking.

No, better not tip the balance by letting the injured cat out of the bag, he decided. He was okay feeling hurt—and jealous—at least he was alive to his sexual being, his desire to possess her, but the thought of facing the holidays alone made him antsy.

"Alright, little lady, time to get up and face the oncomin' day," he said, unhooking Isabel's arms from around his waist, as he pushed himself out of bed.

Isabel glowered and threw a pillow at his head. "But it's Sunday! We can stay here all day if we want to."

"Not if we want Swedish pancakes. Which you are gonna make." He pulled on his underpants and turned around to kiss her. "Even if you don't have any lingonberries."

Isabel tossed another pillow at him which he caught and threw back at her. With a fake snarl of rage, she leapt from the bed and flashed her claws at him, then rubbed up against his chest with her naked breasts. "Well, okay, Mister," she purred, "whatever you want."

Jesus, who was this new sex aggressive woman?

The coquettish look on her face seemed as foreign as the gaze of a stranger's suddenly, as she pranced around him, light on her feet as cat. Seductive, almost surreal in her change of mood—was it still playful or predatory?—she seemed transformed. More youthful, crazier. Was this how she'd been with Charlie?

Before he could further develop this rude train of thought, she'd knelt down, extracted his cock from the fly in his underpants and begun skillfully sucking him off. He was seething with conflicting desires—to stay or go—sink back onto the bed or gently move her head away—but finally—no, quite easily—he succumbed to her ministrations and let himself come. And come, and come. Until he was totally wrung out, and dropped, panting, to knees, hugging Isabel hard to him, before he realized that she was crying.

Patting her back ineffectually, and struggling to make sense of something other than the continuing tremors in his weak-kneed satiated body, Terry realized what a fool he'd been to have thought that Isabel was okay about having any kind of relationship with him, much less a sexual one.

It was Charlie she wanted, no matter that the exalted professor had been reduced to ashes and grit. Charlie's arms, Charlie's mouth, Charlie's cock. Like Osiris', eternally missed, he suspected —he'd read the myths—what else could he do but treat her like a widowed goddess? Someone who couldn't be touched. Isabel = La Belle Isis. Even her backwards name held a clue to his inferiority to her.

"It's not you," she said, after a long drawn-out sob. But of course it was him. Him and Charlie. Two fuckin' heart-breakers. On two entirely different scores.

"Yeah, well, maybe it's me and maybe it's *him*." Terry didn't bother to keep the angry sarcasm out of his voice. Denial of factual material seemed to beleaguer the point, no matter how clichéd. She just wasn't that into him. Not the way he was into her. Or wanted to be into her.

They might as well fuckin' face it. Like Matt, she belonged to a ghost.

Pushing her gently away, Terry rose to his feet and sat down on the bed.

"You mean Charlie?" She finally said.

His laugh was mirthless. "Who else?"

Her green eyes flashed up at him. "I can't help loving him."

"I know."

"No, you don't." Sitting back on her haunches, Isabel stared up at him with the inscrutable face of one of those noble Renaissance ladies her husband had loved.

Was she angry, sad, guilty, bitter—what? What—and who—was she, he wondered, loving her all the more because he really didn't know.

"I spent thirty years with Charlie, since I was practically a kid. We made a good life together and a wonderful daughter who surpassed us in countless ways. Which isn't saying that our marriage was easy. But we endured. We had a track record, not that he'd put it that prosaically. But I would."

She scooted closer to the bed. "Other than Matt—and your mom and dad—who have you been with that long? Who have you ever loved?"

Terry looked down at her, wishing that he'd never brought up Charlie but there it was. Or there *he* was. *Il Professore* himself. Hovering over the room like a looming apparition, taking up all the space.

He could practically see the dude—dashing, even in death. Mister Mcfuckin' Darcy. Handsome as sin, aristocratic, dynamic, professorial, a goddamn learned lecturer. There was no competing with a guy like that, even if he was a ghost.

Terry bowed his head and shut his eyes, wishing he could just disappear. The jolting release of his surprise orgasm, the shattered look in Isabel's eyes, his fomenting anxiety about Matt, made him feel disoriented, trapped in a down-spiraling reality that felt like the high dive off a cliff.

Mustering his fortitude by remembering the unlooked for gift of Isabel's presence in his going-on-middle-aged life, he answered her painful inquiry without opening his eyes. "Nah, I've never loved anybody like that. Like you loved— still love—your husband."

He took her cold hand in his and kissed it with the fervor of a blind man sensing his loved one's disquiet. "Bet you wish it was him, not me, sitting here with you."

"Of course I do!" Isabel cried, disappointing and surprising him, even though he admired her honesty. "But I'm not sorry you're here," she went on quickly, stumbling over her words. "You're bringing me back to life. Making me feel like myself again, even if totally damaged. And I'm so grateful to you. But I can't figure out what you're getting from me."

Isabel clutched his arm with the hand he'd kissed. "How you can be satisfied with so little when you deserve so much."

But life doesn't work that way, he thought, as he pulled her up on her feet then gently pushed her down on the bed so that she was sitting next to him, their hands entwined, bare knees touching. His body was no longer trembling although he felt wobbly as Jell-O inside.

"How 'bout if we get back in bed?" he said after a few minutes of relative quiet in which the neighborhood's morning sounds—cars starting, dogs barking, the whomp-whomp of a basketball on the sidewalk—seemed like far off messages from another planet. Morse codes from another life where time was static, not dangerous and foreboding and riddled with loss.

Lying back on his now cold pillow, with Isabel cradled in his arms, Terry wondered if his chilled limbs would ever feel warm again or the hollow space in his chest fill with anything other than ice. The room felt colder than an unheated winter cabin, even though it was a tepid fifty-two degrees outside, in the middle of a balmy November. And soon Isabel would be leaving him to spend a month with her daughter. Someone he might never meet.

They slept until late afternoon. Or Isabel did while Terry dozed and started awake multiple times, chased into muddled consciousness by a haphazard series of dreams in which Isabel and Matt fought or fucked or ignored him. Isabel's silver-ish bob morphing into Rosie's red curls as she straddled Matt's cock, the tinkle of her voice turning harsh as she screeched out her orgasm.

Matthew was Charlie and then Charlie was Terry. Riding over the top level of the old Alaskan Way Viaduct on his motorcycle. Then crashing over the side of it onto Western Avenue, where a host of hungry seagulls pecked at his eyes while he lay shattered on the pavement, reduced to jagged pieces like his Harley.

"Fuck a fuckin' dog and his mother, too!" Terry extracted himself from Isabel and sat up, forcing himself firmly awake, pushing away his dreams.

He was warmer now but also massively pissed off, as if steam was gathering in his bloodstream, which needed to be capped off or expelled in a super-heated Yellowstone geyser, before it scalded him to death.

He needed to punch someone! Preferably Matthew since he couldn't reach Charlie. And please, please, try not to wake Isabel, so he could get away clean without hurting her.

She roused a little when he got up and dressed, but fell back to sleep while he was in the bathroom, scowling at his face in the mirror, disgusted that he looked like warmed-over shit. No wonder Isabel didn't know what to do with him, before or after giving him the most intense blow job of his life, which had drained all the joy out of him and left him smarting with fury.

Creeping down the stairs, holding his grungy boots so he wouldn't wake Isabel, made him feel like a cad or a cat burglar, navigating his way through the duskish dark so he could make a quick escape without turning any lights on. Padding across the driveway in his stocking feet increased the sensation that he was running away from an important something—an issue bigger than his weird deal with Isabel—but he resisted the inclination to think about what it was.

Endless analytical worrying was Matt's thing, not his. He'd clean out his refrigerator instead or scrub his bathroom floor. And tomorrow morning he'd be back at his janitorial job at the hospital where his body would do all the work and his mind would be free as a bird.

He opened a beer and did his chores with the radio turned up too loud to hear his phone ring. Turning his cell off wasn't an option even though any messages that came in would be waiting for him when he turned it back on. Prudent to leave all channels of communication open even when ignoring them.

Grabbing a couple more beers from the fridge and a microwaved Trader Joe's burrito, Terry hunkered down on his sloppy old couch for the evening when he was done with his desultory housework, washed hands still stinking of bleach, but that was usual.

Netflix. Amazon. Hulu. Acorn. He had 'em all on his Roku, but there was nothing there that interested him, so he clicked on YouTube and browsed around until he found an art channel featuring interviews with contemporary writers which would either enthrall him or bore him to sleep.

And lo and fuckin' behold there was Jackson lounging on a classy red velvet sofa like a bronzed-blonde playboy, and sitting next to him, not Rosie, or some other writer, but Rosie's ex-lover, the luminous trans man from the magic bodega, suave as a 1940's film star in a grey cravat and smoking jacket. The two of them kept touching each other's hands and batting their eyelashes at each other.

Terry sat up straight and turned up the sound.

Holy fuck! Were they fucking each other?

Well, no and yes, it turned out.

The very weird—and almost obscenely beautiful, to Terry's mind—odd couple were writing a book together. Or rather, Brand was writing it, and Alex was providing the background story, the travails of a lesbian who becomes a hetero man, sparing no details about her—his—doomed affair with The Bastard's wife. Poor luscious Rosie, whose body everyone wanted.

"Well, I'll be goddamned." Terry was talking to the television, but he didn't care. Better than calling up Matt, although he was dying to spill the beans about this particular high strangeness involving his friend's romantic nemeses.

Maybe, by some sick of quirk of fate, the unlucky dude was watching, or had watched, this? As much as he wanted Matt to know what the fuck was going on—he fervently hoped not.

"It's a nonfiction work of fiction, much like *In Cold Blood* . . . only not as bloody, of course, until we get to the breast reduction and phalloplasty section, that is." Jackson said, flashing a wicked grin.

"That must have been very difficult for you," the invisible interviewer said, presumably to Alex, but Jackson, ever the ringmaster, went on.

"Yes, it was . . . quite awful . . . having to go under the knife in order to feel like oneself . . ."

Patting his companion's stovepipe-trousered leg in a gesture of solidarity—which looked pretty fictional to Terry—the writer continued his story, in the bold voice of someone who's been victimized by society yet ended up at the top of the heap.

"It wasn't so long ago that a person like Alex would have committed suicide . . ." Here Alex looked skeptical, but remained silent as Jackson described the indignities that trans people face.

"Can you imagine having to chop off your tits in order to fit into the body you were born with?" Jackson shuddered with gruesome delight.

After what seemed like an uncomfortable pause, the interviewer said, "But tell me, Alex, how did the two of you meet? It seems rather unusual that you used to be romantically involved with Mr. Brand's wife. How do you think your former lover feels about your literary partnership with her new husband?"

Jackson jumped in, or rather snaked in with his silky drawl, before Alex had a chance to answer.

"Dear Rosie is absolutely fine with Alex working with me on this . . . to my mind . . . very important book. I've always written from personal experience, as my fans and critics will tell you . . . so it's a gift to have his participation in what I'm sure will be my master work." Another flashy grin, this time directed at Alex.

Terry shook his head in disgust. "Christ on a bike, why doesn't that asshole shut up!"

And then, for a rare moment, the insufferable writer actually did, because his companion finally spoke up.

"Rosie understands me sharing my story with her husband, because it's her story, too," Alex said.

"She left an unhappy marriage to engage in a lesbian affair, not to guide me through a mental health quagmire. My gender reassignment plans were difficult for her, not that she has anything against trans people. And here I am spilling my guts to her husband, which must feel equally weird. But I think she understands that I have to, if I want my truth to be told."

"And of course, she reverted to type," Jackson butted in. "Rosie is classically female, in preferring . . . shall we say . . . an unaltered male form . . ." He chucked nastily, "Except for circumcision, of course . . ."

Shee-it! What an unconscionable jerk!

Terry's previously uncompassionate heart constricted with pity for Rosie's plight. To be so easily dismembered in public, so blithely categorized as a common and predictable female—as a partner—was an affront to her real value and artistry.

Rosie might be a cheat but at least she wasn't a fraud like Jackson, who didn't give a shit about his new muse's emotional wellbeing. Alex was just grist for Jackson's word mill, an extension of his sword-like fountainpen, a necessary key on his QWERTY board—a hapless tool, if an obviously willing one.

There was more writerly palaver, mutual patting, eyelash batting, and fawning questions from the interviewer, before the video came to its merciful end, by which time Terry felt drunk with roiling disgust. Witnessing Brand co-opt Alexander's painful life story, was painful in itself, an unwanted demonstration of pernicious gaslighting disguised as literary élan, which made Matt's creeping paranoia seem tame in comparison.

Pissed that he couldn't—or wouldn't, as yet—tell the Ol' Bean anything about the strange triangular arrangement Rosie was embroiled in, and worried about Isabel, whose downstairs lights hadn't come on yet, he went outside and sat on the stairs of his tumbledown deck to smoke a joint.

Disjointed thoughts swooped through his head, batwings of anxiety and unease about relationships and fate. Bits of old dialogue, unanswerable questions. Why other people's lives were bleeding into his. Why nobody seemed to give a shit about what he wanted, who he was. Other than Good Ol' Terry Thompson, humble batman to the officers in an imaginary British film.

A light flicked on in Isabel's kitchen and two minutes later his cellphone rang. He took a deep drag off his doobie and ignored it. When the phone rang again he took it out of his pocket and turned it off, without looking to see who was calling him. Fuck whoever it was and the interfering horse they rode in on. Even if the horse had a shaggy silver mane like Isabel's.

SECOND TIME AROUND

The sunlight slanting through the window was a shaft from outer space connecting Matthew to a world he'd only seen heretofore in his stoned imagination.

Branch and leaf shapes swayed on the wall like hazy effects from an old black-and-white movie, creating patterns that reminded him of woven fabric. Muted tapestries he'd touched in some hallowed faraway place. Someplace real, yet not real, he'd once inhabited.

He was not stoned or drunk. He was not asleep or awake. Dead or alive. Simply floating in the present moment, inner consciousness honed to a bright point of being.

With a sigh of pleasure he closed his eyes, thrilled to see the waving branches and plant leaves on the inside of his mind, hearing now the scrape of those same branches and leaves on the outside of the window, the distant call of a bird, a dog barking.

A delicious warmth coursed through his veins; even the insides of his eyelids pulsed hotly red under thin pink skin. His body, seemingly permeated with sun, opened up like a flower, until his thoughts fell away, scattered like petals on a soft summer wind.

Then, a tiny shift in perception. The smell of cinnamon. The feel of something wet nosing his palm. A dog's muzzle or a woman's tongue. Someone's voice swimming up from the depths of his unearthly calm.

"Muffins! Wake up! There's muffins and tea. But please take a shower first. You smell worse than Tehuti."

Matthew sat up and looked around, taking in his surroundings with a confused expression. A dim room. A couch upon which he was lying fully clothed under a pink duvet. Madam Zodie batting at her dog with a giant hand that morphed into an oven mitt when he put on his glasses.

"Get a move on!" she cried, herding the stubborn dog off to the kitchen, much as she'd herded Matthew out of the party last night, only rather more good-naturedly.

Apparently the creature had been pestering him. Or sleeping with him, judging from the warm spot on the top of his legs that felt like a body had been lying on him. He shuddered with revulsion. Yet how untouched he'd felt just a moment ago. How purely sublime!

Matthew stretched awkwardly and looked at his Casio before lumbering up from the lumpy old couch. It was later than he'd thought. A few minutes before one. Lunchtime, not brunch time, and the muffins smelled intoxicating to his suddenly ravenous hunger. Like something from his earlier paradise.

By some miracle he didn't have a raging hangover. And he didn't feel stupid and worthless and strained down to nothing but minuscule particles, like he usually did after outlandishly embarrassing contretemps at parties, started by him. He felt like an ordinary guy—a fuck-up, but salvageable.

The sunlight seeping into the steamy seams of Madam Zodie's old-fashioned bathroom smelled like wildflower honey, increasing his joy in what felt like a portentous new morning. As he showered in the old claw-foot bathtub, behind a pretty homemade shower curtain, he even hummed a little tune. *I've got you under my skin.*

Toileted and redressed in his crumpled pajamas, Matthew made his way to the kitchen where tea things, silverware and plates, and jars of jam and honey cluttered the cloth-covered table. A perfect cube of sun-colored butter sat on a red saucer in the middle of the table, like a ritualistic symbol from which everything radiated.

Madam Zodie was standing at the counter next to the stove filling a basket with blueberry muffins. She was wearing a pale-blue flounced dress that reminded him of the 1930's. House-wifey. But not quite. More Myra Loy in *The Thin Man*. Her sneaky dog was nowhere in sight.

"Juice? Orange or pineapple?" she said, gesturing for him to sit down.

"Er, maybe just a cup of strong coffee?"

She brought the muffins and a dish of scrambled eggs to the table and sat down. "No coffee here. Just tea."

Er, okay. Whatever you want, he almost said sarcastically. But he didn't feel sarcastic. He felt tender and warm watching her pour out their Darjeeling. Drop a lemon slice into his cup without asking him if he wanted it.

Breaking open a steaming muffin, he slathered it with butter and apricot jam. The taste of it sent him straight back to childhood. Hot summer days. Fruit juice dribbling down his chin. His mother's Sunday coffee cakes. Her plump body's syrupy scent. Still alive in his olfactory memory.

He sighed with delight, finished the muffin in three greedy bites, and reached for another one.

"God, these are good," he blurted, hoping the ridiculously rhapsodic tone of his voice didn't sound like the bluff tenor of a gauche flatterer. But oh, if he could just have one little bite—one tiny taste—of *her*!

Madam Zodie examined Matthew's face intently for a few moments, then looked away, frowning, as if she didn't like what she saw.

Then suddenly she was smiling again. "Glad you like 'em," she said, passing him the strawberry jam before refilling their teacups.

Another few moments while they ate in silence, this time not looking at or away from him—her gaze diffuse—before Madam Zodie politely inquired, "You sleep okay?"

"Yeah, great!" he said, wiping crumbs off his mouth. "Thank you for letting me crash—I mean sleep here—last night."

Not remembering lying down on her couch, or taking off his shoes, was embarrassing, but less so than memories of how rude he'd been to her at the freaky Halloween cuddle party and their contentious astrological appointment, where he'd pretty much said she was a charlatan.

Madam Zodie was weird all right, but she was more tolerant than most people he'd insulted—and there were many of them, including his most steadfast clients. Only Terry could top her, it seemed.

She smiled broadly for the first time. "Hope you don't mind that Tehuti was sleeping with you. The couch belongs to him. At least in his mind."

Talking about her dog seemed to be a safe subject so they did that for a while, Madam Zodie praising Tehuti's intelligence while excoriating his bad manners. "His possessiveness is a pain in the butt, sometimes, but he's a Cancer with Moon in Scorpio, you know."

She rolled her eyes theatrically, mocking herself. Or was it Matthew?

"Yeah, Astrologer to the Dog Stars, that's me."

She passed the basket and he took the last muffin, after confirming that she didn't want it, wishing he hadn't finished his eggs since he felt so damn hungry. His appetite was on fire. What had she put in the food?

Madam Zodie got up to make another pot of tea. "There's leftover quiche I can warm in the oven. Or I could make you a smoothie?" She set a box of graham crackers down in front of him. "Peanut butter?"

Blushing hotly, Matthew declined her offers, wondering how deeply she could read his mind, what she made of his ravenous hunger. If she thought him a fool. "Well, fuck, yeah!" Terry would have said, if only he were here.

"How's your friend?" she said, seeming to pick up his thoughts again, although of course it was a natural question, given that Terry was—presumably—courting her widowed cousin.

"Uh, I dunno." There was no point in lying.

Madam Zodie brought the refilled teapot back to the table and sat down. "He seems like a nice guy. I met him, you know." No, actually he didn't. But she probably intuited that, and was just trying to screw with him.

Matthew squirmed in his chair, and reached for a graham cracker he didn't want. "Nicer than me, you mean."

"Well, yeah." Madam Zodie guffawed, surprising him. "I mean, fuck yeah!" She wiggled her eyebrows just like Terry did.

He pretended to laugh. Jesus Christ. Was everyone sick of him?

A loud bark at the back door saved him from his wry hostess's amused scrutiny. When she went to let Tehuti in, Matthew got up and began clearing the table, hoping to improve her opinion of him. The dog instantly made a mad dash for him, tugging at the stretched-out sleeves of his wrinkled pajama top, until Madam Zodie shouted, "Lie down!"

"Him or me?" Matthew squawked, both hands glued to his crotch, as he glared at the scolded animal.

Responding to his mistress's firm instruction, Tehuti did lie down, but he still looked like a devil to Matthew. Or one of those weird Wyoming horned lizards who can spray blood from its eyes.

It was obviously time to go.

Matthew backed out of the kitchen into the living room where his coat and shoes were piled on Madam Zodie's throne-like circular chair where she'd reigned like a goddess last night.

Gathering up his stuff desultorily, playing for time, since he didn't really want to say goodbye to the intriguing astrologer—in spite of her crazy dog—he kept thinking about how different she was from Rosie. How in touch with herself she was. Brave enough to wear a ridiculous unsexy dog costume to a fuck party. And to save a no-goodnik like him from—further—embarrassing himself.

He felt like he was speaking French in a terrible accent as he said his thanks and goodbyes to Madam Zodie after calling for an Uber. *Adieu, Mademoiselle,* pronounced with a mouth full of marbles. Might as well have said, "I'm such a stupid dick," which he supposed he was and always would be.

But Madam Zodie was kind.

"My pleasure to have you here," she said, hugging him awkwardly as they said goodbye on the porch. "Go with God, and peace be with you."

Matthew looked down at his feet, not wanting to let go of her. But the next thing he knew he was walking down the steps towards a Toyota Prius driven by a scrawny guy with a grey goatee.

Once home, he changed into jeans and a comfortable old sweater and settled down to work in his office, blocking out the high—and low—lights of last night, taking charge of his errant thoughts which edged so close to romanticism.

The gorgeous visions of earlier that morning were nothing but silly pipedreams. The leaf-shaped shadows on the wall, seemingly so profound, meant nothing. Even his growing interest in Madam Zodie felt flat. Because he wanted it to, but still.

How natural—if not easy—it was to sit at his computer all afternoon until the sun went down at a quarter to five, to crank out snarky emails to project managers he didn't like, to sluff off his attraction to Madam Zodie as if it were a holey old coat that smelled of old dog. To pretend that he wasn't missing Terry. Or his mom.

His mother used to say that being footloose and fancy free was just a front for not being able to commit to anything— how the best part was when you stuck to *something and someone*, did the dance, swirled your partner. Otherwise you just ended up lonely.

Sixth grade square dances had taught him as much, although unconsciously. Holding some lanky little girl in his arms—allemande left and allemande right—bending her backwards, light as a sapling, dipping and tripping over the scarred wooden floor. Feeling, for perhaps the first time, the urge to merge with someone who wasn't his mother. Oh, the pure humiliating joy of it!

But, this wasn't gym class and Madam Zodie wasn't his partner. He was crawling or maybe stumbling, not dancing through life, although Rosie was still kicking up her rosy red heels for Jackson, as well as a wider audience of sophisticated hedonists and burly-q fans. And not only that, she sang.

Remembering Rosie singing on stage, or even in the tub, during one of her hours-long rehearsal baths, gave Matthew a truculent hard-on. She'd sung for him the night they'd met, sashaying across the dirty floor of his old apartment in a sexy black slip, more prototype than caricature of a French chanteuse, in spite of her joking—her voice was that good—sending his heart—and cock—soaring.

Masturbating to a remembered soundtrack—one of his more accessible vices, thanks to his brain wiring—usually worked, but not tonight. He pulled and punched, stroked and hand-humped, milked, and even wrapped his cock in the silky crotch of a trophy pair of Rosie's old underpants, but he couldn't orgasm.

He was dry as a bone. "All comed-out," like Terry said, explaining his long-term celibacy. Which, for some sick reason, cheered Matthew. Going without sexual activity, of any kind, might make him a better man, clear out his darkest fantasies—if it didn't make them more virulent, that is— empty the final dregs of sexist resentment. Maybe he'd even stop working for the patriarchy?

Fantastic thoughts like these accompanied him to bed, which he crawled into at nine-thirty, wishing he felt more virtuous about not being drunk. It took him a long time to fall asleep, and when he finally did, he dreamed of an afternoon garden party populated with figures from a 1930's costume drama, Rosie in a big white hat, Jackson in a polka dot dressing gown like Noel Coward's, servants pouring tea and champagne.

Amongst the upper-crust witticisms and jaded expressions of sangfroid, a lone voice warbled a cheery little tune, calling his attention to the lower branches of a laden apple tree where a bird sat, looking at him. A female robin, judging from its drab russet-colored breast. And a magician, since it could read his mind, and put its own thoughts into it. Birdlike thoughts of flight and survival, nest building and worm retrieval, rainstorms and sunshine upon roofs made of clay.

"What are you going to do about Alice?" the bird trilled, fixing its tiny beautiful all-seeing eye on Matthew. "When are you going to fly after her?"

Standing beneath the apple tree his dream self asked, "Who's Alice?" wanting most desperately to know. But the robin just cocked her head and sang a bit louder, drowning out the sounds of the party—popping champagne corks, Rosie's throaty laughter, the jazz record on the gramophone, the insistent pinging of a telephone.

Startled awake, Matthew fumbled for his phone in the dark, knocking his reading lamp and glasses off the bedside table onto the floor. He couldn't read the caller ID but he was still half in his dream. "Alice?" he croaked.

"Nah. It's me, Ol' Bean."

Terry, for fuck's sake. What time was it anyway?

"Call me back," Matthew said after a few languid beats. "I'm asleep."

"Ever-bawdy knows that." Terry laughed, but his voice was sad. "But wake up long enough for me to tell ya that I just lost my dad."

Matthew rubbed his eyes and sat up, glaring at his cellphone as if it belonged to a stranger. Terry's gravelly baritone voice seemed like a radio signal, calling him out of a nightmare, although his dream had been sweet, not just brittle and cold, when the robin sang about Alice.

"Uh shit. I'm so sorry," Matthew said, and he really was. He'd liked Mr. Thompson a lot, and Mrs. Thompson, too. As a child, he'd wished they were his parents, that Terry was his brother instead of the awful twins.

"Me, too. An' I hate that he died in that gol-dang *home*. Seems like there's no justice, duddn't it?"

"So . . ."

"Yeah, I'm goin' to Mcfuckin' Casper. Leavin' tomorrow just after ten."

Matthew could almost visualize Terry's unspoken invitation hanging in the space between them, in the fuzzy darkness of his bedroom where he couldn't see a goddamn thing without his specs except the glare from his cellphone when he checked on the time. Only a bit after twelve, amazingly. He hadn't slept very long.

"Get me a ticket, too," he finally said, "I'll pay you back later."

"Already did, Ol' Bean." Terry's chuckle was warm, albeit somber, reminding Matthew—yet again—that his old friend was just that. His friend.

And now it was his turn to be one.

They spoke for a few more minutes, confirming their plans with only two or three sarcastic asides about Casper, until, just before hanging up, Terry said, "So what's the deal with Alice? Didn't think she'd be talkin' to ya yet, much less callin' you at midnight."

A little jolt in Matthew's chest. A spark of joy hearing the name from his dream, and yet, confusion. "Who's Alice?" he said.

"Whoa, dude! You must *rilly* be sleepin'! It's Madam Zodie, of course. Her real name is Alice."

SQUARING THE CIRCLE

With its fringed lampshades and faded wallpaper emblazoned with rustic scenes of the Rockies, Matthew and Terry's shabby yet strangely attractive room at the Wagon Wheel Motel, on the outskirts of Casper, looked like a set from an old TV western. The only things missing were seductive saloon girls and rowdy cowpokes playing cards in the corner across from the chenille-covered twin beds.

Easy enough to imagine if you'd ever been to the Wonder Bar.

They had a bottle of whiskey, a large bag of Doritos and four sticks of beef jerky, so they were set for the night, ready to get down to some serious *thinkin' and drinkin'*, before heading into town in the morning to attend Mr. Thompson's funeral.

Terry had often said that his dad would be better off dead than moldering away in the Alzheimer's home, sitting in an overheated room with a bunch of confused incontinents all day, staring out the window at the ubiquitous cottonwoods.

Memory Care Assisted Living—his ass! It was more like assisted brain death. But his father's sudden death two days ago had fazed him.

He took a big gulp of whiskey and sloshed it around like mouthwash, showing his canine teeth as he crunched up the ice shards. "Gol-dang it all, Matt, I gotta tell ya once again, I couldn't hack this trip to Casper without you."

"Any time, brother." Matthew gestured to the map of Wyoming he had spread out on his lap. "What about heading up to Thermop for a soak at Star Plunge? After a decent interval, of course."

They were lying on their beds in opposite directions so they could face each other, Matthew propped up rather awkwardly on a couple of pillows since he didn't have a footboard to lean back on.

Terry rubbed his curly sideburns, then the raspy stubble on his chin. "Gotta meet with my dad's lawyer Monday morning, but we can head out after that. My mom's gonna want me to stick around, but I don't wanna dick with her husband. Dipshit's probably glad my ol' man died."

"Think your mom is?"

"Glad? I dunno. Duddn't seem possible she'd be happy about the fucked up way my dad's life turned out. Even though that's rilly why she divorced him. But I hope she misses the man he used to be, the man she used to love."

"He was a good dad." Matthew raised his paper cup to toast Mr. Thompson and Terry raised his back.

"That he was."

Matthew poured himself another drink and reached across the beds to hand the bottle to Terry. "Mine wasn't," he scoffed, but his laugh was forced.

Terry sighed heavily, sad for both of them. "Sorry Ol' Bean . . . But no, unfortunately he waddn't."

"Sins of the fathers, hey what?" Matthew laughed again, still sounding awkward.

"Yeah, Bean, for the poor ol' orphaned both of us."

Terry rummaged around on his rumpled bed. "Lookee here," he said, tossing Mathew one of the jackalope postcards he'd stolen from the motel office when he was fetching their bucket of ice. The giant jackrabbit-cum-antelope had a pretty redheaded cowgirl, wearing big sharp spurs on her boots, riding on its back.

"Reminds me of you and Rosie." Terry's deep chuckle made a nice counterpoint to the tiny tinkle of ice cubes in their bathroom-size Dixie cups.

"Thanks a lot, dude," Matthew shot back, but he wasn't offended. Sure Rosie had ridden him half to death, but so what; he'd mostly enjoyed it.

"'Member how we used to wonder if we'd ever get laid?" Terry mused, as if his long spate of celibacy was far in the past.

"Yeah, I wanted to stick it to Miss Ravendahl even though I didn't know what to *do* with it when I got it in. She hit me one time for horsing around in the girls' bathroom which made me want to kiss her. No wonder I married a bitch."

Terry tossed some melting ice cubes at Matthew. "Don't defile my lifelong affection for our second-grade teacher by comparin' her to Rosie."

Lurching a bit Matthew reached for the whiskey bottle which Terry grudgingly gave him after a momentary tussle. "Sorry, dude. Less have 'nother drink as night falls down… Good night to get drunk, iddn't it?" Matthew's voice sounded like Terry's now that he was slurring his words.

"Might as well." Terry sighed again, heartily. He missed Isabel, who was dependably comforting, unlike Matthew, who was preoccupied with romantic fantasies when he wasn't warding off panic attacks or drinking too much.

To be fair, he'd risen to the occasion by agreeing to accompany Terry to his dad's funeral in the middle of November. Taking two flights to get to Casper, flying coach which he hated, driving a cheapo rental car, staying in a cruddy motel. Still, asking Matt for advice about Isabel or what to do about his dad's pitiful estate, which he was aching to do, was a crapshoot. So he tried another subject.

"So what's your deal with Madam Zodie anyway? Isabel says she needs somebody to take care of her—the way she takes care of ever-bawdy else—without makin' her feel guilty."

"I don't make her feel guilty . . . Do I?" Matthew scooched down in his bed so he could untuck the faded bedspread from underneath the mattress and pull it over his legs. It was growing cold in the room as the heat powered down; the snowstorm they'd proceeded by a few hours had finally arrived. The flakes curling down under the porch light outside their room unfurled like tattered blue ribbons.

"Fuck if I know. That's why I'm askin' if you're good to her."

Matthew looked uncomfortable, but maybe it was just from sitting backwards on his sagging bed, trying to hold his head up on squished old feather pillows. Terry hoped so. It was too damn late for a fight.

"I've only seen her once since the bullshit astro-chat you made me have with her. Dragged me out of a Halloween party dressed like a dog. Her, not me. She's nice. Too damn nice."

"Nicer than Rosie, ya mean." Terry tossed Matthew a jerky stick but hung on to the bag of Doritos he'd paid for.

"And not as sexy."

"'Cause she isn't a cunt?"

Matthew threw the jerky back at Terry, hitting his drinking arm, luckily missing the Dixie Cup which was once again full to the brim. "C'mon, you know what I mean."

"Oh fer crap sake. Just 'cause Rosie's got bigger boobs and a fat purty ass duddn't mean she's sexier than MZ. Why that little gal's got more love for humanity in her skinny little finger than Rosie's got in her overblown heart of hearts."

Matthew made a fake hangdog face and sneered, "Thanks for the lecture, Dad."

Terry downed his drink, threw his Dixie Cup on the floor, and flipped the switch on his bedside lamp. "Ah, fuck you, man. I'm goin' ta sleep. Don't talk to me about dads."

The eerie pewter light that comes with snow in the night shone through the crack in the curtains and the highway outside was silent. No animal sounds in the snow-dusted fields beyond the motel, no sounds of other patrons. They could have been anywhere in the Rockies, they might have been stuck on the moon. They were back in *Nowheresville*, the cold strange primitive world they'd hoped to stop calling home.

Terry was just nodding off when he heard Matthew whisper, "Sorry," from under his blankets. He didn't respond to his friend's muffled voice, just settled back to let the hiss of the snow and the cold velvet feel of the dark help him to imagine a dreamland where maybe he would see his dad.

They had hangovers when they woke up shortly before seven the next morning, Terry needing to take a much needed piss, Matthew to throw up, both in copious amounts. The fresh start to the day was looking dubious, but Terry, as ever, was pragmatic.

Addressing's his sick friend's bowed head hanging over the toilet, he declared, "What you need is a hearty damn breakfast. Biscuits n' gravy and chicken-fried steak like the good ol' daze will cure ya!" Terry rummaged around his shaving kit while Matthew continued to retch and vomit.

"Hope you brought your own toothbrush, bro. Ain't gonna lend ya mine after that disgustin' sight," he said, stepping into the old-fashioned bathtub shower with his soap on a rope. The ancient metal rings on the plastic shower curtain clattered ominously as he pulled it loosely shut and Matthew groaned accordingly, ever the hapless victim.

Terry vigorously soaped his sideburns. "Close the bathroom door behind ya when yer finally done pukin' in here, okay?" he shouted over the sound of the cascading water, before starting in on an old crush tune from the Wonder Bar jukebox in his gravely baritone. *"Don't It Make My Brown Eyes Blue"* or some such love-struck nonsense. Singing in motel showers always felt so damn good. He could almost pretend he didn't have a hangover.

Matthew dressed in bleary silence after crawling out of the bathroom, pulling on his dress pants while lying back on his bed, Doritos crunching beneath his raised and lowered hips.

The room smelled rotten, or maybe it was just him, even though he'd gargled toothpaste and water, spitting into the rust-stained sink like a punch drunk prizefighter to get rid of the liquor and vomit.

Terry came out of the bathroom, dressed in his usual black T-shirt and jeans, and put on the tweed suit jacket Matthew had loaned him for the funeral. It was too tight in the shoulders and too long in the arms but he didn't complain.

He looked like a spit-shined boy heading off to Sunday school, proud of his grownup clothes.

He swatted at Matthew when Matthew stood up to tuck in his shirt, striking him twice on one arm. "Today's the test, McFucker! Casper's comin' like a goddamn freight train!"

"Stop hitting me!" Matthew pushed Terry's hands away, annoyed. It was infuriating! How could a hungover guy whose dad had just died remain so fucking cheerful? And so goddamn over-organized—he had their day ahead completely mapped out, with travel notes.

Terry's plan was to load up their stuff in the rental car and drive around Casper for a while before heading someplace decent for breakfast. They'd cruise past the Wonder Bar. Swing by Lou Taubert's display windows to check out what fashionable faux cowgirls were wearing these days. Maybe take a quick trip to the wrong side of the tracks to see if Flora's funky little house was still there.

After a leisurely brunch they'd head to the church for the early afternoon funeral then out to the cemetery for Mr. Thompson's burial. If Matthew wanted to bow out of that part, fine, Terry said—if not, then maybe he could be one of the pallbearers?

"Of course," Matthew said, "of course."

There would be family stuff after that, people milling about, a minister to talk to over coffee and cake back at his mother's house, followed by an afternoon of drinking while they set up for the wake.

Matthew was confused. "I thought the wake was the drinking part."

Terry grinned. "Nah, the wake's the crazy drunken fall apart part."

They bundled themselves into the car in their heavy jackets, dressed for cold and snowy conditions, after the trunk was packed. They'd decided to trade last night's cowboy-kitschy motel for a place inside the city limits, closer to Mrs. Thompson's place.

"We'll just drive around after the wake and pick somethin'," Terry suggested, at the wheel of the flimsy rental car as they drove down the snowy highway towards their natal city. Two hungry hungover antiheroes on the way to a demented man's funeral, like a road trip movie, only this day was real.

Terry had a bullish look on his face which meant he'd concentrate all his attention on the road and not much on Matthew. The new snow on the road was distracting but manageable—his seriousness was about other things which he obviously didn't want to talk about.

Matthew rolled his window down a crack to let in some frosty air. Thank God, they had only a few miles to go before they hit the outskirts of Casper. His anxiety level was starting to ramp up; avid anticipation almost always provoked a panic attack.

Something shifted in his guts that wasn't hunger but wasn't yet the sensation of fear. Something wafted through his nostrils, the memory of old-time smells triggered by the flashes of familiar scenery rushing by on the side of the highway. His synesthesia kicking in. He could smell—almost taste—gunpowder and frying meat, sagebrush and percolator coffee. The enticing aromas of Casper. He shut his eyes and deeply inhaled.

RUNNING ON BORROWED TIME

The funeral was fine, the wake not so much, considering the fight between Terry and his mother's new husband, who kept referring to himself as Terry's stepdad.

"I'll fuckin' step on you!" Terry announced, crushing the arrogant pretender's foot under the heel of his motorcycle boot, much to his mother's dismay.

"That's my husband!" the divorced widow—widowed divorcee?—cried, referring to the stocky house painter who was being shoved into the buffet table by her angry son.

"Yer husband's dead!" Terry cried, throwing an ineffective punch. "This dumb-ass dude's an imposter!"

After one of the mourners dumped a glass of beer on the grappling men and the fight finally broke up, there were angry words between mother and son in Mr. and Mrs. Thompson's old bedroom where the house painter now slept.

"You're fuckin' what's-his-doodle in my father's gol-dang bed!" and "Mind your own business, sonny!" and similar oedipal complaints rang through the little house. The mourners eyed each other conspiratorially, anticipating another fight.

Matthew lurked in a corner of the kitchen, drinking longnecks and looking down the neckline of Terry's pretty cousin's low-cut blouse, waiting for Terry to finish up with his mother. He had a hard-on which made him feel disrespectful of Mr. Thompson, but it seemed less embarrassing than having a full-blown panic attack.

He wished Madam Zodie were here to confide in, or maybe to fuck, to relieve his simmering tension. Naturally if she were here, he wouldn't put it that way, but right now he missed her in a physical way. Not that he wouldn't mind talking with her. He downed his Coors, opened another one from the case on the counter, and took a good long swallow.

Getting drunk might help if he didn't get too plastered.

Matthew found the bottle of Stoli Mrs. Thompson always stashed in her freezer, behind a cache of TV dinners, poured a slug into his beer bottle and went to look for Terry, weaving slightly as he walked down the hall towards the master bedroom.

The door was ajar so he could see Mrs. Thompson lying down on her dead husband's old bed in her rumpled funeral dress, and Terry sitting next to her, holding her hand. The little tableau of grieving mother and son reminded him of sentimental war memorials where the lost hero was rendered invisible, and all that was shown of him was his family, eternally mourning him.

"You get some rest now, Mom," Terry said. "Me n' the Ol' Bean gotta get going. Snow's pilin' up and the rental car chains ain't worth shit. We'll be skiddin' down the street like skinned jackalopes 'less we get a move on."

"Trust a Thompson to run out on me." Terry's mother laughed bitterly but her words were wistful. "I never would of left your dad if he hadn't lost his mind, you know. I just couldn't take it anymore. Being somebody he didn't recognize."

"You shoulda told me what was goin' on in your head — in your life—'stead a springin' this new guy on me. Gettin' hitched to fuckin' Green without even warnin' me."

Mrs. Thompson grimaced and laughed, "He's a good man in spite a being a horse's ass sometimes. Not as good as your dad, a course, but his brain works just fine. And he loves me…Or thinks he does."

Terry kissed his mom's forehead. "Guess that's okay for me, if that's good enough for you." He nodded his head towards the doorway. "Here's Matt come to say g'bye."

Matthew tiptoed into the room. Mrs. Thompson scooted herself into a sitting position as he sat down beside her. For a half-second he wished it was his own mother lying between him and his childhood friend, although it was hard to imagine her ever being that thin and used-up looking.

"I'll have a sip a that." Mrs. Thompson took a long swig of Matthew's vodka-spiked beer, then hugged him tightly, her skinny spine a row of radio knobs beneath his clutching fingers.

"You take good care a my boy, now, you hear?" True to her modest West Texas roots, Mrs. Thompson phrased her maternal command as a question, but Matthew felt ashamed. How could she trust him after all the terrible crap he'd put her son through over the long hard years?

"Of course I will," he swore, looking at Terry apologetically, expecting a sarcastic rejoinder, but his sad-eyed friend was smiling.

Terry gave his mother a tender kiss before punching Matthew's arm a bit harder than necessary. "Hey ho, we gotta go, bro.'"

Mrs. Thompson scooted back down into a lying position as the two men got up to go. Terry covered his mom with an old afghan Matthew remembered from years ago, how the finger-sized crochet holes had let in the light when they stuck their heads under it playing hide-and-seek during their sleepovers.

Such terrible things had happened to them since they were those playful little kids. Being orphaned, divorced, taken for granted, losing their self-respect—or not gaining it as it were, since when had either of them really had it?—losing people they loved.

Matthew wondered what all that bad stuff meant about a person's destiny and wished he could ask his mom. She'd know if there was such a thing as fated personal doom, if anyone would—she'd been married to his wreck of a dad for thirty years before being burned alive in a car wreck.

Surely she'd have something wise to say about the unfair distribution of suffering?

Terry closed the bedroom curtains and turned out the overhead light. "See you in the mornin', mom. Get a good sleep, now. Love you."

"Love you, too. Both a you." Mrs. Thompson closed her eyes, then opened them again. "Leave me that drink, okay?"

Matthew set his beer bottle on the bedside table and followed Terry out of the stuffy bedroom, latching the door carefully behind him. They crept down the hall, skirting the wake which was humming along calmly now, and retrieved their coats from the front hall closet then let themselves out of the house.

They stood on the porch for a few minutes, buttoning up their jackets and putting on the homemade wool hats Mrs.

Thompson had presented them with earlier. They both looked as ridiculous as Alice had in her Halloween dog costume but Matthew didn't care. He pulled the fuzzy knit earflaps over his ears and crowed, "We're free!"

Twilight was coming on and the November air seemed almost balmy, compared to the frigid temperature they'd experienced when they stumbled out of the motel that morning. The day had warmed up instead of cooling; there was melted snow in the yard.

"Don't be fooled," Terry warned, as he started the car up. "Gonna be colder n' a witch's tonight. Buckets a snow comin' down."

"Buckets of rain. Buckets of tears. Got all them buckets coming out of my ears," Matthew sang, as they pulled out of the driveway, euphoric to be back on the road, even if they weren't going that far.

"Exactly…" Terry took a deep breath. "And no—I know whatcher thinkin'—but NO, we are not gonna go to the Wonder Bar for Old Times' Sake. We're goin' straight to a damn motel with Mcfuckin' room service."

Shit. Secretly Matthew was relieved, but shit. It got old getting your mind read all the time, feeling that goddamn predictable. Just think what his life might be like if he got hooked up with Madam Zodie—two nosy psychics sneaking around in his mind would be intolerable.

But Matthew decided he wasn't going to think about that possibility or anything else. He was just going to ride along in a relaxed—make that drunken—stupor, like a tired kid in the family car on a Sunday outing, and forget about being in Casper.

It had always been hard to be in Casper, even in the fun days of basement forts and snowball fights. His father's constant griping, and the wind that never let up, made him feel like he was stuck in a toxic dust storm. Even as a tiny kid he prayed that his head would stop buzzing, that his dad would just shut up.

The sky-wide sunsets, the purple hills and ancient rocks, Casper Mountain, his mother, and Terry, of course—these things had all been precious to him while he was growing up. But everything else, including the tired-out teachers and coaches he turned to for succor and refuge, and the Wonder Bar, where he hung out, much to his detriment, when he was older had made him long for some other reality, some other time and place.

Some other state of mind.

Tuned in to her son's disaffection, Mrs. Barker attempted to soothe him with the balm of motherly advice. Out of earshot of his pissed-off father, of course.

"You'll be on your own someday..." she started out, sitting down with on the edge of Matthew's bed one night twenty years ago, a few months before he graduated from high school.

If she'd been able to read the future, she might have added, "sooner than you think," envisioning her fatal car crash, but luckily she wasn't. Instead she saw a map of the world with little flags stuck in it depicting places Matthew might prosper and be happy and Casper wasn't on it.

Matthew remembered how nervous she was, how she'd patted his back as if soothing a colicky baby. Unlike her husband, she wasn't used to giving instructions.

"You don't have to stay here your whole damned life, honey. Go someplace where people have bigger thoughts than the twins and your dad—no offense to my boys, God bless 'em. This town's too damn small for you." Not to mention the Barker's crowded house and Matthew's closet-sized bedroom and his claustrophobic mind which kept threatening to flatten him.

The sick mystery of his parents' more or less harmonious relationship coupled with his mother's kindhearted docility, his dad's inexplicable belligerence, and his brothers continual fighting in their trashed-out bedroom, made Mrs. Barker's suggestion to leave Casper less an option than a necessary directive.

When Matthew finally took her advice a few troubled years later and got the hell out of Casper, his mother's rumpled going away note, written in perfect schoolgirl penmanship on a half sheet of college-lined notebook paper, was tucked inside his wallet, along with her check for fifty dollars he'd never had the heart to cash.

He pulled the note out now—out of a different wallet, of course—and read it to Terry, squinting over the paper in the gathering darkness, although he knew the poignant words by heart.

Be good! Be true to yourself! Remember to relax and have FUN! Love you, XXX Mom

Matthew put the note away and looked at the side of Terry's impassive face staring straight ahead at the roadway, for a good long time before he said, "Are we having fun yet?"

"No, I don't think so." Terry laughed, thank God. For a few seconds Matthew had thought he was crying, even though his cheeks were dry. His dad, after all, was dead.

Matthew's legs felt wobbly when he got out of the car at the motel where he'd waited in the cold while Terry checked in. Luckily they were parked right outside their room. He wondered if Terry was drunk but considering the competent way he'd driven the car through the Wyoming gloaming with snow beginning to fall, he doubted it. Still, it would be miraculous if it turned out that he wasn't loaded. He'd drunk six or seven beers before his fistfight with the house painter.

Terry unlocked the door to their room, number 21, even though it was only the third room down from the office. There'd be no room service here, just takeout pizza from Domino's, and beer and more beer, while they skimmed the TV.

And more maudlin talking, Matthew secretly hoped, wanting to get into the primal- scream stuff with Terry. To share their dirty dark secrets, the pain of their crummy childhoods, apologize for the dumb-fuck things they kept on doing to each other as adults—no, the shitty things Matthew kept doing to Terry, his supposed best friend.

God, how could Terry even stand him? Shouldn't that be the main topic of their next intimate discussion?

"Mind over matter!" Matthew cried as he stumbled into the motel room and threw himself down on one of the beds.

While Terry took off his coat, hauled off his motorcycle boots and rummaged through their cooler for a beer, Matthew experimented with jumping on his bed, testing the springs out. Jouncing around on his knees first, then standing up still wearing his coat, he jumped faster and faster, then more slowly until he found a regular beat, the tempo of a squeaky waltz.

Up and down and up and down he went like a wound-up mechanical doll.

After Terry took a piss he came out of the bathroom with a pissed-off look on his face. "Take yer fuckin' boots off if yer gonna jump on the gol-dang bed! That yer sure-fire way to ward off a full-blown panic attack? Or are you just a stupid drunk bastard?"

"Blasted! Straight to the moon, Alice!" Matthew made one last giant leap, so forceful his head bumped the acoustic ceiling. "Shit on a stick!" he cried and crumpled down on the bed, assuming the fetal position. He wasn't hurt, just out of breathe and surprised.

"Do you need some help, brother?" Terry chucked a boot towards Matthew's bed. "I mean… *Do you need some help, brother*, or are you just foolin' around?" Terry's bovine brow was knitted tightly which was always a bad sign. It was put-up or shut-up time according to that strained look on his kindly face.

Want to know how I'm doing then read my fucking mind, Matthew thought, determined not to say anything. His earlier desire to completely unburden himself had flown as soon as he collapsed on the bed. All he wanted to do now was eat and sleep and maybe call Madam Zodie.

But he relented, to pay back a tiny bit of his karmic debt to the friend he kept wronging, and said, "I don't need Doctor Terry yet, if that's what you mean. So fuck, yeah! Give me a beer."

"You don't need a beer, you need to get your head examined. By somebody's who's an actual head doctor. Seems like you got one too many screws loose."

"Well, fuck you. I don't like to drink beer out of cans anyway. Fucking aluminum poisoning."

Terry chucked his other boot at Matthew's head, but gently, more like a little kid's baseball toss. Matthew caught it and threw it back at Terry's knee where it connected with a dull thud and bounced off.

"You should call Madam Zodie." Terry stroked his voluptuous sideburns like a thoughtful philosopher as he lay back on his crumpled up-pillow, after pulling off his holey socks.

Matthew snorted. "You should call your old lady. See if her social security check has arrived."

"Chicken shit. Yer just jealous which is kinda touching but pretty damn tiresome. It's gettin' kind of old bein' nicer than you. 'Specially since you've always been the lucky one."

Matthew rubbed the sore spot on his head indignantly. "My parents are dead, which is pretty much my fault, my brothers are losers, and my wife left me for a woman who decided to become a man before she got kidnapped by Jackson. What's been so lucky for me?"

"You got to fuck Rosie for one thing. You got to marry her."

"You said that was the stupidest thing I ever did."

"Guess I was wrong."

"Why in the fuck is that?"

"Because you loved her."

"And that's enough?"

"Well I guess."

Terry dug around in the pocket of his jacket which was hanging on the knob of his bedstead and threw something small and metallic at Matthew, which he caught in midair. It was an old-fashioned Big Ben windup alarm clock with bells on the top.

"What the hell! Where'd you get this?" Matthew examined the clock with careful hands.

"Stole it off my mom's bedside table. It used to be my dad's."

"Great! We should set the alarm."

Terry laughed, "Nah, duddn't work. Used to tick away like a charm. Thought you'd like it better if you could fix it so I busted it when I was in the bathroom."

He pulled his Swiss Army knife out of his back pocket and waved it at Matthew. "Ain't it great what a little screwdriver can do?" He tossed the tool on Matthew's bed and took another swig of beer.

CASPER MOUNTAIN

The air was so invigorating, the view so enticing, that Matthew and Terry hollered with joy when they reached the summit of Casper Mountain in their little rental car.

Not much snow for this time of year, so driving up had been easy, although Terry swore most of the way. The *fuckin' piece of shit* Kia had worn-out shocks and skeezy handling, tending to pull towards the left. Annoying, but not too dangerous, since they weren't going too far from town, and the road out and back was familiar.

They got out of the car for a few minutes to gaze at the view and finish the joint Terry had stashed in his carry-on luggage, unbeknownst to Matthew, who was paranoid about airline drug searches. Sucking the filthy pot smoke deep into his lungs along with the clean fresh air made Terry wonder about paradoxes, but he guessed that was why they were here. If you had to put a name on it. Other than a short vacation from death.

Missing Isabel at the same time as he was missing his dad was hellish, but at least he'd had—still had—people he loved, people who loved him, in his three-and-a-half decades of life. Although he wasn't too sure about Isabel yet. Not that he couldn't forgive her for clinging to Charlie's ghost. Her devotion to her dead husband, her struggle with grief, meant that she was a loyal person, not a runner like Rosie—that was for damn sure.

Matt was looking peaky today, but Terry didn't point that out, since he felt a bit peaky himself, in spite of the being back up on the mountain. Memories of his past—and weirdly, his future—seeped into him like a slow transfusion of platelets suffusing his blood with new hormones.

How keenly he felt his desires today, how deeply his sadness, and most painful of all, his nostalgic pull towards the city on the flat plain below the mountain where his dad was now buried. Looking ahead he saw Isabel making tea in her kitchen, himself standing outside, waiting for her invitation to come in.

Surveying the changed yet familiar landscape was like peering through binoculars. Everything that should stay far away seemed much too close. Even the air he breathed now seemed full of oxygenated clues from his past. Infancy, childhood, adolescence, manhood. Body changing, brain getting smarter—presumably—emotional life contracting and expanding with the seasons of his life, and even the weather.

Terry didn't miss the rain in Seattle, but he missed running across the driveway to Isabel's house with raindrops pelting his head, shaking himself like a wet dog in the warmth of her kitchen. That this exact scenario had happened less than a week ago gave him small comfort, since that was the last day they'd touched one another or spoken. He'd sent Isabel a vague text before leaving for Casper but she hadn't responded, which was all right and good, given that he had nothing—or everything—to say to her.

"Ever wish you could start over?" Matt said, pinpointing the nexus of Terry's unspoken thoughts. How everything, good and bad, about their present situations, had its origin in Casper.

Terry took a deep toke, passed the roach to Matt and coughed out his answer on an exhalation of skunky smoke. "What the fuck d'you think, buddy boy?"

"Ouch!" Matthew dropped the joint end burning his fingers and ground it out with his boot heel. Hiking boots this morning instead of the cowboy shit-kickers Terry warned him not to bring, which were still concealed in his suitcase. He stomped back to the car. "Don't call me boy, motherfucker!"

Terry caught up with him and punched him on the arm. "Sez some-bawdy who still wants to diddle his mom!"

"Cut it out!" Mathew punched back, his face turning angry red, but Terry didn't give a damn. "Or what?" he said, climbing into the car, grimacing at his pissed off passenger for a grim few seconds before breaking into laughter.

Sullen silence from Matt while Terry maneuvered the rattletrap car back out onto the roadway, then, "Okay, I'll get off my horse," muttered somewhat grudgingly, followed by a mirthful cry of "Fuck Casper! And both our moms!"

Turning into the parking lot at Crimson Dawn, seemed like turning into another time and place, of hitching posts and horses. The strange old homestead where artist and poet Neal Forsling painted witches, sculpted Anubis-like dogs, and told fairy stories to the children of Casper at her Midsummer bonfires over most of four decades, still reeked of magic in spite of the computer age and the fact that Neal had been dead for forty years.

"Wouldn't ya know it," Terry huffed angrily, when they saw the sign on the door that said the frontier museum was closed October through May, which they should have remembered.

Peering inside the front window, and walking around the perimeter of the little cabin was disappointing, but walking the grounds where fenced enclaves of Forsling's primitive art—statues, seashells and stones—mythic forms and faces— was, as ever, entrancing. The red dirt path cutting through the lodgepole pines, the blonde-brown fields stretching off down the hill towards the blue horizon, the almost absolute quiet, in sharp contrast to the busy city sounds they were used to, rendered the two men silent and thoughtful.

Walking out of the trees into damp stubbled grasses, they made their way towards Neal Forsling's grave, which was enclosed behind an iron-bar fence at the crest of the hill looking down into the valley. Down there was where they'd heard Neal's fictional *Invisible Woodcutter* chopping trees when they were teenagers, perhaps the same side of the mountain where her husband had died in the 1940's, freezing to death on his way to town to purchase supplies.

A beautiful grave, set amongst several others, simple not somber, on which was inscribed, beneath the name Elizabeth Paxton Forsling (Neal), and her birth and death data, on the grey granite marker:

"For my epitaph.
Look around you."
Euripides

And look around they did. "With new eyes," they both would have said, if they were speaking at all, much less poetically. Although that was a lie, when Terry thought about it, gazing across the wide open spaces to the powder-blue sky beyond Neal's grave.

It wasn't a new view of this magic place that enthralled him, it was the renewed sense that he'd been in this luminous spot before, felt the same awesome feelings about magic and art and God. Been humbled, felt love.

Sensing that his friend felt similarly, he started to speak to Matt, but was interrupted by the BRRR of his cell phone. Might be his mom, but no, it was Isabel, calling from that other time and place he'd left behind at the entrance to Crimson Dawn.

Impulsively he answered, "Hullo?" He'd regret the choice later but not yet.

"Terry?" Isabel said, tentatively, as if somebody else might be using his phone.

"Yeah-ah," he said, with the half hitch in his voice that Matt always said came straight from the barrooms of Casper.

"I'm sorry I haven't called. I've been thinking about you a lot. Thinking about us. I just haven't known what to say."

Arching his eyebrows at Matt, in apology for continuing his call, Terry turned away from the grave and headed back down the hill towards Neal's cabin.

"That's ok," he said. Only half a lie. He hadn't wanted to talk to her but he'd fervently wished that she'd call.

"Is it?" Isabel said, apologetic tone morphing into a more challenging one.

Terry paused for a long moment, staring at the gently swaying pine trees behind Neal's cabin. "I guess so," he finally said, knowing that his terse words were hurting her.

"You shouldn't have left when I was sleeping," Isabel ventured. "We should have talked about it."

Terry laughed mirthlessly. "'Bout what? Yer dead husband? Or Lady Chatterley fuckin' the servant class?"

"What the hell! You're just jealous that I had a life before you, that I can love other people."

"Bullshit!" Terry exclaimed, following a script he didn't even like. One that made him seem like a dick.

"I was starting to trust you," Isabel murmured softly, and then, her tone hardening, "But maybe I was wrong. I don't really know you. You could be anyone."

"You know damn well who I am, ma'am." Terry couldn't help a subtle sense of affection creeping into his voice, and realized that he didn't want to. It was exhausting being mad when his heart was hurting so deeply. He missed his dad. He missed Isabel. He even missed Matt who was standing fifty feet away.

Muffled sounds of an indeterminate nature. A likely hand over Isabel's phone. Was she laughing or crying?

"Can you please come over tonight?" she asked, startling him. He'd forgotten she didn't know he was in Casper.

"Nah," Terry said, wishing the answer was yes. "But for sure I'll see you this weekend."

No, I'm not punishing you. I'm saying goodbye to my dad, and communing with nature.

If only he could say that. But he couldn't. Still, there was something more or less true he could say. "Been thinkin' about you, too. Missin' you, even though I don't want to. As for you and Charlie—well, I sorta understand now, how you can't let him go. We'll talk about that later, okay?"

"Er . . . Okay. You'll call me this weekend, then?" Isabel sounded pissed off, which made Terry feel better about being short with her. And sad that he wanted her to her feel guilty, when she'd really done nothing wrong. He'd been pushing her too hard. Almost as bad as Matt chasing after Rosie long after she'd gone, which Isabel—as yet—had not.

She was right here at Crimson Dawn, with him, even though she was just on the phone.

"I promise," he said, giving her back something of what his disappointment in her had effaced. A sense of trust was all he wanted really, on a level higher—or separate—level from the physical, anyway. He didn't give a shit about the sex although he certainly wanted it with her in a compelling way that made his bones ache for her.

But he wasn't going to make her his muse like Matt did with Rosie. That wasn't what Isabel wanted.

Unless she'd been Charlie's?

But he wouldn't think about that.

After saying goodbye, Terry walked back up onto the ridge where Matt was still standing at Neal's grave, gazing out at the electric kind of blue sky they never got in Seattle, with a kid's big grin on his face like he was lost in a pleasurable fever dream. He hadn't seen the Ol' Bean this relaxed and happy since he didn't know when.

"This place makes ever-bawdy feel awestruck," Terry said, once Matthew looked over at him and seemed to come back to himself. "Even the fuckin' heartless vandals who kick up the place sometimes. Too much magic for 'em, I guess."

Matthew laughed and, knowing what was coming, punched Terry on the arm just as he was raising his fist. Terry arched his eyebrows and guffawed, happy to be standing with the man he called his brother, even though his brother was weird enough to drive his car into the back of a truck. On purpose. But they'd talk about that later.

Terry didn't feel much like talking anyway, now that he'd spoken to Isabel. All the words he wanted to say — to her, to Matt, to his dad — had dried up and blown away in the sharp fresh breeze that scoured the mountain top, alternately whispering and roaring through the trees, shaking off pinecones.

But there was idle banter, of course. No way to hang out with the Ol' Bean and not shoot the shit about something or other, which today was Crimson Dawn, Yellowstone Park, which they'd miss since they were flying home, the changes that had taken place in Casper since the last time they were here.

"Piece-of-shit town" Matt called it, but to Terry it wasn't. It was home and fond memories of growing up with his parents before his dad got sick and lost his mind, his touchstone, his lucky charm that looked like a jackalope.

"No, we're *not* goin' to the Wonder Bar," he said, yet again, as they walked back to their car, shooting his wistful friend one of those scowling looks that hyperbolic Matt swore he was famous for. "Stop askin' me, okay? We came for my dad and mom and Crimson Dawn. That's it. 'Less you wanna call on yer crazy twin brothers . . ."

"Fuck off, Keanu. You know damn well I don't." Matthew was sulking which made Terry feel glad. Otherwise he'd have to hit him, harder than the usual punch on the arm, maybe a smack in the face.

Driving back down the mountain, they stopped again at the lookout spot and lit up another joint, sitting in the car this time. It hadn't occurred to them to smoke weed at Crimson Dawn though they'd done that a lot once upon a time. What dipshits they'd been, back in the day. Still were, Terry thought.

A few cars passed them on the road, one full of teenagers passed them and honked. They waved lackadaisically, while passing the joint, and Matthew said something droll about acting their age which made Terry wince in spite of his laughter. He'd never felt so used-up and old as he did today.

All of a sudden he was hot to be back in over-duded-up Wallingford, Seattle, with its crowded rows of new apartments and gentrified McMansions squeezing the older houses half to death. Which was a goddamn shame — and funny — since Casper was by rights his home. But if home was where the heart was, like folks always said, then it was Isabel's kitchen that he longed for. Her bedroom still belonged to Charlie.

"So that was your old lady on the phone?" Matt said, with the kind of knowing smirk that Terry hated more than he hated himself for putting up with such weaselly crap from his best friend since time out of mind. The dude needed a fuckin' facelift. Nicer eyes behind the horned rim glasses, a gentler smile, cheeks that didn't look like an angry cadaver's.

"Get a life," Terry mumbled, more to himself than to Matt, who was deaf to all insults unless they involved Rosie or Jackson, or some tech jerk criticizing his work.

"Why should I? When I can have yours for the asking?" the dumb-ass said, and then Terry slapped him left-handed, leaving a livid red stain on his cheek.

Matthew reared back against his car door, aghast. "You fuckin' bitch-slapped me?" he shouted.

"'Stead a what?" Terry said calmly. "Punchin' ya in the face like a man? Kinda like you did to me only using a goddamn truck to smash in my head. You should feel lucky I'm still your stupid-ass loyal friend not some crazy Tarantino like Brand. So suck it up and just shut the hell up."

Matthew did not shut the hell up. Swearing and sputtering inchoately, he yanked the door open and stumbled out of the car, then began power walking up the road, seemingly numb to the fact that he was weaving drunkenly, and heading back up the mountain.

Terry rolled down his window and yelled, "Yer goin' the wrong way!" but Matthew kept on walking.

Watching him disappear around the bend gave Terry a weird sense of déjà vu. Not that this exact scenario had ever happened before, but numerous instances of Matt stomping off in anger sprang to mind, bathed in the dull glow of unhappy and cynical remembrances that lately defined their relationship.

"Well, fuck you and the lame horse you rode in on," he muttered to himself as he started and revved up the car, hoping the sound of the engine would bring Matt back. But it didn't.

WUNDERBAR

W hat the fuck happened to The Wonder Bar? Gutted, remade, and redone to look like a respectable joint, Matthew's old watering hole bore almost no resemblance to his memories of it, or his former identification of it as his personal hangout.

If he didn't know better, he'd think he was still in Seattle, visiting some gentrified backdrop to his current state of depression.

The exterior was sort of the same, except for the fancy new sign that said *restaurant and brewery*, instead of just Wonder Bar, above the row of old-fashioned windows on the ground floor, which he was peering through now, and four larger windows on the second floor where one of his old girlfriends used to live.

But the interior, from what he could see from outside, through a blurred haze of tears, was nothing like it used to be. The scarred-up old wooden bar, the funky booths upholstered in Naugahyde, the tipsy little tables where card games ended and fistfights started were all gone, replaced by smooth surfaces and a long polished bar as big as a whaling-ship spar.

A steep open metal staircase under a cavernous ceiling led up to the top floor where the cheap-ass apartments used to be. God know what was up there now. Maybe a collection of mummified cowboys who'd lived and died in the bar. Stuffed along with their beer-drinking horses.

Matthew imagined navigating the steps drunk and started to laugh, picturing himself stumbling and soaring into the air over Yuppie patrons quaffing designer cocktails and gourmet beer. Landing in a heap of tarted-up buffalo burgers and French fries with a Howdy Doody grin on his face, and a steak knife poking his ass.

By God he'd do it, too, if the thought of going inside didn't make him want to puke as well as nostalgia cry. Falling down something in a stoned stupor sounded pretty good right about now, although he figured it would put the last nail in his coffin as far as Terry was concerned.

He'd been shocked when he came to his senses while stalking up the mountain and, turning back, found Terry and the rental car gone. He'd expected—almost hoped—that would happen, but still, he'd felt abandoned and bereft, and cold without his hat and gloves, which he'd left in the car with his phone.

He was nearing the bottom of the mountain, trudging along in the middle of the road, when the car with the teenagers reappeared behind him, almost mowing him down. Flagging them down had been easy but convincing them to take him back to Casper, when they were headed South on 251, had required some quick talking and a fifty dollar bill from his wallet which, luckily, he'd kept in his pocket.

Matthew wished he'd asked the kids to take him back to the motel on the north side instead of dropping him off downtown. He had no desire to call an Uber driver from inside the bar. Or to keep standing on the sidewalk looking in, but he couldn't seem to walk away from the scene of what seemed like a terrible crime.

A trio of baseball-hat-wearing men exiting the bar passed him going to their car which had a "Make America Great" sticker on it. Matthew muttered, "Dumb fucks," under his breath, but kept his eyes down. His three-hundred-dollar REI Patagonia parka wasn't going to protect him from their scorn or their fists, which, based on sorry local experience, would likely be deft and merciless.

Deciding to chance taking the bus—even though he couldn't quite remember the name of last night's motel or exactly what street it was on—he searched his pockets for change but couldn't find any.

Damned if he'd go into the ruined bar to get any, though. So he started walking, aimlessly at first, then sparked by a new sense of direction, towards the only place in Casper he'd loved more than the Wonder Bar, the Natrona County library, just a few blocks away, which he hoped was still open Sundays.

An ebullient feeling rose in his chest as he approached the familiar building.

"Howdy," he said, holding the door open for a raggedy duffer exiting the library with an armful of Louis L' Amour books.

"Right back at cha," the old gent said, tipping a tattered cowboy hat at Matthew before tottering away.

Stepping inside the library was like stepping into the past, in as much as he'd spent a lot of time here as a kid, but the atmosphere, while welcoming, felt subtly different than his last stints in high school, poring over outdated computer books. The place had an airy feel now, more cosmopolitan although still small town, because of the elegant way the rooms had been rearranged and repurposed. In spite of the extensive changes in décor its sense of history was still alive, unlike the sanitized Wonder Bar.

Finding the bathroom was easy, facing himself in the mirror once inside was not. He looked like a skeezy guy on the run in somebody else's coat. Stubby red whiskers, red cheeks, ears and chin from walking in the wind, red eyes from crying, red words in his head flashing like traffic lights. All he needed was a red flag to complete the portrait he presented of a man being chased by a bull.

Where were the distracting clowns when he needed them?

"Ha ha." He heard Terry's deep laugh echoed by Jackson's higher one.

He waited for Rosie's sarcastic voice to chime in while he slapped water on his face and washed his hands, but nothing else happened. When a rangy guy and his teenaged son entered the bathroom, teasing each other, Matthew almost shouted with joy, realizing it was them he'd heard laughing.

Feeling somewhat more presentable, and somewhat less worried about his dustup with Terry, he ambled out to the checkout station where a middle-aged librarian was stacking kids' picture books on a cart. Goddamn it if she didn't look like the elementary school teacher he and Terry had crushes on! A bit older and heavier perhaps, but her brown hair was long and shiny and her smile was exactly the same.

"How can I help you?" she inquired.

The pretty woman's name tag said Ms. Wanamaker, but Matthew asked anyway, "Are you Miss Ravendahl?"

"I used to be, why?"

Matthew blushed, remembering the time he got to sit on her lap after another flighty little second-grade shit—a girl—kicked him in the nuts.

"Uh . . . you were my teacher . . ."

The librarian looked at him closely for a moment, then laughed. "Matthew? Matthew . . . Barker?"

"Yeah. But how did you remember my name?"

Ms. Wanamaker laughed. "How could I forget the sweet redheaded boy who was in love with me?"

Matthew didn't remember himself as having been sweet. He'd been angry and anxious and sad, but he *had* been sweet on his teacher, because she had been sweet to him. SWEET. The word twirled in his mind like a helicopter blade, threatening to chop off his head. He needed to get away.

"I'm kinda stuck in Casper," he quickly explained, cutting off further reminiscences. "I need change for bus fare and wondered if you . . . the library . . . could help me." He fumbled for his wallet and tried to hand her a fifty-dollar bill.

She waved his hand away. "We don't have change for that. But hold on." Crossing to the other side of the L-shaped desk, the smiling librarian unlocked a drawer, removed her purse and took several dollar bills out of her wallet.

On the way back to Matthew she picked up a map of Casper off the counter and handed it to him with the money. "The bus routes are on it in red. There's a stop going north two blocks from here, and one going south on the other side of the street."

Carefully pocketing the map along with the money gave him a chance to compose himself before thanking her. The tears that had formed in his eyes would remain unshed. He wished he were a seven-year-old boy again.

Back out on the street he decided to head back to the Wonder Bar to take one last disappointed look at the soulless place, hoping that Terry might be there waiting for him. But there was no sign of the rental car on the street and nobody who looked like Keanu sitting at the bar when he peeked in the window. So, shit, it was back to the mystery motel, if he could find it.

There were two men in identical plaid jackets standing at the bus stop when he walked up behind them. In a dim recess of his mind, he suspected they might be his brothers, the terrible tormenting twins. He prayed they wouldn't look at him, but it was too late, they'd already turned around.

"What ho! It's our shitty little brother," the scruffier of the two said. Frank—or was it Fred?—held out an ungloved hand with dirty fingernails, then withdrew it before making contact.

"Parm me. Been workin' on a fucked-up old beater over at Doof-ball's place. Ya know, that old rat-cellar garage next to where Skeeter's meth lab used to be, afore the pigs tore it down."

The other twin laughed unpleasantly instead of sticking out his hand. Matthew shoved his hands deep into his coat pockets and started to edge away, but the two men caught up with him.

"Hey lil' bro," said Fred—or was it Frank?—putting a dirty paw on Matthew's forearm, "Long time no see. Last time you was here was a real shitstorm, but 'member how you helped us out? If you could do the same this time around, we'd be mighty grateful, wouldn't we, Bub?"

Christ, it was back to the bad old days when Bub and Bub regularly shook him down for Monopoly—and later, drug and bail—money. The fuckers had always wanted something from him, if they couldn't cajole or steal it from their mom. Their dad was the only person they never tried to sweet talk or cheat—one more reason why Matthew had been afraid of him.

But he wasn't afraid of the twins anymore.

Instead of asking what happened to the SUV they bought with their inheritance money, or the Barker's old house that Matthew had pretended to sign over to them, or the various cockamamie schemes they had a habit of investing in, he just walked away while they shouted insults at him.

Shit, now he couldn't take the bus since his brothers might be on it, so he circled back to the library to wait for a later one, ducking into the bathroom without going past the checkout desk. Sitting on the toilet with the lid down wasn't the best place for mindfulness meditation, but it was dark, close and private in the stall which helped his anxiety, like those tight-fitting cattle chutes and "squeeze machines" the autistic inventor Temple Grandin was famous for.

He wondered, not for the first time, if he might have autism. Terry said no, but he wasn't so sure. It might be comforting to have a semi-clear diagnosis about what was wrong with his brain. His soul was another issue.

After twenty-five minutes in the bathroom, he finally crept out, feeling a bit like a pervert, although he'd done nothing but sit, elbow on knee, chin resting on the back of his hand like The Thinker. Not that he'd figured much out.

There was no one waiting to attack him when he got back to the bus stop, although there was a large pile of dog shit on the wooden bench that hadn't been there before. A ceremonial present from his brothers, he guessed, but he just laughed and scooped it away with a handful of leaves. Fuck 'em both and the bullying horse they rode in on.

The bus ride, mercifully uneventful, gave him a few pleasant moments of freedom, observing familiar old haunts and a few new or redone buildings like The Wonder Bar from the smudged-up window, feeling beholden to no one and nothing, least of all the town where he'd been born and, so often, had wanted to die.

He didn't want to die anymore, he suddenly realized. Not in Rosie's toned milk-white arms, as he'd so frequently fanaticized, or in a car crash like his mom and dad, or alone at his computer, stroking out over some complex logarithm. On the other hand, he didn't want to live like he'd been living. In what Madam Zodie—Alice—called his "magic shell of impermeability." At least he thought that's what she said, before she went to bed and left him curled up on her couch like a shrunken fetus.

Towards the end of the line Matthew spotted the rental Kia in the parking lot of a Courtyard by Marriott and got off the bus.

The two-toned-beige exterior looked familiar enough as a stereotypical traveling businessman's haunt, but the bland façade could have graced the outskirts of any small town, rendering it simply a backdrop to his drama with Terry, not a place, like the faux-cowpoke motel, where, on their first night in Casper, their homecoming saga had begun to play out.

Too bad they hadn't stayed put, although likely they wouldn't get robbed or beat up at the Courtyard. The attendant in the lobby managed not to look askance when Matthew asked for the number of his room and a card-key to get in. His name was on the register along with Terry's, which seemed weird, but no stranger than anything else which had happened to them since leaving Seattle.

Standing in the corridor outside room 221, he felt like a fool, and a fool for feeling like one. His typical MO, but the thought struck him anyway with a kind of slow force like an intensification of gravity, pulling him down into his familiar sinkhole.

He stuck his keycard in the slot and opened the door. He hoped to God that Terry was inside. And equally that he wasn't.

TERRY'S GAME

One of Terry's favorite pastimes was a verbal Scrabble game assigning scurrilous nicknames to people who'd pissed him off. Ten letters for Matt, not including the hyphen, in at least three of the nastiest three words Terry could think of that described him.

Cock-breath, that old Wyoming chestnut, seemed the most specifically insulting, if also somewhat inappropriate, unless the dumb-fuck—only eight letters—had actually gone down on the evil prick Jackson. These last crazy days, Terry wouldn't put it past him.

He played the word game in the car driving back from Casper Mountain sans Matthew, skirting downtown in order to avoid the Wonder Bar where he figured the affronted asshole—seven letters—would end up.

Damned if he'd do the loyal-sidekick trick and rush in to rescue his crazy-assed friend like in all those silly Hollywood romances. Back in the literary good ol' days there would have been real sword play between guys like Porthos and D'Artagnan. Now it was all dope deals and doobies, bucket lists and hot chicks, Bitcoin and social ballet. Wedding Crashers, blah fucking blah.

Thinking about running Matt through with a sword wasn't satisfying, though. No use in the rat-bastard—one of the best ten-letter words—dying before apologizing or seeing the light in terms of his selfish behavior. Which Terry worried he'd lately been emulating, minus the abject masochism, with lovely widowed Isabel.

Knowing he was pushing her to commit to him prematurely, passive-aggressively punishing her for her loyalty to Charlie, didn't make things any easier when it came to confronting what was really bothering him. Isabell was at the core of his existential dilemma, but so was Matt. And his dead gol-dang father, that was for damn sure. Him and the Alzheimer's horse he rode in on. And then permanently out.

He was lying on his starched white motel bed, after sending a short, probably confusing text to Isabel, when Matt pushed the door open and came in, exuding the pungent smell of averted disaster, the signature scent of Casper, as far as Terry was concerned.

Terry turned towards the wall, scrunching down on his pillow. Damned if he was gonna say the first words. Even though he was glad to see his old friend in one piece, not chewed up into hamburger like the last time they were here.

Matt sidled into the room, bent at the knees like Groucho Marx, although he wasn't trying for humor, based on the shit-eating grin on his face indicating canine submissiveness in front of a ravening wolf pack.

It was pathetic watching the poor bloke squirm and blush, but also quite exhilarating. "Down on yer knees," Terry wanted to say, wishing he had a whip at hand, or, even better, a PowerPoint presentation categorizing his best friend's flaws in high definition. A taste of his own techno medicine!

Eventually Matt took off his coat and sat down on the other double bed, shoulders slumped like the spineless puppet he was. Terry hawked loudly, pantomiming spitting into his open hand, which he subsequently wiped onto his jeans with a gesture of mordant repulsion.

The fight was apparently on.

"You were just gonna leave me there?" Matt started out, completely predictably. When Terry didn't answer, he took off his shoes and lay down on his bed with his legs flung out like a toddler's. Goddamn, but he was maddening. Nine letters and a fucking exclamation point!

"Guess you know I went to the Wonder Bar," the dork-ass said, again entirely predictably.

"Sure," Terry said. But only in his head. He wasn't talking till the infuriating fuck-wit—seven letters—confessed.

Matt swung a skinny leg towards Terry's bed, like a lazy teenager prodding a drunk friend at a slumber party. Terry wished he *was* drunk, then maybe he would have been passed out when numb-nuts came in. Now he had to make a concerted effort not to look at him, which was annoying.

"I never went in," Matt continued breathlessly, disregarding Terry's silence. "It's a soulless Yuppie bar now. I just stood outside and looked in the window, like fuckin' Oliver Twist . . ."

Terry appreciated the Dickensian reference but didn't respond.

Clueless Matt obviously didn't get the degree to which Terry was pissed off at him. He kept squirming and vogueing on the bed like a Victoria's Secret model caught on the end of a hook, trying to attract the attention of a crusty old seadog who's thrown back a million fish.

There was something incredibly unnatural about the poor dude's need to be liked, when he was regularly so very unlikeable. Yet, given the proper circumstances, and maybe a joint and a bottle of wine, the Bean could be a wonderful companion, someone who never judged you for your failures and creepy shadow side, who took the internal heat for you. Who said, "Brother we're all sinners," and meant it.

Knowing that made it hard to be hard with him, especially as he was such a soft-centered chocolate drop, inwardly squishy and sweet if outwardly a fuckin' hard-edged disaster. Losing Rosie, the love of his mostly loveless life, had shot a hit of poison into Matt's bloodstream—bitter, bitter despair— which hadn't done him a lick of good in spite of his insistence on feasting on it. Gollum with his goddamn ring.

Terry turned towards his friend, hoping that this was the last time they were going to have a fight in a sterile motel room. He wished they were back at the Old Corral, throwing Doritos at each other, and making horny jokes about cowboy girls. Shit, it just felt good to be a drunk cretinous bro sometimes. Shootin' the mindless breeze.

He looked at Matt with a haphazard grin, not quite sure if he was forgiving him, but what the heck. It was almost five p.m. They had a whole night to get through before it was time to check out and go see his dad's lawyer tomorrow morning. Might as well make the best of it. And maybe he could stop obsessing about Isabel.

Terry stretched and yawned like a big hungry cat. "All righty, then," he said. "Pineapple and ham, or pepperoni and jalapeno peppers?"

Matt chortled and kicked his legs, but had the grace to look somber when he said, "Anything you want, mate," without the usual Cockney accent. There were tears lurking behind the rims of his wiry little glasses when he added, "And I *mean* that. Anything you want to make things all right," but Terry didn't say anything, just handed him a box of Kleenex.

The evening unfolded with a certain familiar scenario—beer, pizza, pot and bad jokes—into which the two friends hesitantly inserted some heart-to-heart talks which made both of them tingly with pride and embarrassment.

A fistfight, like in those rocky bromance movies, or a car chase, or the steamy presence of a hooker, would have made things easier than all the psychological crap. Easier to acknowledge and apologize for literal black eyes than all the bad choices and passive-aggressive ploys they'd pulled on each other. Both of them pushovers. Terry to Matt, Matt to Rosie, then Matt to the Rat-bastard Jackson.

"And fuck it, Brand's the only one who's gettin' properly laid," Terry complained, letting the cat out of the bag regarding his ambiguous sexual relationship with Isabel, which the Ol' Bean, for a change, didn't pick up on.

Or maybe he was just being nice. He looked pretty damn cute curled up on his bed with his bright-red hair mussed up from his folded-up pillow. Terry's heart skipped a beat just looking at him, remembering Matt as a kid. How earnest he'd been. And still was.

Matt was just explaining about meeting their second-grade-teacher crush at the library and running into the twin Lords of the Fly on the street, when Terry's cellphone rang. He took it into the bathroom and shut the door before answering.

It was Isabel.

"Hey ho," he said, and then because he was almost drunk, "Well, howdy, ma'am. Mighty nice of you t'call." He sat down on the ledge of the bathtub, and gazed around. Where the hell was his beer?

"Just got your message," Isabel said, "I'm so sorry about your dad. Wish I'd known where you are and why a couple of days ago . . ." Her voice was tender and soft. "How are you holding up?"

Teetering on the skinny edge of the tub was a great metaphor for how he was feeling, but Terry just laughed, as was his usual habit, and mumbled, "Doin' okay, hey, hey, hey. Like the gol-dang Monkees."

Isabel didn't laugh, but somehow he knew that she knew exactly what he was—or wasn't—talking about.

"Duddn't seem that long ago that my dad was my age and I was an eight-year-old boy scootin' 'round the schoolyard with Matt. He's here with me now, a course, 'though it might be better if he waddn't. A goddamn pain in the ass, but my dad liked him. And Matty was good to him back."

"I'm glad he's there with you. How's your mom?"

Terry sighed heavily and brushed an errant curl out of his eyes, which he realized were copiously dripping. "Sick at heart and feelin' guilty as charged. But okay, I guess, 'cept for the fuckin' eejit she married, which I hope she dearly regrets."

Thankfully Isabel didn't argue with this, in spite of being a mom and—he surmised—a feminist. Knew when to keep her critiques to herself, unlike flapdoodle Matt. Ten letters, Terry noted to himself, wondering if Isabel ever played the mean-spirited Scrabble game. What insulting words she'd ascribe to Charlie. What letters she'd pick out for *him*.

"When are you coming home?" she said. Home, not back to Seattle. His heart took another little jump.

He turned on the bathtub's cold water tap and took a swig out of his cupped hand. He wished he'd brought his beer into the can with him, but oh well, probably better not to get drunker while they talked. Isabel deserved at least a modicum of sincerity, considering that she'd called.

"Goin' to my dad's lawyer in the morning, then a goodbye kiss with my mom, and it's off and away to my favorite hyperspace place. The Natrona County Airport. Flight gets in to SeaTac 'bout seven."

Dreamlike images of Casper Mountain, a babbling crick on Hat Six Road, erupting geysers at Yellowstone, buffalos and prairie dogs and Devil's Tor jockeyed for position in Terry's mind, as he tried to say something salient to Isabel about laying his old man to rest in Wyoming. Something that maybe tied him to Charlie. How it was a shame that both of them died.

But all he said was, "My dad was a rilly good guy . . . Gonna miss him," to which she replied, "Yes, I know." And, most likely, she did.

"It'll be good to see you," Isabel said, and Terry said he'd be glad to see her, too. There was yearning in their voices, but something else, too, that he didn't want to think about until he saw her face. Took a long investigative look at it. Kissed her mouth. Or turned away.

Probably time to hang up, he decided, wanting his beer and Matt's stupid placating face, and a look out of the motel-room window into the slushy wet streets where the wind was blowing hard through the cottonwood trees that he'd smelled at the drive-thru liquor store a while ago.

Maybe he wanted to get back in the piece-of-shit rental car and drive till it ran off the road or ran out of gas. Or maybe he needed to run, like an antelope or a deer—not one of those over-fed bread eaters on Casper Mountain—until he collapsed and fell down.

But again, he didn't share these thoughts with Isabel. And wouldn't with Matt. There was nobody he could count on to understand him now that his father was dead.

"So I gotta go," Terry said, hoping that Isabel wouldn't argue with him, at the same time as he wished she was here. Then again, Charlie would've had to come along, too. So forget it. Forget her. But just for a second.

Agreeing to call her as soon as he got home, if only to say he was there, helped cut their conversation short. Sighing with relief after they said goodbye, he took a long piss, then decided on a shower and shave.

His face in the bathroom mirror looked just like his dad's in the photograph he kept in his wallet. Same broad forehead, high flat cheekbones, wide generous mouth, the same Kerouac "On The Road" look in their same-colored eyes, although neither of them traveled much, and preferred motorcycles to cars.

The photograph was snapped by his mom when she was pregnant with Terry, which made it seem providential, as well as nostalgic. As if it predicted his future, based on his dad's. His possible—probable?—propensity for Alzheimer's disease, the slow death of his brain. The humiliating return to infancy under the aegis of underpaid caregivers.

Shuddering, he turned away from the mirror without shaving and stepped into the shower stall.

The hot needles of water cascading down on his head cooled his anxiety a bit, put him back into his body and away from morbid thoughts of his mind going bad on him. Back into wanting several more beers and one of those immortal cupcake things from the liquor store that people bought to feed the deer on Casper Mountain. No healthy vegan donut shops here. No fuckin' hippies either, from what he could tell. Not that he'd seen much of Casper so far.

Except for the cemetery and the mountain, he'd been in a plane and a room and a car and a room and a room and a room—like Paul's grandfather in *A Hard Day's Night*—since they got here. Only Matt had gone out foraging for old haunts, not that it had done him any good. The Wonder Bar's shocking remodel job had done a big number on his head—and Terry's by extension, since the Ol' Bean hadn't stopped carping about it since he returned from downtown.

"Don't give two half-hearted fucks about that gawd-awful place," Terry declared, as he dried himself off, mentally preparing himself for another squabble with Matt. His preplanning was moot, as it turned out that Matt was asleep when he went back into the room, face down on his bed, hair askew, like a toppled down scarecrow.

"Poor bugger,"—six letters—Terry muttered as he covered up his friend's crumpled form with a clean white blanket that reeked of bleach.

Sure he missed the Old Corral's homely dirt and disorder, but the Courtyard's excessive cleanliness was disarming. No hefty cum-stained polyester quilts to tear off before crawling into bed, for instance. And there was an all-you-can-eat breakfast buffet he was looking forward to. Those upside-down DIY waffle machines always thrilled him. And those little packages of fake maple syrup.

Rummaging through his backpack he found an old pair of pajama pants and faded Aerosmith T-shirt with photos of the band when they were young and ungrizzled. He put them on and sat on the bed, drinking beer for a while, waiting for Matt to wake up so he could make him apologize again.

"Ten times ten ain't enough, little brother," he said, prodding Matt's side with an angry finger, but the dork-dog just rolled onto his back and started snoring.

"Sleepin' asshole!" He ranted for a moment, then gave up.

Folded piece of pizza in hand, he stood at the window with the curtains pulled back, looking out at the night lights and the dark sky promising more wind, if not snow, before morning. No smell of cottonwoods seeped through the tiny opening he'd made, no scents of sagebrush or coffee, no sense of the assisted living home, just five blocks from here, where his dad had died, or the cemetery where he was buried.

"Just nothin'," he muttered. He closed the window and went back to his bed, where he sat drinking beer until morning.

SAM SHEPARD'S RIGHT: THERE'S ALWAYS ANOTHER FIGHT

Waiting for Terry wasn't that onerous, but Matthew was definitely going to complain about sitting in the waiting room surrounded by the heads of dead animals and copies of American Rifleman. Graphic reminders of blood and gore belonged in criminal defense attorneys' inner-offices, not in an estate lawyer's suburban enclave. Unless, of course, the lawyer was a Wyoming guy with an obvious penchant for taxidermy.

Scrolling through cellphone text messages offered little distraction from the decapitated antelopes and bighorns, until he came across one from Madam Zodie with a psychic warning for Terry embedded in a message for him.

"Good for you for taking care of Terry," she wrote. "I've sent my condolences through Isabel. Tell him to be careful with the gold and the green when he says goodbye to his mom. Take care. XX Alice."

Hey what?

Matthew read the text several times. Glad for the X's, wary of the message, unsure of his part in helping his friend, and suddenly full of foreboding. What was the deal with Terry's mom? And what did those colors mean?

Fuck it, he was alarmed, but completely stumped. The worst combination for his anxiety disorder and pounding hangover, not to mention his perspicacious personality. Something was rotten in Casper and it wasn't the goddamn cheese.

Terry eventually emerged from the lawyer's office looking uncharacteristically peaked. A bit green around the gills, to Matthew's practiced eye, a bit chastened. Like a kid who's just been whacked on the butt by an irate school principal.

"Let's get outta here." Terry growled, stalking through the exit door faster than Matthew could heave himself off of the couch, and still hang on to his phone and coat, and the faded issue of *People* magazine he was stealing for its photo of Jackson Brand that he planned to burn in the Kia's ashtray.

Terry was halfway across the parking lot by the time Matthew—half running while struggling into his coat—caught up to him and demanded to know what was happening.

"Back off, dude! And fuckin' don't ask!" Terry lunged for the car door, jumped in, and started the engine before Matthew reached the passenger side, pumping with adrenaline, and shoved himself inside.

Terry gunned the motor and screeched out onto the street, driving at the posted limit, yet the Kia seemed to be speeding, racing towards the east side of town.

"Are you okay?" Matthew shouted, flopping around in his seat like a kid's stuffed animal as he fumbled to fasten his seatbelt.

"What's it look like?" Terry shot back, swerving to avoid an unhelmeted bicyclist who shot them the finger as they passed, calling up memories of Seattle cyclists who inevitably did the same thing when drivers were trying to be nice to them.

It wasn't long before they pulled up in front of Terry's mother's house, where they could see Mrs. Thompson standing at the kitchen window, and behind her, the portly figure of the house painter with his fat arms encircling her.

"Fuckin' bastard and fuckin' bitch," Terry intoned in a droning monotone, like some kind of crazy monk, clenching the steering wheel with angry hands as he watched the couple nuzzle, then kiss.

Oh fuck, Matthew thought, wishing Terry would just drive away, instead of doing what was apparently coming next, which was having a big showdown with Green.

But why?

The dumb guy who didn't hold a candle to his dad screwing his mom was sad and bad, but Terry had already picked that fight. The upcoming grudge match was about something else. Something to do with Terry's visit to the lawyer this morning. Something to do with his dad.

Matthew was just about to ask what, when Terry turned to him with a threatening look, barked, "stay there," and got out of the car, unfolding himself from the compact's seat like wary, deliberate bear emerging from hibernation.

Watching his buddy walk up the back steps and into a house where a fight was about to take place gave Matthew the willies and the start of a massive headache. *BONG! BONG! BONG!* The evil chimes in his temples drowned out the voice that said he should be calling the cops, instead of sitting there like a dummy with his phone fingers stuck up the crack of his ass.

Yanking at his hair and clothing gave no relief, ditto checking and rechecking his text messages for more psychic warnings from Alice. He should have told Terry about the original text, but he realized this too damned late. By the time he'd sprung out of the car and run up the steps and into the house to alert his friend, the fight was already on.

Terry and Green were beating the shit out of each other, going for serious blood, not just flailing around like they had at Mr. Thompson's wake. Terry had a streaming gash over his eye, in the same spot where he'd been wounded in Matthew's car crash, and the house painter's blubbery jaw hung askew like a half-broken tree branch.

Mrs. Thompson slash Green shouted for Matthew to watch out when her husband picked up a kitchen chair and began smashing it over Terry's back. But Matthew rushed forward, screaming, "Stop it, you mad motherfucker! I'm calling the cops!"

He blocked the raging creep from hitting Terry again, then kicked him hard, taking careful aim. With a loud clatter the chair fell to the floor, along with the hefty bulk of the house painter, moaning and clutching his balls.

Terry's mom was moaning, too, and crying with big hiccupping sobs. "You could a killed him!" she screamed at one man, then another, including Matthew in her declamatory statement, even though it was clear she was wrong.

"He ain't no killer, ma," Terry said, struggling to his feet from his knees. "Duddn't have the heart for it. But I surely do."

Advancing on Green with three giant steps—and slapping his mother's hands away as she reached out to hold him back—he bent down and grabbed Green by the neck.

"Tell me the truth about you and my dad!" Terry roared, squeezing the fat man's throat even tighter as he struggled to rise from the floor.

Terry's mom could only rush to her husband's defense verbally since her son stood in her way. "You're just jealous!" she cried, but there was doubt in her trembling voice which Matthew picked up on.

Oh, God, there was really something bad going on here that was going to break Mrs. Thompson's heart.

Helping her to sit down at the kitchen table, after dismantling the broken chair that Green had beat Terry with, Matthew sidled across the floor and put a retraining hand on his friend who was still clutching the painter's neck.

"Not worth the trouble of you landing in jail . . ." he whispered hoarsely, gently tugging at Terry's right arm.

"Get away from me. I got business here," Terry snarled, but he loosened his grip just a trifle.

"Go on and tell it like it is," Terry ordered the struggling house painter. "Go on an' confess to my mom what a cheatin' scumbag you are. How you ripped off my dad."

The putative stepfather choked and grimaced and finally loosened his tongue after Terry jerked his head around a bit. "I didn't do nothin'! Nothin' that hurt your dad. It was his choice to give me the money!"

Terry laughed cynically, which meant he was dangerous.

"My dad's lawyer had your I.O.U. from my dad's safety deposit box. Ten thousand bucks you stole, you fuckin' weasel!"

Mrs. Thompson Green gasped. "Is it true, Greg? Did you steal money from poor deranged Ted?"

The house painter tried to gurgle an answer but Terry held his throat tight, like a farmer grasping the neck of a dead turkey he was carrying home for Thanksgiving.

"Let him speak!" Terry's mother, oddly regal in a purple polyester housecoat, commanded, and her son, however disapproving of her collusion with his enemy, slowly obeyed, freeing his captive.

"Yeah! Yeah!" the fallen man mumbled, rubbing the raw marks on his throat with a pudgy, but claw-like, hand. "So I borrowed money from a friend," the traitor spat out. "What's it fuckin' to ya?"

Terry stepped closer to his mother while the guilty bastard floundered, and said, "You never paid it back. And you never told my mom. You took advantage of a righteous guy. And you were supposed to be his friend!"

"Well, maybe I did," the piece of shit sputtered out of his battered jaw. "Maybe I goddamn did. But Ted never missed the money. He practically gave it to me, no strings attached, except I fuck his old lady. But I was 'sposed to wait till he was gone."

Green had the grace to look contrite at this dire point, but his stricken wife wasn't buying his excuses, based on the murderous way she was glaring at him.

The tension in the room, which had reached an unbearable point in spite of the break in the fighting, was broken by her slapping Green's face and kicking at his shins, once he'd managed to heave his bulky frame from up off the floor.

"Bastard! Liar! Worthless asshole!" she shouted, clawing at him. "You slept in Ted's bed—and married me!—after you ripped him off. Knowing he'd forget you owed him the money. Knowing he'd forget me." She slapped him again. "How can you live with yourself?"

Matthew had just stepped forward to propel his fuming friend out of the house, when the house painter grabbed a heavy glass canister off the counter, and hurled it full force at the back of Terry's head. It hit with a terrible crack.

And down Terry went to the floor.

Mrs. Thompson screamed in terror. The victorious Green just gawped.

The next few moments were a blur as Matthew rushed to Terry's collapsed form—much smaller than it was two minutes ago, as if his body had instantly shrunk.

Blood was puddling under Terry's head, but he was still breathing, thank God.

"Come back, buddy! Come back!" Matthew exhorted, stroking his unconscious cheek. "Please! Please! Come back!"

Slipping his coat—surprised he was still wearing it, everything had happened so fast—under Terry's lolling head, he checked the wound, bleeding copiously but smaller than expected, then pressed gently down on it with one of the empty coat sleeves.

"You'll be all right. You'll be all right," Matthew crooned, vaguely aware of the repetitive words, everything coming in twos as if to confirm his distress.

At the same time as he was wailing those begging words, Matthew's mind was jolted into another world. The usual PTSD-induced marquee letters were flashing in his head but they weren't spelling anything out, just zapping his brain with electricity which, oddly, felt kind of sensual.

At the center of his interior vision a bright light was beckoning. Maybe his soul was changing places with his dying friend's? Maybe he was dying himself?

His outer perceptions, reduced to pinprick, managed to zero in on the guilty house painter sidling away from his wife.

"Call 9-1-1!" he shouted, lunging at Green and grabbing his cumbersome thighs like a roided-out thrower shouldering two thick poles for a caber toss, bringing him down to the floor with a resounding thud that shook the whole room.

Straddling the musk ox's massive chest, Matthew shouted for Mrs. Thompson to bring him a knife. She grabbed a carving knife out of a yanked-open drawer, shoved it blade first at Matthew, then rushed towards her fallen son, screaming into her cellphone.

"Move, motherfucker, and I slit your fat throat," Matthew hissed, holding the kitchen knife over the thief's sweaty pink face. The creep crying and blubbering now, saying he was sorry, Terry's ashen-faced mom kneeling beside her son's body, pulling on his motionless arms and hands, trying to revive him.

Matthew's brain felt like it was fizzing now. The sensation was no longer sensual. Simply the barbed perception of doom. Sharp as a giant tattoo needle.

Pressing his knees harder into the big man's chest, Matthew brandished the knife threateningly, then cut a small nick in the jerk's broad cheek, deep enough to hurt but probably not disfiguring.

"One inch of your stinking flesh that even twitches before the cops get here and I'll chop off your balls and eat them on toast," he vowed, breathing what he hoped was pure poison into the creep's bawling mouth.

"And your spleen and your worthless gizzard."

And every fucking thing else.

There's a moment of stasis and quiet after every terrible event, terrifying in itself for its seeming normalcy, as if you've always been at the bottom of a deep dark pit and long ago copped to the fact that you'll never get out.

When the fatal car crash, or the sudden massive heart attack, or the pernicious treachery of childhood disease and death rips your world—and your loved ones—apart, and you think, "I should have expected this," then you've been at the bottom of that very special well where time stands still yet drowns you.

That's where Matthew was when the cops and medics arrived. Inside the static abyss.

Watching Green being frisked down and handcuffed and pushed into a squad car, watching Terry's limp body being lifted onto a stretcher, watching Mrs. Thompson scramble into the ambulance behind it, made Matthew feel wobbly, yet he was still standing when they all drove away, sirens blaring, as he shivered in his shirtsleeves on the sidewalk.

One of the cops—had there been two or three?—had brought him his bloody jacket before Terry's mom locked up her house, and the savvy ambulance driver had made sure to search Terry's pockets for the rental car keys so Matthew could drive behind them to the hospital, but he did not move to follow right away.

Slumping down onto the gravel parking strip, loose as ragdoll, he began to sob, covering his eyes with his palms. Then stopped abruptly, since no tears came out, just sweat rolling off his brow, mixed with blood where Green had clawed at him, funneling down to his lips.

Suddenly, over those awful mingled tastes and scents, he smelled the cottonwoods Terry had been talking about last night. Shallow root systems, dangerous branches in high winds, yet people in Casper—and elsewhere—kept planting them because they smelled so good. Like sunny days and butterscotch ice cream. And the Barker's and Thompson's backyards.

How weird that he'd forgotten that, until Terry reminded him.

The scary storm-tossed tree limbs, the piles of golden leaves for jumping in, the tents and outside forts and homemade wigwams shunted up against the base of creaking swaying monsters, one in each neighboring yard. And their lovely tree-perfume, spritzed into the air along with floating clouds of cotton fluff, foretelling sun instead of rain.

How glorious those trees had been!

Yet, when Terry had smelled cottonwoods in the queue at the drive-thru liquor store, they'd reeked of old age and death, he'd said. Not that their fragrance was any less paradisiacal than he remembered, just much more complex, like everything else that floated to adult consciousness after sorrow and loss.

Terry had rubbed his sideburns ruefully, laughing at his own conundrums while chugging a beer. "Gotta keep hydrated, bro," he'd said, a lopsided grin splitting his face into two unequal parts. Turned-up mouth and downturned eyes in which unshed tears were swimming.

Those sad eyes. That well-loved face covered with blood. The stark vision of his friend dropping to the scrubbed linoleum floor, near noiselessly compared to the house painter's gigantic thud, brought Matthew scrambling to his feet. Head spinning, heart pounding, throat dry—still in shock, certainly—but he had a mission.

Vaulting into the driver's seat of the rental car, he started the engine, and turned up the radio, giving in to an old superstition that what was playing now would define his future.

Twinkly sounds of a synthesizer, a strumming guitar, and then a man's tenor voice singing Terry's favorite song, with the lyrics about everybody you love dying someday, that Matthew had always hated.

"Fuck! Fuck! Fuck!" he shouted, pounding hard on the steering wheel.

He snapped off the radio, pulled the car out onto the street and headed for the hospital.

GOIN' BASS-ACKWARDS

The Wyoming Medical Center—or The Memorial Hospital of Natrona County, as it was known when Matt was born there thirty-six years ago—wasn't the type of place Terry had in mind when he was thinking about checking out a couple of landmarks before leaving Casper.

Yet here he was lying on a gurney in the stately old hospital's ER, being examined by a short blonde pregnant doctor who kept calling him Terrance, which wasn't his name. He considered correcting her but the only sounds that emanated from him were mumbles and croaks that scraped on his ears.

"What am I doin' here?" he thought, while the doctor prodded him, although, even hazy with confusion, he supposed that was obvious. He was hurt in some way or he wouldn't be in the hospital. Or maybe he was deathly ill with some virus, although he couldn't remember coughing or vomiting.

He must have passed out, fainted or fallen, since his head felt woozy and his lankly limbs torpid, and somewhere in his mind a clock was ticking ominously, counting off random thoughts. None of them containing any usable clues to his present condition. None of them comforting.

The pregnant doctor, bending over him with her tiny flashlight and dangling stethoscope, smelled like sweet sweat and sour perfume, the arresting scent of autumn cottonwoods leaves incinerated in oaky burn barrels. He could see the caked line of her foundation makeup where it ended under her chin.

"You been workin' too hard," he wanted to say, feeling sorry for her for some reason, but couldn't muster the effort to speak. A drink of water to wet his parched throat was all that he wanted. And a brief explanation for how he'd ended up in the hospital, although that probably wasn't important in the long run, he guessed.

It was about that time that he recognized the crumpled up form of his mother, grave as a grieving pietà, huddled in a chair at the side of the room, staring beseechingly at him.

"Hey, Ma," he managed to drawl, flicking a jittery glance at her. And instantly the inert twiggy little scarecrow woman—that he suddenly saw that she was—sprang to maternal life, jumping up from her chair to join the doc at his side. Shrieking with joy, "You're alive!"

And yeah, he probably was. Although everything seemed pretty dreamlike. Weird how he had a terrible throbbing headache at the same time as his head felt entirely disconnected from his body. From his inner essential self. But if he was dead he wouldn't be in so much pain. He felt a tiny surge of relief.

He let his eyelids droop for a moment, but closing his eyes didn't seem to soften his present reality, even though he tried repeating a soothing mantra, and visualizing Isabel leaning over him instead of the pregnant doctor.

All he could see was his dad's grave at the cemetery and a scared fat man shouting invective at him. And now he remembered. The nasty shock in the lawyer's office. The fight with Green at his parents' house. The Ol' Bean's vain attempt at calming him.

Sighing deeply he opened his eyes.

He could see and hear fine—at least to his scrambled mind—but that didn't seem to alleviate Doctor What's Her Name's fears. She kept frowning and squinting at him, even after he'd told her his name, the date, and the salutary fact that he knew who the president was.

"You're pretty damn lucky," she finally said, slapping Terry's thigh encouragingly, Wyoming style, cowgirl to injured horse. "You're going to be all right. But we're going to do some tests—a CT scan and MRI, maybe—and keep you locked up overnight. Hope you're okay with that. But too bad if you're not!"

"Right, mom?!" She shot a meaningful smile at Mrs. Thompson, then went out to the unit station to order the appropriate tests.

Matt arrived, right after the doctor exited, bursting into the examining room like a man on fire looking for the nearest extinguisher. He rushed to Terry's side, after throwing his bloody jacket on a chair and side-stepping Terry's mom.

"Goddamn it, you're alive!" he shouted, to which his dazed buddy shakily replied, "That's what ever-bawdy keep sayin'."

Matt looked like a washed-up piece of shit from a scummy sea of turmoil, bleached white by a malevolent sun, hair sticking up like shredded pieces of plastic fish netting. Like he really had been doused with water from a firehose or sprayed with retardant.

"Well, look what the dog's dragged in," Terry said, wishing for a crazy second that his agitated friend would leave the tiny room where the wall of curtains between the adjoining cubicles seemed to be pressing in on them. Then, seeing the rapturous relief on the Ol' Bean's face, he was glad he was there.

The reunited friends were just starting in on an expletive-filled postmortem of their terrible morning, when the doctor returned with a nurse who looked a black Ricky Gervais.

"This nice guy here's gonna take you to the imagining room," she said, gesturing to the pudgy nurse, after giving Matt what looked like the stink eye, but was probably just a quick assessment of his mental and physical health. After all, she'd just stitched up a nasty head wound from a fight he was likely involved in.

"You most certainly have a concussion," Doctor Malden—Terry had finally taken note of her nametag—continued. "Which I'll discuss with you in more detail after your CT scan. We want to make sure your brain's not bleeding." She grimaced theatrically here which made Terry warm to her. That and the scuffed up square-toe cowboy boots she was wearing under her maternity scrubs.

Terry was about to ask if she'd bought 'em at Lou Taubert's when her pager went off and she hastily left the room, leaving him feeling like a smitten guy whose blind date has run out on him.

But it was kind of fun being wheeled down the hall on a gurney, with his mom and Matt trotting obediently along beside the nurse who kept joking with them.

Pointing to his name tag which said "Dave Wilson", the Ricky guy said, "That ain't my real name, but so what?" winking broadly at Mrs. Thompson to put her at ease. Her returning smile was strained but genuine.

But Matt was never at ease. Not here in the gol-dang horse-pistol, as Terry's dad always called hospitals, nor any place else, which made Terry feel kind of pissed. Pretty damned hard to deal with his damned concussion and rest like the good doctor ordered around Matt's worrisome vibes.

"How 'bout you take my mom down to the cafeteria and buy her some coffee," Terry suggested when they reached the imaging room, shooting Matt one of his bullish looks that said he meant business.

"Better than sitting around here." Nurse Dave arched his eyebrows encouragingly, and gestured to the dreary waiting room, where a disconsolate man sat holding a woman's pink purse on his lap, and another man was reading a newspaper, muttering to himself.

Matt and Mrs. Thompson started to object, but after an encouraging nod from the nurse, they wandered away down the hall, timid as Hansel and Gretel without breadcrumbs to follow, in search of bathrooms and coffee.

"Thanks, man!" Terry said, flashing a conspiratorial smile as Dave wheeled him into the imaging room.

Under the watchful eye of a starchy female technician, the suddenly serious nurse helped him onto the CT table and the strange procedure began.

Being slowly sucked into the body of a gigantic X-Ray machine was pretty science-fictiony, but Terry felt okay if he pretended he'd done it before. Maybe on some other planet where people's true motivations could be mapped by electronic radiation.

Wadn't so bad lying there with his head stuck inside a mechanical donut, he decided, forcing himself to look up when he wanted to shut his eyes. And vice versa, when the tech reversed her directions.

In a weird way, there wadn't much difference between lyin' here on his back, pinned inside a machine like overaged caterpillar stuck in a squeeze-box chrysalis, and moppin' floors every day at his dead-end janitorial job.

Both were a goddamn drag.

What really got Terry's goat—and what was left of his mind—was knowing his dad had been ripped off by the duplicitous dick who was fucking his mom. Wadn't the stolen money that pissed him off, or even the outright fraud. It was the two men having been friends, at least according to his dad.

Poor deluded Theodore Thompson, whose mind had turned into a jumble of tangled connections. Like his was now apparently. He'd had a few concussions as a kid. Pretty bad one time when he got beaned by a poorly-aimed baseball. But Terry had never felt quite as peculiar as he did right now. Confused. Beat down. Sore in body and mind.

He was suddenly glad to be in the hospital. If not safe from the medical terrors in his head, at least having them seen to by professionals. His brain kept repeating silly phrases and he knew it was spizzing like Matt's. He wanted to say the words out loud but he'd been told to keep perfectly still. A swarm of vicious swear words toyed for first place in a hierarchy of ridiculousness with words that didn't make any sense.

"Idn't it weird what can happen to people's minds?" he wanted to say, giving voice to his tumultuous thoughts. Envisioning Nurse Dave's disappointment, and the tech's probable frown, he clenched his teeth and shut up.

"Relax your jaw," the seemingly omniscient technician ordered anyway, making him want to bite her.

"Shee-it!" Terry suddenly exclaimed, realizing that no one had notified Isabel that he was *in here*. That he might be brain-damaged. Although, on the bright side, that hadn't been established yet. His concussion was supposed to be temporary.

"Please don't move!" ordered the exasperated technician. "Or we'll have to start again."

"Yeah, hang in there, *Terrace*. I mean *Terrance*," counseled Nurse's Dave's jolly voice, from somewhere outside the creepy metallic circle that had eaten Terry's head.

Eventually the tiresome imagining process was completed and Terry was wheeled up to the second floor by the nurse, who turned out to be a proud Casper native, third generation.

"One of the first black families in Casper. And not a janitor in the whole damn bunch, no offense. Pharmacists and shopkeepers. Middle-class Wyoming people. Like you." Dave explained as he readied Terry's room and got him into bed.

Terry lay back on the over-bleached hospital pillows after Dave fluffed them. "How do you know that?"

"What?"

"That I'm middle-class."

Dave wrote something on a chart after checking Terry's pulse. "Well, aren't you?"

Terry shrugged, which hurt his neck. Or maybe it was his shoulders that were wrecked.

"Guess so. Then again, maybe not. My dad worked hard all his life providing for his family. But it was always a struggle based on the oil market and boom-and-bust times in

Casper. My mom was a housewife, which I think is purty cool now, but still . . ." Terry's voice trailed off.

He felt tired and increasingly disembodied. He had to sleep or he'd be as brain challenged as Matt.

And sleep did come, after Dave, nursing duties done, left the room in a sweet little cloud of good humor, bidding him goodbye after cheerily advising him to stay the heck out of Casper.

It was dark when Terry woke up. For a second he thought he was back in the emergency room with the pretty blonde Doctor, coming to after getting his head stitched up.

No, no, he was home in bed with a stinging headache and a deep ache in his skull that felt dangerous. And God, he was hungover and thirsty.

Next thing he knew he was back in a dream again, although he wasn't quite sure he was sleeping. Maybe he was in some kind of alternate reality, like the hapless heroes in the time- travel stories he liked to read in the lunchroom at work about guys who end up in the wrong historical era or cosmic dimension, then don't want to leave or get stuck.

Everything was pleasantly fuzzy and floaty and surreal. He was in the company of cotton-candy angels. Or maybe he was dead. In spite of the scan and the doctor.

He could see his mom and Matt sitting on either side of his bed when he opened his eyes, scratching his trusty sideburns fiercely to make sure he was actually awake and not just wandering about in a dream story.

"Hey Bean," Terry said.

Matt snapped to alert attention although he'd been dozing. Mrs. Thompson likewise. Pulling their cheap plastic visitor's chairs closer to his bed, they began showering him with information, interspersed with joyful ejaculations about how lucky he was.

"You coulda been killed," Mrs. Thompson moaned. "By my *husband* . . ."

Gently patting her hand, like a baby patting a dog, Terry told his mother to hush. "I'm all right, Ma. Ever-thin's okay. Dudn't matter what happened before. Or who did what to who. Just gotta be here now. Like *good ol' walleroo* . . ."

"Er, pretty sure he means Ram Dass," Matt quickly put in, to Terry's mother's confused look of concern.

Her son was babbling and her second husband was a bully and a swindler. Dear God, but you had to feel sorry for her, Terry thought. Although for a brief selfish moment, he was not. She'd married Green. Put his dad in a home. Given him and Matt hats that looked like bumble bees. Fuck her and the lame-brained horse she rode in on.

A lot of what his mom and Matt said over the next half hour went over Terry's head, but most of their news was good. No bleeding in his brain had been noted on his CT scan, no signs of additional head trauma, nothing that might result in seizures or aneurisms, his mother reported, tripping over her words as she quoted Doctor Malden.

But there were things he couldn't do until his concussion receded. No reading or looking at screens for the next few days. No strenuous exercise and no work for a couple of weeks until Terry passed muster on a neurological exam. No stress, no fighting. No drugs or alcohol. And no riding his Harley.

"In short, a boring damn life," Mrs. Thompson said, laughing and crying from relief, and Terry started crying, too.

His heart felt near to breaking although he was glad he was alive.

Matt was going to turn in the Kia for a better rental car so they could drive back to Seattle, instead of going by plane which could fuck with Terry's concussion. They'd stay at the Marriot until Terry felt ready to go, take it slow and easy on the way home, and stop whenever they needed to. Maybe check out Yellowstone.

"A spontaneous road trip," Matt said, trying to put a good face on things, which Terry appreciated, although the idea of traveling eleven hundred miles in a strange vehicle, with a disorienting concussion, and a driver he pretty much didn't trust, made him exceedingly anxious.

It was weird watching Matt's eyes as he rattled on about their rearranged travel plans, but Terry couldn't stop searching for signs of distress in the amber-colored orbs which looked so much like an owl's. The poor guy ought to be in the hospital, too—maybe in the psychiatric ward. He looked like a little swizzle stick that had been stirred so hard it had broken.

Terry turned his face towards the wall and shut his eyes when his mom started talking about the house painter. He didn't want to know that Green was in jail. He wanted to know that the man had been cut to pieces, like a dismembered whale in a Japanese fishing village, after his oversized head was bashed in.

His befuddled statement about things not mattering and being here now was an out-and-out lie. Terry wanted to kill the guy. He just couldn't think how.

But he'd figure that out before they left Casper.

His mind kept wandering from point to point, person to person and none of it made any sense, except for passing sensations—the bleachy pillowcase next to his face, the smell of coffee on his mom's breath when she bent down to kiss him, the numbness in his chest when he tried to visualize Isabel.

The thought of her made him open his eyes and fix them on Matt. "Has she heard the news?"

"Who?"

Matt was fidgeting with his glasses which must have been bent in the fight. But he was buying for time, not trying to fix them, because it was obvious that Terry meant Isabel. The only other woman who cared about him was his mom, sitting right here in his room.

Terry enunciated his words very carefully. Matt was a fuckin' idiot. "*Isabel*. Didja call Isabel? Does she know I'm in the fuckin' horse-pistol?"

Matt mumbled something weird about Madam Zodie that Terry couldn't quite catch, followed by a pathetic, "No. I'm sorry. I didn't call her," and some histrionic handwringing.

Snorting disdainfully, Terry sat up higher, jarring his head painfully. The stitches on the back of his head hurt, and he felt like he wanted to puke, but he could still punch Matt hard on the arm, so he did. Twice.

"Ow!" Matt reared back but not too far—he knew he had it coming.

"So Isabel dudn't know what the hell's going down back here in Casper. Just thinkin' that I haven't called like I said I would." Terry slugged Matt's arm again. "Wouldja just get a hold a her, dude? I can't use my phone."

"Yeah. Yeah," Matthew said, looking more than usually uncomfortable.

Terry's mother asked, "Who's Isabel?" but Terry didn't answer.

Drifting back to sleep after his loved ones were shooed out of his room by a conscientious nurse who said Dave had gone home, Terry dreamed he was fishing with his dad. Big fat trout—the kind that had all but disappeared in the last twenty years, according to Mr. Thompson's last coherent letter—leapt and frolicked in a deep stream near Alcova Dam.

Almost jumping onto the two men's baited hooks, as if dying to be caught, the trout writhed and twirled, scales flashing in the sun, a thousand little points of silver and green, reminding Terry of the glittery baubles in his mom's old jewelry box.

One big gem dove and spun and another one formed the connecting link in a long chain of causal activities. Terry's fate was bound up with the fish and then he was one of them. Swimming in the water. Heaving his body. Thrashing his powerful tail.

"Dive deep!" A passing fish, leaving a colorful trail in the water, called out to him.

"Die! Die!" shouted another one, squirming on the end of his father's fishing hook.

"You're safe," the smallest fish said, swallowing a tiny minnow.

He called out to Isabel in his mind, awash in hard to catch memories.

With a choking sound, Terry woke up and peered into the eerie room, half-lit by the lights from the nurses' station, wondering if the teeming river had drowned or saved him.

SHORT STRANGE TRIP

B ack at the motel, Matthew drank down a beer in one thirsty gulp, sitting on his unmade bed, still dressed in his bloody coat. The stains on it looked like Rorschach blots. Crushed flowers. Red insects. Cochineal. Weird that wearing his best friend's dried blood didn't make him feel sick. Maybe he was in shock.

Terry was recovering in the hospital, Mrs. Thompson was safely back at home, and Green was locked up in jail. Good things all, but not quite good enough for Matthew to fully relax or take off his clothes to sleep. He kept analyzing the terrible events of the day, with an eye to his eventual guilt.

He should have told Terry about Madam Zodie's prescient warning. Kept him away from the truculent house painter. Hit Green a whole lot harder when he had him down on the floor. Remembered to call Isabel.

So many things he should have and could have done—back in Seattle, over a metric fuck-ton of years, as well as in shit-stormy Casper—to be a better friend, a wiser and better man. He'd pretty much failed when it came to Terry, never mind Rosie and his screwed-up brothers, or his dead father and mother who'd never come back.

It seemed insane that everything had changed on a dime—or ten thousand bucks—that morning, less than fifteen minutes after entering the lawyer's office. The good-hearted legacy Terry had expected from his father's modest estate turned out to be something dark. Evil comes in all kind of well-meaning packages, but knowing that didn't help.

He fished another bottle out of the Styrofoam beer chest's pool of melted ice water, then lay back against the varnished headboard on a stack of flattened pillows on which had rested hundreds of troubled heads. Happy ones, too, he reckoned, remembering motel sex with Rosie at her athletic best, squatting over his tongue on muscular haunches, facing backwards while she sucked him off.

The sexy memory made him wish he could call her but for only a tiny second. Rosie was sucking and fucking Jackson now, in The Bastard's own bed, as well as expensive hotels, presumably. She didn't belong at a tacky cowboy motel or even at the middle-class Marriot. She was a rising star now, ascending on a rising cock, and he was nothing but an unwanted chauffeur for a friend he always betrayed.

He dialed Madam Zodie's number, putting off calling Isabel like he'd promised for as long as conscientiously possible. Watching his trembling fingers adjust to speaker phone felt weird. His hands didn't feel like they belonged to him even though they hurt from being savagely wrenched by Green. Even his palms were bruised.

Madam Zodie—Alice—must have been doing something mind altering before she answered. Checking out horoscopes or reading Tarot cards. Her voice sounded dreamy and distant.

"Hey, Matthew. How's it going?" she said, in a vaguely abstracted tone.

Matthew wanted to hem and haw, prolonging the pleasant moment where they almost seemed like friends, but he rushed on, uttering the self-damning words. "Terry's in the goddam hospital! I didn't tell him what you said."

"How is he? What happened?"

"His mom's crazy husband threw a jar at his head and he's got a bad concussion," Matthew explained, "CT scan didn't show anything else. He's staying in the hospital overnight but he's doing all right, I guess."

"Does Isabel know?" Madam Zodie said, a harder edge to voice.

Matthew blushed even though he was invisible to her. "No," he said, feeling guilty again.

"I'll text you her number. Do you want me to call her first?"

"I'm not totally inept. I can do that myself," Matthew said, lying about his basic self-definition while defending himself. He wanted Madam Zodie to like him even if he didn't like himself.

After a brief silence, Madam Zodie said, "It's not your fault, you know. You can't stop bad things from happening just because someone like me gives you a vague warning to watch out. I just wish I'd seen what was coming more clearly."

The rest of their conversation flashed by in a blur. Matthew felt like he was skydiving, plummeting down fast as he recited the details of the morning's sordid fights between Terry and the house painter and the house painter and him.

He pictured Madam Zodie curled up on the couch where he'd drunkenly slept on Halloween night, listening to his tainted words, and wished he was "sitting in a tin-can," calling her from the moon over a KU satellite band.

Maybe then she wouldn't seem so remote; there'd be a reason for her distant voice. And the butterflies in his chest wouldn't seem like caterpillars worming their way towards his innards.

"I might call you back after I talk to Isabel," Matthew ventured, when it was obvious it was time to hang up.

As soon as she said, "That would be good," in an efficient professional voice, he knew for sure that he wouldn't.

Feeling rebuffed, he stammered, "goodbye", and sat awhile peering into his empty beer bottle as if he was waiting for a genie to come out.

A pint of Jim Beam next to the lamp on the bedside table twinkled at him in a friendly manner, but he reached into the cooler for a beer instead, trailing his sore hands through melted ice water to soothe them, wishing he could dunk in his head.

Summoning his courage, he punched Isabel's number into his phone, after picking up her contact info from his text messages, hoping it might be easier talking to her than it had been conversing with her enigmatic and strangely desirable cousin.

But he stuttered when Isabel answered the phone, faltered when she started crying as their awkward conversation progressed, impotent as a child to comfort her. Chastened by her genuine concern for his injured friend—which seemed somewhat excessive, until he remembered she'd been recently widowed—Matthew struggled to explain the whole bloody day to her.

The severed animal heads on the walls of the lawyer's office, the berserker fight between Terry and his crooked "stepfather," Mrs. Thompson's contagious terror, Green's final attack, the medics and the cops and the hospital. The whirlwind pace of domestic disaster. The surreal yet familiar feel of it all.

The explanatory words tumbled out of his mouth, the phrases higgledy-piggledy, preceding his thoughts. He could feel a migraine coming on, or maybe a stroke, but worse, he could feel Isabel's distress snaking around his heart, squeezing hard.

"Promise you'll call me if Terry gets worse," she said, her voice, husky from crying, sounding so different from Madam Zodie's arch tone, yet so much the same.

Matthew picked up the whiskey bottle, unscrewed the top and took a big slug. "Terry's gonna be okay," he said stubbornly, almost believing it himself.

There was mayhem and madness everywhere and things that would never be right. But he didn't share that little bit of nihilism with Isabel since she was already worried sick. Score one for his higher self.

His lower self, however, wanted another four or five beers, but the cooler was empty when he stuck in his hand. It was imperative to get to the drive-thru liquor-store before he collapsed, but Isabel—Goddamn or bless her—had started to talk, so he listened politely, suppressing his urge to hang up.

In halting then sped-up words, she told him about being widowed before Terry came into her life. How her grief over her husband's death had rendered her incapable of joy and trust. How she was haunted and lost and frightened of love itself.

Isabel finished her poignant soliloquy by declaring, "I don't want to love Terry. But I do."

"He'll be happy to know that," Matthew said, and after that it was easy to say he would call her with an update tomorrow and to finally hang up.

Leaving the bedside lamp on, he went outside, glad that the room opened directly onto the deserted parking lot, where there was nobody looking at the blood on his jacket, just a few cars with Wyoming license plates and the feisty little Kia that was starting to feel like a friend.

The trip to the liquor store was quick, just five or six minutes driving through dusky streets, with the heady scent of wind-whipped cottonwoods streaming in through the open window, reminding him of what Terry said about everybody's past having a particular smell—Terry's, of course, being those fragrant trees.

Matthew loved the smell, but it wasn't his.

Sagebrush, red dirt, his mother's cowboy coffee—Folger's coffee grounds steeped in a big enamel pot, his father's nervous sweat, his brothers' sweaty socks, the thick black stinky coat of their crippled old Labrador—and always, beer and marijuana—perfumed his fondest, and worst, memories of Casper.

"Coors," he said to the clerk at the drive-thru liquor-store window, even though he preferred fancy IPA's. He always drank Coors in Wyoming.

Longneck twelve-pack and Ranch Doritos in hand, he started back to the motel, planning on taking a scalding hot shower before he got completely drunk, but at the crossroads of two main streets he took the wrong turn, letting his subconscious guide the Kia to the last place on earth he wanted to be. The Barker's old home.

Goddamn muscular memory, he groused, as he pulled up to the familiar curb, no longer on his broken-down paper-route bicycle, no longer worried about the state of his family inside, yet drawn inexorably towards the hated house as if by a powerful magnet.

He parked the car and turned off the ignition, rendering the dark familiar street creepy and silent. Inside the front room of his childhood house, dim lights shone through the heavy ceiling-to-floor curtains which had made him claustrophobic but his parents always liked.

Imaging his brothers curled up inside the fetid semi-dark like two evil chipmunks in the bole of a tree made him shudder with revulsion. Before he could stop himself, he was out of the car and walking up the front steps to the old screen door that used to have a long rip in its right side, letting in flies. The wooden door was metal now with nary a tear in sight. Score one for the feckless boys.

The front door opened from inside before he had a chance to knock. One of his brothers—Frank or Fred—stood there with a devilish smile on his mottled face, saying, "We been expecting you. Come in, brother."

Palpitations and panic attacks aside, Matthew didn't want to go into his old house without some kind of guarantee that he'd come out alive, but he stepped through the entryway into the living room anyway, saying, "I come in peace," which was sort of a lie.

Matthew's other brother was lounging on a rather nice-looking modular couch in front of a gigantic TV, and the one who'd let him inside pranced about the surprisingly tidy living room like an agitated otter playing hostess, exhorting him to "sit the fuck down!"

After a moment's hesitation, he did, lowering himself into his mother's tipsy old rocker, while the otter brother plopped down on the couch next to his remote-wielding twin.

The two guys leaned back against the couch cushions looking placid and sensible, entirely different creatures than the hostile monsters at the bus stop menacing him earlier that day. Matthew surveyed them with a skeptical eye as if pinpointing the glitches in a computer program, and said, "I don't know why I'm here," adding manfully, "But it's good."

"Yeah, man," it seemed like Frank said. His hair was a tiny bit thicker and darker than his twin's, but their jutting brows were the same. Goddamn Neanderthals, Matthew thought, feeling ashamed.

Frank pinned Matthew with a squinty-eyed look which could have been taken as hostile. "What took you so long to get here?"

"Pussy," Fred hissed with a curl of his lip, before shooting a sideways paw at his brother for an awkward high five.

Matthew accelerated his nervous rocking, feeling infantile. "The last time I was here you said it was my fault mom and dad died and I didn't deserve my one third of the house. So I gave it to you guys. Remember?"

The twins nodded in unison.

Matthew was pretty sure it was Frank who said, "Dude, you always thought you was better n' us, but yer just another lost boy from Casper tryin' to make it in the big ol' world and it don't look like you done it so well."

"Frankly," he winked at his twin here so he must have been Fred, "You look like a raggedy ol' carcass a broke-down cougar dragged in from the scrub brush. What the fuck happened to you, anyway?" Fred's laconic voice dropped into a conspiratorial tone. "'Zat blood on yer jacket?"

The other twin snorted with laughter and began rolling a joint.

"We was just messin' with you at the bus stop but you shoulda seen yer damn face. Pale as Cinderella's snow-white tits, pussy-boy. Laughed our asses off all the way home rememberin' how easy it is to spook ya. Case a too many nerves, like mom always said."

"But maybe that don't matter too much when yer knockin' back Starbucks with Bill fuckin' Gates and Jeff fuckin' Bezos?" Frank suggested, taking a big hit off the doobie he'd just lit before passing it to Fred.

Fred sucked down some skunk smoke. "How fuckin' rich are ya, anyway?" he sputtered, after a series of hacking coughs. He handed the joint to Matthew. "Did ya bring any beer?"

"Uh, yeah . . . there's a twelve pack in the car." Matthew started to rise to go outside—maybe to escape—but Fred said no, he'd get the beer, just give him the goddamn car keys.

"Door's unlocked," Matthew said. He sat down again, feeling doomed.

Fred tromped outside in his ratty old mukluks, leaving the door wide open behind him, as usual. The resulting blast of cold air made Matthew shiver and pull his jacket closer around him. Or maybe it was the way Frank was looking at him—alternately dagger-like and confused.

Frank gestured at Matthew to take a hit and pass the joint. "You didn't bring us that beer, did ya?"

"Sure I did," Matthew said, glad, then sorry he was lying.

Once Fred was back and the door was closed, and he was drinking a thirst-quenching beer, Matthew felt a little bit lighter, a little bit brighter in spirit, than he had at the Residence Inn. Those awkward phone calls with the cousins had just about done him in. Not to mention the terrors of the previous ten hours in which Terry could have been killed.

Drinking beer with his brothers—unimaginable just twenty-four hours ago—and sitting in the living room of the family house he'd gladly escaped, felt surreally normal. He could almost imagine his mom and dad sitting on the tired old Penney's sofa the twins had replaced with the spiffy modular couch. Hear their voices, see their hands touch, oddly conjoined, as usual.

By the looks of it, the house seemed middle-class, respectable, well cared for if a bit shabby. The woodwork could use a coat of paint and the familiar tweedy rug had several worn spots. There was a pile of socks on the floor, two bags of chips and a Tupperware bowl of popcorn on the coffee table amidst the pot paraphernalia, and a few skin magazines peeking out from under the couch, but all in all it was a nice clean atmosphere.

Watching the twins chug their misappropriated beer and cram chips in their mouths in the clean domestic setting, it seemed almost reasonable to think that they'd changed somehow, were no longer potential monomaniacal savages of the kind that strung up Matthew Shepherd, or even the clueless dumb-fucks they'd proved themselves to be year after year.

They had a nice little well-kept house, some kind of income—at least partially lawful, he hoped—and, aside from this morning's bus stop debacle, seemed disinclined to fuck with him. They seemed friendly—or friendly-ish, almost civilized.

Maybe they'd actually changed. Could he trust them?

One more swig of beer. One more toke. One more stoned squinty-eyed look between Frank and Fred, excluding him. Was pretty much all it took for him to decide that no, maybe not. Maybe he could not actually. Now or ever. Trust them. He wasn't that goddamn fucking drunk yet. Or that stupid.

Memories of his brothers sitting on his chest, spitting in his face, skimmed the shallows of his mind like sharks surfacing to bite him. The creepy heebeegeebees the twins always gave him were back in gleeful force, demons with pitchforks, destroying his cautiously optimistic mood with a few well-aimed thrusts.

The lit up marquee in his head was flashing its seizure-inducing warning sign, just like it had that very morning, at the Green's. "GET OUT OF THE HOUSE! NOW!"

He stood up suddenly to go, setting the old rocking chair bouncing hard against the back of his legs, reminding him of his brothers' synchronized habit of kicking him when he was down.

"Where ya goin' Matty-boy?" Fred said, in the sneering voice that Matthew remembered from childhood as their father's own when he was pissed. And he was always pissed at Matthew.

"An' where's yer bum boy Ted?" Frank threw in, pretending not to remember Terry's name after thirty years of complaining about his "faggot" love for Matthew. "Back in Skedaddle fuckin' yer bitchy ex-wife, I betcha!"

Shit. Same old. Same old. Matthew sighed and started to amble towards the door, but he wasn't actually ambulatory.

His legs were as wobbly as cooked pasta. He could feel them collapsing onto the floor.

The twins bolted off the couch, quick as defenders against an armed intruder, and grabbed him by the arms. To steady or strangle him, he wasn't sure which. He flung himself against his brother's beefy carcasses like a man trapped in a speeding off-rail cattle car, braying like a branded steer, "Get away from me! Get away!"

Matthew's brothers kept tight hold of his arms as he struggled to fight them off. One pushing him towards the door, one pushing him towards the couch.

"*You* get away! Ya filthy fuckin' traitor! You get the hell outta this goddamn house where ya left us to rot with our crazy ol' mother!" Frank or Fred screamed in his face, showering him with rancid spittle.

"Who loved you the best. Stupid bitch," the other brother put in, unnecessarily.

Somehow Matthew's legs re-inflated themselves and his hands, hitting out at his brothers, connected with first one, then the other one's face—not hard, but effectually, enough for them to release their tug-of-war grips and swipe at their noses as if set on by horse flies.

"Hold on, lil' bro! Ya don't have to go," one of them cried as his twin sucker-punched Matthew's back. Or tried to. Frank and Fred were hardened fighters but their bodies were soft, and Matthew's, while rangy, was hard. Plus he didn't give a good goddamn who hit him or why. All he could think about was Jackson. And his dad. And these two toasted morons who could probably kill him if they tried.

But they wouldn't. Which made him stronger than them, his drunken brain boasted, right before he passed out.

BREAKFAST WITH THE BARKER BROTHERS

Waking up in his old bedroom in the Barker house wasn't as weird as waking up to the sound of his twin nemeses, standing next to his bed, discussing what they were going to do with him when he woke up with a mother of a hangover.

"Prolly needs Starbucks and all we got is Folgers," one of them said.

The other one snorted, "Tough shit. We got bacon and eggs. That'll fix him right up."

Matthew opened his eyes. He was lying prone, head pounding like a jackhammer. "And toast," he heard himself say into his pillow, before turning his head to look at his brothers. "Can I have some toast?"

"Fuck yeah," said the brother he recognized as Fred, since he was wearing a gas station shirt with his name on it, underneath the motto: "Conoco 24/7."

"Hey, bro', we got strawberry jam. Smucker's, not mom's, but so what." Frank punched Matthew's bare arm, reminding him of Terry. Fuck! He needed to call the hospital and check on him ASAP.

He rubbed his punched arm. What happened to his clothes?

Frank punched him again, a little bit harder. "Take a piss and warsh the drool off n' yer face. Lucky fer you, we warshed the puke outta yer clothes. Didn't we, brother?"

Crap on a stick, there were too many brothers in this fusty old room, seemingly preserved in amber since he left it. Matthew struggled to sit up, eying the Peter Frampton and Metallica posters on the walls with alarm. Had he really been a lovesick teenaged head-banger? What happened to his Elvis Costello records?

Once ensconced in the rinky-dink, lemon-colored 50's-era bathroom, he stood under the shower for fifteen blissful hot minutes, marveling that he hadn't been killed by Green or bludgeoned to a pulp by his brothers, that Terry was in the hospital not him.

He scrubbed his head fast, trying to wash away his hangover with a bar of Irish Spring, buoyed by the poignancy of his present location. Being in the one place of solace he'd ever found in the Barker house. The bathroom. With its reliable lock on the door.

Matthew went into the kitchen, wrapped in a towel, asking where he might find his clothes. The proud old green Formica table—worth at least five hundred dollars in a high-class junk shop in Seattle—was covered with plates of tasty looking breakfast food.

Frank pulled Matthew's jeans, shirt, underpants, and socks out of the kitchen dryer while Fred poured thick slugs of black coffee into gigantic mugs emblazoned with rampaging bears. "Grizzly County!!" the mugs said in bright orange lettering. In the background, geysers that looked like burnt marshmallows erupted in thick white smoke.

"At yer specific command," said Fred, setting a platter of crisp buttered toast down in front of Matthew after he'd dressed and sat down, barefoot, cold feet somehow grounding him. Making it harder to run away.

But he didn't want to run. He wanted to eat and eat to feed the hangover worm in his guts. The over-medium eggs cooked in bacon grease, the cracking rashers of pork, the sweet crunchy, then glutinous mass of the nutty toast and jam, comforting as Seattle Sunday brunch in a time warp.

Shoveling food into his mouth like a starving convict, in jail with the twins—also starving, judging by how greedily they ate—the tiny portion of Matthew's mind that didn't feel gluttonous admonished him to be wary of his brothers' unexpected hospitality and kindness. They might have spiked his plate with poison or spat on it, or some other egregious offense.

They were mean motherfuckers. Yet how silly they looked with jam and eggs on their faces. Slurping their thick-as-shit coffee. Burping and farting and snorting as they chewed and laughed and bellyached about the losers in Casper. Which they were definitely not, they staunchly declared. They didn't do meth anymore. They had jobs!

"Me and the brother," Frank said, as if he had only one, "Well, me and him were thinkin' about opening our own garage. Even though the local economy still purty much stinks. Same's it always did. We're good with trucks and people like our work."

Frank took a big bite of toast and nodded sagely at Fred before glaring at Matthew. "Duddn't matter what any-bawdy says about our non-existent business sense."

"I never said that," Matthew declared, springing to his own defense, however pointlessly.

Neither of the twins ever listened to him even though they swore they did. Quoting back ancient insults he supposedly tossed out at them with the insouciance, if not the wit, of

Oscar Wilde, getting his words all wrong. Mistaking satire for the truth and truth for fiction and anger for hurt. Just like their mixed-up dad.

"Nah. Never mind," Fred said, playing go-between for a change. Although far back in their childhoods, he'd occasionally gone against his twin and championed *him*, Matthew suddenly recalled, remembering Fred's secret late night tutorials in how to get Frank's goat.

Frank had been the hard one to beat or satisfy, although both of the twins were indefatigable about maintaining a strict fraternal hierarchy in which baby brother was their unwilling slave. But on some level, Frank too had gone to bat for Matthew, back in the Barker house past. Stepped in to catch the punishment when their father was primed to go on a verbal attack aimed at Matthew.

Matthew gulped down the last of his bacon with a lump in his throat, remembering those fraternal salutary times with a frisson of distress that he'd forgotten them for such a long time. Most of his adult life, seemingly. Every good memory of growing up with his brothers had been ruthlessly, then routinely, suppressed so that he could keep thinking of them as irredeemable oafs, guilty of every sin against their family. Against him.

Yet he'd been the stupid one. Tried to run away from home when there is no running away from blood or *terroir*—the particular topography and climate of one's past. Or the smell of cottonwoods, he thought, starting to get up to call Terry at the hospital, then sitting down again to share the bad news about his bashed-in friend with the twins.

They seemed somewhat concerned but philosophical. Fred said, "Tough luck. Poor bastard." And Frank said, "He still a fag? Iddn't too good to be gay around here." And then Fred said, "Bad news about his mom's new man. Never did trust me no house painters. Alkies and huffers, most likely." He was smoking a joint and doing a crossword in an old Sunday paper while Frank cleared the table.

What the fuck day was it anyway?

Matthew scratched the stubble on his face, wondering if he looked as crummy as he felt. Eating the massive breakfast had stopped the roiling in his belly but a leaden headache lingered on, making him feel like he had a metal cap pulled down tight on his skull like one of those old chainmail helmets.

Leaving his brothers to clean up the kitchen, he went back in his old bedroom to call Terry. No answer from Terry's cell phone, so he called the front desk at the hospital and got switched through to the nurses' station. A familiar voice answered. Thank God. Nurse Dave.

"'Bout time you called in. Your friend Terry's raring to get out of here. Needs a decent cup of coffee, I guess, and some of your rain. Said the wind kept him awake all night." Dave chuckled appreciatively. "That dude's got some fun stories about Casper, though. Witches up on the mountain, ghosts at the Planetarium, and such. Cool stuff I never knew."

Matthew's anxiety level rose at the mention of witches—a subliminal reminder of Madam Zodie, perhaps—then dropped when Nurse Dave said that Terry would be ready to be checked out at noon, just forty minutes away. He was getting a final exam before discharge, which was why he hadn't answered his phone.

The nurse's cheerful voice went on in a bit more business-like tone. "We'll go through everything you need to know about taking care of Terry while you're driving him home. Give you a list of potentially worrisome things to look out for. But we're pretty sure he's going to be fine. So just get here by noon. Okay?"

"Roger that!" Matthew sighed with woozy relief as the tight muscles in his neck and scalp released.

No bags to collect, just his blood-stained jacket, and red-dirt-stained running shoes which he put on after regarding himself in the pockmarked bathroom mirror where his mother used to put on her drugstore makeup, the coral lipstick and Chantilly cologne her husband always liked.

He looked like shit, although not quite as execrable as he might have, if he'd gone back to the motel and kept on drinking last night, not eaten the surprisingly delicious breakfast his brother's had made, not slept in his familiar old bed, with his feet hanging out of the covers—too hot as usual, in spite of the low-forties temperature.

Saying goodbye and thank you to the twins, who stood in the doorway beaming at him benignly, after solemnly pumping his hand, felt almost as surreal as his encounter with them at the bus stop, or the fight at the Green's house the day before.

"Thought we was gonna kill ya, but you was wrong," Fred said, punching Matthew's sore right arm for emphasis.

Frank nodded his big shaggy bison-like head. "Yeah, we're not the same mud-suckers we used ta be. Couple dee-vorces and stints in the clinker kinda changed our minds about how to live our piss-ant lives." A wicked grin, showing the gap between his crooked front teeth, the same gap as Fred's. "But we still hate ya, little brother."

Tears welled in Matthew's eyes. "I hate you, too," he said. And in some ways he still did, but in better newer more loving ways, he didn't. He might not be exactly feel comfortable with the twins, but his fear of them was gone. They were his brothers, after all, not monsters.

His little surge of comforting elation was immediately capped by Frank's parting words. "You'd a come home for Christmas, like you promised ya would, mom and dad wouldn't a died comin' ta see you. An' ya didn't even come to their funeral . . . You had your damn fool head stuck so far up yer purty wife's ass ya couldn't see straight."

Frank put his meaty paw on Matthew's now slumping shoulder, Fred looking on with an unreadable smirk that might or might not have been compassionate. "No-bawdy blames ya for stickin' to her like flies on shit—even though you were a terrible fit—or your slick urban life that mom said was so good fer you. But ya shoulda come home, brother. Mom needed you."

"After ya went off to the big damn city, everything went ta hell," Fred put in, looking objectively sorrowful. "Leastwise, when it came to our folks. Dad was holed up in the basement fixing old radios while me and Frank were runnin' wild. And Mom was lonely as hell 'cause she missed you so much. Which she sure as shit let us know."

Crap. No, don't tell me that now, Matthew wanted to say, hating them all over again for killing his memory of his mom as a contented soul who loved her life even though she had a difficult husband and horrible kids and never got to do a goddamn thing she really wanted to. But all he said was, "Crap," as he stared wide-eyed at his brothers.

So this was goodbye.

Afterwards, driving to the hospital, he cried for his mother and father, and his tired yet true twin brothers, for Mr. Thompson and Terry and Terry's mother, and Isabel and her dead husband, for enigmatic Alice who was Madam Zodie, trying to make sense of the world.

No tears for Green. Or Jackson or Rosie. Although those would come later, when he was safe at home in bed, leaning back on his own pillow, looking out through wavering curtains at dim stars trying to twinkle over city-lit Lake Washington, exhausted from the trip back from Casper. Relieved to have brought Terry safely home. Then he would shed tears for everyone.

But first things first. A semblance of order. Increments of moving time. Not to say that forethought and foreshadowing, aftereffects and altered states, foresight and hindsight, presentiments or the lapsing of linear time, had no meaning or purpose here.

But, for Matthew, now had to simply be *now*—him pulling into the hospital parking lot, him getting out of the car, walking down the hall to the nurses' station. He couldn't stand what might happen to his brain, already blinking with the dreaded white strobe light of neural anxiety, if he let it overheat with visions of the future or memories of the past. It—he—might explode.

No alternative universes. Just this place. Here and now. Is what he told himself as he entered Terry's room.

AIN'T ALRIGHT

Matt wanted to go to the hot springs at Thermopolis but Terry didn't want to. Nor did he want to drive through Yellowstone on the way back home.

Casper to Billings, where they'd stay the first night, then Billings to Coeur d'Alene—a longer traveling day than the day before, but they'd be closer to home, then on to Seattle—was the only route he wanted, Terry said, fixing Matt with a bloodshot eye.

Turning their trip into a week-long vacation, like Matt suggested, was out of the goddamn question. Three days and two nights on the road was all Terry could handle, concussion or no. Back in the day they'd made the trip in Terry's granddad's classic old Ford in under twenty hours, eating Stop and Rob hotdogs in the car, stopping just to pee and fill up the gas tank. If Terry had his druthers, they'd do the same now, but, thanks to doctor's orders, he didn't.

He made a few concessions to the dictates of his physical health, but he wasn't going to be a day-tripping wimp. Yeah, Matt could drive, and they'd steal one of the motel pillows so he could stretch out on the backseat of the obscene new over-sized rental car, but that was about all Terry would agree to about going home.

Grey-faced and haggard looking, Terry sat silently for most of the first day after they drove out of Casper, pottering up Highway 25, until Buffalo where it joined Interstate 90, in the huge SUV that was supposed to be comfortable but wasn't. Every time Matthew wanted to step on the gas and take advantage of the behemoth's surging horsepower, Terry said, "Cut it out," or "Slow down," so they meandered along in the slow lane like a couple of geriatrics lost in the opposite of hyperspace.

Chivalrously Matt ignored the irony of slowing their pace when Terry was so hot to get home, but couldn't help glancing at his morose passenger with obvious concern from time to time, which should have pissed Terry off, but apparently didn't.

"Take a picture. It'll last longer," Terry finally said, but there was no bite in his sarcasm. He sounded wrung out, which he was.

Everything Terry saw and heard made him feel sick. The rumble of the SUV's big engine, the roar of accompanying traffic, the vast swathes of desolate landscape interspersed with the august beauty of the Big Horn Mountains, the moth-eaten antelope and deer foraging behind rickety snow fences.

His head hurt, his body hurt, his mind hurt; the house painter's assault having done its work to undermine him. Although his heart hurt for other reasons than being on the receiving end of hammering fists and Green's egregious betrayal of his dad and mom. He desperately and despondently missed Isabel.

But Terry was a practical man.

No matter how much he longed to speak to Isabel, to apologize for his insensitive and selfish behavior, his jealousy of the intensity of her grief, there was no way in hell he was going to call her when he was on the road with Matt, dependent and impaired, unable to speak in anything but the shorthand monosyllables of an injured freak.

She deserved better than that.

Lying in his hospital bed last night, with his phone clutched in his shaky hand, he'd tried to talk himself into calling, but all he'd managed was a text, "Know you're thinking of me. I'm thinking of you," which he quickly erased. The first statement was a huge assumption. The second innocuous. *Shee-it.*

Isabel probably didn't want to talk to him anyway, although Matt had said she was concerned about him, had cried during their awkward phone call. But the real reason Terry couldn't call, which he tried, unsuccessfully, to hide from himself, was that he was scared. Scared of saying the wrong thing, scared of scaring her off with his rearranged thoughts—due as much to the exigencies of his father's death and being in Casper as to his brain-altering concussion—and, most debasing of all, scared of Isabel herself, and what she already meant to him.

Which is what? he asked himself intermittently but regularly as the SUV head north then east from Wyoming to Montana, Matt's hand's loose on the wheel but a tight expression on his face, as if there was something he needed to say but couldn't. For once in their friendship there was no small talk just a pervasive uneasy quiet when they weren't listening to country-and-western songs or classic-rock radio.

Terry alternately dozed and daydreamed in the front seat, ignoring the makeshift bed in the back, the stolen blanket and dented motel pillow that had soaked up his tears the night before he went to the lawyer's office. When he wasn't worrying about his uneasy relationship with Isabel, or the safety of his mother when Green got out of jail, he thought about his father, reliving childhood days when he felt as if the two of them were parts of a unified pair, big and little versions of the same self, the prototypical Thompson male.

No time was spent thinking about his relationship with Matt, a gratifying change from the recent usual, although Terry was grateful for his old friend having defended him from Green. He had less confidence in the Ol' Bean's driving abilities but had ceased giving a shit about imminent danger since it was everywhere.

They ate "whiskey burgers" and fries at the Main Street Applebee's in downtown Billings at six o'clock then headed for a motel in the chilly November dark. The wind was up and the air smelled of snow, the external car thermometer registering 37 degrees, dropping a degree by the time they parked the SUV in the lot at the Best Western.

Terry was too tired to take a shower, so he dabbed at his face and teeth with a wet washcloth, and then crawled rather than fell into bed, rickety as a rheumatic old man. Matt kept pacing the floor and taking hits off the big fat joint he'd stolen from the twins. It was obvious Matt wanted to talk, but there was nothing really to say, as far as Terry was concerned. He rolled over, turning his back, and soon sleep had him, blotting out everything but the dream.

Big yellow stars twinkling in a deep blue sky. Forked lightning, peals of thunder, then the crackle of an old Bakelite radio like Matt liked to fix. A howling wolf. A sobbing child. His mother's voice whispering, "Hush." Flower petals falling on black wet streets like shreds of rubber confetti. His Harley, equipped with translucent wings, soaring aloft like a dragonfly. Roiling images, arresting sounds, and none of it sensible, even in the lucid dream state in which he found his consciousness piqued by the ridiculousness of reality.

Why am I having this dream? Terry wondered. Not *why am I in it*. For he was not in the dream, merely watching and listening from outside, as if parked in a car at a drive-in, watching an old horror movie. All night long—or what seemed like all night—he surfed the surface of the dream, never diving in, never coming to any sort of recognizable shore.

Waking in the dark, blessedly free of the disjointed images and sights, Terry checked the steal-proof built-in alarm clock at the side of his bed and found it was eleven p.m. Matt's bed was empty but there was a sliver of light at the bottom of the bathroom door which meant he was probably taking a piss or getting ready for bed.

"Hey, Ol' Bean!" he cried, suddenly afraid of the dark. Where the fuck was that weird table-lamp switch? Where was his fucking phone?

No answer. Maybe Matt was taking a shower? But there was no sound of running water or the low hum of a hairdryer. Terry yelled again and again, but there was no answer. Why couldn't Matt hear him calling?

Fumbling with the slippery bedcover which had wound itself around him like a rank cocoon, Terry struggled out of bed and tottered to the bathroom door, pushing it open a crack.

"Matt?"

Opening the door wider, letting light stream into the room, he stepped onto cold linoleum. Blinking in confusion, scalp prickling with fear, he gazed around the tiny bathroom.

Except for the normal porcelain fixtures and a wadded-up towel on the floor, it was empty.

What the fuck!

Navigating by the 100-watt light of the tiny bathroom, he made it back to bed, where he sat on the edge, shivering, and nauseated, but too confounded to get back under the covers.

Ok, he told himself, Matt's probably gone to get some ice, or a Coke from the vending machine in the motel lobby where there was also a gigantic flat-screen TV. Perhaps he was hunkered down with a candy bar, watching the late-night news. Or chatting up the pretty concierge who'd checked them in four hours ago.

Wobbly with exhaustion, reeling from the lingering doomsday sensation he'd carried since the moment right before Green's well-aimed kitchen missile hit him smack in the head, he looked down at his hands, surprised to see he was clutching his phone.

Taking this as a sign, he dialed Isabel's number, abstractly wondering if dialing was still the right term to use, since he was no longer turning a disk simply pressing a digital keyboard. His thumping heartbeat had quieted down a bit, which was good, since he could hardly hear Isabel's voice over the roaring in his ears which he hoped didn't mean he was having a stoke.

Gol-dang it, when did he get so damned paranoid?

"It's *me*," Terry said, pleased that he could lay claim to that intimate pronoun, even if she didn't love him.

"Oh Jesus!" Isabel yelped. "I've been thinking about you day and night. Wondering how you're doing since I talked to Matthew. Kind of going out of my mind, to tell you the truth. Wondering if you'd ever call me."

"Told ya I would." Terry was shocked by his gravelly baritone. Had he always sounded this much like a cigar-smoking drunk? Yet he went on, somehow impervious to the enormous effort it took him to talk, to form the formless words of an abject apology, at the same time as he was screaming inside. Unsure of everything. Missing his dad.

"Shee-it," he began, hating his crassness when he wanted to be delicate.

At the same time he wanted to mutter "I done ya wrong,'" like a hoary ol' cowpoke, and move on to the good part, where Isabel forgave him before he spelled out his sins. His awful male chauvinism, his abandonment of her, his insatiable desire for sex.

Terry paused, hoping Isabel would play out his fantasy with instant absolution, but she was silent, waiting for him to go on.

"I did you wrong and I'm sorry for runnin' away. For not callin' you before I left for Casper. Or after my mom's jerk of a thievin' husband clobbered my stupid head. For being a real insensitive prick plus a dick and a cad and a crumb-bum."

Isabel laughed. "Crumb-bum. That's a new one for me."

Terry sighed with relief. "Dunno 'xactly what it means either, but it's me. I'm just sorry, like I said. And I need your forgiveness."

Another inscrutable silence from Isabel, even though it was brief. He used to think he could read her. But now he didn't think that he could.

"You have it," she blessedly said, easing his heartache, before increasing it again by adding, "But I'm still angry at you. Which is really hard when you've been hurt and are faraway. Yet another conundrum of our brief relationship, wouldn't you say?"

There were so many things Terry did want to say about conundrums and love but he just didn't have time. The key click in the room's metal door had signaled Matt's return just a few moments before.

The interloper tiptoed through the semi-dark room like a stealthy parent checking on a sleeping child. Swearing sotto voce but vociferously after banging into chair, Matthew sat down on the floor, muttering inanities, apparently unaware that Terry was sitting up in bed attempting to talk on the phone.

"Hang on a minute," Terry whispered to Isabel, before growling, "Fer cryin' out loud," at Matt, whom he pretty much wanted to hit, but the dude was too far away.

"Who's cryin'?" the drunk ass said, falling over into a floppy fetal position, frustrating Terry who wanted to stay in bed without further disturbance while he finished his difficult call.

Recognizing the necessities of his present ridiculous reality, Terry slid out of bed and crawled into the bathroom, where he sat with his back against the door, bare-assed on the cold linoleum, shivering and pouring sweat from the palms of his shaking hands. Turning on speaker-mode, he put down his slippery phone.

"Sorry about that," he said, prosaically, when he wanted to say something pretty and profound like *Il Professore* might say, wooing Isabel with Renaissance poetry crooned in the original French.

Isabel's voice was tight. "Are you all right?"

"Yeah . . . No . . . I dunno . . . Duddn't seem like, huh?" Terry babbled stupidly, staring down at his phone with a rigid intensity, willing his sudden upsurge of jealousy to melt away, so he could stop picturing Charlie serenading Isabel.

"No, it doesn't," Isabel said, in what seemed like a more loving voice. But maybe it was just friendly concern. "Are you in bed? How's your head? Maybe I should talk to Matthew?"

Terry chuckled through chattering teeth. "Dude's drunk on his ass. I'm sittin' in a shit-hole, thinkin' I should take a bath to warsh the Wyoming off." And to warm up. He was freezing.

Isabel laughed for the second time in their truncated conversation, transforming his mirth from frantic to fondly familiar. What a woman! If only he could say that he loved her!

And—throwing caution to the wind of the bathroom's moldy old fan—Terry would have, too. If only Matt hadn't started yelling, "What's going on in there?" while hammering hard on the flimsy door.

Terry put a hand over his phone, in a pointless attempt to disguise the ruckus. "I'm takin' a shower!" he yelled, cursing his friend's bad timing.

"I really gotta go," he eventually confessed, when Matt kept pounding on the door. "Call you when we get home." *We* not I. As ever, joined like balls to a dick like Matthew.

"Get the fuck away!" Terry cried, after ending his call, free now to rage and swear without embarrassment. The fire in his head that might have been lust or love a mere moment ago had turned to treacly loathing, for he suddenly hated Matthew with a sour sweetness that felt unendurable.

Who else made his life so gol-dang miserable? Who else shit in his face? No other selfish martyred little shit on the planet came close to the Ginger Menace in his neurotic need to be loved. His ability to suck the dear life out of everything.

Door hammering turned to claw-like scratching. Terry imagined Matt nosing the door like a cat. "I don't hear any water running in there," Matt hissed disconsolately, and then, getting no answer, raised his voice to a shout, "I'm responsible for you. Please! Let me in!"

Terry almost felt sorry for Matt but he didn't give in. He just got up and turned on the taps. He needed a bath—not a shower—a complete baptismal emersion—peace and quiet—a place to think—and the door was locked, thank himself not God—so all he said back to his panicky friend was "See ya after I'm done!"

Impossible to stretch out full length in the tiny little tub, and leaning back meant that his knees stuck up like bony islands in the hot soapy water, but for almost ten minutes after Matt stopped his infernal pounding, he was as content as he was dejected and mortified.

Thoughts flying and fluttering—dragonflies and butterflies, intransigent birds—Terry let his mind float free until the water cooled from scalding to hot, then got out of the tub and dried off.

Opening the bathroom door a crack, he looked out. As predicted, Matt was fast asleep on his bed, still wearing the wool winter cap that Mrs. Thompson had given him.

A sliver of fear pierced Terry's heart at the thought of his mom, but he manfully and sadly suppressed it. When they'd said goodbye that afternoon, she'd confessed that she was planning on taking Green back when he got out of jail.

She'd made her damn bed, let her lie—sleep—die—in it.

Back in bed, Terry scrunched up his pillows so he could half recline, half sit up, in order to watch some TV, even though he wasn't supposed to. His warmed up body felt almost relaxed, but his tired brain was still reeling. He needed something to focus on besides his passed out buddy's rough breathing. A digital mandala or some such. An image or images to soothe him.

He scrolled through the channels, stopping to watch a few seconds here and there of seemingly interchangeable programming. News, weather, cowboy stuff—this was Montana—on local broadcasting. Cooking and sports and reality shows, dorky comedies and gritty dramas on cable and Netflix. Same old. Nothing new.

Until like a magic trick gone awry—or maybe fantastically realized—one set of familiar faces popped into view as the electronic pictures flipped by.

Christ on a bike! It was Jackson and Alex again! Jackson and Alex! And Rosie!!

Terry gawped at the terrible trio being interviewed by Anderson Cooper, who seemed absolutely delighted by them. Brand was writing a Broadway burlesque show for Rosie at the same time as he was finishing up his Capote-esque literary collusion with Alex. Rosie's two lovers sat on either side of her, but Jackson was the focal point of attention.

Icy blonde Jackson with his barbed smile, glamorous Alex with his Zoot suit and coils of inky black hair, red-and-white Rosie with her impressive décolletage and come-hither smile. Each personality soft and sharp. Aggressive and docile.

They seemed as exotic and mysterious—and dangerously beautiful—as angels to Terry, watching them for less than a minute, before he sprang out of bed, and shook Matt by the shoulders, shouting, "Ya gotta see this! Wake up, dude! Wake up!"

But, alas, to no avail. Matt snorted and muttered and turned on his side, before opening his eyes in confusion. "Wha'?" Matthew mumbled, looking towards where Terry was pointing.

But there was nothing to see except a promotional news ad with the CNN logo. The interview was done.

Terry laughed bitterly. Struck once again by life's ironies. How people's lives bled into each other. And occult coincidences and synchronicities took roundabout—often maddening—ways to reach individuals. The lack of pattern consistency hurt his head.

He patted Matt on the shoulder, whispering, "Go back to sleep, buddy."

CHERRY PIE

asy Peasy. No. *Easy Breezy*. Like the Cover Girl slogan on that "Top Model" show Rosie used to watch. That was how it was supposed be between him and Terry. Even when they were fighting. Or Terry had a concussion. Or they were stuck in a shit-hole town.

Best friends for life take it easy on each another. They talk the same talk.

But Terry wasn't talking. He was silent.

Fucking worse than yesterday, Matthew thought, as he aimed the corpulent SUV up the left-hand lane of the highway, wishing that Terry would just say something.

Maybe comment on the Western-type scenes that peeled away from view as the car hurried past, speeding through the hinterlands of their lives. The borderlands between Wyoming and Seattle that they'd traveled together so many times. Where they'd felt the delicious pull of both ends of an irresistible axis. The coming and going, departing and arriving, leaving and staying places. Where everything, bad and good, became part of one's personal geography.

But, no. Terry just gazed at the dashboard as if in a trance, drumming his fingers on his thighs in a half-manic rhythm that made Matthew feel nuts. It was all he could do to not clock him. Or pinch him, maybe. Clocks were for fixing not hitting with.

Matthew gripped the steering wheel hard and whistled through his teeth, red cowlick bobbing like Woody Woodpecker's topknot as he shook his head in disgust.

"So, okay, I get that you don't want to talk. But at least turn on some music so I can hear myself think," he said lightly, trying not to sound hostile. "Your noble silence is deafening."

Terry sniffed. "Nothin' noble about it, brother." Terry always called Matt *brother* in a sarcastic tone when he was mad.

Matthew sniffed back but not as expressively. "Just tell me if you're okay."

Terry turned slowly towards Matthew then back towards the passenger window. He didn't seem to be looking at anything in particular, just swiveling his head like a predatory bird, waiting for something edible to appear in his concentrated line of vision.

"Yea-ahh, sure, ya betcha. I'm fuckin' fine," Terry said, elongating the words. He reached forward and switched on the radio.

"Ooh you'll wait a long time for me. Ooh you'll wait a long time."

The deceptive refrain streamed into the car, filling Matthew with instant nostalgia and a whisper of longing for Rosie before Terry changed the station to an NPR news report about yet another White House debacle.

"The bludy sinking ship o' state, captained by our braw commander," Matthew joked, in the goofy highlander accent that usually got a laugh, but his taciturn companion didn't respond.

Matthew sighed, resigned to the chilly atmosphere of Terry's stubborn silence, as well as the chilly weather. There were flakes of snow settling on the windshield as they headed into Idaho, but nothing to worry about. He'd driven through a hundred crazy snow dumps in Casper and other Rocky Mountain environs, stoned and drunk, and done fine.

His drunk driving days were over, he reminded himself, sneaking a quick look at the left back side of Terry's head where nine neat sutures decorated the center of a baseball-sized ring of cleanly-shaven scalp. Terry looked like a mangy pirate, or a wounded Civil War veteran—or, more attractively—one of the guys from The Band, back in the basement days of jammin' with Dylan.

Terry's head wound was rather fetching, in a sick kind of way, but Matthew didn't comment on it, for the same reason that he maneuvered the big rental car down slippery I-90 as warily as a conscientious school-bus driver. He must not cause any more accidents! Any more pain! Make Terry hate him again!

How he was going to achieve these lofty negative goals— since it's harder not to do something than to do it—Matthew didn't know. But he'd keep his mind on the road. Keep Terry safe. Keep trying to be a Jordan Peterson kind of guy. Diligent, responsible and caring. Instead of negligent, selfish and resentful.

Yet resentful thoughts teemed in his mind. The missed trips to Thermopolis and Yellowstone, Terry's worrying silences, even his brothers' unexpectedly semi-respectable working-class life in the house he'd falsely given over to them back when they didn't deserve it. Rosie's defection, Jackson's coy sadism, his stupid consulting job's boring yet demanding clients. On top of the bad news out of D.C. and the global maelstrom.

Mathew sighed loudly again. *How come life's never fair?!*

"Know whatcha mean, dude." Terry said, apparently reading his mind, but no conversation followed until they stopped for gas and something to eat at a truck stop a few miles outside of Missoula.

Neither of them had eaten much at the motel's "complimentary" breakfast buffet that morning, and Matthew was famished so he ordered a buffalo burger and double-chocolate shake, while Terry, shaking his head at the trucker-type menu, asked for a piece of pie, "any kind'll do."

"And a cuppa black coffee. An' a beer," he amended. "Long as it iddn't Coors."

When the waitress brought him a thick triangle of under-baked crust oozing bright-red filling under a greasy dollop of whipped topping, Terry just smiled politely and said, "Cherry, is it? Think I might save it fer the road," before covering the plate with his napkin.

Watching Terry take alternate sips of cold beer and hot coffee with the patient deliberation of a permanent invalid, while he sucked up his gut-busting burger and shake with diminishing gusto, made Matthew feel guilty and sad.

"You gotta *eat* something. You can't just drink your lunch. And you're not supposed to be having alcohol," he admonished his stubborn friend.

But Terry just looked back at him angrily and sneered, "Sez who? The guy who runs on chocolate and suicide/maybe homicide?"

Matthew choked down his greedy mouthful of grilled onions and burger meat. "What the fuck!" he sputtered, aghast at the charge, what it said about him. Who he was. *Or used to be.*

Because he wasn't that crazy selfish immature jerk who drove his car into the side of a truck anymore. The guy who threw good-hearted Terry over for evil-minded Jackson. The dumb-ass who stalked his ex-wife. Who didn't go home for his parents' funeral and lied to his brothers about their inheritance.

No. He was different now. Or, well, sort of. He knew what he lacked. What he shouldn't run after.

And anyway, Terry was almost—almost—as fucking culpable as he was for everything bad and weird that had gone down between them—or to them—in the past couple years, wasn't he?

Matthew was just about to point that out, when Terry muttered, "Aw, sorry, man. I did forgive ya, didn't I? Let's just forget it."

"No, let's not," Matthew said, firmly, even though all he wanted was peace and calm before driving I-90 in what was soon to be rush hour.

Migraine sensations poked at his forehead, sharp pinfeathers of distress which Matthew manfully ignored, in order to confront or console, his hunched over friend. Terry's face looked skeletal because of the deep circles under his eyes, and the blankness in their pupils which had no life in them.

Wishing he could masterfully orate, or at least subtlety express, his self-conscious explanatory thoughts, his genuine declarations of love—where he was not and never would be Terry's adversary—Matthew paused, waiting for the magic words that would absolve him permanently, but they wouldn't come out.

So he just said, "I'm sorry." Hoping not to have to explain himself, hoping for mercy. But Terry just laughed.

"Shee-it. But yer a dumb motherfucker!" Lively sparks lit up Terry's eyes like firecrackers while he cackled gleefully and reached for his pie.

The sudden change in his demeanor was so astonishing that Matthew leaned back and stared at him in wonder, but Terry didn't seem to notice. He shoveled in his awful pie as fast as he could eat it, much like a starving dog.

Terry licked his plate clean before nodding sagely at Matthew. Sagely, yet stupidly, Matthew thought, wondering if the concussion had rendered him dumb in all senses. If his old friend—the *real* Terry T. Thompson—would ever come back.

Terry took the last swig of his beer, ignoring his lukewarm coffee. Pinning Matthew with sharpshooter's eyes, he said, "Ever consider that *sometimes* other people's bothersome shit ain't about you?"

Matthew shifted uncomfortably in his vinyl seat, feeling penned inside the grubby little booth, wishing they were back in the car. The wonderfully thoughtless joy of automatic driving had been a nice antidote to invasive soul searching.

But he'd complained about Terry's silences. Maybe they needed to talk.

"What do you mean?" he asked, trying not to sound defensive.

"Ya never ask me a gol-dang thing about me an' Isabel. How we're doin' together. Who she is. Duddn't even seem like ya give a shit about her cousin, even though she rescued yer ass from that Fellini-esque fuck party, an' she has yer number down pat, astrologically."

Terry stabbed at his paper placemat with his dirty fork, still holding Matthew's gaze. His handsome hollowed out face registered something close to disgust, but his next words were kind.

"I'm sick a feelin' sorry for you, Ol' Bean. Yer freaky and impaired, but yer gonna be fine. Just as long's you remember the rest of us . . ." Terry waved his fork and pointed it straight at Matthew. "And no, don't say yer drivin' me home and make a thing outta that. 'Cause you owe me."

Matthew hung his head to escape Terry's probing gaze. Yeah, well, of course he owed him.

A last-minute trip to Casper after a last-minute death. A last-minute tackle to stop the rampaging Green. A last-minute trip to the hospital. And a last-minute thousand-mile drive home.

None of his unplanned responses to unplanned things were going to cut it when it came to paying off his debt to his friend. Matthew knew that. But wished it could remain unsaid.

"Why are you doing this to me?" he complained, hoping to see a familiar refrain in Terry's lopsided smile, but there was no smile on his face, just anger and a little bit of fear.

And suddenly Matthew, too, was a little bit afraid.

"Maybe we should get a move on?" he said, beginning to scoot out of the tight little booth, but Terry put a restraining hand on him.

"Wait a second there."

Matthew's guts clenched as Terry stood up, waiting for Terry to hit him. But Terry was just fishing for his bulging wallet which was crammed with old snapshots he'd pinched from his mom.

"Lookee here," he said, handing one of the crumpled little pics over to Matthew as he sat down again. Two teenaged boys, one red-haired and scrawny, the other dark-haired and burly, grinned at the camera goofily.

"My dad just gave us beer money," Terry said. "'Member?"

Matthew laughed, relieved that the haunted look had faded from Terry's eyes. "Sure I do."

Terry picked up his coffee cup and set it down again. "Well, see, that's how we're 'sposed to be. Happy for each other. Not slittin' each other's throats."

Matthew felt rankled again. "What? I'm not slitting your throat."

Terry shook his head and drawled earnestly, "Wall, no," sounding like Jimmy Stewart in *A Wonderful Life*, which was when Matthew knew he'd been had. Terry was smiling again. Thank God!

Matthew sighed with relief and looked around for the waitress to bring them the check. But Terry wasn't done.

Handing Matthew the crinkled up old photo, he said, "Keep it," he said. "You been real good to me lately after a hell of a time. An' I'm grateful for that. But it duddn't mean I'm gonna let ya off the damn hook. I need ya to rilly *see* me. And ever-bawdy else. So keep yer head outta yer ass from now on, and look around at other people. Okay?"

Matthew blinked hard to hold back his tears. "Okay."

Terry punched him gently on the arm, which felt comforting, and continued the longest cautionary speech he'd given in some time.

"You had Rosie for a purty long time. An' I didn't have anyone. But I wasn't a goddamn Incel. My dry spate was totally my choice. I was hopin' for love, same as you. Now I've got it. Or think I have. An' I need ya to be happy for me."

"But you don't seem happy. You seem miserable," Matthew interjected and Terry punched his upper arm again, only much harder, as per usual.

Terry scowled and pulled on a lock of hair that was stuck to the edge of the raggedy Band-Aid on his forehead. The dead look was gone from his eyes. His new look was incendiary.

"Don't be stupid. My dad just died. My mom's married to a sociopath who gave me a concussion. My lady's in love with her dead husband. And yer still a goddamn moron."

Terry stood up and snatched at the check in Matthew's hand. "Let's get out of here," he said. "I need to call Isabel."

HOMECOMING

B ack out on the road things got easier. Terry even wanted to talk a bit more after they reached what he called Idy-Ho and the rugged yet subtly softening landscape seemed more like the Pacific Northwest, less like the high prairies and Rockies they'd left behind.

Their third night in a motel was restful, since neither of them got drunk, and there was nothing pressing to fight about. They'd chatted inconsequentially about their driving day like an old married couple while they got undressed.

Driving out of Coeur D'Alene the next morning and on to Spokane, where they ate breakfast at Denny's, seemed like crossing a dividing line. The dour heaviness of their trip seemed to lift so that they could breathe more freely, Terry thought, watching Matt's steady hands on the wheel with admiration.

By the time they got to Snoqualmie Pass that afternoon, they were laughing and passing the joint that Fred had tucked into Matt's jacket pocket when they said goodbye, what seemed like a hundred years ago, Matt declared.

For a guy who liked fixing broken clocks, the Ol' Bean was funny about actual time, but Terry said it *did* seem like a long time ago that they were getting the shit kicked out of them in awful old Casper. Days, not years ago, but he didn't say that. It was pointless to argue with stoned people.

Weird, though, how he kind of missed the place, Terry said. Because that's where he'd buried his dad.

Matt's dad and mom had gravesites in Casper, too, only what was left of their burned up bodies had been cremated. But Matt never talked about that. He talked about his low-life brothers, and ragged on Rosie, then Alex and Jackson, but his folks were forbidden topics.

Terry didn't miss Mr. Barker, but his sweet tooth missed Matthew's mom every so often. She'd made a great banana cream pie and raspberry-filled donuts that were to die for. She'd been soft and squishy like her homemade desserts while Matt's dad had been a lean mean stick of a man. The opposite of Mr. Thompson.

Missing his dad made Terry feel heartsick, but in most ways he was glad his old man was dead. Witnessing his father quickly succumb to the ravages of Alzheimer's—and they were ravages, in spite of the media cliché—had been like watching a magical landscape of safety and joy become riddled with some horrible life-eating disease of mythic proportion.

There was no safety in a world like that, he said to Matt, and Matt concurred, noting that there was no safety in any kind of world at all, except maybe the tiny little planet of true friendship to which they both belonged.

"After some big fuck-ups, cock-breath," Terry added, happy to be giving Matt some non-hostile shit again, to be free, if not once and for all, then for now, of his grudge-bearing anger.

Feeling angry made Terry feel angry, instead of guilty like Matt, but that didn't mean he liked being overtaken by wrath. He'd been mad at Isabel for preferring a dead man to him, for rejecting what he suspected—or fervently hoped—was real love, but mostly because she wouldn't let him rescue her. His resentment had been typically masculine.

Not that he was calling himself a misogynist. Or whatever it was that he, most probably, was not, and Matt most probably was, when it came to women and sex. These days it was hard to know if having balls and a cock automatically made you a paternalistic autocrat or a disorganized little boy making messes in psychological corridors.

But Terry couldn't jibe with that. He was clean and tidy by nature—and he cleaned up crap for a living—and, in spite of his tender love for his mother, he wasn't a mama's boy. Regardless of his macho biker's appearance, he was a clean-cut guy, whereas poor Matt was a down-and-dirty dude, far more disreputable than Terry could ever be. Or want to be.

And that was the God's honest truth.

Matt was the rebel not him. Matt, who wanted the world to be different, who thought people should be brighter and smarter, who yearned for a utopian society unmarred by trauma, whereas Terry mostly didn't give a shit that the planet was going up in flames. Not that he didn't care. He was just trying take care of his own tiny little corner of the world.

Terry was musing on these kinds of simplified self-analyses when he realized that they were not only back in Seattle, they were back in his neighborhood, driving down North 45th Street. Had he been asleep—or comatose—ever since Issaquah? Which was the last place he remembered passing by on the freeway. Where had the miles gone?

Matt turned the huge SUV down Ashworth, drove a few blocks, and pulled into the driveway separating Terry's yard from Isabel's. Switching off the powerful engine, he excitedly announced, "Hey, buddy! We're home! Or well, you are."

"Wait a second, dude," Terry gasped, wrenching the car door open so he could lean awkwardly out and vomit the undigested residue of that morning's Denver omelet onto the soggy parking strip.

He groaned miserably and sat back in his seat, wiping his mouth, waiting for the sick feeling in his head and stomach to cease, hoping Isabel hadn't witnessed his body's—inner character's?—latest profound embarrassment.

"Jesus, man! You're falling apart," Matt said, patting Terry's trembling knee affectionately. He'd become very motherly of late, Terry thought, wondering what that boded for their future relationship. More mayhem and madness, only the cloying kind? Matt hot on his heels, day and night, asking if he'd eaten properly or taken a detoxifying dump. *Shee-it.*

Shuddering inwardly, but still grateful for his best friend's help, Terry sat glumly in the car while Matt removed his luggage from the trunk and set it on his porch. Backpack, beer cooler, the plastic carryall from the Casper mall where they stopped for coffee and car snacks. Not much to show for such a momentous trip, he reckoned. No red dirt from Crimson Dawn, no family souvenirs, nothing from his dad except the little cache of photographs he'd stolen from his mom.

His injured head throbbed forcefully as he extricated himself from the ridiculous car, reminding him that he did, in fact, carry a significant marker of the trip on his person. Ugly, bludgeoned bruises and itchy stitches, not romantic saber scars, but still, they added up to something. Didn't they? A big statement—about what?

Of course—and thank God—it started raining when he said goodbye to Matt, after refusing his offer to come in the house and get him well settled in.

"I can take care of myself," Terry insisted, pasting a grin on his face, as they stood on the warped steps of Terry's scrappy little hundred-year-old house.

After lifting his face to the drizzling sky, the Ol' Bean had regarded him somberly through rain-streaked glasses, before slapping his back fondly, and saying, "Welcome back to Rain City, brother. Call if you need me. Any time."

Terry's face was also wet and not just from the rain. "Thanks for everything. *Brother*," he answered. This time the word wasn't an insult.

Aside from the weather, this was no place to chat, although there were many things left to say. They were both tired and anxious to be home, and Matt still had some driving to do in the oncoming dusk. So they parted with handclasps and backslaps and stupid remarks, like men friends often do.

"If we'd a had tails, we'd wag 'em," Terry wryly remarked, turning back to the walkway that led up to the porch after he unlocked his door.

But Matt had already reached the car. He honked three times and then drove away.

And now Terry was alone.

He removed a meagre stack of ads and bills from his mailbox, then went inside and shut the door. The empty house smelled musty, not rank. He'd remembered to take out the garbage and pour out his milk before departing in what was probably a rush but seemed like slow motion.

The half-expected call from the care home, his needy plea to Matt, the mind-numbing flight, the wake and the funeral and his confrontation with Green, the fact that his dad wasn't there, would never be there, played out in his memory in quarter time. His life had been over-cranked—or, in a digital sense that Matt would like, time-stretched.

Too bad it was real, not a movie. If it were, then Isabel would be here right now. Or maybe she would have been with him the whole time in Casper. Sitting at his side at the funeral. Sitting on his grieving mother's bed. Giving the wicked house painter a piece of her mind.

Being the heroine to his hero. The star of their own movie show.

"That strong-willed Scorpio woman can do anything she damn well wants," Madam Zodie had said of her seemingly fragile cousin. But could she? What about giving the boot to her dead husband?

There was beer in the fridge but he made himself a pot of tea and toasted some stale bread, which he spread with peanut butter and some apricot jam Isabel had made before Charlie died. Although he was superstitious, there was no taste of incipient death in it, just a summery tart sweetness that reminded him of Isabel.

He wanted to call her but he knew that he should sleep first, so he washed his face and hands, stripped off his clothes and got into bed, leaving his bedroom light on, so Isabel could see that he was home. If she was looking over at is house, that is. If she was waiting for him.

Terry's headache mercifully stopped throbbing as he drifted off to sleep, but his heart-ache expanded as he dreamed.

For there was his dead father and dead Charlie sitting around heaven in woven basket chairs, wearing white flannels and sipping tropical drinks like gents in the British Raj. Unseen but malevolent, Jackson Brand lurked just off the skyline, muddying the stark sunshine of the dream.

A chorus of chirruping birds turned into Rosie's sexy contralto, then morphed into the churning of vast ocean waves. A tsunami of sensations washed over him, picking him clean, until he was nothing but an energetic vibration.

No sound. No air. Yet not quite nothingness. There was definitely something illuminative there. In the void. Was it sadness?

Then he heard Isabel's voice whispering softly in his ear, "I'm here, sweetheart. I'm here," breaking the unearthly silence.

Terry opened his eyes and there she was, kneeling beside his bed with her cold hands resting on his naked chest. Isabel. "You left the door unlocked," she said. She was real!

Terry pulled Isabel up onto the bed so he could take a good look at her. It seemed like a long time ago that he'd gazed at her thick silvery hair, her somber yet mischievous eyes, the scar on her chin from a bicycle fall when she was ten. Forty years ago, yet there it still was. The tiny crescent he found so endearing.

He cupped her chin in his sleep-warm hand, and said, "Gol-dang it, I missed you," before kissing her slightly moist lips. Her face was wet. She wasn't crying now, but she had been.

"Jesus, look what they've done to you!" Isabel whispered, as if a malevolent cabal of mischief makers had been wreaking havoc with his body since his car crash with Matt, not just the weaselly house painter.

Terry reckoned she was right, but didn't say anything. Maybe he'd ask Madam Zodie about that. If his personal demons were real.

He leaned back on his pillow, holding Isabel close to him. Her solicitousness felt comforting, yet he couldn't relax, knowing that he wasn't prepared to see her, that he didn't know what to say. He was still in a sleep-induced funk where his brain was focused inward. On his weirdly discomfiting dream.

He breathed in Isabel's inebriating scent, wondering if she could smell sadness and death and treachery on him, instead of the sweet fragrance of cottonwood blossoms that he carried in his mind. Aside from Red Dawn, it was his best memory of Casper.

Images from his dream floated into his consciousness when he closed his eyes. A montage of muted colors and bright blacks and whites. The dead men's lightweight flannel trousers. The azure dome of heaven. The velvety-grey smoke cloud that was Jackson, looming on the blank horizon.

He opened his eyes, feeling obtuse and sleepy, happy Isabel was lying there with him, with her head on his chest, but worried about her, too. What in the world could he give to her out of his meagre little store of love and forgiveness to help relieve her ongoing pain? Maybe his own pain could wait.

But there was something he needed to ask her, had been needing to ask since the first time she told him about her husband. What an impressive man he'd been. Respected scholar, great father, devoted partner. The kind of guy Terry's father had been before his brain fizzled out. Responsible, sensitive, fun. Someone people looked up to.

Terry hemmed and hawed, then just blurted it out. "Do you think Charlie would be okay with me?"

Isabel stiffened in Terry's arms, but answered casually, "Sure, he'd like you. He'd like you a lot. You're a man's man, after all," she said, drawing back to look at him.

Just a few minutes ago her eyes had been mossy green, soft and inviting. But now they were glassy and hard, with little chips in them like newly cut emeralds. Yet they were amused looking, which made him confused. Was she or wasn't she pissed at him?

"C'mon now, whaddya mean by that?" Terry sat up straighter, pulling the slipping down sheet Isabel's body had displaced back up to his waist so she wouldn't see his cock, which resembled a wilted flower against his sinewy thighs.

Isabel slid her butt toward the end of the bed, enlarging the space between them. Wordlessly fiddling with the little knobs of raised chenille on Terry's old-fashioned bedspread, she seemed to have receded into herself, so that she was a stranger again. A helpful neighbor who'd come to check on him rather than his lover.

Although maybe they never had been *lovers* at all, even though they'd—sort of—had sex.

"What don't you get?" she said. Was there a hostile tone in her voice or was she just playing with him?

"Shee-it, I dunno. Charlie likin' me, which seems weird under the circumstances. And the "man's man" thing—well, that just seems like crap. No offense! I was really just wonderin' whether he'd approve a me—my character—if he'd think I'm good enough for you."

"Well, how the hell would he know? He's fucking dead!" Isabel shouted. It was the first time she'd yelled at him.

Maybe now we're gettin' some place, Terry thought. Although, judging from the angry look on Isabel's face, maybe not.

Still, he wasn't deterred. They were gonna have this conversation, whatever came of it, even though he wasn't really sure what it was all about. Insecurity? Jealousy? Love? Yes and no to all of it.

Terry stretched out his hand which Isabel didn't take. "I'm sorry about that," he said, and he was, even though Charlie's early demise had benefitted him greatly.

"Yeah, me too." Isabel whispered. "But Charlie wasn't perfect, you know," she went on, in a louder voice, still looking down at the bedspread. Although her face seemed impassive, there were tears on her cheeks.

Terry couldn't resist saying "How so?" even though that was asking for trouble. Charlie's imperfections being far superior to his own sterling qualities, which he'd have to concede upon inspection, no doubt.

"Well, he was a know-it-all and a pedant, which I guess is the same thing." Isabel chuckled mirthlessly. "And he didn't like rock n' roll. Plus he liked full-figured operatic-type women, which I'm obviously not." She paused for almost a minute while Terry waited for her to continue.

Jesus, maybe pluperfect Charlie was a douche after all?

But instead of expanding on her husband's seemingly minor imperfections, Isabel said, "I was his student, you know. Nineteen when I met him and he was thirty-one. He used to call me his "dirty little nugget," because of my working class roots, even though I was as almost as cultured as he was. My field was modern American history, which he found rather dull."

She paused again, without glancing at Terry. "After we got married, he polished me up pretty nicely so I could be a good academic wife. I was smart and well-read, but I was young, so it took a while."

Isabel's story trailed off and Terry was glad. He didn't want to know that she'd had a self-sacrificing life, that she'd been married to a possible narcissist. That Charlie was a heartless dry-as-dust intellectual.

But she started up again. "Don't get me wrong. We were happy. *I was happy*. It was okay for him to be the brightest star because I didn't want to be. Being a wife and a mother, and working for my brother, was enough for me. Charlie took advantage of my lack of personal ambition, I suppose, but I don't have any hard feelings about that. I—we—made the right choices."

Ok, so Charlie wasn't a weasel, just an entitled prick, who loved being adored by his students, and writing arcane history books which nobody ever read or bought, while his wife slaved away for his benefit in companionable silence.

"No, it wasn't like you think," Isabel said, once again, like her fey little cousin, reading his mind. Why was it that so many women could do that?

Rubbing his sideburns thoughtfully—they were shaggy and needed to be trimmed—Terry sat up higher in bed, so his face was on the same level as Isabel's and their eyes could meet and lock, which, after a beat, they did.

Looking so deeply into her eyes was almost painful; this time it was him who looked away first. "Duddn't matter what I think," he said, somewhat disingenuously, for he was thinking a hundred different things about why he hated Charlie. And why he was glad he was dead.

Terry picked at the cotton tufts on his bedspread, unconsciously mimicking Isabel. "I didn't have a girlfriend for a mighty long time," he said, changing the topic at hand, or possibly just adding to it, since the topic, really, was love.

"Yeah, I was celibate for purt near three years 'cause I was mad for my best friend's wife—and I do mean mad, as in bonkers—as well as mad at myself—cause I didn't just have the hots for Rosie. I loved her."

"Jesus," Isabel whispered. He couldn't tell if she was shocked or simply surprised.

"Nah, Matt never knew," Terry went on, answering her unspoken question. "Although he probably could a guessed. I did a lot of bad-mouthin' their marriage, and a lot of shade talk about Rosie, when I shoulda been lookin' after myself. Findin' my own woman to be with. Maybe marry."

His laugh was rueful. Because he wanted to say, "And then came you," which not only sounded dorky, but assumed a lot about her reciprocal feelings, which he might be wrong about.

Isabel leaned forward and clasped Terry's hands, pulling him closer. "You're kind of a fool, you know," she said, tenderly. "No wonder you get knocked about so regularly. Defending Matthew. Defending your mom. People keep taking advantage of you. And I'll bet Rosie was flattered that you loved her. Am I right?"

Terry grimaced theatrically then tossed out a rueful smile. "Fuck yeah, she knew, but I never touched her, even though she came on to me a lot when things with her and Matt were slidin' down the shit-hole."

Isabel rolled her beautiful green eyes, which had returned to their softer shade. "So beautifully put," she laughed, mocking him.

And somehow, at exactly that moment, Terry knew that everything between him and the woman he loved was going to be all right.

DINNER WITH THE FOLKS

Entering his deserted living room gave Matthew a shock. It looked and felt like a dentist's waiting room, empty and lifeless and more than vaguely threatening. Dove grey furniture of the ergonomic kind, a sleek gigantic sofa, and none of the cozy kitsch that Rosie had decorated the room with, back when they hung out in it together, binge watching Netflix.

He threw his jacket on the back of a boring looking chair and set his expensive leather travel bag down on the polished floor. In its zippered compartment lay the deed to the Barker house that he'd stolen out of his dad's old file cabinet in the den while his clueless brothers cleaned up the kitchen after breakfast.

The twins had never asked for legal proof of the purported property transfer of three years ago, which had pleased him immensely, even though he didn't want any part of the house. Lying about signing his portion of the house over to them seemed pointless in retrospect, since they'd never know that he'd fooled them until one of them died. Or they tried to sell the house, which was unlikely.

The crazy trip to Casper had been an eye-opener when it came to seeing his brothers as pretty much the same as him. Psychologically challenged little boys who'd grown up to be regular guys, if by regular, one meant self-deluded, emotionally fragile, ever hopeful for better outcomes than they felt they deserved.

The empathy and sense of identification that had risen in him had been sludgy and tainted with bitterness, but it was real. And it hadn't gone away on the trip back to Seattle. So tomorrow he'd download a warranty deed, sign his share of the house over to his brothers, get the form notarized, and send it off to the Natrona County Clerk's office, and that would be that. For now.

No need to inform his brothers of something they thought he'd already done. No need to run it by Terry, since making things right had been his idea, when bereaved Fred and Frank were wandering around the outer limits of Wyoming after their folks died, getting their heads done in with hard drugs and low-life women. Thank God—or something-or-other— they'd eventually decided to go home.

Perching on his streamlined couch, didn't give Matthew the safe feeling his brothers apparently now had in their cozy little house—which once would have bugged him, but all he wanted was a place to sit when Terry came over, and a firm surface to jerk off when he wasn't roiling in bed, dreaming about Rosie. Maybe tomorrow he'd buy a cheap sofa from IKEA and give this pricy one to Goodwill, if Terry didn't want it.

He took off his shoes and went into the kitchen, which felt a trifle bit friendlier than the cheerless living room. Rummaging in his near-empty fridge, he found three outdated cheese sticks and a couple of beers, which he drank very slowly since he was too tired to go to the grocery store.

Watching YouTube videos, ensconced in the ratty old armchair in his office, was slightly relaxing, but not as soothing as he hoped it would be. His brain was spinning with ideas. All of which would have to wait until tomorrow, except maybe calling Madam Zodie, if he could hang on to his balls while she lobbed metaphysical insults at them.

He fiddled around for a while, checking how many emails were in his consulting inbox without reading any of them, writing a beer-heavy grocery list, looking through his desk for pot. Bad habits were one thing, he thought, as he bent over to take off his stinky socks, but bad timing was something quite other. Something that could ruin your life.

Like not going to Casper for Christmas even though his mom begged him to. Like marrying Rosie when she was hot with ambition, and expecting her to be happy, singing in bars for a pittance, living a tiny little suffocating life. Like swerving his car into a truck full of hippies when he wasn't even that drunk. And messing with a bastard like Jackson.

Madam Zodie could look into that, if she wanted to. Not that he'd insult her by suggesting that she consult for him. Been there. Done that. All wrong. But it would be nice to get her take on the downs and upsides—if there were any—of misplaced timing, if only to remind himself that the tendency to be early or late, in a fateful sense, was universal.

"Well, fucking crap on a stick," Matthew muttered, gazing at Madam Zodie's contact info on his phone for a long time before finally pressing her number.

Stuttering and stammering—just like he was supposed to, based on their ramshackle history in which he was always a jittery jerk-off, if not quite a villain—he squeaked, "Hello," when she answered, followed by "Hi," which could have been "High," for how stupid he sounded. Like an embarrassed kid caught with a porno mag.

Cursing himself, Matthew modulated his voice, so that he almost sounded adult.

"I was thinking about you while we were driving back from Casper. Er, well, I was thinking about you before that. The whole time we were there. Wondering how you're doing. If everything is going okay."

He cleared his throat awkwardly, hoping he didn't sound like a guy who was getting ready to hawk and spit. Women always hated that. Among other gauche manly things.

"Everything is great. I'm fine,' Madam Zodie said cheerfully, without further exposition.

A sudden vision of a tall dark man, some kind of lithe gypsy violin-playing type, wielding bow and penis like magical wands, rose up behind Matthew's third eye, stabbing him with a hot pang of jealousy.

Jesus, was that—*some man*—what she was so damn fine about? Of course not, he chided himself. He wasn't a fucking mind reader!

"Don't get any big ideas," Madam Zodie said, reading his mind or pretending to. "It's been pretty much same old, same old for me. Except for trying to keep Isabel from freaking out about Terry. Poor guy! I'm so glad that he's okay."

Yeah, well, Terry was sort of okay, if you didn't count his disorienting concussion, his dad being dead and his mother being hitched to the duplicitous house painter. And vomiting on his parking strip as soon as he got home.

Another sharp pang—this time of brotherly concern—poked at him menacingly, but Matthew shrugged it off, telling himself it was just his usual pointless worries and not any valid concern about the state of his battered old friend that was bothering him.

He'd made sure that Terry was okay before he drove away from his house an hour ago. He was just tired and hungry, that's all.

Matthew and Madam Zodie chatted desultorily for few more minutes. Matthew exclaiming over the unexpected foreignness of Wyoming; Madam Zodie, over the growing damage to *Lesser Seattle* from gleaming techno-domes and scattershot homeless encampments.

"But you already know about that," she laughed. "Not like you've been gone for years and years. But maybe it feels like it?"

Well, yes—how typically perceptive of her—but he didn't say that, instead he said, "I'd like to see you sometime. Like right now."

A pause—not quite long enough to be reassuring—then Madam Zodie said, "I'm in my sweats working on charts. Anyway, it's late and I don't feel like going out or having company. Maybe another time?"

It was obvious she didn't want to see him, spur of the moment or any time, based on their awkward experiences, Matthew thought, feeling his heart sink.

And his cock, too, not that he'd had a hard-on. Just twinges of desire dotted with clots of anxiety, similar to how he'd felt when he first met Rosie. A sort of falling upwards— at the same time as tumbling mercilessly down—sensation that made him feel like a storm-blown insect. A moth not a butterfly. Clumsy and bumbling.

"Okay, then," he said carefully, wanting to end the call.

Another pause from Madam Zodie, this time a longer one, then, "My parents are coming up from Oregon for the weekend. If you can handle tomorrow evening with two elderly hippies and their doted-on offspring, then please join us for fried twigs and tofu."

He didn't want to spend an evening with Madam Zodie's parents and her cantankerous dog, but he wanted to see *her*, so he accepted the invitation with alacrity and rang off, feeling so uplifted that he sang "Brown-eyed Girl" in the shower, even though it was green eyes he was thinking off.

Lying in bed, clean and warm, Matthew gazed into the dark until his eyes adjusted to the contours of the room, feeling as cocooned as an astronaut in a spacesuit. Safe but slightly uncomfortable, as if tethered to a spacecraft by unbreakable cords. Missing something or someone on earth. Hurtling someplace incredibly fast. But where?

Rosie's dazzling face swam into view, floating in murky space, then Madam Zodie's shining even more brightly. Then, oddly his mother's, round as the moon, with a quizzical expression in her smile, which burned away when he shut his eyes, unwilling to look at her.

Inside his mind images of women leapt and frolicked like aggressive dolphins—this time erotic ones and none of his mother—until he was forced to masturbate to calm and appease them, lying spent afterwards, feeling pleasantly hollow as he lay in the warm shallows, drifting towards sleep.

After a restful descent into a sweet nighttime underworld of infant-like slumber, he awoke refreshed and raring to get on with his day, willing the hours to pass quickly until it was time to see *Alice*.

Should he call her that or stick to Madam Zodie, he asked himself obsessively as he dressed, and drove to her house, arriving on the dot of six o'clock, dry-mouthed with apprehension.

He brought flowers—not roses for personal reasons—and a bottle of domestic white wine he'd snagged for twenty bucks. More appropriate for earth-firsters than the sixty-dollar bottle of French Sauvignon Blanc he'd usually bring to a dinner party, he guessed.

Standing on the landing outside the house, he inhaled the spicy scent of the chrysanthemum bouquet to fortify himself. He felt oafish in his plaid flannel shirt and REI rain jacket, as if he were only pretending to be a guy who changed his own tires and swabbed his own toilet. The wad of money in his wallet made him feel like a spoiled one percenter instead of a dweeb from Wyoming with working-class origins.

He knocked on the door softly, tamping down unpleasant memories of banging loudly on Jackson's in the dead of the night. He put a friendly smile on his face, hoping he looked harmless and normal.

Madam Zodie answered the door wearing a long white chef's apron over an ankle-length cotton dress. She'd obviously just come from the kitchen—her face was flushed and he could smell the aroma of roasting chicken in her flyaway hair when she stepped forward to greet him.

He thrust the wine and flowers at her, surveying the good-looking middle-aged couple standing behind her with a mixture of appreciation and dread.

"Hey, Matthew, come on in." His hostess kissed him lightly on both cheeks and patted his arms briskly as if she was patting her dog, then gestured to the lanky dark-haired man and the small blonde woman in the entryway who were gazing at him.

"This beautiful lady is my mom, Marianne, and that big galoot's my dad, Chet. And of course you've already met Tehuti."

Tehuti sniffed Matthew's pant legs with a look of distain, but Madam Zodie's parents smiled benignly when they shook his hand, increasing his hopes for a good evening.

Marianne looked vaguely Scandinavian and a little bit wild, like a mischievous elf. The wiry grey hairs in her messy blonde coif stuck out like errant crochet loops, which apparently she didn't mind. When she clasped Matthew in a motherly greeting, he warmed to her immediately. Perhaps she was a potential ally!

Long-limbed Chet reminded Matthew of his gangly dad — if his dad had been an easy-going guy instead of an angry control freak, who would have died from a rage-induced heart attack, if he hadn't croaked in the car crash. Robust Chet looked like he'd never die, whatever the circumstances.

"MZ's told us some good and bad stuff about you," said twinkly-eyed Chet, as they walked into the living room to sit down on the couch. "Good to know you're a man of two minds. So many people have only the one."

Marianne's laugh sounded just like her daughter's. "Oh, Chet. Ever the Gnostic philosopher," she retorted fondly, saving Matthew from making a silly comment about schizophrenia.

They made small talk while passing around a frosty pitcher of sangria and plates of cheese and crackers, while Madam Zodie went back and forth tending to dinner. It was impossible not to compare the easy way she related to her parents with the uncomfortable relationship Matthew had with his family. He felt envious of their easy comradery at the same time as he felt thrilled to have been included in such splendid society.

"Come 'n' get it!" Madam Zodie called, carrying a platter with the perfectly roasted chicken in from the kitchen. She set it down on the dining room table where a simple green salad and a loaf of warm rosemary bread were waiting. Chet took the seat at the head of the table while Matthew and the women scooted in around him, giddy as hungry children.

When everyone was settled, Chet folded his hands and solemnly intoned, "Dear God and Goddess, for good food and friends we thank you," then happily cried, "Dig in!" as he picked up the carving knife.

"Chateau San Michele! One of my favorites!" Marianne enthused as she poured Matthew's wine offering into their glasses. She might have been fibbing about enjoying the local brand, but Matthew took her comment as a sign he was winning her over and beamed semi-besottedly, wondering if she'd make a good mother-in-law.

They passed the food around and ate in silence for a few moments, savoring the meal after enthusiastically complimenting the cook. When conversation started again, Matthew realized he was beginning to feel rather relaxed. Or at least not on the verge of a panic attack.

Chet told a story about driving his old VW bus through the Rockies, back when he and Marianne were selling leather goods at county fairs and singing for beer in hippie bars. How the vehicle just chugged indefatigably up and down mountains, like the Little Train That Could, even though it rattled and banged like it was falling apart and skittered sideways in every whiff of the wind.

"My old car crapped out up on Togwotee Pass," Matthew cried, emboldened by the wine and possessive memories of his homeland. "Luckily I had *Zen and the Art of Motorcycle Maintenance* along with me. I was up shit crick, but at least I had something to read!" Terry's tattered old copy, not his, but at least he'd said something real.

"Hear! Hear!" Chet patted his breast pocket as if looking for cigarettes. "'Spose you had a couple of joints on you, too?" He laughed uproariously and took another bite of his chicken leg.

"Oh, dad!" Madam Zodie said in a mocking voice, pretending to be embarrassed. Being a disarming kid looked good on her, the same way it did on her mother.

"So, you're uh, Isabel's sister, is that right?" Matthew asked, turning to Marianne, who was regarding her husband with the fond smile of an affectionate wife.

"No, I'm Isabel's' aunt. Her mother, Solveig, was my sister. So Isabel and Alice are first cousins. Not Alice and Isabel's daughter, Emily."

Matthew shook his head in confusion. "I never did get that family stuff. Different generations . . . first and second cousins . . ."

"Nobody really does! But the generations are kind of staggered in our family since we're all born ten years apart, beginning with me and Solveig." Marianne cast a sly look towards her daughter. "No babies after Emily. Although I'd really like a granddaughter!"

Madam Zodie rolled her eyes, but continued her mother's story. "Aunt Solveig would be seventy this year if she was still alive. Mom's sixty. Izzy's fifty. I'm forty and Emily's thirty. No males born since my grandfather's time. Just us crazy females. A real gynocentric bunch!"

Chet hooted and stomped his feet. "Hear! Hear!"

When all the food, including an apple tart for dessert, was eaten and conversation about the usual subjects—the dismal state of world affairs and the addictive joys of streaming media—had dwindled to a trickle, Chet announced that it was time to call it a night, levering himself awkwardly up from his chair, seemingly less a man than a disjointed skeleton.

Lolling against the table while he took a final swig of his wine, he seemed as laissez-faire and loose-limbed as the scarecrow from Oz or a stoned Abe Lincoln. "No more postprandial drinks for your tired old dad and mom," he declared, as the rest of them rose to their feet.

"Me thinks some lovebirds might like to be alone." Chet grinned a comic leer at his wife before pulling her into a warm embrace and reaching out for Madam Zodie, who centered herself in their arms. Matthew stood apart from the tight familial hug, wishing he was snug inside it, like the yolk of a Cadbury egg.

Matthew grabbed Chet's bony hand, pumping it frantically, as the foursome walked towards the closet where the coats were stashed. "So great to meet you," he warbled, in what seemed like a strangled voice. Maybe he was just tipsy. But he definitely sounded like a dork.

"If I'm ever in need of an IT person, I'll contact you for advice." Chet said, whacking Matthew's shoulder with his free hand, a little more gently than Terry.

"Oh right, dad." Madam Zodie scoffed, shooting Matthew an apologetic glance, which did little to ameliorate his budding sense that affable Chet might be dangerous should anyone mess with his daughter.

Marianne took hold of Matthew's hands as the two of them said goodbye. "You know, you could be good for her," she said, in an unexpectedly steely voice, nodding towards Alice as she pulled him closer.

"But you'll have to get to know yourself better. *'Gnothi seauton'* is the first principle. Just ask Chet," she whispered into his ear. And then she kissed him goodbye.

Madam Zodie nudged Matthew with her elbow after she closed the door on her departing parents, leaving them suddenly alone.

"You okay?" she said, stepping closer to him in the narrow entryway, then stepping back, as if reconsidering something she saw in his face.

Matthew arranged his features into a smile. "No, I'm fine. Your parents are completely amazing. So much different than mine . . ."

His voice trailed away as they walked into the living room and sat down on either end of the couch, half-way facing each other. The air in the room felt weirdly charged but not wholly uncomfortable.

After a few minutes of companionable silence, in which Madam Zodie continued examining him in the inquisitive manner of a kindly zookeeper, she got up to fetch the pot of tea brewing in the kitchen, and brought it to the coffee table along with tea things and a bottle of whiskey.

After sitting back down again and removing her socks, even though the night was chilly, she filled two china cups with rich black tea infused with a sweet herb he couldn't identify and handed one over to Matthew.

The tea smelled like Madam Zodie, or she like the tea, which scared him. Making sensual associations about people was how his obsessions started.

"Have you looked at my chart again?" Matthew asked as she added generous shots of Bushmills to their teacups.

What a stupid thing to say! But what *did* her mystic's green eyes see about the kind of person he was? Whether he could be trusted? Or loved?

"Well, of course. But if you want my professional opinion you'll have to make an appointment." She was mocking him, but it felt good.

Madam Zodie stretched her legs towards Matthew's end of the couch until her bare feet touched his thigh. Well away from his crotch, he noticed, guessing that the only intercourse they'd be enjoying tonight would be mental. And, spiritual, of course, her stated forte—yet, wasn't there a physical attraction? It was always part of the dance.

The Bushmills and tea tasted good and the whole night seemed flavorful and full of promise. A good omen for sex, once upon a time, but not right now. For Alice—*yes, Alice*—for didn't she seem like a creature from Wonderland, with her Victorian dresses and imaginative way of thinking?—wasn't giving him any indication that she was interested in him in that way. Unless treating him to dinner was her form of foreplay, which he fervently hoped that it was.

On that note, a compliment issued forth from his lips, tingly from tea and whiskey as if he and Alice had been kissing.

"That was a really good dinner you cooked!" he blurted, hearing the alcohol in his voice and his longing for her. Shit.

Pretty soon his tongue would be hanging out like her crazy dog's and he'd be drooling on her.

Alice smiled and poured him another dram of whiskey. "Glad you liked it. And my folks." She raised her teacup at him in a sweet little toast. Her eyes were sparkling.

Matthew suddenly felt like he was up in the stars, staring back at her, knowing—crazily—that she was meant to be in his life. Alice was like a tiny little bright dot on earth from his freaky vantage point, glowing like a supercharged Christmas light, like a beacon in the night calling out to him. And he was going to answer, by God, even if it—she—killed him. Like Rosie almost had.

"You're looking at me pretty googly-eyed," Alice said, nudging Matthew's hip with her foot, half-way breaking his autoerotic spell, but not quite. Part of him was still stuck up in the stars even though his body felt soft and languid next to her.

Reaching out with trembling fingers, he took her cold feet in his hands, gently massaging them until they were warm, letting all his silly thoughts about forever float away as he brought himself back down to earth.

To the great *here and now* that Terry had been fuzzily talking about in the hospital. Although that, too, belonged to the stars, Matthew reckoned, since the moment was cosmic, and eternity meant timelessness, not time going on forever, even though sometimes he wished that it would.

"You can stay here tonight, if you want to," Alice murmured, voice low, eyes closed, not looking at him deliberately, he supposed, yet the short string of words made him feel exposed and vulnerable.

"Yes, please," he said, letting go of her feet so he could reach for her outstretched hands.

TERRY'S TURN BUT MAYBE NOT THE LAST CHAPTER

What a difference a day makes.

Terry had always loved that song. The wistfulness of his own rendition while he soaped the breakfast dishes, after Isabel went home, disappointed but didn't surprise him. He'd always been a shitty singer in spite of his masterful baritone.

The world seemed so much brighter now that he was back home with Isabel. Yet there were murky specks of darker thoughts circling in his head, pinpoints of pitch that shone blackly on, like stars in an inverted sky. Reminders of the disquieting dreams he'd had about midnight fires and medieval spires since she told him about Charlie.

He'd been so gung ho, so hot to possess Isabel before his father's death and the fucked-up funeral trip to Casper, but now he wondered if he'd created a big karmic mess by following his heart's unlikely tug to her. So many questions remained to be answered about the essence of their relationship and its unfathomable future. And of course there was the problem of Charlie. Undead even though he was dead.

Terry wasn't ready to address those tricky questions quite yet, or talk about his thoughts which seemed flaky and venal and selfish, even though he cared very much for Isabel. And, very likely, loved her with a love that would last. But they were still in the wild-animals-sniffing-each-other stage, following each other's scent on the shifting breeze, getting closer slowly as they moved through the landscape.

He and Isabel hadn't had sex last night, but lay wrapped in each other's arms for hours, talking and kissing, provoking both his desire for her and his desire for sleep which had finally won out.

He'd dreamed he was walking on eggshells, then sliding on them, then gliding high up in the clouds, like a man in a Chagall painting. Floating along, shining and weightless, he looked down at the earth, where he could see Isabel standing in a field below holding a handful of flowers. Reaching across a thousand miles of dappled space, he plucked the bright bouquet from her fingers and tossed it heavenwards. Isabel cried out his name when the petals came scattering down on her in a downpour of soft-colored lights.

He woke up awash in memories of the floral shower which, fading quickly, morphed into impressions of rain. He scooted out of bed, careful not to wake Isabel, and drew back the curtains, glad for small synchronicities when he saw raindrops spattering the window.

Smiling to himself, he'd gotten got dressed in the bathroom, then gone down to the kitchen to make coffee, reveling in the quiet familiarity of his modest little house until Isabel, charmingly dishabille in his ratty old bathrobe, joined him.

"Hello you," she said, giving his shoulders a quick hug before sitting down at the table where he was doing the Sunday crossword.

"Hello *you*," Terry said, enjoying the intimacy the pronoun suggested, and the sight of Isabel in his too-big robe. Half silly, half sexy. Still warm from his bed.

"Haven't started on breakfast yet." Terry put down his newspaper and handed her the steaming cup of Arabica he'd already poured. "You look like could use a good shot of caffeine."

Isabel's soft laugh was sleepy. "Thanks. It seemed like a short night. But I'm glad I spent it with you."

"Me, too."

Watching her sip her coffee with the abstracted air of a fey Parisian drinking café au lait in a Belle Époque cafe, it was hard to believe that his dream last night wasn't real. There was something painterly and other-worldly about Isabel, even at her most prosaic in his ill-fitting clothes. Something that pulled at him. That made him look.

Her family resemblance to her more occult cousin Madam Zodie was, as ever, pronounced. Sharp jutting cheekbones. Forest-colored eyes. A lightweight look to her bones. Two peas in a pod, some might say. But they'd be wrong, he thought. There was no one exactly like Isabel.

Her maddening ambiguity seemed as attached to her as her skin, but Isabel always been honest with him. Too honest, it seemed, when she began laying out her plans for herself and their chancy relationship while he gulped downed his coffee, wishing it was a magic elixir that would make her shut up.

"I'm going to Emily and Deepak's for Thanksgiving, and I'm probably going to stay for Christmas," she said, laying her hand gently over his. Terry didn't say that he already knew this.

"The timing's hard since you just got back, and I'm really going to miss you. But it will be good for me to get away for a while. Get some perspective. Figure out where I want to go from here. On my own. And with you."

For a ridiculous instant Terry thought "where" meant an actual place. A town or city to which she—or they—could escape and start a new a new life. But what about Isabel's allegiance to her dead husband, and his own new tussle with grief? She needed to run away and he needed to hunker down after the terrible onslaught of Casper. There didn't seem to be any place in the world that had their conjoined names written on it.

In the back of his mind, where his headache had started up again, he heard Matt's ridiculous Cockney accent, admonishing him not to get his bollocks in a twist over Isabel's stated plans. Stupid advice from a guy whose life was predicated on worrying, so Terry ventured on. Into the conversational trap he knew was waiting to snap off his legs and arms.

"So yeah-ah," he started, hating the gravelly hitch in his voice. "You're gonna leave Seattle for a gol-dang month while I just hang around here with my busted head up my ass waitin' for you to come back. Ain't blamin' you for wantin' to visit Emily. I think it's a good idea. But you're right, the timing fuckin' sucks."

Terry pushed his chair back and stood up to cook breakfast so Isabel couldn't see his face while he was rummaging in the fridge and parked at the stove frying eggs. He probably looked angry even though he wasn't. Or was he? But, for sure, he was downright sad.

He didn't want to see her face either, although he hoped she was mad instead of looking at him with that patient expression she sometimes had when his swearing got out of hand. Her maternal side wasn't what he wanted this happy, then sad, early morning.

Aside from asking Terry if she should set the table—to which he coldly replied, "No, thank you"—Isabel didn't say much while he finished basting the eggs and toasting stale bread, for which he deliberately neglected to provide any of her homemade jam.

He knew he was being a dick when he slammed down their silverware and set down their plates so clumsily that the rickety table shook a bit, but he didn't care. Fuck her and the about-to-bolt horse she rode in on, he thought, sitting down to his half-burnt toast and greasy eggs with a sigh which he hoped Isabel would pick up on.

But all she did was smile at him kind of goofily, as if he was the one with the flea up his ass, not her with her sudden intentions and stupid damn plans that made so much sense that he hated them.

"Well, go on then," he said, sopping up the last of his too-runny eggs with a charred piece of crust while Isabel was still taking her first tentative bites without saying how awful the food was. "Just tell me when you're gonna leave so I can get ready for the backdraft when you're gone."

Isabel put down her fork. "Jesus, Terry. I'm going to visit my daughter, not moving to a foreign country. I'll be back by the first of the year, maybe sooner, depending on how I feel. I've never really liked staying in other people's houses for more than a couple of nights, but Emily wants me there. We haven't talked about her dad in depth since she came home for his funeral, and that's something we need to do."

"Well, maybe you could talk about my dad for me, so I don't have to?" Terry said, attempting a lighthearted laugh, but his voice was tight and his heart was racing in a weird kind of arrhythmia that seemed like the doomed palpitations of love.

He got up from the table to clear his plate while Isabel finished eating, sorry he was being rude, but unable to face her. Isabel hadn't seemed to mind, but she was weird that way. So full of unsaid things even when she was taking full bore. Nothing like when Matt got ticked off—no fireworks just a long slow burn that was treacherous.

Still, he was pretty sure that wasn't the deal. She hugged him goodbye after she ate the last of her horrible eggs and toast, and replaced his robe with her own less evocative clothes, saying, in a calm tone of voice, "We'll talk more about this later. Whenever you want," before she walked out the door. Not mad then. Just set on her version of things.

When the dishes were done and the counters wiped off, Terry sat down in Isabel's chair—still warm from her body seemingly, although she'd gone a while ago. Resting his open palms on his thighs, he closed his eyes, imagining her sitting on lap while his cock was inside her, calling out his name when she came like she had in his dream.

He tamped down the lovely fantasy out of respect for their apparent impasse, and the lost art of chivalry which probably went out when Charlie died. Time to call Matt, he guessed, but didn't get his phone out of his shirt pocket. Just sat there for a good ten minutes letting the sexual images drift off, not looking for something to replace them, not really wanting to *see* anything at all—about *whatever*—right now.

Perhaps he just wanted to *feel.* But, then again, *no.*

No, he did not.

Feeling too much was gonna kill him.

Or turn him into Matt, which was already happening, based on the weird way his brain was firing and the fact that he couldn't tell his ass from a hole in the ground anymore. Or his asshole from the cosmic vortex that was sucking him in, inch by creepy inch, until he disappeared into a teaming mosh pit of chaos that might spell the end of his new romance.

But what the fuck was the antidote?

Not tinkering with his motorcycle, apparently. Which he did eventually—to no avail, in terms of the bedlam in his head—trying not to sneak looks over to Isabel's house, while he crouched, cat-like, in the driveway, wishing he could find solace in combustible machinery, wishing he could find solace in her.

He wasn't a goddamn stalker but he felt like one, at the same time as he felt like a hermit holed up inside himself, or a solitary yogi stuck in a cliff-top cave, blind to the spectacular view.

"Crap on a fuckin' stick," he muttered, borrowing the Bean's favorite epithet, as he buffed up his Harley's already shining front fender, adjusted the mirrors, scraped pine pitch off the flame-colored gas tank.

Living under the wide swath of evergreen green trees which shaded his front yard and part of Isabel's had its seasonal benefits and deficits. But today the downside moved to the fore as he polished the cleaned-up tank, wishing he could rub out his worries with a well-placed smear of solvent. Knowing he could not, as the dark of the gloomy tree-shaded afternoon descended upon his head like a grim benediction.

In the end—or what seemed like the end, even though it was only five o'clock and not even dinner time—Terry did call Matt. Or rather, Matt called Terry, and Terry called Matt back, after letting the call go to voice-mail, while he covered up his bike and took his tools inside the house, vowing that someday he was going to have a real garage and not just a gol-dang driveway.

"What ho, Slow Joe Crow bro," Terry said, sounding stupider than he meant to, but what the hell, he couldn't just come right out and say he was having second thoughts about Isabel, could he?

When he was—supposedly—being a brave exemplar for ghost-fucking Matt, pursing a real present-tense woman instead of a serial cheater from a tortured marital past. Not that Rosie was simply a cheat. She was smart, arrestingly beautiful—the woman of his dreams, if he'd ever let himself do much more than admire her cynically from a false afar, hiding behind his loyalty to Matt.

But yes, he'd always wanted to make love to Rosie. Caress her freckled skin. Breathe in her alluring essence, smoky as vetiver under rose-petal musk.

Which put a crimp in his talking to Matt about anything involving Rosie and sex unless his observations were strictly Pythonesque. As in, "she's a real goer, iddn't she?" But, somewhere, deep inside, he'd wanted Rosie to love him.

Rosie. Who'd always mocked and poked at and joked about him.

"Terrible Terry Thompson!" she would sneer, every time he made a fool of himself, tripped over a chair leg, spilled beer on his shirt, farted in her and Matt's elegant grey living room.

And he'd poked back, to her face and behind it, right in front of Matt.

"Bitch." Terry would mutter, whenever Rosie made a triple word score using her Z during a contentious Scrabble game, or bested him at pool at an old-timey dive bar, sneaking a quick look at Matt to see if he minded. And the dumb fuck never did.

Funny how all this old shit kept bubbling up in his mind, like mud pots at Yellowstone, since he got his goddamned concussion. How quickly his thoughts ran, even when stumbling. Careening through his brain in the three or four seconds it took Matt to reply to his dumb conversational opening with a dorky "What ho!" of his own.

After various remarks about being glad to be back in Seattle—"a classier shithole than Casper" both laughingly agreed—the two friends fell into their new routine, discussing Terry's health, prompted by Matt, still conscientiously enjoying his nursemaid role.

"How'd you sleep? Is your head okay? You still puking?" Matt rattled off. He didn't ask about Terry's heart.

"I'm doin' all right," Terry said, even though his head throbbed with morbid thoughts about his poor dead dad rotting away in his coffin, and Isabel's dead husband watching them from the southeast corner of her bedroom ceiling whenever he and Isabel were in bed.

"Can't kill a ghost with a gun," he muttered, as Matt moved on, not hearing—or ignoring—his off-the-wall comment.

Burbling about Madam Zodie—Alice—the same way he'd gushed about Rosie in the heady first days of their love affair, the formerly wretched dude seemed happier than he'd been for a good long time.

"I'm going over to her place tonight," Matt proudly announced, adding, not altogether convincingly, "Unless you need me for something, that is?"

"Ah, fuck you, brother," Terry said, feeling jealous and annoyed, pissed that Matt couldn't—or wouldn't—sense his distress and rush to his side, with pot and pizza and a ton of old movies from Scarecrow Video.

Attempting to brush off his negative feelings, Terry asked what was up with Alice these days. Had she been hangin' out much with Isabel?

"How should I know?" Matt snapped. "We don't talk about her social life. And how come you get to call her *Alice*, anyway? You don't even know her."

"Uh, yeah, like you really do, *bud*," Terry scoffed.

"Don't call me bud. And I do know her! I do."

"Okay, then tell me what Tarot deck she likes, or how she got to be an astrologer, or why she's puttin' up with a cock-breath like you, when there are at least a million guys out there who are better n' you . . ."

"What the fuck?" Matt stammered, sounding hurt rather than angry, which Terry almost wished that he was, so they could get in a raging fight.

The Ol' Bean was on the cosmic elevator up, while he was going down fast, like a kid on a rain-drenched slide, which felt like a total rip-off. He'd been trying to live a righteous life for the last three years and look where it got him. Still scramblin' and scrapin' for a living and a life while Matt, as usual, managed to snag a quick lift to the top of the pops.

However comforting it might feel to blame his bruising anguish on his inconvenient concussion, Terry was pretty damn sure that wasn't the case, although somehow his grief for his father and his insecurity about Isabel didn't seem to add up to the massive black cloud bearing down on him.

Maybe it was just life itself that was suffocating, he thought, listening to Matt rattle on. Madam Zodie this. And Madam Zodie that. Interspersed with admiring quips about Alice. As if he was talking about twins.

"Hey, are your old lady's eyes the same weird color of green?" the dumb-ass finally said, pushing Terry's polite-listener's stoicism over the edge, so that he said—or rather drawled, rather creepily, "Nah. They're nothin' like Rosie's," bringing the whole conversation to a close.

After he switched off his phone, Terry started to laugh, thinking about how he'd stuck Matt with a romantic conundrum, for Rosie's eyes really were green, mixed with sharp flints of blue. Rosie's eyes had the magnetism of a predatory animal, while the cousins' sly glances were soft and inviting.

Kind of weird to think about the Ol' Bean changing his anima type from Celtic temptress to Nordic forest spirit, although he'd most likely just expanded his repertoire—which Terry hoped did not, and would never, include Isabel.

He swept the floors and dusted the furniture, doing housework karaoke as he cleaned, thinking yet not thinking about Isabel and Rosie and the power of obsession, wanting to be cleanly aware yet unable to grasp his ultimate predicament.

What was it exactly?

Aside from life itself?

Eventually he put down the old T-shirt he'd been using as a dust rag and lay down on his couch, burying his hands under the throw pillow on his stomach like a giant marsupial.

Isabel. Rosie. And yes, he had to admit, Alice.

How odd to want to fuck all of them, one after the other, or in tandem—if he had three cocks—to want to hold and suck and possess—to sink, to drink, to think of nothing but flesh and fat and the stink of semen on their breasts and lips, the grinding of hips, mouth-to-mouth breathing, the resuscitation of his soul. The atomic end to his celibacy.

Not just odd, but ridiculous, he decided, laughing harder and harder at the gross depictions that assaulted him, until his eyes were swimming with tears, and he thought he'd faint from the great blast of heat irradiating his root chakra and the stream of bodily and out-of-body sensations vying for possession of him.

To want. To need. To yearn. To fear.

To be grounded. To be free. To be held. To be safe.

To be something to someone. To be something for someone.

To be nothing at all.

Rain was falling outside. He closed his eyes, feeling sleep come. Perhaps he would dream about Isabel.

THANKSGIVING

What a difference a year makes.

Terry didn't know if there was a song like that, but if there was he was going to sing it. Top of his lungs, maybe, or no, crooning it like Ol' Blue Eyes, his dad's favorite singer. To Isabel, up close, that night on the couch after dinner when all her guests had gone home.

He checked his face in the bathroom mirror, pleased that the scars on his forehead had faded. His beard was neatly trimmed, sideburns too, and there was a twinkle in his eyes that was true. He no longer looked like a grizzled prizefighter.

He was wearing a pale-blue button-down shirt that he'd ironed instead of his usual black Henley. And fancy new underpants—bikini not Y-front—which he'd bought with Isabel in mind even though they were a bit uncomfortable. She wouldn't care that he was wearing old jeans when she discovered he was dressed as a lover.

One last grin at his beaming reflection, then he padded barefoot into the kitchen to pack up the stuff he was taking next door for Thanksgiving. A bottle of Hennessy cognac, some fancy mixed nuts, a wedge of Manchego cheese. He poured himself a glass of beer before adding a jar of pickled peaches to the bag, a seasonal gift from his mother that he didn't particularly want.

With fifteen minutes to spare before it was time to leave the house, he sat down at the table to finish his beer, and toy with his memories of everything that had happened in the past year since Isabel hared off to Emily's for Thanksgiving and Christmas.

A bit like peering at his face in the mirror, he thought, only looking from the outside in. The way he felt when he read a sci-fi book that seemed particularly relevant to his life—kind of creeped out, yet oddly illuminated.

He stroked his sideburns meditatively. Here he was, still alive and kickin' after the long tortuous twelve months post the Casper debacle, in which he'd quit his janitor job, had a mini-breakdown, and breakup and reconciliation with Isabel, disappearing into the deepest darkest part of himself while Isabel looked on, transfixed, yet unable to help him.

His Big Fuckin' Man Struggle, as he now thought of it. Able to laugh at himself a little, like he had in the dim old days before the nasty double bashes to his head let the bright light of brutal self-examination stream in. Sins, fears, doubts and sorrows, all shining like atomic suns on his inner retinas and everything else as blurry as an Etch A Sketch drawing.

No wonder he hadn't been able to see Isabel clearly. Or himself. When all he could see was Eros versus Thanatos in everything he thought and did, in every aspect of life. Sex and death. Sex and death. The ancient indivisible couple. Or maybe just one entity with two faces, like him and his bathroom mirror.

Terry sipped his beer, careful not to drink too fast. No way was he gonna embarrass his hostess tonight by getting drunk in front of her daughter. Emily seemed nice when he met her last night, as did Deepak, her husband, but as dutiful children concerned for their mother, he knew they'd be watching him. He didn't mind if they saw a bit of awkwardness in his manner as long as they didn't compare him with Charlie, who'd probably quoted Dante when he was drunk.

How much had Isabel told Emily about their relationship, anyway? Did she know about their fights? Their early problems with sex? The fact that Isabel didn't want to marry him—at least not yet? Some things were sacrosanct, personal, Terry thought, although he'd never advised Isabel to keep their love affair secret.

As if on cue, one particular memory floated up in his consciousness at the same time as he was checking the clock. Almost time to go, but the image held him fast. It wasn't the only turning point for him and Isabel, but it felt indelible because of the vivid location. The olfactory hit of Puget Sound. The murmur of the in-coming tide. Children shrieking as they ran along the beach. A blue uncompromised sky.

He and Isabel had walking at Golden Gardens last summer, a few months after getting back together, holding hands as they navigated the rocky shingle, when she'd startled him by saying, "I don't mind you being jealous of Charlie, if you don't mind me being jealous that you'd like to fuck Alice. But I do mind not knowing if you're going AWOL again."

"What d'ya mean? I'm here, ain't I?" Terry had said, glibly self-righteous, in spite of the fix he'd left her in last winter and spring when he'd emotionally and mentally checked out.

Avoiding her calls when she came back from Minnesota. Working on his Harley at Matt's. Keeping his blinds down so she couldn't peer into his house. Exasperating Isabel—and himself—with the intransigence of his bullheadedness.

Holding onto his resentment of Charlie while he grieved the death of his dad, when he should have been sticking to her and trying to work things out.

She shot him a sideways glance, wistful rather than menacing, but it pierced his heart when she let go of his hand and began walking away from him back up the beach towards the parking lot. He'd fumbled after her, nearly tripping on wet stones in his haste to grab back her hand.

By the time he caught up with her, Isabel was leaning against the fence railings on the little wooden bridge near the turtle pond, staring down at the red-eared sliders that were lined up side by side on floating logs, basking in the noonday sun.

He'd wished he were down in the murky water with the relaxed-looking turtles, instead of stuck up on land, trying to get closer to Isabel when all she'd show him was her back. The short dress she was wearing was the same color as the patches of moss on the logs, her concentration away from him altogether tortoise-like, as if she were slowly yet inexorably creeping away from him in the private green field of her mind.

For a crazy moment Terry wanted to fall to his knees in front of her, but there were teenagers who flounced by on the footbridge aiming their cell phones at each other, so he stifled the impulse. He leaned forward until he could smell the familiar perfume of her hair and neck, but did not touch her.

There'd been nothing and everything to say. About sex. Commitment. Fear and love. The fact that he didn't want Alice anymore. That maybe he never had. But all he'd said was, "I am here for the long run." And he'd meant it. And everything it implied.

After that everything seemed to get easier between them. The sex, the talking, the lovemaking—which was how he thought of their eventual success at intercourse—even their fights which less and less centered on Charlie and other insoluble ghosts.

Sunday mornings in bed, making love before breakfast. Danish movies at the Nordic Museum. Walks at Discovery Park, jaunts around Green Lake. An entire afternoon dedicated to Scrabble and Monopoly. Cheeseburgers from Dick's Drive-in, chocolates from Dilettante. A sly hand up Isabel's skirt while riding downtown on the Monorail. Slick kisses in the back of Uber cars, all hot tongue and soul.

The sensual pleasures were inestimable, the psychological benefits ditto, and the whole cranky process of getting to know one another finally began to flow, swift and sure as a deep fount of water.

Now here he was, about to attend an intimate family gathering with Isabel and her family and friends. Finally comforted and comfortable—well, almost—after months of fearing that, in addition to losing Isabel, he was going to lose himself to the worst of his post-concussive symptoms.

Headaches, paranoia, distrust of his trusty motorcycle. Messages from his dead father in the form of odors of unknown origin. An obsession with birds. And always, the terrible fantasies about coitus and cunnilingus with women he couldn't have. Even after he started having intercourse with Isabel.

But oh the joy and sublimity of that! The feel of the hot core of her body accepting the essence of his. The sense that he'd finally come home to her.

The achievement of his deepest desire had turned the tide of the arousing images that repeatedly washed over him, but it took a few months for the pornographic deluge to firmly withdraw.

Happy as this new state of sexual affairs made him, Terry had struggled. Supposed he was struggling still, although that didn't seem to matter today when he felt so sweetly fulfilled.

Leaving his janitor job to work as fry cook meant ten hours a day standing on his feet, but not much moving around. After just a couple of months he'd gained ten pounds, added a Jesus-y beard to his sideburns and cut his curly hair short so the hairnet he had to wear in the restaurant kitchen didn't look like a holey Rasta hat.

When he came home at night his hair stank of grill grease and meat and his arms ached like a motherfucker. The new routine was staggering in its senselessness and he was broke to boot, but he was rejiggering his life, so he forced himself to think it was worth it.

Offering himself to Isabel in his compromised state had seemed dishonorable. But, somehow, after their tacit agreement at the turtle pond, a sort of confidence took root in his psyche and he opened himself up to her, expecting both the best and the worst. Which they'd had. And so far survived.

"These are the good ol' times," Terry chuckled to himself, as he rose from the table to put on his boots before carrying his holiday contributions next door. He'd had enough of remembering and dissembling the past. Enough of what the I Ching calls "chewing on old meat." He wanted fresh turkey and stuffing.

Isabel and her female guests were rushing around the kitchen when he arrived at her open back door. The smoke alarm had gone off at some point apparently, but the warm kitchen smelled delicious not burnt, and there was a hint of butter-drenched herbs in the air that made his mouth water expectantly.

"Hey, Terry!" Alice yelled from her post at the stovetop where she was mashing a big pot of spuds. Emily and Alice's mom, Marianne, also greeted him warmly, taking the bag of food from his arms, pouring him a glass of wine, patting his back affectionately.

Only Isabel seemed wholly distracted, but then, she was the widowed hostess with a lot going on—and he was just a guest, he reminded himself. She had the big roasting pan in her hands, minus the resting turkey, and was pouring drippings into a smaller pan to make gravy. There was a smudge of flour on her nose and cranberry stains on her apron. She looked wonderful.

"Anythin' I can do to help?" he offered, but Isabel shook her head.

"It's all under control," she said. And then, with a more present smile, "So glad you're here, Terry. Why don't you join the menfolk while we finish up?" which made him feel slightly uncomfortable, since he didn't know Deepak and had only met Chet maybe twice.

But the Ol' Bean was here, so, with a bit more confidence, wine glass in hand, he went through the hall to the living room. No football on TV, thank God, just the three men sitting around the coffee table eating chips and guacamole which didn't seem very Thanksgiving-like to Terry.

He almost went to fetch his Manchego cheese, but Chet and Deepak stood up to shake his hand and Matt gave him a brotherly hug before starting in on some story about the dreadful green-bean casserole his mom used to make.

Following his own sage advice, Terry sipped his white wine, waiting for the night to begin, even though it already had. When the women's kitchen duties were finally done and they joined their partners for the promenade to the dinner table, he realized that what he'd hungered for, aside from the food, was the zing of their feminine laughter.

He took Isabel's hand as they entered the dining room, and whispered, "I'm glad I'm here," and he was.

Isabel sat down at the head of the table with Emily, Deepak and Chet taking seats to her right, and Alice, Matt and Marianne taking seats on her left—while Terry claimed the end of the table where the thirteen-pound turkey sat directly in front of him, since he'd volunteered to carve it.

 Looking down the beautifully set table, Terry saw that Isabel was smiling proudly and patting her daughter's hand—for once, completely un-sphinxlike. Then holding her wine glass aloft, she announced in her warm melodious voice, "Emily has something to say," to which her beaming son-in-law added a hearty, "So do I!"

Emily and Deepak clasped hands, their faces glowing in the candlelight. "We're going to have a baby!" they cried, shedding tears of expectant joy as they stammered out details of their birth plan.

Trust Chet to set the proper mood of jubilation after the grand announcement. "A toast!" he shouted, spilling wine on the damask tablecloth as he splashed their glasses with Rosé.

"To babies and love and my niece's happiness and good health! And her husband's, of course. Deepak, you the man!"

Terry's eyes watered as he took in the congratulatory faces, including Matt's, which looked inordinately smug, although the dude hardly knew Emily and Deepak. Hardly knew Isabel either, for that matter, having been involved with Alice to the exclusion of all else for the past many months. For a second, Terry wanted to punch the smile off his face. But what good would that do? It wasn't the Ol' Bean's fault that he felt so discombobulated.

Isabel was going to be a grandmother.

The information shouldn't have floored him, but he was stunned.

She'd never have his child, or grandchild with him, Terry thought, feeling resentful and needy and guilty at the same time as he felt pleased for Isabel and her family, of which he was not—and might never be—an integral part.

There'd be no chips off the old Wyoming block destined to love motorcycles and stretches of wide open road and red-dirt witches' haunts and moonlight on Lake Union—as seen from the Salmon House when a little bit tipsy—ever growing inside of her. Being born into this world of sorrow and joy. Looking as beautiful as Isabel. As goofy as him. Boy or girl, it didn't matter. The kid would never exist.

The visceral realization of this awful truth packed such a punch that he almost dropped the carving knife that he hadn't realized he was holding. Suffused with self-pity, he sawed at the turkey while bowls of mashed potatoes and stuffing—and his mom's pickled peaches—were passed around the table by happy people who suddenly seemed so much more present than him, burbling with baby talk and anecdotes about parenting.

"Emily was the sweetest little child," Isabel declared, eliciting a burst of laughter from Alice who said, "No, she was a pain in my babysitting ass with her all her infernal questions."

"Like you weren't?" Marianne said, waggling a motherly finger at Alice before grinning at Chet.

Deepak held his wine glass up to Emily. "Our baby will be fortunate to have such a brilliant and inquisitive mother."

"And a dad who's good at changing diapers," Emily said, giving her husband a grateful look.

Faces lit with candlelight and the starshine of welcome news, the hubbub of excited talk emanating from the rest of the group seemed like a warm cloak enfolding them, while Terry sat in the cold and dark, staring at the brussel sprouts on his plate, wishing he could throw them at someone.

Exchanging a quick look with Isabel, across what seemed like the vast swath of the laden dinner table—almost a continent it seemed—he wondered if his selfish thoughts were obvious to her. Or the rest of her family, which seemed to include Matt since he kept referring to Chet as his future father-in-law and making coy remarks to Marianne, who laughed indulgently.

Isabel was still smiling, but Terry thought she looked a bit tense, which he interpreted guiltily, or maybe narcissistically, as concern about him. So he stepped up his game and began babbling about random shit to reduce the strain he was probably putting on her at the first Thanksgiving dinner she'd hosted sans Charlie.

After the leftovers were cleared away, and pumpkin pie and cognac were served, the next incendiary bomb was detonated. By Matt, rising from his chair with a self-satisfied look and proudly exclaiming, "Alice and I have some more good news. We're pregnant!"

The royal WE. The biological impossibility of it. The wrong grammatical syntax. *Shee-it.* Even Alice looked pissed at Matt's temerity in making the announcement that should have been hers. She rolled her eyes as he sat down. "Too bad this dumb-ass dad has morning sickness," she said.

Terry hacked and coughed, wishing he could spit out his jealousy, while everyone shouted out congratulations and advice. Marianne, beaming delightedly, put her hand over her daughter's cognac glass. "Don't drink that!" she commanded, "Give it to your dad. He's going to be a grandfather!"

"And that's going to help?" Alice laughed, hugging her joyful mom.

After that, the night was a blur, even though Terry didn't get drunk. Wine and cognac, followed by several beers after Isabel's guests departed did nothing to improve his mood or inebriate him. But he was flummoxed about how to get high when he didn't have any marijuana with him, and he was afraid to go home, in case he did something stupid.

Alice and Emily had done a spot-on job cleaning up the dining room and kitchen, leaving nothing for him to do to work off his nervous energy. He wandered around the living room feeling itchy and restless, while Isabel locked up the house, trying to focus on something other than envious feelings about the happily expectant couples.

Isabel came into the room and collapsed on the couch in front of the fire—expertly laid and tended by Chet, although that was usually Terry's job on a chilly autumnal evening. He sat down beside her and took hold of her hand, wondering if she was disappointed in him. Or worse, coldly pissed off.

But she seemed happy enough, if a trifle subdued, so he guessed she hadn't picked up on his shameful thoughts. Maybe she was just missing her daughter and son-in-law who'd gone off to Alice's to spend the night. He hoped she wasn't missing Charlie.

Her small hand in his felt so vulnerable, he was suffused with a terrible longing. He wanted to eat her alive, skin and bones and breasts and heart, chew her into tiny bits of perfumed flesh. Chanel Number Five mixed with a stiff whiff of cottonwoods. Metaphorically speaking, but still. His hunger for her terrified and exhilarated him.

As did his humiliating desire to impregnate her which made him feel like a crass barbarian. Not bloody likely that she'd be up for a natural or IVF pregnancy at the age of fifty.

In the firelit room Isabel's face waved and flickered, her expression changing and shifting, her liquid gaze fixing first on his mouth, then on his eyes, then on his mouth again, as if she were going to kiss him.

Terry leaned towards her expectantly but she let go of his hand, closed her eyes, and lay back, hair spread out on the cushions like a laudanum-stoned Pre-Raphaelite, seemingly, yet enchantingly, exhausted. Once again, he was reminded of the mystical quality she shared with her outré cousin.

"A fine pair we are," she said, after a short while in which he examined her languid form, waiting for her to stiffen up and tell him to go home.

Isabel's voice was low and dim, half as bright as the fire. "I saw your face when you heard that Emily and Alice are pregnant. You looked the same way you did when you came back from Casper. Like a man who's been hollowed out."

Terry chuckled mirthlessly, imagining his scarred old head shooting up in alarm like a mule deer that's scented his hunter, even though he didn't move. Stark images from his bereavement trip home rose up in his memory, piqued by the leaping flames in the fireplace, followed by a swirl of pictures from his early life, his boyhood in Wyoming, the creased face of his dad.

The pop and sizzle from slightly damp logs reconfigured the images of harsh sun and deep snow and bone-chilling winds into interior depictions of rain. Looking away from the fire towards the living-room windows, he realized that it was coming down buckets outside. The swish of wet leaves on a window pane, the drumbeat of furious drops, the odd tingle in his head that came on when the weather was like this, reminded him that he was here now, not back in the past.

Not waiting for something or someone. Not aching to leave home.

"So, okay," he suddenly said. "I'm not the right guy for you and you're not the right gal for me, maybe. But who fuckin' cares? The age thing duddn't matter, even though maybe the babies do. But I can get over that, I'm purty sure. I love you and you love me. It's you I want. *You.*"

Isabel gently squeezed Terry's hand, then brought it up to her face so she could kiss the once-broken fingers, the Nazca lines of his palm, caress his wrist with her thumb. She had tears in her eyes but she didn't look stoned anymore.

"Guess it's time for us to figure out where we're going from here," she said, giving him a tremulous smile that made her look younger than him. Or the way Terry guessed he looked with his heart all aflutter, hopeful and scared.

For a weird second he wished Alice was there to translate her cousin's unspoken intentions, but then Isabel punched him on the arm like he always hit Matt, only much softer.

"Yes, I do mean together, Terry. If that's what you want."

ANOTHER NOVEMBER

Six-month-old Isadora Belinda Barker's eyes were changing from newborn blue to green. Not the woodland hue of her mother Alice's green eyes, but the sparkly aquamarine of Rosie O'Hara's, her father's ex-wife's.

Her wispy hair was strawberry-blonde but it was likely she'd end up with flaming red tresses like the captivating woman Matthew hoped to forget. And Matthew himself and his long dead mother—and most likely some of Alice's Viking ancestors—so she was cursed to go through life, sans hair dye, as someone who stood out from the crowd. As a bona fide flame-haired ginger.

Matthew worried about the genetic mutation his daughter had apparently inherited as a redhead, but Alice didn't seem to mind. She said biology wasn't destiny just window dressing. The real self was metaphysical. And besides, red hair and pale freckled skin were beautiful things. Just look at the gorgeous depictions of auburn-haired vixens that artists had painted over hundreds of years.

But Matthew didn't want a fox for a daughter, just a normal ordinary girl.

Watching Isadora reach for Tehuti while the old dog snuffed around the couch in search of dropped movie-night popcorn. Listening to the yabba-dabba-do sounds of her baby talk. Inhaling the sweetness of her baby scent—clean scalp and mother's milk and something indefinable that smelled like innocence—made him glad he'd married Alice. Made a baby with her.

This incomparable, wonderful, magnificent baby, who was sitting on his lap now while he read *The Very Hungry Caterpillar* to her. Laughing at him with such bold eye-to-eye contact, that it seemed like they'd been friends, not just father and daughter, for much longer than she'd been alive. Since time out of mind, in a way. The same way he felt about Terry.

Matthew was pretending to be a hungry caterpillar, munching on the corner of the book and waggling his eyebrows at Isadora, when Alice came into the living room, fresh from her Skype reading, looking worn out, which meant her consultation had been challenging.

"Hey Groucho." She flashed a weary smile and plopped down on the couch, reaching for Isadora.

"Lovely Miss Izzy," she said, nuzzling the small silky head as the child squirmed in her arms then settled down to nurse, looking drowsy eyed.

Matthew reached for Alice's hand. "Everything go okay with your reading?" he asked, knowing she'd extemporize without giving away anything about her client's specific problems or identity. She was good that way. Trustworthy. A free spirit, but the honorable kind.

Unlike some people, he couldn't help thinking grudgingly.

Alice laughed her wounded-healer laugh—a slight little barb tipped with no-nonsense compassion—and gave him a shorthand version of her last ninety minutes.

"Another Saturn-dominated person who has to do everything the long hard way and can't tell the difference between apprenticeship and slavery. Needs to get a grip on how to be his own master with something approaching joy. But then, don't we all."

Alice shook her head ruefully, then stretched out with the now dozing baby on her lap, pressing her feet against Matthew, signaling her possible desire for a foot massage. He let out a happy sigh as he pulled the slipper socks from her feet, fantasizing about sex in the afternoon while the baby was asleep.

Alice smiled apologetically, then scooched herself off the couch, holding the baby tenderly as she walked towards their bedroom, leaving Matthew holding her socks.

"Izzy's going down for a nap and then I'm calling Isabel while I get started on dinner. And hey, maybe you should call Terry? You guys haven't talked in a while."

Well, no they had not. Not person to person, anyway, although he talked to Terry in his head pretty constantly. Alice this and Isadora that. And, every once in a while, confidences about himself that weren't about his precious family and home or his boring-ass software job.

How he still fantasized about Rosie sometimes. How, even now, he imagined tonguing her succulent white flesh, lapping up her essence, inhaling the rose-petal scent of her. It wasn't real desire, just the residue of his old obsession, but it felt weird and uncomfortable.

Back in the day when he was actually fucking her, Matthew hadn't minded talking about Rosie and sex, in that godawful jokey frat-bro way he and Terry used to keep intimate confidences from getting too specifically particular.

He'd even bragged about how much pussy he was getting at home, and the superiority of said pussy, as if his wife's private charms could be quantified—the sudden memory of which had filled him with self-loathing one of the first times he changed his new baby-girl's diaper. Cleaned her tiny vulva. Turned the word into *vulnerable* on the synesthetic screen in his head.

Worrying about Isadora's ability to withstand the sexism that he'd no doubt continue to exemplify, however unconsciously, was terrifying. If he couldn't protect his daughter from himself, then what hope did he have in controlling her experience of the androcentric world she'd been born into?

Almost none, Alice said. But he could help her to be strong enough to deal with it.

Matthew stretched out on the couch, willing his stupid mind to stop obsessing and kvetching and to count his blessings, even though they seemed too fresh and miraculous to be true.

Alice's low voice followed by raucous laugher wafted in from the kitchen as he watched the moonfaced clock on the mantelpiece tick off the minutes of the dwindling afternoon. The strange feeling he'd had on this very same couch, the morning after the debauched Halloween party two years ago, flickered into his consciousness. Not peacefulness exactly. Not joy. More like the awe-fullness of being transported to another planet. One much different, and better, than earth.

Being in Madam Zodie's house—for it was still hers of the arcane name, regardless of his welcome occupancy—felt like being in the boudoir of a temple priestess, with its bowls of potpourri and joss sticks burning on the hearth, and gauzy curtains made of the kind of sinuous fabric an Egyptian queen might wear on a wall of peeling hieroglyphs.

No need to read the titles of the occult tomes in the built-in bookcases on either side of the tiled fireplace, or rummage through her impressive collection of Tarot cards and painted boxes of twinkling crystals, to feel that there was magic here. Not just in the scented air, gradually infiltrated with the aromas of thyme and lemon from her kitchen, but any place where Madam Zodie—Alice—chose to be.

Not that she was perfect or inhuman or particularly blessed with incredible foresight, regardless of her purported psychism. She'd married him, hadn't she? Given birth to his child. Who might, for all they knew, be similarly afflicted with his brain's weird wiring, in addition to the redheads' genetic mutation he tried not to worry about.

Matthew's love for his family, and his growing sensitivity about women—for which his wife jokingly harassed him—made his occasional fantasies about Rosie seem, if not wholly craven, then embarrassingly pointless.

That he'd ever fucked and re-fucked and double-and-triple-fucked her over a period of almost six years, seemed as bizarre as a fourteen-year-old boy in Casper fucking Rhianna at the local bowling alley. It just couldn't happen but it had. His experiences with Rosie had marked him mind and body, but the only way to erase their seemingly indelible effect was to pretend that she was dead and her greedy ghost had been vanquished.

And to never talk about her with Terry again.

And, oh Jesus. *Terry.*

What the fuck was dummkopf doing slinging hash in a breakfast joint in Podunk Central Washington anyway?

Fucking dude didn't even look like Keanu anymore. Last Facetime conversation they had, Terry had long corkscrew electric hair, intense eyes over clean-shaven cheeks which had thinned out over the past year, making his grim seem more wolfish than when he was sporting his New Testament beard, or the few streaks of day-old stubble he wore back when he was a janitor.

In truth, Terry had looked pretty damn good and he still had his magnificent sideburns, but he didn't look like himself anymore—or the self he used to seem to be—since how could you tell who somebody really was, if that person wasn't you?

"The great fucking conundrum," Alice said, coming back into the living room, with her phone held to her ear and a tray full of dishes. Shrimp with sour cream on rye crackers. A few slices of Jalsburg. Two tall shot glasses of Aquavit.

Setting the Nordic antipasti carefully down on the coffee table, she whispered, "Be right back," blowing Matthew a kiss before sashaying back to the kitchen, exaggeratedly wriggling her lately less-than-slender hips, while laughing into her cellphone.

Suspecting that Alice's call with her cousin might last for several more minutes—particularly if they were talking conundrums—he dug in his pocket for his phone, figuring he ought to damn well be in on the conversation between the west side and east side of the Cascade mountains, where the Dashiell-Thompsons now lived.

Not that Terry and Isabel were married yet or going by the same name, but they were definitely a couple now. The couple who got away.

He absentmindedly popped a cracker into his mouth, spilling a glob of sour cream onto his chest, and keyed in Terry's number, which rang for so long he was sure it would click into voicemail.

"Wonderin' how long it was gonna take ya to call me," Terry said, when he finally answered his phone. "Your turn this time, asshole, an' it's been awhile."

"Yeah, sorry. Been kinda busy with my kid," Matthew countered, feeling kind of pissed off that Terry didn't get where he was coming from. What he was doing now. Living in a new home. Being a father.

Ignoring Matthew's sarcasm, Terry went on blithely. "How's she doin', your sweet little girl? Izzy—'zat what you're callin' her?—not Alice. Though I mean her, too, a course. How're *you* doin', by the way?"

"Fucking fine, fine 409," Matthew said, repeating their mantra from when they were kids calling each other on tin can walkie-talkies from their hidey-hole basement clubhouse.

"Alice and Isadora are good, too. And yeah, we're calling her Izzy—or Alice is. I kind of like Dora, although I appreciate the homage to Isabel. Alice wanted to name her Isis, for Christ's sake. Can you dig it?"

Terry laughed appreciatively. "Yeah, I can just picture that on her passport. Too bad nobody knows a fuckin' thing about mythology anymore. World could use a couple of ancient goddesses takin' things in hand about now."

"How are *you* taking things? You and Isabel?"

A slight pause, before Terry answered, saying nothing the same way Matthew had. "Uh, we're doin' okay."

"Yeah, right. Come on, what's up with you guys? Toiling away in the sticks, not getting hitched—seems like you're kind of in limbo. No offense."

"Funny how 'no offense' means you're givin' me shit. Dipshit." Terry's voice was low and growly, but not hard, so he wasn't angry.

But there was something else he wasn't saying, even when he began describing his new life in brief, but sardonic, detail. Erratic restaurant shifts. Isabel's bigger-than-his paycheck from the college where she worked as a bookkeeper. The ridiculously low amount they were paying to rent a nice house on the outskirts of town—half the cost of a dump in Seattle. The burns he got cooking French fries.

"Blah blah, yada yada," Matthew mocked, wishing Terry would just spit it out. Come clean about his disillusionment with the older Isabel, his sadness about their not having kids.

But all Terry said was "Fuck you and the smug horse you rode in on," followed by a long meaningful silence in which Matthew could hear Isabel's laughter in Terry's background in concert with Alice's tinkling cackle emanating from his.

"No really. I want to know what's going on with you. If you're doing okay."

Terry's laughter was light yet brutal.

"*Rilly*? Got your beautiful wife and new kid, your cozy little house and your sweet-ass security contracts, and you still wanna know how crappy I have it. Same as you did back when I was scrubbin' shit off hospital floors and you were scrubbin' code with a few tappy taps of your fingers like a goddamn gentleman. What's your definition of solidarity, anyhow?"

"That's not fair!" Matthew shouted, even though Terry was right. He *had* gloated over the differences in their lives. Felt superior because of his white-collar status, the fat wads of cash in his money clip, his sexy chanteuse of a wife. He'd pitied his celibate, ruggedly independent best friend.

And maybe, just maybe, envied him.

But he couldn't say that now that they'd got off on the wrong foot. And there really wasn't time to get into anything deep before he'd need to get back to Alice anyway. Set the table. Uncork the wine. Check on the baby.

Terry let out a genuine guffaw. "Can hear ya reelin' out yer unassailable excuses, but hey man, ain't necessary to keep defendin' yourself. I know your black heart inside and out, and I don't give a damn that you're a self-centered piece a shit 'cause I love ya anyway. Most of us dudes take the cake when it comes to being clueless 'bout other people anyway. Doncha think?"

Matthew's laughter sounded relieved even though he wasn't, but now wasn't the time to harp on his niggling concerns, so he mumbled some anodyne crap about the differences between men and women, and asked how things were going with Isabel.

"Yeah well, it's good between the two of us, but there's nothin' to do here but work our asses off and come home at night dog-tired 'though we ain't got a dog. Just good ol' Delilah the cat who's still hangin' in. But I don't think she likes this new setup that much. We can't let her out in the yard in case a murderin' coyotes."

Jesus, now Terry was talking about dogs and cats. Not really saying anything. Although maybe he was, underneath his intransigence. Making Terry talk when he didn't feel like it had always been hard, but he'd always given Matthew free rein to spout off, which sort of made up for the verbal imbalance, but not quite.

Matthew meant to say something funny about Tehuti, keeping the conversation light, but instead he blurted out, "You guys should some back! You can get new jobs! Break the lease with Isabel's renters! Borrow money from us if you need to!"

Terry sniffed disdainfully. "Shee-it, dude. Purty sure me and Isabel can figure this out. We're goin' to Minnesota to visit Emily and Deepak for Thanksgiving. Check up on little Charlie. Bring him some old books that belonged to his grandfather—although what an infant's gonna do with a treatise on Chartres Cathedral's beyond me. Anyhoo, when we get back to E-Burg, we'll do some brainstormin', but it looks like we'll probably move."

Matthew took a celebratory slug of Alice's Aquavit, since his was all gone, and crammed two more shrimp-laden crackers into his mouth in his new-found enthusiasm. His old buddy was coming home!

"That's great man. I can't wait!" he said, preparing to end the call with some kind of inspirational aphorism like 'do what you love and the money will follow', or 'follow your heart'—bullshit, of course, but knowing Terry, he'd appreciate the sentiment, understanding that Matthew meant it both seriously and ironically.

But the call wasn't quite over yet, because Terry started snorting the way he did when he was high, pretty much laughing his ass off before Matthew could ask what was tickling his funny bone. Finally, gasping for breath after taking what sounded like a big hit off a joint, Terry said he had some news about Rosie and the cock-breath Bastard that Matt might enjoy. Something about a video.

"'Less you're sick a those jerks," he added.

A sharp little twinge in his chest, followed by a similar stab to his guts, tweaked Matthew's consciousness, but he told Terry to go ahead anyway, hoping the story was short.

"So yeah, man, there's Brand, dressed like a cross between Oscar Wilde and Alistair Crowley, all velvets and silk, sittin' on a gilded couch. And there's Rosie, wearin' a white little Victorian hooker dress, stuck on his lap like they're fuckin'. Hair fallin' all down her back while he's kneadin' her ass, and she's moanin' like they're actually doin' the act. But hey, maybe they was . . ."

Terry took another expressive hit off his joint.

"Then the camera pans to the side and what d'you know, she's pregnant. Belly stickin' out, tits as big as the moon, while the dude is suckin' her neck like a gol-dang vampire. And she's lookin' like she's in heaven—or maybe hell—'cause her eyes are rolled way back in her head. And the whole damn time there's this little kid music tinklin' away on one of those old-fashioned toy pianas and a buncha eerie voices chantin' some weird crap about scarlet women. "

Terry let out an expansive breath of stunned admiration. "The whole dang thing was surreal."

Matthew clawed at his glasses, in the vain hope that removing them would block out the evil banner of obscenely illuminated words that were suddenly flapping inside him like a wind-tossed kite. *BITCH. BASTARD. ASSHOLES.* Each letter as distinct and alarming as a magical alphabet designed for cursing people. All shimmering and glittering in scarlet red like the costume Rosie was wearing in the last act of *Miss Communication* the night he was stalking her.

Pushing down his anger at Terry for presenting him with this latest obscenity—and the migraine lurking in its oily wake—he blurted, "Send me the link!" before gulping down the last of Alice's Aquavit, wishing that she'd left the whole bottle with him so he could chugalug it.

"Sure thing, brother," Terry said, so cheerfully that Matthew wanted to slug him. There was a hidden barb beyond the snarkily ubiquitous 'brother.' Not knowing what it was made him paranoid. Still, this was no time to ask if his cunning old friend was pissed at him.

Isadora was stirring, dinnertime was minutes away, and he needed to stop seething—and visualizing, and remembering, and hating and yearning and wondering why the good things in his life, his marriage, his kid, couldn't just stay that way. Untouched by his neuroses, his past, his worries about his friendship with Terry, and Terry himself, even though the damn dude was laughing again.

Restraining the urge to ask what the fuck was up with Terry being in regular media touch with Rosie and her Bastard husband—when those people were in *his* karass, were *his* concern—Matthew said, "Time to eat. Gotta go." Glad for the excuse to get off the phone, even though a little voice in his head said he should hang on and get the big picture.

But the big picture always sucks, so he delivered a friendly goodbye.

"What ho, bro. Catch ya later." Terry's voice sounded a bit hoarse—probably from laughing so much—and laconic, ironic, and kind. No matter what was going down with the man—or him—Terry was always kind.

Matthew chided himself for forgetting that indisputable fact, even for a kneejerk instant, feeling yet again smaller inside himself than he should be, a mere grain of sand instead of the shining constellation that Alice indicated he was, astrologically.

Then again, soul was bigger than psychology, wasn't it? Maybe, over many lifetimes, he'd become a better friend, but he doubted it. "Same ol' selfish bullshitter" was more his likely evolutionary outcome, like Terry always swore he was, after one of their ridiculous fights. But he could try, couldn't he?

DINNER AT HOME WITH THE WIFE AND KID
OR "WITH MY BODY, I THEE WORSHIP"

Matthew wanted to call Terry back the instant they concluded their call. Get to the bottom of what Terry was doing in Bum-Fuck Washington. What he was doing with his life.

But it really was time to eat.

Matthew set the table while Alice rushed around. Mashing potatoes, steaming green beans, putting the succulent brown chicken and roasted carrots on a serving platter, between trips to the bedroom and bathroom to change Isadora's diaper, and bring her into the living room to play on the rug with Tehuti.

In spite of being so ferociously busy, Alice looked less frazzled than she had after her consulting appointment, which Matthew ascribed to her call with Isabel, since he hadn't done a thing till now to help with dinner. He wondered what her cousin had said to make her so cheerful. She smiled and swatted his butt when she passed by him in the tiny kitchen.

Finding cloth napkins to put on the table, and decent bottle of wine, made him feel more supportive, a bit less like a privileged male jerk, which was ridiculous since Alice, for all her archetypal insights into gender issues, didn't really see him that way.

"When you get out of your mind and into your heart, you're almost as sweet as Terry is," she'd said one memorable time, making Matthew proud of himself and jealous of his friend, who looked like—but wasn't—a hell-boy like him.

Getting his mind out of the way was pretty damned hard even at the best of times. Like Sunday dinner with his wife and kid, which he cherished. The freaky keyboard soundtrack to the obscene video of Rosie and Jackson he'd vividly imagined had mercifully exited his brain—although it would inevitably come back—leaving a hole in his head shaped like Terry.

Once he got Isadora strapped into her highchair and sat down at the table, he couldn't stop thinking about their phone call, realizing with a jolt followed by a murky sinking feeling, that Terry hadn't actually said Seattle when he'd talked about moving.

"Don't you think that's pretty much for Terry and Isabel to decide," Alice said, stressing the three syllables of Isabel, as if they were incantatory, when he brought up the topic of the mismatched couple's potential future. Whether or not they would move.

"Crazy couple might end up anywhere!" he complained.

To which Alice answered, "And well they should. That's what lovers do. Go where life—the gods—fate—or just pure chance calls them. It's their right, you know."

"I didn't say she was fucking Yoko Ono," Matthew protested, defending himself against the implied accusation that he was blaming Isabel for Terry's ongoing problems, even though he probably was.

"Good if you did. I love Yoko!" Alice declared, launching into a heated defense of creative feminism.

Isadora, delighted with the bowl of mashed potatoes on the tray of her highchair, showered her mother and father with rapturous smiles while they argued, maintaining composed voices—which Matthew and Rosie had never done, having never had an impressionable infant at home counting on them to be civilized. Not that the presence of anyone, young or old, had ever stopped them from shouting at one another.

"Well, gee, this is a wonderful meal," Matthew said, only slightly sarcastically, attempting to change the topic towards something less incendiary than the shadow side of gender politics.

But Alice was adamant. Forgoing the typical astrological analysis which always disarmed him, she charged back into the conversation about Terry and Isabel with brio as she made her point. Which was that he was a gormless idiot.

"You think Terry having a sexy young muse would save him from having to deal with his shit? His grief, the ramifications of his long-term celibacy, his crazy loyalty to you, the whole weird thing with his mom?"

She spooned mashed carrots into Isadora's mouth then wiped the baby's sticky face. Took a long deep drink from her wineglass, looking at Matthew over the rim, assessing, yet not assessing him.

An unfamiliar smile played at the corner of her mouth. Was she drunk? Or simply smirking at him?

"And how about you sand me?" she went on, in the calm inquisitive voice she used with her clients that inevitably entranced him, although its bittersweet undertone stung.

Matthew squirmed in his chair, pretending to pick up his fallen napkin although it was parked on his lap, covered with chicken grease. Thinking fast, but not fast enough. What the hell could he say?

Sitting up slowly, without looking at his wife, he barked, "Cut it out!" at Tehuti who was waiting for food to drop from the baby's highchair and licking Isadora's feet.

He wished he could say the same thing to Alice. Stop her from asking any question about the two of them. Their relationship. Marriage. Their love affair.

They *were* still having a love affair, weren't they? Amidst the turmoil of two careers and a demanding, if delightful, baby and a too small house in a neighborhood overrun with new apartment blocks and homeless encampments.

Still having interesting sex, still snuggling together in bed at night, while she wrote in her journal and he pecked away on his laptop. Izzy—Dora—tucked in her crib in the corner, Tehuti snoring away on his dog bed beside her. The crazy modern jangling world and all its indignities and horrors shut out tight as each night fell, proceeded, and concluded with a dawn that these days seemed hopeful.

Tearing himself away from these lightning fast thoughts, which had, nevertheless, created a lag in the conversation, Matthew forged ahead with his answer. Something along the lines of: "We're fine. We're married. We have a baby. We love each other. We're different than Terry and Isabel."

He'd hoped for better words. Something more romantic. But that was all he had.

He raised his eyes to Alice who was still gazing keenly at him, forcing himself to return her look. Eye to eye. One to one. Like the grown-up man he was trying to be.

"Okay, so you're pissed at me," Matthew said, hoping that was all it was. A silly little fight of no consequence and not a bloody showdown.

The sound of Alice's laugh was beautiful, no matter that it was dry.

"Just because we have it easy right now," she said, gesturing towards the well-fed baby, their excellent dinner, and him, her half-drunk husband, "doesn't mean it isn't going to get hard. Or easier for Isabel and Terry, over the course of time. Nobody's got the key to eternal happiness. We're all just trying to pursue it. Something that doesn't exist."

She smiled and stroked his hand. "Besides, they seem pretty happy to me, bar finding the right place to live, which is hard at the best of times. And maybe for them, it is. The best of times, I mean."

Yeah, of course she was right. Like she always was. Or almost.

After finishing the rest of their meal—in a blessedly more relaxed atmosphere—and cleaning up, and getting Isadora ready for bed in her red polka-dot nightie, it was time for the tired couple to snuggle up on the couch with their baby. Sated and drowsy and warmed by a flickering fire in the drafty old fireplace, they cuddled together for a few moments before Tehuti leapt up from his spot on the rug and joined them.

My little family, Matthew thought fondly, closing his eyes as something approaching rapture crept over his intertwined recumbent form, the mingled sounds of mammalian breathing filling his system with serotonin, draining it of cortisol. He wanted to, but couldn't fall asleep, because of needing to tend the fire.

He was a husband and father now. And yes, even oddball Tehuti's protector. He must keep a watchful eye out. The thought thrilled and chilled him in equal measure. Proud and humbled, he thought also of Terry, his very best—perhaps his only true—friend. And how much he missed him.

A week or two ago he'd taken Isadora to the Wallingford playfield near Terry's old house, sitting on a bench with her tucked into his jacket, while he watched a motley group of kids run through the squelchy grass playing tag with each other.

Shrieks of laughter amidst the rough and tumble, an occasional shout out to a cellphone-glued mother—that, and the organic snacks the moms doled out—made the scene seem contemporary even though he and Terry had played the same way thirty years ago.

Pretty soon it would be his daughter's turn to run and cavort, contest and be contested over some awesome juvenile sport, take her place on the field with the other little blighters flinging themselves around in reckless abandon.

The lovely yet awful thought—for how fast she would grow!—too goddamn fast!—had made him get up from the bench and start to walk back towards his car which he'd parked a few blocks down the street.

After a bit of fumbling and grumbling, he managed to extract Isadora from her baby pack and fasten her into her car seat, before the rain which had been threatening all day started to pelt down on his head.

Pausing to watch for traffic before stepping around the back of the car to get to the driver's seat, he'd heard Terry's commanding voice say in his head, "Look down!"

So he did. And there, beneath the telephone pole on the corner, right next to where he was standing, someone had stenciled *YOU ARE WITH ME EVEN WHEN YOU ARE NOT* in light green paint on the sidewalk.

Breathless—almost stabbed—by the sentiment, he'd hunkered down a few moments and cried. Missing so many people. Terry. And his mother. Rosie, and what she'd meant to him. Even his fucked up dad and incomprehensible brothers seemed like they might be there with him, if only as cautionary characters. In this weird play that was his life.

The sudden memory of that poignant experience was electrifying. His heart was beating a mile a minute from the onrush of adrenaline, but he didn't move. Just focused his dilated eyes on the glowing embers of the dancing fire until the fight-or-flight sensations receded. But there was something he needed to do.

Careful not to wake his sleeping companions, Matthew reached across the baby for his phone which he'd left on the coffee table along with his last glass of wine. He carefully dialed, punching in the numbers from memory, like a promise to remember his vows.

"Terry?"

"Uh yeah?"

"Are you coming back here?"

"I dunno. Maybe so. We're stoppin' off in Casper on the way home from Emily's. Asshole Green has some money for me. But that ain't why we're goin'. Just need me some a that Wyomin' wind in my hair, ya know. We might stay awhile. Like I said, I dunno."

"I really love you, you know. I mean, you do know that, don't you?"

The familiar cowboy sniff. Or maybe a fulsome sigh. Then the baritone laugh, less a chuckle than a rumble, full of something more complicated than joy, but loving, all the same.

"Sure I do. Duddn't matter how much time goes by. Or who marries who. Love ya, too. *Dear Boy*."

Matthew snorted in happy relief. "Fuck you!"

"An' the horse I rode in on," Terry replied. Both of them sounding happy now, in spite of things left unsaid.

"Give my love to Isabel. I'll talk to you soon."

"Done an' dusted," Terry said.

"Goodnight."

A tiny pause filled with understanding, then, "G'night."

ACKNOWLEDGEMENTS

Grateful thanks to my daughter, Natasha Priess, for always supporting my writing and being honest in her praise and criticisms. From childhood onwards, she was a talented author with an intelligent distinctive voice. I look forward to being reunited with her in some future life and to, once again, enjoy reading her imaginative stories and sharing our innermost thoughts.

Heartfelt thanks to my dear husband, Mikal Priess, for teaching me so much about metaphysics and the mysteries of love and sex. I deeply miss our road trips to Wyoming where he was born and raised, and all the other thrilling adventures and intimacies we shared over many intense and rewarding years.

Sincere thanks to my friend and mentor, Leslie Hayertz, for her invaluable editorial and personal advice when I was struggling with writing and publishing this novel. I could not have done those arduous things without her capable assistance and good humor.

Delighted thanks to Brian Jelgerhuis for creating the gorgeous ECSC book covers and logo for Benny Bee Books, and to Alan Clark for his original drawing of the "Emerald City" which graces the front cover. Having one's written words and ideas translated into beautiful art is truly an awesome thing.

Belated thanks to Brandon LaFave for his helpful organizational advice when this novel was an unwieldy 750 page manuscript, and to my mother, Margaret Montague Bell, for instilling an abiding love of reading and writing in me when I was a child.

Amiable thanks to my first readers for their perceptive comments, and to friends and family members who managed not to comment on the inordinate amount of time it took me to finish my manuscript.

And finally, appreciative thanks to the unknown person who stenciled "You are with me even when you are not" on a Seattle neighborhood sidewalk. I felt the same way as my character Matthew did when I saw it—stunned by the truth of this simple little aphorism.

ABOUT THE AUTHOR

Susannah White, a native of the Pacific Northwest, where she still resides, worked as a cook, bookseller, editor, homeschool teacher, childbirth program coordinator and astrologer, before settling down to write An Emerald City Sex Comedy.

www.ingramcontent.com/pod-product-compliance
Lightning Source LLC
Chambersburg PA
CBHW030832110726
47900CB00006B/1859